Being beautiful is no guarantee

of happiness in this

world. Strive instead for elegance,

grace and style.

ELEGANCE

Born in Pittsburgh, Kathleen Tessaro studied drama before emigrating to London.

She is married and lives in North London. *Elegance* is her first novel.

Praise for Kathleen Tessaro:

'Ultra-smart and classily edgy, this is the glitz novel brought up to date.' *Sunday Times*

'It is friendship, not elegance, that proves Louise's real saviour, and the friendships that develop through the book are drawn carefully and with insight.' *Independent*

'This is a book all women will identify with, and you'll adore Louise, who's every bit as charmingly neurotic and nutty as Bridget Jones.' *Glamour*

'Funny, charming and a certain bestseller.' *InStyle*

'It's surprising that this is Kathleen Tessaro's first novel as her style shows the confidence and ease of a more seasoned writer. A charming, entertaining novel.' *Punch*

'A perfect pick-me-up.' *Cosmopolitan*

'A brilliant read with fashion advice thrown in.'
New Woman

'A charming and unusual romance.' *Guardian*

'Superb, original… hilarious.' *Irish Tatler*

It's a freezing cold night in February and my husband and I are standing outside the National Portrait Gallery in Trafalgar Square.

'Here we are,' he says. But neither of us moves.

'Look,' he bargains with me, 'if it's dreadful, we'll just leave. We'll stay for one drink and go. We'll use a code word: potato. When you want to go, just say the word potato in a sentence and then I'll know you want to leave. OK?'

'I could always just *tell* you I want to leave,' I point out.

He frowns at me. 'Louise, I know you don't want to do this, but you could at least make an effort. She's my mother, for Christ's sake and I promised we'd come. It's not every day that you're part of a major photographic exhibition. Besides, she really likes you. She's always saying how the three of us ought to get together.'

The three of us.

I sigh and stare at my feet. I'm dying to say it: potato. Potato, potato, potato.

I know it's a complete cliché to hate your mother-in-law. And I abhor a cliché. But when your mother-in-law is a former model from the 1950s, who specializes in reducing you to a blithering pulp each time you see her, then there is really only one word that springs to mind. And that word is potato.

He wraps an arm around me. 'This really isn't a big deal, Pumpkin.'

I wish he wouldn't call me pumpkin.

But there are some things you do, if not for love, then at least for a quiet life. Besides, we'd paid for a cab, he'd had a shave, and I was wearing a long grey dress I normally kept in a plastic dry cleaning bag. We'd come too far to turn back now.

I lift my head and force a smile. 'All right, let's go.' We walk past the two vast security guards and step inside.

I strip off my brown woolly overcoat and hand it to the coat check attendant, discreetly passing my hand over my tummy for a spot check. I can feel the gentle protrusion. Too much pasta tonight. Comfort food. Comfort eating. Why tonight, of all nights? I try to suck it in but it requires too much effort. So I give up.

I hold out my hand. He takes it, and together we walk into the cool, white world of the Twentieth Century Galleries. The buzz and hum of the crowd engulfs us as we make our way across the pale marble floor. Young men and women, dressed in crisp white shirts, swing by balancing trays of champagne and in an alcove a jazz trio are plucking out the sophisticated rhythms of 'Mack the Knife'.

Breathe, I remind myself, just breathe.

And then I see them: the photographs. Rows and rows of stunning black and white portraits and fashion shots, a collection of the famous photographer Horst's work from the 1930s through to the late sixties, mounted against the stark white walls, smooth and silvery in their finish. The flawless, aloof faces gaze back at me. I long to linger, to lose myself in the world of the pictures.

However, my husband grips my shoulder and propels me forward, waving to his mother, Mona, who's standing with a group of stylish older women at the bar.

'Hello!' he shouts, suddenly animated, coming over all jolly and larger than life. The tired, silent man in the cab is replaced by a dazzling, gregarious, social raconteur.

Mona spots us and waves back, a little half scooping royal wave, the signal for us to join her. Turning our shoulders sideways, we squeeze through the crowd, negotiating drinks and lit cigarettes. As we come into range I pull a face that I hope passes as a smile.

She is wonderfully, fantastically, superhumanly preserved. Her abundant silver-white hair is swept back from her face in an elaborate chignon, making her cheekbones appear even more prominent and her eyes feline. She holds herself perfectly straight, as if she spent her entire childhood nailed to a board, and her black trouser suit betrays the causal elegance of Donna Karan's tailoring. The women around her are all cut from the same, expensive cloth and I suspect we're about to join a kind of ageing models' reunion.

'Darling!' She takes her son's arm and kisses him on both cheeks. 'I'm so pleased you could make it!' My husband gives her a little squeeze.

'We wouldn't miss it for the world, would we, Louise?'

'Certainly not!' I sound just that bit too bright to be authentic.

She acknowledges me with a brisk nod of the head, then turns her attention back to her son. 'How's the play, darling? You must be exhausted! I saw Gerald and Rita the other day; they said you were the best Constantine they'd ever seen. Did I tell you that?' She turns to her collection of friends. 'My son's in *The Seagull* at the National! If you ever want tickets, you must let me know.'

He holds his hands up. 'It's completely sold out. There's not a thing I can do.'

Out comes the lower lip. 'Not even for me?'

'Well,' he relents, 'I can try.'

She lights a cigarette. 'Good boy. Oh, let me introduce you, this is Carmen, she's the one with the elephants on the far wall over there and this is Dorian, you'll recognize at least her back from the famous corset shot, and Penny, well, you were *the* face of 1959, weren't you!'

We all laugh and Penny sighs wistfully, extracting a

packet of Dunhill's from her bag. 'Those were the days! Lend me a light, Mona?'

Mona passes her a gold, engraved lighter and my husband shakes his head. 'Mums, you promised to stop.'

'But darling, it's the only way to keep your figure, isn't that right, girls?' Their heads bob up and down in unison behind a thick cloud of smoke.

And then it happens; I'm spotted.

'And this must be your wiiiiiiife!' Penny gasps, turning her attention to me. Spreading her arms wide, she shakes her head in disbelief and for one horrible moment it looks as if I'm expected to walk into them. I dither stupidly and am about to take a step forward when she suddenly contracts in delight. 'You are adoooooorable!' she coos, turning to the others for affirmation. 'Isn't she just adooooooooooo-orable?'

I stand there, grinning idiotically, while they stare at me.

My husband comes to the rescue. 'Can I get you ladies another drink?' He tries to attract the bartender's attention.

'Oh, you perfect angel!' Mona smoothes down his hair with her hand. 'Champagne all around!'

'And you?' He turns to me.

'Oh yes, champagne, why not?'

Mona takes my arm proprietorially. She gives it a little cuddle, the kind of disarming squeeze your best friend used to give you when you were ten that made your heart leap.

My heart leaps now at this unexpected show of affection and I half hate myself for it. I've been here before and I know it's dangerous to allow yourself to be seduced by her, even for a second.

'Now, Louise,' she has a voice of surprising power and depth, 'tell me how you're doing. I want to hear *everything*!'

'Well . . .' My mind races, desperately flicking through the facts of my life for some worthy gem. The other women look up at me expectantly. 'Things are good, Mona . . . really good.'

'And your parents? How's the weather in Pittsburgh? Louise is from Pittsburgh,' she mouths, *sotto voce*.

'They're well, thank you.'

She nods. I feel like a contestant being introduced on an afternoon quiz show and like any good quiz show host, she helps to jog me along when I dry up.

'And are you working right now?'

She says the word 'working' with the kind of subtle significance that all showbiz people do; there is, after all, a world of difference between 'working' and having a job when you're in 'the profession'.

I know all this but refuse to play along.

'Well, yes. I'm still with the Phoenix Theatre Company.'

'Is it an acting job? Our Louise fancies herself as a bit of an actress,' she offers, by way of an explanation.

'Well, I *was* an actress,' I blunder. No matter how hard I try, she always catches me out. 'I mean, I haven't really worked in a while. And no, this isn't an acting job, it's working front of house, in the box office.'

'I see,' she smiles, as if she can discern a deeper meaning I'm not aware of. And then Dorian asks the most dreaded question of all.

'Have we *seen* you in anything?'

'Well, of course I've done the odd commercial.' I try to sound casual, shrugging my shoulders as if to imply 'who hasn't?'

'Really?' She arches an eyebrow in a perfect impersonation of a woman impressed. 'What commercials?'

Damn.

'Well . . .' I try to think. 'There was the Reader's Digest Sweepstakes Campaign. You may have caught me in that one.'

She stares at me blankly.

'You know, the one where they're all flying around in a hot air balloon over England, drinking champagne and searching for the winners. I was the one on the left holding a map and pointing to Luton.'

'Ah ha.' She's being polite. 'Well, that sounds fun.'

'And now you're working in the box office.' Mona wraps the whole thing up in a clean, little package.

'Yes, well, I've got a couple of things in the pipeline, so to speak . . . but right now that's what I'm doing.' I want my arm back quite badly now.

She gives it another little squeeze. 'It *is* a difficult

7

profession, darling. Best to know your limitations. I always advise young women to avoid it like the plague. The simple truth is, it takes more discipline and sacrifice than most modern girls are willing to put up with. Have you seen my picture?'

Keep smiling, I tell myself. If you keep smiling, she'll never know that you want her to die. 'No, I haven't had much of a chance to look around yet; we've only just got here.'

'Here, allow me.' And she pulls me over to a large photograph of her from the 1950s.

She's incredibly young, almost unrecognizable, except for the distinctive, almond shape of the eyes and the famous cheekbones, which remain untouched by time. She's leaning with her back pressed against a classical pillar, her face turned slightly to the camera, half in shadow, half in light. Her pale hair falls in artfully styled curls over her shoulders and she's wearing a strapless gown of closely fitted layers of flowing silk chiffon. It's labelled, '*Vogue*, 1956.'

'What do you think?' she asks, eyeing me carefully.

'I think it's beautiful,' I say, truthfully.

'You have taste.' She smiles.

A press photographer recognizes her and asks if he can take her picture.

'Story of my life!' she laughs and I make my escape while she poses.

I look around the crowded room for my husband. Finally I spot him, laughing with a group of people in the corner. He has two glasses of champagne in his hands and as I make my way over, he looks up and catches my eye.

I smile and he says something, turns and walks towards me before I can join them.

'Who are they?' I ask, as he hands me a glass.

'No one, just some people from one of these theatre clubs. They recognized me from the play.' He guides me back towards the photographs. 'How are you getting on with Mums?'

'Oh, fine,' I lie. 'Just fine.' I turn back and look but they're gone, swallowed by the ever shifting crowd. 'Didn't you want to introduce me?'

He laughs and pats my bottom, which I hate and which he only ever seems to do in public. 'No, not at all! Don't be so paranoid. To be frank, they're a bit, shall we say, over-enthusiastic. I don't want them boring my charming wife, now do I?'

'And who might that be?' I sound much more acerbic than I'd intended.

He pats my bottom again and ignores me.

We pause in front of a photograph of a woman smoking a cigarette, her eyes hidden by the brim of her hat. She leans, waiting in a doorway on a dark, abandoned street. It must've been taken just after the Second World War. There's something unsettling in the contrast of the shattered surroundings and the pristine perfection of her crisp, tailored suit.

'Now *that's* style,' my husband sighs.

Suddenly it's too hot. I feel overwhelmed by the crush of people, the smoke, and the sound of too many over-animated conversations. Mona's waving to us again but I allow my husband to walk over to her and make my way into a smaller, less crowded room off the main gallery instead. There's a flat, wooden bench in the centre. I sit down and close my eyes.

It's foolish to get so tense. In another hour, it will all be over. Mona will have had her moment of glory and we'll be safely on our way back home. The thing to do is relax. Enjoy myself. I open my eyes and take a deep breath.

The walls are lined with portraits – Picasso, Coco Chanel, Katharine Hepburn, Cary Grant – rows and rows of meticulous, glamorous faces. The eyes are darker, more penetrating than normal eyes, the noses straighter, more refined. I allow myself to slip into a sort of meditative state, a spell brought on by witnessing such an excess of beauty.

And then I spot a portrait I don't recognize, a woman with gleaming dark hair, parted in the middle and arranged in a mass of black curls around her face. Her features are distinctive; high cheekbones, a Cupid's-bow mouth and very black, intelligent eyes. Leaning forward, with her cheek lightly resting against her hand, she looks as if we've happened to catch her in the middle of the most engaging conversation of her life. Her dress, a simple bias-cut sheath, is made from a light satin that shimmers against the dull material of the settee and her only jewellery is a single strand of perfectly matched pearls. She's not the most famous face or even the most attractive, but for some reason she's undoubtedly the most compelling. I get up and cross the room. The name reads: Genevieve Dariaux, Paris, 1934.

However, my solitude is brief.

'There you are! Mona's sent us to find you.' Penny comes strolling in on the arm of my reluctant husband.

Stay calm, I remind myself, taking a much-needed gulp of my champagne. 'Hello, Penny, just enjoying the exhibition.'

She leans forward and waggles a finger in my face.

'You know, Louise, you're very, *very* naughty!' She winks at my husband. 'I don't know how you can let her drink! You're both as bad as each other!'

My husband and I exchange looks. Come again?

She leans in further and drops her voice to a stage whisper. 'I must say, you look amazing! And this,' she continues, feeling the fabric of my dress gingerly between her thumb and forefinger, 'this really isn't too bad at all. I mean, most of them look like absolute tents but this one's really quite cute. My daughter's due in May and she's *desperate* for something like this that she can just pad about in.'

I feel the blood draining away from my head.

She smiles at both of us. 'You must be sooooooooooooo pleased!'

I swallow hard. 'I'm not pregnant.'

She wrinkles her brow in confusion. 'I'm sorry?'

'I am not pregnant,' I repeat, louder this time.

My husband laughs nervously. 'You'll be the first to know when she is, I can assure you!'

'No, I think I will,' I say, and he laughs again, slightly hysterical now.

Penny continues to gape at me in amazement. 'But that dress . . . I'm sorry, I mean, it's just . . .'

I turn to my husband. 'Honey?'

He seems to have found a point of fascination on the floor. 'Humm?'

'Potato.'

I don't know what I thought he'd do, defend me somehow or at least look sympathetic. But instead he continues to stare at his shoes.

'OK.'

I turn and walk away. I feel like I'm having an out-of-body experience but somehow manage to gain the safety of the loo. A couple of girls are fixing their make-up as I enter, so I make a beeline for an empty stall and lock the door. I wait, with my back pressed against the cool metal and close my eyes. No one ever died of humiliation, I remind myself. If that were true, I'd have been dead years ago.

Finally, they leave. I unlock the door and stand in front of the mirror. Like any normal woman, I look in the mirror every day, when I brush my teeth or wash my face or comb my hair. It's just I tend to look at myself in pieces and avoid joining them all up together. I don't know why; it just feels safer that way.

But tonight I force myself to look at the whole thing. And suddenly I see how the bits and pieces add up to someone I'm not familiar with, someone I never intended to be.

My hair needs a trim and I should really dye it to get rid of those prematurely grey strands. Incredibly fine and ashen coloured, it drapes listlessly around my head, forced to one side by a faux tortoiseshell clip. My face, always pale, is unnaturally white. Not ivory or alabaster but rather devoid of any colour at all, like some deep sea animal that's never encountered the sun. Against it, the bright red smear of lipstick I've applied seems garish and my mouth far too big – like a gaping, scarlet gash across the bottom third of my face. The heat of the crowd has made me sweat; my nose is glistening, my cheeks are shiny and flushed but I haven't any powder.

And my favourite dress, despite being dry cleaned, has gone hopelessly bobbly and is, now that we're being honest, shapeless in a way that was fashionable five years ago, though definitely out of style now. I remember feeling sexy and confident in it when it used to just skim the contours of my figure, suggesting a sylph-like sensuality. Now that I'm ten pounds heavier, the effect is not the same. To finish it all off, my shoes, a pair of practical, flat Mary Janes with Velcro fastenings, make my ankles look like two thick tree trunks. Faded and scuffed, they're everyday shoes, at least two years old, and really too worn to be seen anywhere but inside my own house.

I'm forced to conclude that the whole effect does rather shout, 'Pregnant woman'. Or, more precisely, 'This is the best I can do under the circumstances.'

I stare at my reflection in alarm. No, this person isn't really me. It's all just a terrible mistake – a Bermuda Triangle of Bad Hair day meets Bad Dress day, meets Hippie Shoes from Hell. I need to calm down, centre myself.

I try an experiment.

'Hi, my name's Louise Canova. I'm thirty-two years old and I'm *not* pregnant.'

My voice echoes around the empty loo.

This isn't working. My heart is pounding and I'm starting to panic. I close my eyes and will myself to concentrate, to think positive thoughts, but instead the images of a thousand glossy black and white faces crowd my mind. It's like I'm not even of the same species.

Suddenly the door behind me opens and Mona walks in.

Triple fucking potato.

She leans dramatically against the basin. 'Louise, I've

just heard. Listen, she didn't mean anything, I'm sure, and besides, she's blind as a bat.'

Why does he have to tell her everything?

'Thanks, Mona, I appreciate it.'

'Still,' she comes up behind me and pushes my hair back from my face with two carefully manicured fingers, 'if you like, I could give you the name of my hairdresser, he's really *very* reasonable.'

My husband is waiting when I come out. He hands me my coat and we leave the party in silence, finding ourselves standing in the same spot in Trafalgar Square less than thirty minutes after we arrived. Scanning the street for any sign of a cab, he takes a pack of cigarettes out of his pocket and lights one.

'What are you doing?' I ask.

'Smoking,' he says. (My husband doesn't smoke.)

I leave it.

The yellow light of a cab lurches towards us from a distance and I wave wildly at it. It's misting now. The cab slows down and we get in. My husband throws himself heavily against the back seat then leans forward again to pull down the window.

Suddenly I want to make him laugh, to cuddle him, or rather to be cuddled. After all, what does it matter what I look like or what anyone else thinks? He still loves me. I reach over and put my hand over his.

'Sweetheart? Do you . . . do you *really* think I look OK?'

He takes my hand and gives it a squeeze. 'Listen, Pumpkin, you look just fine. Exactly the way you always do. Don't pay any attention to her. She's probably just jealous because you're young and married.'

'Yes,' I agree hollowly, though it's not quite the effusive sea of compliments I'd hoped for.

He squeezes my hand again and kisses my forehead. 'Besides, you know I don't care about all that rubbish.'

The cab speeds on into the darkness and as I sit there, with the cold wind blowing against my face, a single, violent thought occurs to me.

Yes, but I do.

What is Elegance?

It is a sort of harmony that rather resembles beauty with the difference that the latter is more often a gift of nature and the former a result of art. If I may be permitted to use a high-sounding word for such a minor art, I would say that to transform a plain woman into an elegant one is my mission in life.
—*Genevieve Antoine Dariaux*

It was a slim, grey volume entitled *Elegance*. It was buried between a fat, obviously untouched tome on the history of the French monarchy and a dog-eared paperback edition of D. H. Lawrence's *Women in Love*. Longer and thinner than the other books on the shelf, it rose above its modest surroundings with a disdainful authority, the embossed letters of its title sparkling against the silver satin cover like a glittering gold coin just below the surface of a rushing brook.

My husband claims I have an unhealthy obsession with second-hand bookshops. That I spend too much time day-dreaming altogether. But either you intrinsically understand the attraction of searching for hidden treasure amongst rows of dusty shelves or you don't; it's a passion, bordering on a spiritual illness, which cannot be explained to the unafflicted.

True, they're not for the faint of heart. Wild and chaotic, capricious and frustrating, there are certain physical laws that govern second-hand bookstores and, like gravity, they're pretty much non-negotiable. Paperback editions of D. H. Lawrence must constitute no less than 55 per cent of all stock in any shop. Natural law also dictates that the remaining 45 per cent consists of at least two shelves' worth of literary criticism on *Paradise Lost*, and there should always be an entire room in the basement devoted to military history which, by sheer coincidence, will be haunted by a man in his seventies. (Personal studies prove it's the same man. No matter how quickly you move from one bookshop to the next, he's always there. He's forgotten something about the war that no book can contain, but like a figure in Greek mythology, is doomed to spend his days wandering from basement room to basement room, searching through memoirs of the best/worst days of his life.)

Modern booksellers can't really compete with these eccentric charms. They keep regular hours, have central heating and are staffed by freshly scrubbed young people in black tee-shirts. They're devoid both of basement rooms and fallen Greek heroes in smelly tweeds. You'll find no dogs or cats curled up next to ancient space heaters like familiars nor the intoxicating smell of mould and mildew that could emanate equally from the unevenly stacked volumes or from the owner himself. People visit Waterstone's and leave. But second-hand bookshops have pilgrims. The words 'out of print' are a call to arms for those who seek a Holy Grail made of paper and ink.

I reach up and carefully remove the book from its shelf. Sitting down on a stack of military history books (they will migrate if you're not careful), I open to the title page.

Elegance

By Genevieve Antoine Dariaux

it announces in elaborate script and then, underneath:

A complete guide for every woman who wants to be well and properly dressed on all occasions.

Dariaux. I know that name. Could it be the same woman I saw in the photo? As I leaf through the book, the faint fragrance of jasmine perfume floats from its yellowed pages. Written in 1964, it appears to be a kind of encyclopaedia, with entries for every known fashion dilemma starting with

A and going through to Z. I've never before encountered anything quite like it. I flip through the pages in search of a photo of the author. And there, on the back cover, my efforts are rewarded.

She looks to be in her late fifties, with classic, even features and heavily lacquered white hair – Margaret Thatcher hair before it had a career of its own. But the same black, intelligent eyes gleam back at me; I recognize the distinctive, imperious set of her mouth and there, luminous against the fitted black cardigan she's wearing, is the trade-mark strand of impeccably matched pearls. *Madame Georges Antoine Dariaux*, the caption below the photo reads. She doesn't look directly at the camera with the same beguiling candour of her earlier portrait, but rather beyond it, as if she's too polite to challenge our gaze. Older now, she's naturally more discreet, and discretion is, after all, the cornerstone of elegance.

I turn back eagerly to the preface.

Elegance is rare in the modern world, largely because it requires precision, attention to detail, and the careful development of a delicate taste in all forms of manners and style. In short, it does not come easily to most women and never will.

However, in my 30-year career as the directress of the Nina Ricci Salon in Paris, my life has been devoted to advising our clients and helping them to select

*what is most flattering. Some are exquisitely beautiful
and really need no assistance from me at all. I enjoy
admiring them as one enjoys admiring a work of art,
but they are not the clients I cherish the most. No, the
ones that I am fondest of are those who have neither the
time nor the experience necessary to succeed in the art
of being well-dressed. For these women, I am willing
to turn my imagination inside out.*

*Now, would you like to play a little game of
Pygmalion? If you have a little confidence in me, let
me share with you some practical ideas on one of the
surest ways of making the most of yourself – through
elegance, your own elegance.*

At last, I have found my Holy Grail.

It's only 4 pm, but it's already growing dark when I leave
the shop. I weave through the streets; down Bell Street, over
Marble Arch, across St James's and then into Westminster,
clutching my magical parcel.

Big Ben chimes in the background as I push open the
door and am greeted by the sound of a Hoover.

My husband is home.

There's something about the persistent, draining, in-
cessancy of domesticity that signals a call to arms for my
husband. (Those who know him only as a rising star of the

London stage are, in fact, blind to his most astonishing talents.) Each day finds him bravely battling the enemies of filth, disorder, untidiness and decay with renewed determination. A resourceful soul, he can transform any sort of disarray into a clean, habitable environment, usually in under half an hour.

He can't hear me as I come in, so I poke my head into the living room where he is furiously forcing the vacuum over the parquet wood floor (he claims to be able to actually *see* the dust settling on it, so remarkable is his sensitivity to that sort of thing) and shout to him.

'Hey!'

Switching off the Hoover, he rests his arms against its handle, with the same masculine ease of a television cowboy leaning on a fence. He is a man in his element, setting the world to rights.

'Hey yourself. What've you been up to?'

'Oh, nothing really,' I fib, concealing the brown paper parcel behind my back. In the face of my husband's never-ending schedule of home improvements, spending an afternoon ferreting around old bookshops seems like a kind of betrayal.

'Did you return that lampshade?'

'Ah, yes . . .' I confirm, 'but I couldn't find anything better, so they gave me a credit note.'

He sighs, and we both look mournfully at the pale marble lamp Mona gave us a month ago.

In every marriage there are certain ties that bind. Much more substantial than the actual marriage vows, these are the real-life, unspoken forces that keep it glued together, day in and day out, year after year, through endless trial and adversity. For some people it's their social ambitions, for others their children. But in our case, the pursuit of the perfect lampshade will do.

We are bound, my husband and I, by a complete, relentless commitment to the interior decoration of our home. And this lamp is the delinquent, drug-addicted teenager that threatens to destroy our domestic bliss by refusing to coordinate with any ready-made lampshade from a reasonably priced store. It's incredibly heavy and almost impossible to lift. We are doomed to a Sisyphean fate: forever purchasing lampshades we will only return the next day.

My husband shakes his head. 'We're going to have to go to Harrods,' he says gravely.

Harrods is always a last resort. There will be no 'reasonable' lampshades at Harrods.

'But you know what?' he adds, his face brightening. 'You can come with me and we'll make a day of it if you like.'

'Sure,' I smile.

Lampshade Day – certain to be right up there with the Great Garden Trellis Outing and the Afternoon of a Dozen Shower Hoses. 'Wouldn't miss it for the world.'

'Great.' He forces one of the windows open, relishing

the gust of cool air. 'Of course, you'll be glad to know I've had considerably more success here while you were away.'

'Really?'

'You know those pigeons that roost on the drainpipe just above the bedroom window?'

'Yeah . . .' I lie.

'Well, I've attached some barbed wire around the pipe. That's the last we'll see of them!'

I'm still trying to place these pigeons. 'Well done you!'

'And that's not all. I've got some fantastic ideas for draining the garden path which I'm going to draw up during the interval tonight. Maybe I can show them to you later?'

'Sounds brilliant. Listen, I'm just going to do some reading in the other room. Maybe you'll look in on me before you go?'

He nods, surveying the living room contentedly. 'It's all coming together, Louie. I mean, the place is really starting to shape up. All we need is that lampshade.'

I watch as he switches the Hoover back on.

There is always one more lampshade, one more set of authentic looking faux-Georgian fire utensils, one more non-slip natural hessian runner carpet. Like Daisy's green light in the *Great Gatsby*, these things call to us with the promise of a final, lasting happiness, yet somehow remain forever out of reach.

Retreating into the bedroom, I close the door, kick off my shoes and curl up on the bed.

The bed is enormous. It's actually two single beds that are joined in the centre. 'Zipped and Linked' is what the man at John Lewis called it. We needed a bed that was big enough so that we wouldn't disturb each other in the night: my husband twitches like a dog and I can't bear noise or any sort of movement.

'You are *sure* you want to sleep together?' the salesman had asked when we briefed him of our requirements. But my husband was adamant. 'We've only just been married,' he informed the offending fellow haughtily, implying a kind of rampant, newlywed sex life that could only just be contained within the confines of a solidly made double bed. So now he twitches away somewhere west of me and I slumber, comatose, half a mile to the east.

Climbing underneath the duvet, I remove the delicate volume from its brown paper bag. I'm on the verge of something very big, very real.

This is it.

I open to Chapter One.

And the next thing I know, I'm asleep.

When I wake up, he's already gone to the theatre. There's a note on the kitchen table. 'Were snoring, so didn't bother to wake you.' My husband is nothing, if not concise.

This is bad.

The truth is, I sleep far too much – wake up late, take naps in the afternoon, go to bed early. I live with one foot dangling in a dark, warm, pool of unconsciousness, ready at any moment to slide into oblivion. But it's just a little bit anti-social, all this sleeping, so I try to hide it.

I make toast. (I believe that's what's known as cooking for one.) Then climb back on board the bed. Turning to the first letter in the alphabet, I try not to get butter on the pages.

A

Accessories

You can always tell the character of a woman by the care and attention she lavishes upon the details of her dress. The accessories worn with an outfit – gloves, hat, shoes, and handbag – are among the most important elements of an elegant appearance. A modest dress or suit can triple its face value when worn with an elegant hat, bag, gloves, and shoes, while a designer's original can lose much of its prestige if its accessories have been carelessly selected. It is indispensable to own a complete set of accessories in black and, if possible, another in brown, plus a pair of beige shoes and a beige straw handbag for the summer. With this basic minimum, almost any combination is attractive.

Of course, it would be ideal to have each set of accessories in two different versions: one for sport and the other dressy. And in this regard I cannot restrain myself from expressing the dismay I feel when I see a woman carry an alligator handbag with a dressy *ensemble merely because she has paid an enormous sum of money for it. Alligator is strictly for sports or travel, shoes as well as bags, and this respected reptile should be permitted to retire every evening at 5 pm.*

And here, as in no other department, quality is essential. Be strict with yourself. Save. Economize on food if you must (believe me, it will do you good!) but not on your handbags or shoes. Refuse to be seduced by anything that isn't first rate. The saying, 'I cannot afford to buy cheaply,' was never so true. Although I am far from rich, I have bought my handbags for years from Hermès, Germaine Guerin, and Roberta. And without exception, I have ended up by giving away all the cheap little novelty bags that I found irresistible at first. The same is true of shoes and gloves.

I realize that all of this may seem rather austere, and even very expensive. But these efforts are one of the keys, one of the Open Sesames that unlock the door to elegance.

I look down at my own handbag crumpled in a heap on the floor. It's a navy Gap rucksack – the kind that seems to attract bits of dried biscuit to the bottom, even if you haven't eaten a biscuit in months. Needless to say, it could do with a wash.

Or a glass of milk.

I wonder if it qualifies as a sports bag. I can remember purchasing it in the 'Back to School' department several seasons ago and feeling quite elated that I'd managed to resolve all my handbag dilemmas in a single swoop. It would never occur to me to buy more than one bag, in more than one colour or style.

The only other one I own is a squashed maroon leather shoulder bag I bought in the sale from Hobbs four years ago. The leather has worn away and the framework of the bag is exposed; however I'm too attached to it to throw it away. I keep pretending that I'm going to have it repaired, even though it's gone out of style.

The more I think of it, the more hard pressed I am to think of any accessories I own that might be described as even remotely stylish, let alone first rate. Certainly not the collection of woolly brown and grey berets I live in, so practical because they won't blow off your head during the windy London winters and because they're invaluable for those days (always on the increase) when I haven't washed or even combed my hair. I like to think of them as 'emergency hair'.

I find myself gazing at my feet, or rather at the pair of well-worn beige plimsolls that adorn them. It's been raining and they're soaked through. The fabric's worn away above my big toe and I catch a glimpse of the green and red Christmas socks underneath. (My mother sent me those.) I give my big toe a little wiggle.

My nose is running and as I fumble for a tissue in my raincoat pocket, I discover a pair of mismatched black gloves I found on the floor of a movie theatre two weeks ago. They seemed like quite a find at the time but suddenly it's clear, even to me, that I've obviously *not* been lavishing enough care and attention on the details of my dress.

Elegance may be in the details but my situation appears to be a little more serious than that. Clearly, drastic action is needed. I resolve, in an unprecedented burst of enthusiasm, to begin my transformation with a thorough cleansing of my closet. Systematically working my way through, I'll weed out the elements that don't flatter me. And then I'll be free to construct a new, improved look around those that do.

Fine, let's get cracking! I fling open my closet door with a dramatic sweep of my arms and nearly pass out from hopelessness.

I possess a rail of items gleaned from second-hand clothing stores all over the country. Everything in front of me symbolizes an element of compromise. Skirts that fit around the waist but flare out like something Maria Von Trapp would wear. Piles of itchy or slightly moth-eaten woolly jumpers – not one of them in my size. Coats in strange fabrics or suit jackets with no matching skirts bought simply because they fit and that in itself is an event.

But that's not the scariest thing. No, the thing that completely stuns me is the colour. Or rather the lack of it. When did I decide that brown was the new black, grey, scarlet, navy and just about any other shade you can name? What would the *Colour Me Beautiful* girls make of that? Or Freud, for that matter?

I stare in fascinated longing at the bold, crimson drawing room of the house across the street but my own walls are magnolia. Matte magnolia, to be precise. And now here it is: the dreadful consequences of playing it safe. I have the wardrobe of an eighty-year-old Irish man. That is, an eighty-year-old Irish man who doesn't care what he looks like.

However, I won't be put off.

I open my underwear drawer.

I dump the entire contents on the floor.

I sift through the piles of runned and not too runned tights (the only kind I own), the baggy knickers, the ones with the elastic showing, and the bras I should never have put in the washing machine which now have bits of deadly under-wire poking through them. I diligently make piles of keeps and non-keeps.

Done.

I go to the kitchen, grab a black bin liner and begin to fill it. A strange, unfamiliar energy infuses me and before I know it, I'm working my way through the rest of my clothes.

Piles of ugly, vague, brown garments rapidly disappear. I throw away jumpers, jackets, and every last one of the *Sound of Music* skirts. Here's another bin liner: in go the worn out shoes, the natty scarves. Now the maroon leather handbag from Hobbs. I can buy a new one. Beads of perspiration run down my face and in my cupboard empty hangers clash together like wind chimes. I tie the tops of the bags together and drag them out to the garbage bins at the back of the building. It's dark; I feel like a criminal destroying the evidence of a particularly gory crime.

Finally, I stand in front of my near empty wardrobe and survey the result of all this effort. A pale pink Oxford shirt swings from the rail, a single black skirt, a navy fitted pinafore dress. On the floor in front of me, there's a small pile of just about wearable underwear.

This is it. This is now the basis of my new wardrobe, my new identity and my new life.

I take a Post-it from the desk in the corner, write on it in bright red marker, and stick it on the corner of the wardrobe mirror.

'*Never be seduced by anything that isn't first rate,*' it reminds me.

No, never again.

I'm on the train headed for Brondesbury Park to see my therapist. It's my husband's idea; he thinks there's something wrong with me.

After we were married, I began to have recurring nightmares. I'd wake up screaming, convinced there was a man at the foot of the bed. The room would be exactly the way it was in waking life and then all of a sudden, he'd be there, leaning over me. I'd chase him away but he'd return every night without fail. After a while, my husband learnt to sleep through these nightly terrors, but when I started to cry during the day and couldn't stop, he put his foot down. He explained to me that I had too many feelings and I'd better do something about it.

When I get to my therapist's house, I ring the bell and am admitted into a waiting room, which is really part of a hallway with a chair and a coffee table. There are three magazines and have been ever since I started therapy two years ago: one *House and Garden* from spring 1997, and two copies of *National Geographic*. I can recite the contents of all of them. However, I pick up the copy of *House and Garden* and look again at the cottage transformed into a treasure trove of Swedish antiques using nothing but Ikea furniture and a few paint effects. I'm falling asleep when the door finally opens, and Mrs P asks me to step inside.

I take off my coat and sit on the edge of the daybed that is her version of a couch. The room is muted, sterile. Even the landscapes on the walls have an eerie calmness, like lobotomized Van Gogh's – no wild, swirly, passionate mayhem here. I like to think that behind the glass door that separates her office from the rest of the house, there lies an explosion of primitive phallic art and dangerous modern furniture in a riot of vivid colours. The chances are slim but I live in hope.

Mrs P is middle aged and German. Like me, her fashion sense lacks a certain *savoir-faire*. Today she's wearing a cream-coloured skirt with a pair of knee-highs, and when she sits down, I can see where the elastic pinches her leg, causing a red, swollen roll of flesh just under the knee. The German thing doesn't help. Every time she asks me something, I feel like we're enacting a badly-scripted interrogation scene from a World War Two film. This may or may not be the root of our communication problems.

I sit there and she stares at me from behind her square-rimmed glasses.

We've come to the impasse: part of our weekly routine.

I grin sheepishly.

'I think I'll sit up today,' I say.

Mrs P blinks at me, unmoved. 'And why would you like to do that?'

'I want to see you.'

'And why do you want to do that?' she repeats. They always want to know why; there's not really a lot of difference between a therapist and a four-year-old.

'I don't like to be alone. I feel alone when I'm lying down.'

'But you're not alone,' she points out. 'I'm here.'

'Yes, but I can't *see* you.' I'm starting to feel really frustrated.

'So,' she adjusts her glasses further back on her nose, 'you need to "*see*" someone in order not to feel alone?'

She's speaking to me in italics, throwing my words back at me, the way therapists do. I won't be bullied. 'No, not always. But if I'm going to talk to you, I'd rather be looking at you.' And with that, I push myself back on the daybed so that I'm leaning against the wall.

I start to pick at the bobbles in the white chenille throw that covers the bed. (I'm intimately acquainted with these bobbles.) Three or four minutes drag past in silence.

'You do not trust me,' she says at last.

'No, I don't trust you,' I agree, not so much because I believe it to be true but because she says it is and after all, she is my therapist.

'I think you need more sessions,' she sighs.

Whenever I don't do what she wants me to do, I need more sessions. There were whole months when I had to come every day. This is normally as far as we get; for two years we've been arguing about whether or not I should be allowed to sit up on the daybed. But today I have something to tell her.

'I bought a book yesterday. It's called *Elegance*.'

'Is it a novel?'

'No, it's a kind of self-help book, a guide that tells you how you can become elegant.'

She raises an eyebrow. 'And what does "becoming elegant" mean to you?'

'Being chic, sophisticated. You know, like Audrey Hepburn or Grace Kelly.'

'And why is that important?'

I feel suddenly frivolous and girly – like a female member of the Communist Party caught reading an issue of *Vogue*. 'Well, I don't know that it's important but it's worth striving for, don't you think?' And then I spot her beige, orthopaedic sandals.

Maybe not.

I take another tack. 'What I mean is, they were always pulled together, never unseemly or dishevelled in any way. Every time you saw them, they were perfectly groomed, faultlessly dressed.'

'And is that what you would like, to be "pulled together, never unseemly or dishevelled in any way"?'

I think a moment. 'Yes,' I say at last. 'I'd love to be clean and chic and not such a terrible mess all the time.'

'I see.' She nods her head. 'You are not clean. That makes you dirty. Not chic. That makes you unfashionable. And a terrible mess. Not just a mess, but a *terrible* mess. So, you feel you are unattractive.'

She makes everything sound so much worse than it is.

Still, she has a point.

'Well, no, I don't feel very attractive,' I admit, wincing inwardly as I say it. 'The truth is, I feel the opposite of attractive. Like it doesn't matter what I look like.'

She peers at me over the top of her glasses. 'And why doesn't it matter what you look like?'

A thick wave of unconsciousness swims up to meet me. 'Because . . . I don't know . . . because it just doesn't matter.' I try unsuccessfully to stifle a yawn.

'But surely your husband notices,' she insists.

I wonder what she means by 'notices'. Is this some kind of euphemism? Does her husband 'notice' her in her knee-highs and skirt?

'No, no he's not that way,' I explain, pushing the unwelcome vision of them 'noticing' each other from my mind. 'He's really not interested in that sort of thing.' My eyelids are at half-mast now; it feels like they weigh a ton.

'And what sort of thing is that?'

'I don't know . . . bodies, appearances, clothes.'

'And how does that make you feel?' she persists. 'That

he is not interested in your body, your appearance, or your clothes?'

I think for a moment. 'Tired,' I conclude. 'It makes me feel tired. Anyway, why should he be interested in those things? He loves me for who I am, not the way I look.' I'm sinking further and further into the daybed like a deflating balloon.

'Yes, but love is not just a feeling,' she continues, undeterred. 'Or an idea. It's completely natural that there is a physical side too. You are young. You *are* attractive. You are . . . falling asleep, am I right?'

I pull myself up with a jerk. 'No, no I'm fine. Just a little drowsy. Late night last night.' I don't know why I bother to lie. Perhaps what she says is true: I don't trust her.

'Well, in any case, time is up for today.'

As soon as she says it, I start to revive.

I leave, head straight to the newsagent's on the corner and buy two Kit Kats. I eat them in rapid succession, waiting for the train. I'll never get this therapy gig. Can't wait till I'm cured and have been given some sort of certificate I can show my husband.

A disembodied voice comes over the intercom to announce that, due to signalling problems, the next southbound train will be in twelve minutes. I sit down on a bench in the corner and take the copy of *Elegance* from my bag. A gust of wind rustles through it and the book falls open on a page from the preface.

From my earliest childhood, one of my principal preoccupations was to be well dressed, a somewhat precocious ambition that was encouraged by my mother, who was extremely fashion-conscious herself. Together we would go to the dressmaker and select combinations of fabrics and styles that ensured our outfits were entirely original and impossible to copy.

I think of my own mother and of how she hated shopping, dressing up or looking at herself in mirrors. Not only did she not aspire to elegance, but I believe she suspected it as a pursuit. It was at odds with the aesthetics of her strict Catholic upbringing, belonging as it did to the world of movie stars, debutantes and divorcees.

Pale and bespectacled, with short dark hair she cut herself, she preferred to spend most of her time in Birkenstocks and plain, loose trousers, maybe because in the male dominated world of science in which she excelled, fashion was of little practical use. However, in text book Freudian fashion, her unlived dreams and ambitions spilt out onto my sister and me. She longed for us to become professional ballet dancers, paragons of grace and discipline, and we trained for hours every day after school to that end. She indulged us in bizarre shopping trips, made more surreal by the fact that we rarely seemed to buy any actual children's clothes. It was as if she was taking us shopping for her *alter ego*.

It's a Saturday morning. My mother's just picked me up from ballet class and we're in Kaufmanns department store in Pittsburgh. I'm about twelve, but already I'm sporting a pair of high heels, 'wedgies' to be exact, with thick crepe soles and a denim wrap-around skirt, just like my idol, Farrah Fawcett in 'Charlie's Angels'. Like all the girls in ballet school, I want to look like a prima ballerina. We cake on tons of foundation, eyeliner and mascara and roll our eyes around like silent film stars on acid. We're dying swans with our exaggerated posture, ridiculous turnouts, and scraped back hair-dos. It never occurs to us that make-up that's meant to read on stage to the last row of the Metropolitan Opera House might not be suitable for street wear.

My mother and I are shopping in the eveningwear section. It's 10:30 in the morning and we're looking at sequins and taffeta. She's going to a formal Christmas party with my father and we're here to shop for her, but she can't bear to look at herself or try anything on. I carry gown after gown into the changing room, where she's slumped on the stool in her bra and girdle, cradling her head in her hands. 'You put them on,' she says and I do, preening and posing like a midget version of Maria Callas. My mother is a ghost, thin and shorn next to my drag act. 'You're so slim,' she says, as I shimmy into a pink sequined sheath dress. 'You look good in everything.'

We spend hours wading through piles of silk and satin and in the end she buys me a black sequined top and a cream coloured marabou jacket at vast expense, which I wear over my school uniform, despite the fact that it lands me in detention for a month.

My mother buys nothing.

And after we shop, we go to the chocolate counter and buy a pound box of Godiva chocolates, which we eat on our way back home in the car. My mother and I don't do lunch. Lunch is, after all, fattening. So we sit in the front seat of the car, not looking at one another, cramming chocolate into our mouths instead.

By the time we get home, the excitement of shopping is gone. Vanished. Mom is suddenly furiously angry and I'm filled with fear and shame. She gets out, slams the car door and strides across the garage into the house, where I can hear her yelling at my brother. She yells for no reason – because a towel is badly folded or because the television is on. She yells because she hates herself; because she's spent $300 on evening clothes for a twelve-year-old; because she's so livid she can't contain it any more. She throws something but misses.

I hear her storm upstairs and slam her bedroom door. Getting out of the car with my bags, I take the now empty chocolate box with me. It's important that no one should see it. And I walk, or rather waddle the way dancers do, into the house. My brother's there, crying, and there's a pile of glass and plastic that used to be a clock around him on the floor. He looks at me with my Kaufmanns bags and the Godiva chocolate box and I know that he hates me. I stick my chin in the air and walk on. I am a bad person. I am a very bad person.

My mother doesn't go to the Christmas party. She has an argument with my father and spends the evening locked in her room instead.

Closing the book, I get up and walk down to the end of the platform. In the corner, where the cement gives way to rubble and grass, I turn and throw up the two Kit Kat bars.

The light is softly dimming and I notice, as I wipe my fingers on a clean tissue, that the birds are singing, the way they do sometimes at dusk on early spring evenings. They sound impossibly hopeful.

And suddenly it occurs to me, that maybe my mother and I have something in common.

Maybe I come from a long line of women who felt like a terrible mess.

B

Beauty

Since time began, women have sought after beauty with all the passion and vigour of Menelaus pursuing Helen into Troy and often with similarly violent results. And why shouldn't they? Being beautiful has always been synonymous with owning the world on a string and what girl would not wish that?

Sadly though, only God and nature can make a beautiful woman and, to be perfectly frank, most of us do not and never will fall into that exclusive category. Perhaps you think I am being a little hard? Maybe I am. But I am of the philosophy that it is best to face the facts about oneself, especially the most unpleasant ones, early on in life and make peace with them rather than to waste years in nervous agitation pursuing goals and expectations far beyond our reach.

Besides which, being beautiful is no guarantee of happiness in this world. I have known many beautiful women whose own inelegance and lack of breeding rendered them so hopelessly unattractive, that it would've been simpler and less painful for them if they had been born plain. A woman must have a very strong character not to become distracted by her own unnatural power to excite attention everywhere she goes. And there is nothing more tragic than the sight of a badly ageing beauty who never had to develop her wit or imagination in order to amuse her companions or who always relied upon the excellence of her figure rather than the elegance of her clothes to make an impression. They are poor company and almost invariably develop 'champagne chins'.

While beauty, in its purest physical form, is nature's gift alone to bestow, elegance, grace and style are infinitely more democratic. A little discipline and a discerning eye, along with a generous helping of good humour and effort, are all that's needed to cultivate these admirable qualities. And a plain girl who spends a little time in honest self-reflection and who applies herself with diligence to the improvement of her mind and character, will awake soon enough to discover that she has blossomed into a fully fledged swan. The time she spent alone and undistracted by the world will fortify her, the discipline she learnt will carry her into old age with grace and courage, and above all, she will possess compassion, which

*never fails to make a woman more attractive to those
around her.*

I reach across to my bedside table and pick up the Post-its
and a pen, while taking another sip of my tea. Of all the
pleasures in this world, reading in bed in the morning with
a fresh, steaming mug of tea has to be the most luxurious.
I prod the mountain of pillows behind me into a more
yielding shape and lean back.

To be beautiful. There are days when I feel fairly confident that I'm attractive but am I or could I ever be beautiful?
Or am I one of those women who are better off facing up
to the 'unpleasant facts of life'?

It's not really a question a girl should ponder before nine
in the morning, still suffering from bed head and wearing
her favourite faded Snoopy night-shirt. (I couldn't quite
bring myself to throw it away.) I push it from my thoughts
and resolutely peel off another Post-it. 'Beauty is no guarantee of happiness,' I write firmly, 'strive instead for elegance,
grace and style', and then paste it next to the other one on
the wardrobe mirror. My husband, who's getting dressed
to do a radio play at the BBC, sighs wearily.

'I sincerely hope we're not going to become one of those
"happy-clappy households" with charming little inspi-
rational signs posted everywhere.' He reaches for a pair of
navy chinos and a worn Oxford shirt his mother bought

him two Christmases ago. 'I don't want our home looking like the Sunday school meeting room of a church hall.'

'And what would you know about Sunday school meeting rooms?' I parry lightly. 'Anyway, when you close the wardrobe door you can't even see them.'

'Still,' he persists, slipping his feet into a pair of ancient loafers, 'I think that's enough. I don't want to dress in the morning faced with a thousand slogans declaring "I am enough" and "This too shall pass" or whatever pop self-help jargon is being bounced around these days.'

'Fine,' I say, more to end the conversation than anything. 'I'll keep them to myself.'

And it occurs to me that if he's going to be out all day, it's a perfect opportunity to renew my membership at our local gym. Bending down, I search underneath the bed until I locate my old gym bag, covered in dust, complete with a pair of twisted old trainers still lurking inside.

Perfect.

But my husband hasn't finished yet. He removes the most recent Post-it and examines it more closely. ' "Beauty is no guarantee of happiness – strive instead for elegance, grace and style." What's all this about, Louie? You're not going all funny, are you? How are things going with your therapist?'

I'm certain I still own a pair of sweatpants somewhere and there must be a matching sock for this one. I rummage through the laundry basket.

'No, I'm not going funny,' I assure him, as I sift through

piles of dirty clothes, 'and things are fine with my therapist. I'm just trying to make the most of myself, that's all. It's something I'm doing for me.'

He looks unconvinced, so I change my tack. 'What I mean to say is, I just want you to be proud of me.'

His face softens. 'But, Pumpkin, I'm already proud of you. You're a very good girl,' he says, kissing my forehead and patting me lightly on the head. 'You're a very good girl and a very good Pumpkin.'

'Yes, thank you,' I say, smiling back at him. 'Only, would you mind terribly not calling me Pumpkin?'

He looks at me as if I'd just slapped him across the face. 'Not call you Pumpkin? What's wrong with Pumpkin?'

'Well, I know you mean it as a term of endearment but it's just so fat sounding. So round and heavy. Couldn't we have another name? What if you called me something like Sweetheart, or Angel or . . . or, I don't know, what about Beauty?'

He frowns at me.

'OK, well, what about Pretty? My Pretty? That's nice, isn't it?'

'I've always called you Pumpkin. You *are* my Pumpkin,' he says firmly.

'Yes, I know, but we're allowed to change a nickname, aren't we?' I try to pacify him by wrapping my arms around him but he sidesteps me and reaches over to pull his jacket from the back of the bedroom chair.

'You can't just make up a new nickname because you feel like it. After all, I'm the one who has to say it. And "My Pretty" sounds like a pantomime pirate.'

'Yes, fine. But all I'm asking is that perhaps I could have a more attractive nickname . . . I don't know . . . if it has to be a food then what about Sweet Pea? A pea is a lot smaller than a pumpkin.'

'I am not some ageing Southern belle, Louise.' And he sighs, pressing his fingers to his forehead and closing his eyes to concentrate. 'Right,' he says at last, 'what about Sausage? It's my final offer.'

'Sausage!'

'I'm English. You knew that when you married me. I cannot call my wife Sweet Pea or Sugar or My Little Dumpling or any of the other gourmet, internationally recognized terms of endearment.'

'But you can call me Sausage?'

'Well, not just Sausage. My *Little* Sausage.' He smiles. 'I think it's sweet.'

Now it's my turn to look unconvinced.

He shrugs his shoulders. 'Besides which, I really don't have time for this right now. I must be going.' He strides into the hallway and grabs his script from the small round table by the door. Leaning forward, he plants a quick kiss on my forehead. 'I'll see you when I get back tonight, Sausage.'

The door slams shut.

I walk back into the bedroom and stare at the dusty gym

bag and curly old trainers. What's the point of going to all this effort if at the end of it, I'm still not beautiful and the most flattering thing my husband can think to call me is Sausage?

The siren song of the duvet begins to call me, luring me back into bed, away from the gym and this pointless pursuit of self-improvement. After all, I have only a few precious hours on my own to spend in a state of complete oblivion before he returns. My breathing begins to slow and my eyelids droop.

And then I see it, the little yellow Post-it my husband was examining earlier, floating like a butterfly near my pillow. 'Beauty is no guarantee of happiness – strive instead for elegance, grace and style.' I pick it up and paste it back on the mirror.

'I am not a pumpkin,' I say to my reflection. 'Or a sausage.'

And I pick up my gym bag and leave the bedroom as quickly as possible.

While I still can.

C

Comfort

The idea of comfort has invaded every domain; it is one of the categorical imperatives of modern life. We can no longer bear the thought of the slightest restriction, physical or moral, and many of the details which were considered to be a mark of elegance some years ago are condemned today for reasons of comfort. Down with stiff collars, starched shirts, cumbersome hats, and heavy chignons! Practically the only die-hards to resist are women's shoes.

However, if women continue to seek comfort above all twenty-four hours a day, twelve months a year, they may eventually find that they have allowed themselves to become slaves to the crêpe-rubber sole, nylon from head to toe, pre-digested meals, organized travel, functional uniformity, and general stultification. When comfort becomes an end in itself, it is the Public Enemy Number One of elegance.

It's 7:15 on Friday morning and I'm getting ready for work. Although part of me still clings to the dream of being an actress, I earn my real money selling tickets in the box office of a small, self-producing playhouse in Charing Cross.

My husband is asleep on the other side of the bed and I get dressed in the dark. There's not a lot left in my wardrobe to choose from so I put on the navy pinafore dress and the pink Oxford shirt. The dress is figure hugging and very tight, which is why I haven't worn it in years. As I zip it up, my spine becomes erect, encased in the rigidly tailored bodice. I try to revert to my normal, semi-slouched posture and nearly asphyxiate myself. Next, I slip into a pair of dark brown stilettos I wore at my wedding. They're the only pair of high heels left after the Great Cull, and suddenly I'm tottering around the flat like a little Marilyn Monroe. After so many days in cheap plimsolls and baggy chinos, it feels very unusual. I comb my hair into a side-parting, pin it back with a rhinestone clip and then apply a soft red lipstick. Leaving the flat, I catch a glimpse of my reflection in the hall mirror.

Who is this woman?

I'm going to be late. But what I fail to take on board is the tremendous restriction of movement created by pairing a long, straight skirt with a pair of high, strappy heels. This ensemble is fine for staggering around the flat but obviously not meant for long-haul journeys. The faster I try to walk, the more I look like a wind up doll. The only way to move forward at all is to transfer my weight in a slow, rolling motion from one hip to the next. The dress is now in control; it dictates when I arrive at work and how. So, I sashay forth precariously, swaying gently as I go.

There's something about a slow moving female in the middle of rush hour traffic. Everyone, everything changes. And I discover that moving slowly is one of the most powerful things you can do. It's different from being infirm or depressed. The dress makes sure I'm bolt upright, imbuing me with a look of haughty dignity, as if I'm above petty concerns like being at work on time. I appear to be walking because it amuses me, not because I have to. And in the sea of darting pedestrians around me, I have become majestic.

If you're going to walk that slowly, you might as well smile. And here's where it gets really interesting. Cab drivers slow down, even though their light is green, just to let me cross the road. The policemen in front of the Houses of Parliament say, 'Good morning' and tip their hats. And the tourists who cluster so frustratingly in front of Big Ben with their cameras step aside politely, as if they've suddenly found themselves in the middle of a great big living room and they've only just discovered it belongs to me.

Yes, the world is my living room and I'm a gracious hostess passing through, checking to see if everyone's all right.

I have a look around. That's another advantage of

moving slowly, plenty of time for browsing. The air is delicate and sharp, the sunlight crisp and wholly benevolent. Breathing deeply, or rather, as deeply as the dress permits, a strange, unfamiliar awareness descends upon me.

Everything's all right. Everything really is all right.

As I saunter into the theatre foyer, my heart's pounding and my cheeks are flushed. I notice my hand as it pushes against the brass plate of the box office door; it seems small and delicate and pretty. For a moment, I'm not quite sure it's mine. But it is mine. And it is small and delicate and pretty.

Colin's there, waiting for me. I have the keys to the box office door.

'Well, look at you!' he says, kissing me on each cheek.

I smile archly. 'Whatever can you be referring to, Mr Riley?' I unlock the door and switch on the lights.

'Whatever, indeed! Let's put the kettle on and then I want to hear all about it!'

Something amazing has happened. I'm no longer invisible.

Colin's my best friend. He doesn't know it, but he is. He's always chiding me about how unapproachable and distant I am, but in fact, he knows more about me than my therapist and husband combined. A reformed 'West End Wendy', he used to be a dancer in *Cats* until a tendon injury put his spandex unitard days firmly behind him. He can still do an impressive pirouette when he wants to but now he contents himself with teaching seated aerobics to the over-sixties in his local community centre (he loves it because they all call him 'The Young Man') and working part-time in the box office with me. We share not only a love of dance and theatre, but also a very similar Catholic upbringing, with what sounds like exactly the same sadistic nuns (or their relations) rapping our knuckles on different sides of the Atlantic.

'So you got dressed today! What's this all about? Having an affair?' He automatically examines the inside of the kettle for encroaching lime scale. The office kettle is de-scaled twice weekly and the mugs sanitized with bleach when Colin's bored. We're used to coffee that both fizzes and removes the stains from your teeth.

'Hardly!' I switch on my computer.

He takes a small plastic bag out of his rucksack, removes two well-wrapped plastic containers and pops them in the fridge.

'What's for lunch today, Col?'

That's another one of his passions; he can't resist food that's been marked down in supermarkets because the sell-by date has nearly gone. Consequently, his lunches consist of daring taste sensations, dictated by the contents of Tesco's reduced section.

'Today we have a fantastic piece of roasted lamb that's only just slipped by its expiry date but smelled fine this morning, and a small salad of roast peppers, rocket, and new potatoes – although the rocket's not as lively as I'd like it to be. But then you can't have everything.'

Colin's a good cook but you have to have a cast-iron stomach to dine at his house.

'So,' he looks me up and down, 'what's the story? You look amazing. Coffee or tea?'

'Coffee, please, easy on the bleach. There's nothing to tell, really. I cleaned out my closet, and this is what I had left. You like?'

'Very much so, Ouise.' (He always calls me Ouise, pronounced 'weez-y', the name Louise being too long and complicated to say in its entirety.) 'And it's about time. I was beginning to fear for your sex life. What does Himself think?'

'He hasn't seen me today, he was asleep. And you know I have no sex life. I'm married.'

'Well, I'd buy yourself some extra condoms, darling, and be prepared to walk bow-legged for a few days. He's going to think it's Christmas!'

'Colin Riley! Don't be wicked!' I laugh. 'Remember, the Baby Jesus can hear you!' But inside I feel strange, almost sick. I don't know if I want to go there again.

But that's another dangerous thing about being Catholic; we believe in miracles.

When I get home that evening, I decide to give it a go. After all, it's been a long time. The flat is empty, but I spot my husband poking about in the back garden, wearing a pair of rubber gloves. Sneaking into the bathroom, I fix my hair and adjust my make-up. It's so rare that I do this. It's so rare that I even try to be interesting to him any more. I'm not quite sure what to do with myself or how to begin, so I go into the living room and perch on the edge of the sofa.

It's like waiting in a doctor's surgery.

My husband and I puzzle over this room; obsess about it. We spend endless hours trying to rearrange it so that it feels warm, comfortable and inviting. We make drawings, sketch plans, cut out little paper models to scale and move them around on pieces of paper with all the intensity of two world-class chess masters. But the result is the same. Wind howls around the sofa. An ocean of parquet stretches between the green armchair and the coffee table. (I've seen guests land on their stomachs reaching for a cup of tea.) And the dining room table lurks in the corner like an instrument of torture rescued from the Spanish Inquisition. (Dinner parties confirm this to be true.)

I pick up a magazine and am flicking through the pages when he comes in.

'Hello!' he calls.

'Hey, I'm in here!' My throat is tight so it comes out a bit higher than normal.

He pokes his head round the corner. Still wearing the rubber gloves, he's now got the bedroom waste-bin in his hands.

'Louise,' he begins.

'Yes?' I rise slowly so he can see the full glory of my form-fitting dress, smiling in a playful, naughty way. It's a risk. Either I look like a complete sex goddess or Jack Nicholson in *The Shining*.

My husband stands immobilized. He looks cute and confused in his faded, baggy sweatpants. I giggle and take a step forward. 'Yes,' I say again, only softer this time, like I'm answering a question, not asking one.

We're standing quite close now; there's only the wastebin between us. I can smell the damp warmth of his hair and the clean, fresh perfume of the clothing softener we use on his sweatshirt. I gaze into his eyes and for a moment everything shifts and melts. I'm smiling for real now, with my whole being and I know I don't look like Jack Nicholson. Raising my hand, my pretty, delicate hand, I move forward to caress the gentle slope of his cheek, when suddenly I see something that stops me.

As my hand draws closer, his body tenses. He's standing just there in front of me, but somehow, without ever moving, he begins to recede. A look sweeps across his face, hardening his features into a façade of detachment. It's the look of every child who has been forced to endure an unpleasant but unavoidable physical punishment; a spontaneous expression of utter resignation.

I step back in amazement, my hand poised in the air like a Sindy doll. My husband looks up in surprise and our eyes meet. The air around us condenses into a vacuum, thick with shame and humiliation, impossible to endure.

My husband is the first to recover, his face a mask of indignation.

He holds up the waste-bin. 'Louise, what is *this*?'

I look at the contents of the bin. I'm staring at it but I seem to have a hard time seeing it. 'Garbage.' That's the best I can come up with.

He reaches in, pulls out a printer paper box and wields it aloft. 'And this?'

He's really got me now. 'More garbage?'

He rolls his eyes and sighs the sigh of all sighs. The 'shall I repeat this for the mentally impaired?' sigh. 'All right, look.' He places the crumpled box back into the bin. 'Now what do you see?'

My eyes are welling up with tears. I blink them back. 'I see a box in a bin.'

'No, Louise, what you see is a box taking up the *whole* of the bin. Every single bit of room.'

'So what? It's a bin. Empty it!' I despise him. There's no way I'm going to cry. Ever.

'And who's going to do that? Me, that's who.'

'Not necessarily.'

'Please!' He rolls his eyes again. I'm married to a Jewish mother.

'You don't have to. You don't have to be the self-appointed garbage monitor. Somehow we'd survive.'

'You just don't get it, do you? All I'm asking is that when you have an extra large piece of rubbish, could you please use the kitchen bin. All right? Is that understood?'

'An extra large piece of rubbish.'

'Yes. And don't be that way, you know exactly what I'm talking about.'

'Of course.' I feel cold. I want to climb under the covers and go to sleep.

'So, we're in agreement?'

'Yes, large garbage in big bin. Understood.'

'It's not much to ask.'

'No, it certainly isn't.'

He turns to go, but pauses when he reaches the door. 'That dress . . .' he begins.

'Yes?' Heat rushes to my face and I wish I weren't so pale, so transparent.

'It's . . . what I mean to say is, you look very nice.'

I stare at him across the sea of parquet. 'Thank you.'

'But if you want to change into something more suitable, maybe we can start clearing that path in the garden. After all, it's really a job we should do together.'

He lingers by the doorway, waiting for some sort of response.

There's nothing to say.

'Well, whenever you're ready, then.'

He turns and walks back into the garden.

And I am alone.

That night, I stay up and read, searching for clues through the pages of *Elegance*. There must be a way out of this. Someone as wise and experienced as Madame Dariaux must be able to advise me. I'm certain, quite certain, it wasn't always this way. If I can just find the key, the moment I should've turned left instead of right or said yes instead of no, then I'll be able to understand what I did wrong.

And then the rest is easy.

I simply reverse it.

D

Daughters

Little daughters are understandably the pride and joy of their mothers, but they are very often also, alas, the reflection of their mother's inelegance. When you see a poor child all ringletted, beribboned, and loaded down with a handbag, an umbrella, and earrings, or wearing crêpe-soled shoes with a velvet dress, you can be certain that her mother hasn't the slightest bit of taste.

It is a serious handicap to be brought up this way, because a child must be endowed with a very strong personality of her own in order to rid herself of the bad habits that have been inculcated during her early years. The more simply a little girl is dressed — sweaters and skirts in the winter, Empire-style cotton dresses in the summer — the more chic she is. It is never too early to learn that discretion and simplicity are the foundations of elegance.

When I was about nine, I was taken out of my Catholic day school and sent to an all girls' preparatory school. There I met Lisa Finegold, who became my best friend for a year and a half and my fashion idol for a lifetime. Her mother, Nancy, was from New York, which made her sophisticated. Pencil thin, with long brown hair and elegant features, she moved as if she were made of fine bone china.

My own mother was experimenting with unisex dressing that year, to my intense mortification. She'd read a book on Communist China and been so impressed by the austerity of their lifestyle, that she emulated it by wearing the same red tartan trouser suit every day for a month. (This was in the seventies). While Nancy Finegold never ventured from the house in anything but stilettos, my mother regularly rounded us all up for long, rigorous hikes in the woods, dressed in thick moccasins she'd made herself and one of her favourite Greenpeace tee-shirts. I longed for her to grow her hair long and even dug out an old wig she'd bought in the sixties but she stubbornly refused to alter her trademark crop. 'It's not that important,' she'd say. But I couldn't help secretly wishing she was from New York and made of bone china too.

Lisa had her own bedroom, complete with a huge, extra frilly canopy bed, just like in *Gone With the Wind*. It had pillows covered in lace that you didn't sleep on; they were just for show. Rows of beautiful china dolls were carefully seated along her mantelpiece and in the corner stood a mahogany and glass display case filled with her collection of porcelain miniatures.

Then there were Lisa's clothes, which her mother bought in massive shopping sprees in New York. Most of them were dry clean only and hung on silk-covered hangers in neat rows. Everything was pressed, clean and, more amazingly, the right size. She didn't own a single hand-me-down.

Until I met Lisa, all my friends were exactly like me. We shared rooms begrudgingly with our siblings, drawing invisible lines down the centre of the floor, not unlike the battle lines of the Civil War, in a vain effort to gain some autonomy and an identity of our own. We slept in bunk beds on pillows you put your head on and could drool over and that were machine washable for when you got sick. Even the furniture was made out of hard-wearing, wipeable surfaces, the kind of furnishings you could jump off of or on to without a second thought. And our collections were living: spiders, slugs, bugs, and worms. They were displayed in jars and cardboard boxes stored in the cool mud underneath the porch steps in the back yard. There are many back-yard badges of courage, of which touching and capturing a gigantic slug after a thunderstorm is only one.

During recess, Lisa and I would link arms and walk round the edge of the playground in endless circles (Lisa never ran or played tag or did anything involving sweat), and I would ply her for more and more details about her day. I dreamt regularly of my own parents dying in a horrible car accident and, at the height of my inconsolable grief, being adopted by the Finegolds and becoming Lisa's sister.

The first time Lisa asked me home to play, I felt like I'd fallen into a dream world. The housekeeper answered the door and was wearing an apron, just like Alice on the *Brady Bunch*. She made us lunch and not only was it hot, but it consisted of spaghetti and home-made sauce she'd actually cooked herself – not out of a jar. If that wasn't enough, we even had tapioca pudding for dessert, which was sweet and bumply and, Lisa claimed, made with frog's eggs, which is why she wouldn't touch it and why I got two helpings.

Finally we went up to Lisa's room and sat on the bed. It was quite a concoction when fully made; you couldn't really touch it without ruining the effect, so we sat along the edge, not in the middle. Lisa smoothed down the folds of her skirt and looked bored. (This was her most attractive quality, her incredible capacity for boredom.)

'Why don't we play dolls?' I suggested, eagerly eyeing her marvellous collection. I'd already chosen which ones would be ballerinas and which ones would be possessed by the devil. *The Exorcist* had come out that year and although we were too young to see it, my brother and sister and I were fascinated by the idea of being possessed, vomiting green stuff, and speaking in scary voices. Also, it contrasted nicely with the ballet theme.

'Why don't we make the ones with dark hair be possessed and all the blonde ones ballerinas?'

There was a moment's silence and Lisa looked at me like I was retarded.

'Or the other way around?' I was flexible.

'You don't *play* with them,' she said. 'You just *look* at them.'

I wanted to ask why but my desire to impress her prevented me from calling attention to the fact that I wasn't completely *au fait* with the etiquette of owning china dolls.

'Oh yeah. Right. OK, well, why don't we make a miniature world underneath the bed? We can take all the miniatures out of the cabinet and if we get some green tissues, we can make a pond and then we can use the bedside table and it's like they go into the World of the Giants . . .'

I could tell by the pained expression on her face that I was losing her.

'Louise,' she began, and then stopped.

Lisa couldn't explain her world to me any better than I could understand it. And she had never had to before. Finally, like a child reciting a catechism, she said, 'Some things are to look at, not to touch.'

'Oh.' I didn't get it at all.

She smiled at me. So I smiled back. We sat there smiling at each other, both thinking the other insane.

'I know,' she said at last. 'Let's go up to the attic and dress the dog in baby clothes.'

Luckily, there are some human experiences that transcend cultural divides.

Then one day, the Finegolds invited me out to dinner. In honour of the occasion, I wore my best dress, which was made to my exact specifications by Grandma Irene. We chose the pattern and the material together, a crisp white cotton covered in bright blue and red flowers, and she made little cap sleeves trimmed with lace and smocked the front of it by hand.

I brought the dress to school with me on a hanger and hung it in my locker. Occasionally, I'd show it to one of the other girls but I wanted it to be a surprise for Lisa, certain that once she saw me in it, she'd come up with the idea of us being sisters all on her own.

After school we went to her house and played, which, that day, consisted of taking all the miniature figures out of the glass cabinet, looking at them and then putting them back in exactly the same way. After a while, we heard someone come in and Lisa said, 'It's time to get ready.' We put on our dresses, brushed each other's hair and went downstairs. Lisa didn't say anything about my dress and I didn't say anything about hers, which was in black velvet with a creamy satin sash. It was understood that we both looked fabulous.

In the kitchen we found Dr Finegold eating tapioca pudding from a serving bowl in the refrigerator. Tall and slim, with black, wavy hair, a romantic moustache and soft, dark eyes, he was easily the most beautiful man I'd ever seen. He owned an enormous collection of tortoises that he kept in various tanks and plastic pools in the basement, which I thought were cool but Lisa thought were gross. And best of all, he loved to play the piano.

'Daddy, don't do that,' Lisa admonished half-heartedly. (Even her parents were just minor irritations.)

'Our little secret,' he said, tossing the spoon into the sink. 'I know; why don't I play you girls a little tune?'

We went into the living room and he began to play. I danced around the piano and we laughed, egging each other on. I'd turn a pirouette and he'd shout, 'Go on, do another one!' He'd do a massive run and I'd clap and make him do it again. Lisa wasn't very good at dancing; it was part of her whole horror of physical activity, so she stood by the side of the piano, sulking and being bored. Dr Finegold sang 'Mona Lisa', which I thought was hysterical and Lisa ignored him. All in all, we had a great time.

We didn't even hear Nancy come in but suddenly she was there and Dr Finegold stopped playing. I stood beaming and panting to catch my breath. This was it, I'd just turned four pirouettes and was wearing the most beautiful dress in the world. If ever they were going to want to adopt me, it was now.

Nancy Finegold stood in silence in the doorway. 'I think you girls ought to get ready,' she said at last.

'We are ready, Mama.' Lisa's voice was unusually quiet. She turned to me. 'Is that what you're wearing?'

I nodded. Was this a trick question?

She turned her back to me and spoke to Lisa. 'Don't you have something she could borrow?'

I felt myself go cold; the way you do when someone talks about you as if you were a chair.

'Nan!' Dr Finegold interrupted.

She registered him with distaste. 'Don't be so dramatic, Mel.' Bending down to examine my dress more closely, she smiled sweetly. 'That dress is fine, Louise, but Lisa has one that will be better.'

'Mom!' The horror on Lisa's face was unmistakable; she'd obviously never been asked to share anything before.

Nancy Finegold was a genius trapped in a world of idiots. She sighed in exasperation, rolling her eyes in the grown-up version of Lisa's favourite expression. 'All right, fine! What about a cardigan then?'

Dr Finegold walked away and Lisa stared dejectedly at the floor.

In her full-length mink coat and slender high heels, Nancy seemed too thin to stand upright for long. Her huge brown eyes scanned the room for any sign of affirmation or weakness and, finding nothing, she opened her mouth to speak but nothing came out. She closed it again in such a way that she reminded me of a ventriloquist's dummy and for one terrible moment I thought I would laugh. Her exquisite hands clenched in frustration and then fell limply by her side, the gold bangles rattling against one another, as if someone had suddenly let go of the strings.

I couldn't bear it. 'I'll wear a cardigan,' I offered.

She stared at me for a moment and then smiled, triumphant. She gave Lisa a shove. 'Go on. Run upstairs and grab one of your blue cardigans.'

Lisa extracted herself with all the speed of one of my giant slugs.

Now there was just the two of us. I stared at her, but she didn't look at me. Instead, she knelt down and pulled up my knee socks, folding the tops over in two perfectly even strips. I could smell her perfume, her hairspray and the musky, almost aluminium scent of the fur coat she wore as she smoothed down my hair with her hand. I had wanted to be touched by her for months, to run up and wrap my arms around her, to bury my head against her shoulder and tell her how much I loved her. And now, at last, I was the whole focus of her attention. And I couldn't move.

Some things are to look at, not to touch. Nancy Finegold was one of them.

We went out to dinner and I wore the cardigan.

My father came to pick me up in the old brown family station wagon and when I jumped in the front seat, I felt free and very, very old.

'How'd it go, Pea?' he asked. 'Did they like your dress?'

'I don't think they understood it, Da.'

He laughed. 'What's there to understand?'

'Everything,' I said.

Absolutely everything.

E

Expecting

The period during which a woman is expecting a baby is not always, it must be admitted, the most propitious one for elegance. A bad complexion, an expanding waistline, a silhouette becoming a bit awkward towards the end, all add up to an image that is not always a joy to contemplate in the mirror. But since almost every woman is obliged to go through it at one time or another, it is better to accept the situation with good humour and to make the most of it.

A good plan is to buy only a few things for your maternity wardrobe and to wear the same dresses over and over again until you are quite fed up with them. This way you can give them away afterwards without the slightest regret. Above all, don't try to have them taken in at the seams after you have recovered your normal figure. The clothes you have worn throughout these long months will disgust you for the rest of your days.

My husband and I are entertaining friends, a couple we haven't seen in a long time. We haven't seen them because they have children, twin girls. My husband and I don't do children very well; no matter how much we try to hide it, we're clearly horrified. I keep staring at them like I'm going to pass out and he's permanently on guard, brandishing a washing up cloth like he's ready to mop up toxic waste. Very quickly the couple feel as if they've defiled the sanitized sanctuary of our pristine living room and decide that the twins need to go home for a nap after only forty-five minutes in our company. Everyone's relieved, even the babies, who are only nine months old. Their faces noticeably relax as they're loaded into the car.

Our friends are all having children now; we're the odd ones out. They've stopped asking us about it; stopped smiling and saying, 'But surely *someday* you'll want a family.' By now it's obvious that only an act of God could make us parents. We wave to them as they drive away, and then walk back into our barren household – the one with the dust-free living room and the bed the size of Kansas.

'Thank God that's over,' my husband says, bending down to pick up something from the floor. It's a single, pale blue baby sock, still warm and smelling of baby. He hands it to me. I don't know what to do with it or where to put it, so I throw it away.

'Yes,' I agree. 'Thank God.'

The first time I was pregnant, I was sixteen and it was

before the creation of home pregnancy tests. I had to see a doctor to tell me what I already knew. You don't have to have been pregnant before to know that there's something strange going on. I was throwing up in the mornings and, in fact, all through the day and I started noticing strange discharges I'd never encountered before. Things smelled different, tasted wrong, and I'd gone off pizza. For the first time in my life, I was forced into paying attention to my body. I was possessed, like in *The Invasion of the Body Snatchers* and it wasn't going to go away.

I couldn't go to the family physician – not to the same man who'd vaccinated me against smallpox and measured my growth against a chart on the wall covered with smiling, cartoon animals. I was sick but I had to hide it. But by now I was used to hiding all the most important facts of my day.

I was used to hiding the fact that I threw up my food after each meal by going upstairs to the guest bathroom and sticking my fingers down my throat. I was used to hiding the little black speed pills I took every morning, the ones I bought from Sarah Blatz, a fat, red-headed girl who played on the girls' field-hockey team and who was prescribed them by her doctor to lose weight. And I was used to hiding where I went in the evenings from my parents, what I did and especially who with.

My friend Mary took me to see her doctor, a female physician in another part of town. She had a growth chart on her wall too, but she'd never measured me before, so that was OK.

Mary was frightened; she wasn't used to concealing things or maybe she was just used to covering up all the normal things, like that she'd gone all the way with her boyfriend, the one she'd been going steady with for a year and a half, or that she'd got drunk at a friend's party last Saturday and had to spend the night.

I didn't have a boyfriend; I got pregnant from a guy who never called again and I was drunk every Saturday night.

After school, Mary drove me to the doctor's in her mother's custom built silver Cadillac, the one with the horn that played the theme from *The Godfather* when you pressed it. (Her father was in the meat trade.) Every once in a while she'd press it and we'd laugh; more out of politeness than anything else. She was obviously trying her best to cheer me up and I was grateful for her kindness.

The doctor took a blood test and examined me as I sat in my little paper gown on the crinkly paper strip that covered the examining table. The office was on the 7th floor of a modern block, overlooking the traffic that led into the mall below. I concentrated on the pale blue of the sky as she felt my breasts and shook her head sadly.

'They're pregnanty,' she announced. 'We'll get the test back tomorrow, but I can tell you right now, you're pregnant.'

I know, I thought. I know.

Mary wanted me to tell her mom because that's what she would do. But I knew I'd have to do the rest on my own. I made an appointment, but had to wait another month before I could have the abortion.

In the meantime, I told my parents I had an ulcer, which they believed without questioning. Every morning at around 4:30 am, I was sick. And every morning, my father woke up at 4:15 and made me a small bowl of porridge to settle my stomach, which he placed by the side of my bed. Then he'd pad off upstairs in his red robe, feeling his way in the darkness to catch another hour and a half's sleep. He never asked if he should do that; he just did it. Like so many things in our house, even acts of kindness occurred in silence. I wondered if he would do the same thing if he knew the truth. I think he would.

My skin got bad and my mouth tasted metallic. In my locker at school, I kept an enormous box of saltines, which I ate in the hundreds. My diet diminished to saltines, mashed potatoes, and porridge. Anything else was just too exciting. No matter how much I ate, I still got sick. And no matter how often I threw up, I was still hungry. I was more afraid of gaining weight than of being pregnant.

The operation cost two hundred and thirty dollars. My parents gave me two hundred dollars in cash after I managed to convince them that I needed a new winter coat and the rest of it I paid for out of my allowance.

Finally the day came, a Saturday morning in early March. It was raining, softly misting when I left the house.

I told my parents I was going to go shopping with my friend Anne and then I drove myself to the clinic and checked in. It was early, around 9 am. The waiting room was full of flowered cushions, pleasant prints, and bright, soft colours. There were little clusters of people – a young couple holding hands and whispering to each other, a girl with her family. They'd obviously tried to make the waiting room as sympathetic and normal looking as possible, but despite that, no one wanted to look at one another.

You had to meet with a counsellor before you did it. They took us in one at a time, in such a way that you never passed any of the other women in the hall. I was led into a little office where a young woman with short brown hair was waiting for me. I cannot remember her name or how she introduced herself but I can remember her deliberate, almost institutionalized kindness. And I recall her asking if I was alone and saying 'yes'.

My mouth was dry and sticky. The office was like a closet, with no windows. There was a table and two chairs and a chart on the wall with a diagram of the female anatomy. Even here they'd done their best to make it seem normal and wholesome by painting the walls pink. It was like a beauty parlour for abortions. There were no sounds at all in the room, no traffic noise, no distant conversations. Just the woman and me.

'I'm here to tell you about the operation and what to expect,' she began.

I nodded.

She took out a red plastic model of a uterus cut in half. 'This is a model of a uterus,' she said.

I nodded again. I wondered where she'd got it, what kind of company made these sorts of things, and what other models they had in their catalogue.

She started to talk and point at the model. I could hear her voice, and see her hands moving, but my mind had gone numb. I just stared at the plastic uterus, thinking how red it was and how a real one couldn't possibly be that red.

'Excuse me,' I interrupted, after a while. 'I'm going to be sick.'

'Of course,' she said.

I went and threw up in a little cubical next door. There seemed to be cubicles everywhere – clean, little rooms filled with women throwing up. When I came back, she continued where she left off. She was obviously used to people throwing up in the middle of her presentation.

'During the operation, what we will do is remove the lining of the uterus, creating a kind of non-biological miscarriage. You will have all the symptoms of a miscarriage – heavy bleeding, cramps, and hormonal imbalance. This will make you feel a little more fragile than normal. It's important for you to rest afterwards and take it easy for a few days. Is someone coming to pick you up?'

I stared at her.

'Did you drive yourself?' she repeated.

The room was perfectly still. She had no make-up on. I tried to imagine her in a bar, talking to a stranger, way past closing time. I couldn't.

She waited. She was used to waiting.

I started to open my mouth; it tasted like yellow sick. I closed it again and tried to swallow.

'Would you like some water?'

I shook my head; it would only make me throw up again.

'You don't have to do this,' she said at last.

She was looking at me with her clean, fresh face, the face of a mother on a children's aspirin commercial.

I started to cry and she was used to that too.

I hated myself because I knew we would all be doing it. She passed me a Kleenex. Twenty minutes from now, she'd be passing a Kleenex to someone else, the girl with the boyfriend perhaps.

'Maybe you'd like to think about it some more,' she offered. Freedom of choice.

'No.' I was done crying. 'I've made up my mind.'

It was exactly as she said it would be. An hour later I was lying in a hospital version of a La-Z-y Boy chair, drinking sugary tea and eating biscuits.

Four hours later I was shopping for a new winter coat with my friend Anne, using a credit card I'd stolen from my parents.

'Your ulcer seems to be better,' my father remarked a week later.

'Yes, Da. I believe it's gone.'

And it is gone. Until the next time.

There's a coat that hangs in the front hall cloakroom of my parents' house. It's a single-breasted, navy blue winter coat; a classic cut in immaculate condition. It's been there for years but no one's noticed. It has never been worn.

F

Fur

If women are honest with themselves, they would admit that the fascination they feel for furs is not only due to the warmth they provide. After all, a fur is never just a fur — it is also, more than any other garment I can think of, a symbol, and a mink coat is the most easily identifiable symbol of them all. It stands for achievement, both for the man who bought it and the woman who wears it, as well as status and undeniable luxury. It has been said with a great deal of truth that a mink is the feminine Legion of Honour.

Furs are important milestones in a woman's life, and in general they are purchased only after a great deal of thought and many comparisons. So make your selection with care. After all, men come and go but a good fur is a destiny.

There's a story about a famous opera diva rehearsing for a production of *Tosca* at the Met. At the end of the rehearsal, she sends her dresser to collect her things and the poor woman comes back clutching a black wool coat.

The star is appalled. She tosses her head and fixes the woman with an icy stare. 'Honey, you know I don't wear no *cloth* coats!'

Divas and minks have a lot in common. You have to kill something to make a mink. Its beauty is horrible to behold. Divas are like that too. And while you don't have to be a diva to wear a mink, it helps.

I got my first mink when I was nineteen years old. It was given to me by a friend of my mother's, whose own mother had recently died of Alzheimer's. She'd been a tiny woman and no one else in the family could wear the coat. Or wanted to.

It was a full-length mink; glossy, heavy, stinking of musk when it rained. It was the most un-PC garment it was possible to own. And yet it had both authority and a powerful, threatening, glamour. People reacted violently to it; they were infuriated, offended, jealous, or lustful. It was a coat of almost biblical symbolism. It hid nothing, accommodated no one. If you hated it, it was there to be hated. If you loved it, it couldn't care less. The very thing that made it repulsive was the same thing that gave it its splendour. And it fitted me like a glove.

The trouble with a coat like that is it can take over your

life; dominate your whole personality. If you don't know who you are, you can easily become a mink coat.

I had a boyfriend at the time. He'd been a car thief in high school and was now two years ahead of me in drama school. He wore a denim jacket that had been in police chases, that still had bloodstains on it from when he'd been arrested. Badly worn, it hung together in places by threads.

We looked like brother and sister, he and I, with the same pale hair and green eyes. Neither of us knew who we were or who we wanted to be, so we became actors. We spent our nights eating at an all night diner called Chief's, he in his threadbare denim and me in my mink, smoking cigarettes, drinking beer with our eggs, and arguing about iambic pentameter and if Pinter was really a genius or just a fraud. We were going to be great actors, famous and rich. We made up stories about ourselves, wore costumes, acted in scenes. And we were our own favourite characters.

Only, I was always the mink and he was always the denim jacket. We met wearing them, parted wearing them and despite all the drinking, fucking, and fighting, we just couldn't manage to take them off.

He performed Romeo in his end of term project with a black eye. He got it smashing in the face of a man who propositioned me in an all night drinking club over the Christmas break. It was three o'clock in the morning. We'd been drinking since six. The man had said something I hadn't quite heard and then all of a sudden we were outside in the bitter cold.

They rolled around in the frozen black snow in the middle of the road, punching and kicking, blood forming pale pink pools between the patches of dark grit. A crowd gathered and cheered them on; shouting and jeering – full of exactly the kind of people you'd expect to be strolling around at three in the morning.

I hated to be upstaged. Pulling the mink around me tightly, I walked away, staggering in my high heels over the snowdrifts to the car.

We were doing a close up, just the mink and me, when I saw him running towards me, limping. His nose was bleeding and his knuckles smashed. The guy had been wearing a ring and the side of his face was cut.

'You cunt!' he shouted across the car park. 'You filthy, fucking cunt!'

So, we're starting with Mamet.

DENIM JACKET: I fucking defend your fucking honour and you fucking walk away!

MINK: Get in the car.

DENIM JACKET: Fuck you!

MINK: Get in the fucking car!

DENIM JACKET: I said, fuck you! Or maybe you didn't fucking hear me. Maybe you were too busy walk-ing the fuck away!

MINK: I didn't ask you to fight him, did I?

DENIM JACKET: No man takes that.

MINK: It was about me!

DENIM JACKET: No man fucking takes that, understand? You're my girlfriend. A man says something to you, he says it to me. Understand?

MINK: Fuck you!

DENIM JACKET: Fuck you too.

> (Pinter pause.)

DENIM JACKET: You walked away.

MINK: I couldn't watch you do it, Baby. (Tears welling up in eyes; gin tears; three o'clock in the morning tears.) I just couldn't watch you get hurt.

> (Grabs me by the shoulders; moving rapidly into Tennessee Williams territory now.)

DENIM JACKET: You gotta have faith in me, Louie. Please. (Bloody head on mink.) I need you to have faith in me. (*sotto voce*) I need you, Baby. I need you.

> (Curtain.)

Only the curtain never fell.

We broke up just before I came to England, exhausted. I discovered I wasn't a diva, that I didn't have the endurance for grand opera. And there are only so many ways you can say 'Fuck you' to someone before you start to really mean it.

I had imagined that passion, drama, and love were all

one and the same – proof that the others existed. But the opposite was true: drama and passion are just very clever disguises for a love that has never taken root.

I gave the mink away to a friend in New York. It was a heavy coat to wear and I was relieved to get rid of it. But very soon after it was gone, I began to feel that something was missing.

I thought I could change my character as easily as I could change my coat.

But I've been searching for the right one ever since.

G

Girl Friends

It is a good idea never to go shopping for clothes with a girl friend. Since she is often an unwitting rival as well, she will unconsciously demolish everything that suits you best. Even if she is the most loyal friend in the world, if she simply adores you, and if her only desire is for you to be the most beautiful, I remain just as firm in my opinion: shop alone, and turn only to specialists for guidance. Although they may not be unmercenary, at least they are not emotionally involved.

I particularly dread these kinds of girl friends:

1. *The one who wants to be just like you, who is struck by the same love-at-first-sight for the same dress, who excuses herself in advance by saying, 'I hope you don't mind, darling, and anyway, we don't go out together very much, and we can always*

telephone beforehand to make sure we don't wear it at the same time, etc. etc. . . . You are furious but don't dare show it and you return the dress the next day.

2. *The friend with a more modest budget than yours, who couldn't dream of buying the same kind of clothes as you (the truth is that she dreams of nothing else). Perhaps you think it is a real treat for her to go shopping with you. Personally, I call it mental cruelty, and I am always painfully embarrassed by the role of second fiddle that certain women reserve for their best friend. Besides, her presence is of absolutely no use to you at all, because this kind of friend always approves of everything you select, and will agree with even greater enthusiasm if it happens to be something that isn't very becoming.*

3. *Finally, the friend who lives for clothes and whose advice you seek. This spoilt and self-confident woman will monopolize the attention of the shop assistants, who are quick to scent a good customer. You find yourself forgotten by everybody, trying to decide what looks best not on you, but on your friend.*

Moral: Always shop alone. Women who shop with their friends may be popular, but elegant they are NOT.

I'm on my way to Notting Hill to see a friend I write with, Nicki Sands. We began working on a screenplay together about a year ago. Neither of us is really a writer, which is probably why we aren't making a lot of progress on the project. We meet up religiously twice a week, loitering around in a kind of career cul-de-sac. However, writing does provide us with a useful alibi, instantly deflecting any embarrassing questions such as, 'So, what do you do?'

Nicki used to be a model in the late seventies and early eighties and now she lives with a record producer in an enormous double-fronted house in Notting Hill. They openly despise one another. Neither one of them is obliged to work, so they while away the hours wandering from room to room, looking for new ways to torture each other.

I arrive around 10:30 to find Nicki and Dan milling about in their Santa Fe style kitchen. They own a cappuccino machine that neither of them can work and are standing in front of the faux adobe woodburning hearth and indoor barbecue unit holding their empty cups.

Every once in a while, one of them will have a go and the other will provide a running commentary.

'That's right, put the coffee in and turn the knob . . . No! No, no, no, no, no!'

'Shut up!'

'Jesus, you're doing it wrong *again!*'

'No, I'm not!'

'Steam, there's meant to be steam!'

'Shut up! What is it with you?'

'What is it with me? What *is* it? I've been up since six and I still haven't had a fucking cup of coffee!'

Reading the instructions is considered cheating.

After a while, Dan gives up and makes a Nescafé. The three-hundred-pound triumph of Italian engineering has won again. Nicki and I decide to go out for coffee and discuss plot development. But what we really do is sit in Tom's, a café and organic food shop around the corner, and hash over Nicki's failing relationship in detail.

'He thinks he looks young!' she hisses at me, leaning dramatically across the table, as if discretion were a consideration. 'I mean, he said to me the other day, "I don't think I look a day past thirty-five." I nearly choked on my cappuccino!' (They must have been out.)

She's speaking to me but her eyes never leave the door, just in case someone thinner, prettier, or more chic walks in. This almost never happens. I'm just beginning to confide in her that I think maybe my husband and I might have a serious problem too, when suddenly she screams, grabs my arm violently and yanks me across the table. 'My God! Louise!' she gasps. 'That's the handbag I was telling you about! There!'

I smile and nod.

I'm used to Nicki by now. And I'm used to her ignoring me.

Nicki is one of those women who only has one girlfriend at a time. She wears friends out with her constant demands for attention but is too competitive to tolerate more than one extra female in her life. I've known this for a while. However, cultivating friends has never been my forte. Although I'm perfectly sociable – happy to spend an hour or so in idle chit-chat with any number of people, the thing I'm not terribly good at is the kind of honest self-revelation and shared intimacies that are the backbone of a lasting female friendship. I long to be open and informal, if only my life weren't such a mess. But now is not the time. After all, if I started confiding my innermost problems to someone, I'd have to do something about them. And I'm not ready for that yet. Someday, when I've pulled myself together, maybe I'll have a real chum of the heart.

In the meantime, I'm not expected to share any deep personal confidences with Nicki; I'm only required to show up and tag along. And tagging along will do me just fine. It's easy, undemanding – we talk about nothing more taxing than new lipstick formulations and, even though I could never afford it, the benefits of Pilates versus Hatha yoga techniques. And there's a certain amount of glamour involved in these weekly escapes. I enjoy basking in the chaotic splendour and excess of Nicki World, complete with multi-million pound homes, £100 face crèmes, and £4 organic lattes, while clinging perversely to the reassuring knowledge that, for all their money, Nicki and

Dan are still incredibly unhappy. When your own life remains a baffling, unresolved puzzle, there are few things more comforting than to be surrounded by fellow struggling souls.

When we've downed enough caffeine to bring us to tears, we walk back to Nicki's and dump our bags in the Moroccan style living room. Almost everything that Nicki and Dan lose is eventually discovered lying camouflaged against the overwhelming profusion of kilim cushions that populate this room. They've even managed to create curtains out of old Oriental carpets, so that sitting in it is like being swallowed by a giant carpet bag.

Then we climb up to Nicki's Victorian study and she sits in front of her computer, which folds out from a unit made to look like an antique dressing table, and I sit on the daybed. The daybed is an original, painfully uncomfortable and obviously designed to keep Victorian ladies very much awake.

'OK. Right.' Nicki turns on the computer, clicks into our file and pages down to where we left off.

'Here we are, page fifteen,' she announces triumphantly.

No matter how much work we do or how often we meet, we're always on page fifteen.

'OK, so how did we leave it then?' I try to gather my enthusiasm.

'Jan was just about to reveal to Aaron why she'd left home.'

'Oh, yeah. Good. And what did we decide about that?'

Nicki checks through the notes we made at coffee.

'You know, I don't think we came to any firm conclusions about that one.'

'Did we have any ideas?'

She flicks through again. 'I'm not really seeing anything that can be called a *solid* idea.'

'Oh. OK. Never mind.' I haul myself out of the sagging centre of the daybed. 'Right. Let's get brainstorming!'

The room goes dead. A dog barks somewhere in the distance. Nicki gnaws at a hangnail.

Suddenly, like the voice of God, the sound of Dionne Warwick singing 'Walk On By' floats down the stairs. Nicki's on her feet in a flash.

'My God, I can't *believe* he's doing that now! The bastard!'

'Doing what?' I ask.

'He's playing Dionne Warwick!' she shrieks. Flinging the door open, she screams up the stairs. 'I know what you're doing, you bastard! I *know* what you're doing!'

'My God, Nicki, what's he doing?' I'm missing the point badly.

'He's *exercising*!' she screams, rolling her eyes. 'Don't you understand? The bastard will be bouncing all over the treadmill next!' She cradles her head in her beautifully manicured hands. 'I'm getting a tension headache. I can feel it right *here*.' She points to the top of her left temple. 'I can't work this way. I just can't. Do you mind? I *have* to get out of here.'

So we go shopping.

Shopping with Nicki takes stamina. It takes patience. And it takes great fortitude.

I'm fine as long as we stick to coffee shops and her house but as soon as we go shopping, real, proper clothes shopping, the enormous gulf between her life and mine is ruthlessly revealed. Suddenly all the cuddly *Hello!* glamour and intimacy we've shared evaporates and I'm keenly aware of a sharp, insurmountable shift in status.

Firstly, she's tall, incredibly slender, with long legs and a handsome bust. So it's like, well, like shopping with a model.

Secondly, she shops at Prada and Loewe, Harvey Nichols, and Jo Malone – stores well beyond my meagre budget. I'm used to doing my Columbo impression, shambling around the changing rooms of Harvey Nichols in my second-hand trench coat while she parades through the department in her knickers, grabbing piles of garments in all conceivable colours and styles. The shop assistants love her. They look upon me as a badly groomed pet.

Occasionally, Nicki encourages me to try something on. There are awful moments, embedded in my memory, of standing in front of a changing-room mirror in a badly fitting dress, my legs unshaven, wearing a pair of worn out plimsolls, only to have Nicki emerge from the neighbouring cubical in exactly the same dress (but a size smaller), looking, yes, like a model.

It's the shop assistants I feel for most. They avert their eyes and smile and lie. The minutes stretch like years while they desperately try to make a sale to one of us, to both of us, and then neither of us.

Nicki frowns, pouts and checks for non-existent panty lines while I crawl backwards into the cubical, desperate to hide again under my trench coat and brown beret. Later, I help her carry her bags from the shop. She smiles and pats me on the head and I listen to how hard it is to find clothes that fit when you're really a size six and nearly five foot nine on the way back home in the car.

If she shot me, it would be quicker and less painful.

That's our normal routine, only it's about to change.

Thanks to Madame Dariaux, the next time I meet her, I'm not wearing a brown beret or my second-hand trench. And I've already been shopping. By myself.

I've been thinking about it for a while; building up to it. Normally, I don't even allow myself to window shop; I tell myself I don't have the money and therefore it's torture even to look. Or I tell myself I'm too fat; I'll shop when I'm taller (when I'm five foot nine and a size six). But ever since I wore the navy pinafore dress into work, Colin's been hounding me, calling me 'The Vixen'. And then on Saturday, the most extraordinary thing happened.

Someone noticed me.

A man.

I was on my lunch break and famished. Not just hungry but ravenous. I'd run to Prêt à Manger and bought a tuna salad and a chocolate brownie. Then, back in the theatre, I hid inside the empty auditorium, tucked away in one of the ancient red velvet boxes to eat. Eating is, in fact, putting it politely. What I was actually doing was savaging my food, complete with little grunting noises; leaning in close to the plastic container for maximum intake in the minimum amount of time. It was the kind of eating a girl only does on her own, usually in front of the television, dressed in a pair of pyjamas she hasn't been out of all day. Except, I wasn't alone; there was someone watching me.

I didn't recognize him. Wearing jeans and a faded blue sweatshirt, he had dark, almost black hair and brown, heavy eyes.

He just stood there, hands crammed into his pockets, staring at me. And when I caught sight of him, I nearly choked on a caper.

'That's a funny place to eat,' he smiled.

Oh God, a techy, I thought disparagingly. One of those guys who paint scenery while exposing their bum cracks. Piss off and leave me alone.

'If I go upstairs, they'll nick my brownie and I'm really hungry,' I explained curtly. I turned my attention once again to the total annihilation of my feast but he continued to stand there, digging his hands ever deeper into his pockets and rocking back and forth on his heels.

'Are you new here? I don't recognize you,' he continued amiably.

'No. I work in the box office.' I finished each sentence like I was finishing the conversation but he lingered on, enduring my silence and indifference. I picked lamely at my food. He was putting me off my stride – I felt self-conscious and all too aware of the fact I was eating my tuna salad with a spoon.

He asked me some more questions, about the box office hours and what I thought of the company, but mostly he stared at me. I couldn't figure out what he was doing but it made me nervous and uncomfortable. Eventually, I threw my salad away and made my excuses. Back in the box office, I ranted to Colin about my ruined lunch.

'Well, my little Vixen, what do you expect?' he laughed, pouring me a cup of sugary tea. 'He likes you.'

'Me?! Get *real*, Col.'

'Face facts, Ouise. The man fancies you. And by the way, he isn't just a techy: he's our new hot-shot director and his name's Oliver Wendt. Bit of a dish, if you ask me.'

I felt odd – slightly ill, tingly and adolescent.

'Fancies me?' I echoed.

Colin gave me a hug from behind. 'Yes, Louise. Fancies you. Better get used to it.'

When I left the theatre at the end of the day, Oliver

Wendt was having a cigarette on the front steps of the building.

For someone I'd never noticed before, he suddenly seemed to be everywhere.

'Good night, Louise,' he called after me.

I stopped and turned. 'You know my name.'

'That's right,' he said, stubbing the cigarette end out under his heel. 'And my name's Oliver, so now you know mine.' He was looking straight into my eyes. I felt my heart pounding in my chest, echoing around the seemingly hollow recess of my head. I turned away and smiled to myself.

'Good night, Oliver,' I called, and as my voice drifted off behind me, I felt sure he was smiling too.

I walked home as slowly as I could, reluctant to lose the buzz of adrenaline that coursed through my limbs. And that night, as I lay beside my husband in bed, for once I didn't fall into a coma of sleep.

Sunday I got up early, long before my husband was conscious, and made my way to Oxford Street. I went to Top Shop and wandered around the cavernous store for hours, mesmerized by the video screens, pulsating music, and vast selection of clothing.

At last, after trying on what was easily half the stock, I settled on a pair of steely grey, wide-legged trousers and a pale pink, fitted cardigan top. Then, invigorated by my purchases, I walked across the street to Jones and bought a pair of black ankle boots with a kitten heel. And suddenly, in a single afternoon, the thing I had never allowed myself to do was done. The brown beret and second-hand trench coat were gone and I emerged, butterfly-like in all my Top Shop glory.

Monday, I'm due to meet Nicki in Tom's at noon. I get to Tom's a little late, and Nicki's already there, guzzling a latte with all the desperation of a junkie. She looks up and I wave. But instead of waving back, she just frowns at me. Something's wrong with this picture.

'Sorry I'm late,' I say, piling my coat on the chair between us. 'Been here long?'

She's examining me, her eyes registering every detail of my being. 'You look different,' she concludes.

'Yes,' I smile, pleased she's noticed.

'Those trousers are *new!*' This is not an observation but an indignant accusation.

'Yes.' I pull out a chair and swivel my hips proudly.

'When did you go shopping?' she demands.

'On Sunday.'

I sit down and a young man with spiky hair and an apron comes over to take my order.

'And what can I get for you?' He's smiling and his eyes are gleaming. Normally I have to wave my hands in the air like an air traffic controller before anyone takes any notice of me, so this makes a nice change. I smile back.

'What's good today?' I ask.

'Well . . . there's the soup, which today is roasted red pepper and avocado, it's a cold soup but then,' he winks at me, 'you seem like a cold soup kinda person.'

'Do I indeed!' I giggle.

Nicki can't stand it. 'We don't have time for that! We've got work to do.'

'I could bring it right away,' he offers. So accommodating.

'That would be great, and an orange juice please. Thanks.'

'No trouble. Freshly squeezed?'

'Of course.'

'I should've known,' he smiles.

'Excuse me!' Nicki throws her cup down onto the saucer. 'I ordered something almost twenty minutes ago, if you don't mind!'

'Certainly.' He winks at me again as he leaves. Nicki's outraged.

'The service here is appalling. And the food's gone right downhill. God, I've had enough of this. Come on.' She slaps a fiver down on the table. 'Let's go to Angelo's instead.' She pulls on her black Prada duffel coat and storms down the steps.

'I'm sorry,' I say to the spiky-haired young man, as I run to catch her up at the door.

Nicki's cooling her heels in the street. 'Listen, let's just go home,' she says. 'I can make us something to eat.'

'Fine,' I agree and we walk to her house in silence.

When we arrive, Dan's sending a fax in the kitchen.

'Hey, Louise. You look great! Have you lost weight?'

'No, thanks, Dan. Just got some new trousers.'

'They're really cute. Turn around.'

I do a little pirouette and Nicki rolls her eyes. She throws her coat on top of the dog and pushes past us.

'For God's sake, Dan. They're just a pair of trousers,' she hisses, chucking things out of the fridge onto the counter.

'Where'd you get them?' he persists.

'Dan!' She pelts some organic, vine grown tomatoes into a wooden bowl. 'Who cares?'

'Top Shop,' I tell him.

'Top Shop!' He stands amazed. 'My girls shop at Top Shop!'

'No, they do not.' Nicki slams the fridge door. 'No one you know shops at Top Shop.'

'They do now. How much were they?'

'Nothing, thirty-five pounds.'

'No way!' The whole concept of buying a garment for as little as thirty-five pounds is new to him.

'Dan, leave us alone. We've got work to do,' Nicki commands, pointing to the door.

But he lingers on, unfazed. 'Why don't you shop at Top Shop, Nicks?'

'Don't call me Nicks.' She's chopping something with a knife and pieces are flying everywhere.

'Come on,' he persists, 'why don't you buy a cute pair of trousers like Louise?'

She turns, knife raised, eyes narrowed into two tiny little slits. 'Because, my darling, I don't need to shop at Top Shop. I can afford to buy decent clothes from a proper designer. We all do the best we can with what we have and Louise has done very well. It's not easy for girls on a budget and then of course, certain figures are, shall we say, more challenging than others.' She turns back and the knife hits the cutting board with a crack.

For a moment, there's absolute silence. Dan stares at Nicki in disbelief.

'My God, but you're a rude bitch,' he says at last.

Nicki turns around again and looks at me. Her eyes are dead, like a shark. 'I didn't mean it that way. I just meant . . .'

Dan turns to go. 'I'm sorry, Louise. I really am.'

'Don't you dare apologize for me!' she shouts after him.

He's gone and the kitchen is quiet. 'So.' She turns to face me, smiling. When she speaks, her voice is like honey. 'Would you like tuna in your salad?'

'No. No, thank you,' is all I can say.

She swivels around and continues chopping. 'Suit yourself.'

Nicki and I never get beyond page fifteen. We decide we have artistic differences and have gone in different directions. We never noticed it before, but now it's all we can see.

Considering that I used to see her twice a week, I should miss her more than I do.

H

Husbands

There are three types of husbands:

1. The Blind Man, who says, 'Isn't that a new suit, darling?' when he at last notices the ensemble you have been wearing for the past two years. There really isn't any point in discussing him, so let's leave him in peace. At least he has one advantage: he lets you dress as you please.

2. The Ideal Husband, who notices everything, is genuinely interested in your clothes, makes suggestions, understands fashion, appreciates it, enjoys discussing it, knows just what suits you best and what you need, and admires you more than all the other women in the world. If you possess this dream man, hang on to him. He is extremely rare.

3. *The Dictator, who knows far better than you what is becoming to you and decides if the current styles are good or not and which shop or dressmaker you ought to go to. This type of man's ideas on fashion are sometimes up to date, but most often he has been so impressed with the way his mother used to dress that his taste is, to say the least, about twenty years behind the times.*

Whatever type of husband you have, my advice is to make the best of it and to try to tame your expectations of him. Even the most devoted man is bound to be distracted at times and forgetful, despite all the efforts you have made to charm him. If you are wise, then you will allow it to pass unnoticed. It is better to develop a strong sense of your own style than to rely too heavily on the opinion of another . . . even that of your husband.

I'm handing my husband, the Blind Man, a fresh cup of tea.

I walk across the living room and place his cup on the small round table beside him.

He looks up.

'You've lost weight,' he observes.

I stand like a rabbit frozen in the headlights of a car. 'Yes,' I concede.

And for a moment I think he's going to notice. For a

very long second it looks like he's going to register the fact slowly but surely everything about me has changed. I'm wearing my hair differently. I've bought several new items of clothing. I've started to seriously go to the gym. For weeks now I've been making dozens of tiny little adjustments and silently waiting for some sort of response.

And now here it is; he's noticed.

And then, just as quickly, I don't want to know. After years of being invisible, the sudden spotlight of my husband's attention is too much to bear. It infuriates me.

As it happens, I'm in luck.

'Don't get too thin,' he says, disappearing again behind the Sunday papers. I breathe a sigh of relief. I'm safe.

I pick up the Style section of the *Sunday Times* and perch on the edge of the sofa with it. Wait a minute. Why is that a relief? What are my motives for changing the way I look if I don't even want my husband to notice?

I'm doing a pretty good imitation of a woman reading the paper, but what I'm really doing is gathering my thoughts about me.

I'm changing. Fast. It started off gradually enough, but now it's snowballing. I can't explain it; things that were perfectly acceptable a minute ago are suddenly intolerable. At first it was only the clothes but now it's seeping into everything – the way I eat, sleep, think. I steal a glance at the figure hidden behind a wall of newsprint on the other side of the room. Here's the rub: can I hide it from him? And do I want to?

I can hear him chuckling. 'That television show Clive's in has got *terrible* reviews.'

Clive Foster is my husband's arch-rival and we hate him. I say 'we' because this is part of the glue that keeps the relationship afloat. There's a kind of camaraderie in tearing successful people down, like a shared hobby. And Clive is one of our favourites. Not only is he a similar physical type to my husband, which means they're always up for the same roles, but he's also considerably more successful. If that weren't reason enough, they're at present sharing a stage night after night in *The Importance of Being Earnest*. My husband spends most of the evening trying to upstage him and Clive retaliates by cutting off his laugh lines. It's an ugly business. But mostly we hate Clive because he's out there, enthusiastic and determined and that's deeply threatening to people like us.

He laughs again. 'My God! They've even singled him out! "Clive Foster is horrifically miscast in the role of Ellerby"! Splendid!'

'Poor Clive,' I murmur.

Poor Clive?

Unexpectedly, I feel for Clive. Yes, Clive, who used to be the household embodiment of all that is evil and loathsome. Suddenly, getting what you want, thrusting yourself centre stage and taking risks doesn't seem so offensive. What is distasteful is the way we hide behind our own sterile mediocrity and take pleasure in the failings of someone who at least has the courage to try.

That's when I start to lose the plot.

'Poor Clive,' I say again, only louder this time.

The paper comes down and my husband looks at me like I'm crazy. 'Poor Clive? What, are you mad? The man's a beast!'

Here's where I should chime in. But I don't.

'And why is that?'

'Louie, what's wrong with you? You know why.' The paper goes up again.

I feel a totally unreasonable fury building inside me. I should let this go. I should allow it to pass unnoticed. But I don't. 'Pardon me . . . I seem to have forgotten exactly why Clive is so offensive.'

No response.

Come on, let it go. I pick up the Style section for a second time; then, for reasons beyond my control, put it down again.

'Is it perhaps because he's not the way you would like him to be? Because he has the balls to be openly ambitious?'

The paper stays in place; his voice resonates behind it. 'You're being ridiculous. I'm not having this conversation with you.'

'Not having this conversation? Not *having* . . . you don't get to choose which conversations we have or don't have!'

The paper remains. 'I don't need to talk to you when you're being unreasonable.'

I can feel myself flushing; my heart is pounding so loudly I almost scream the next words. 'I'm not unreasonable!'

He snorts from behind the paper. 'Listen to yourself.'

I lose it. Before I know it, I'm on the other side of the room, tearing at the paper that divides us. My husband stares at me with a mixture of horror and disbelief. When I speak, my voice is hoarse and I have a hard time catching my breath. 'Don't you *ever* ignore me again! Conversations are over when we are done talking. *We*!'

My hand is crumpling the paper, shredding it. He grabs my wrist. 'Fuck off,' he says, matter-of-factly. 'Fuck off, Louise.'

I reel backward. He's smoothing back the paper with his hand and I reach forward, grab the whole section and throw it across the room. He's going to notice me now.

'If you don't want to talk to me, why did you marry me in the first place?'

He stares at me in disgust.

'You call this talking? Is this what you call the art of conversation?' He turns hyper-English. 'I'm perfectly happy to talk to you in a calm, reasonable manner.'

'No, you're not! I just tried and all you said is, "I'm not having this conversation with you." We are *never* having this conversation. We've *not* had more conversations than anyone I know! And why are you the arbiter of all that's

107

calm and reasonable? Why can't we have an unreasonable conversation? Why can't we say anything we want?'

He's cold and calm, blinking at me with his pale blue eyes. 'Like what?'

I start to feel foolish, awkward. And then it comes out – out of nowhere. 'We never fuck.'

The world melts; goes all Salvador Dali. I've reached new heights of absurdity. He laughs at me in amazement. 'What's that got to do with Clive or his TV show?'

I'm crazy – I sound crazy. But what I'm saying is true. I say it again.

'We never fuck.'

He stops laughing, quite suddenly, like Anthony Hopkins playing a psychopath. 'So what. Plenty of people don't have sex all the time.'

My breath is slowing and I'm calming down. I say another true thing. 'You're not attracted to me.'

He considers this. 'You're a very attractive woman, Louise, when you're not behaving like a banshee.' He shrugs his shoulders and employs his customer service voice; the one he uses to extract refunds from unwilling sales assistants. 'I'm sorry that I disappoint you sexually. I obviously don't have the same sex drive you have.' The word 'sex' hisses with disdain.

I feel ashamed for being so base. Only, I'm tired of feeling ashamed.

I say one last true thing. 'I don't think my sex drive's unusual.'

He stands, walks to the door and smiles graciously. 'Then it's me.' He does a little half bow. 'I am The Defective One.'

He rises above me and my brute animal sex drive. I am, after all, common – from Pittsburgh, where people fuck and fight and fart. The Three Fs.

'Where are you going?' I sound plaintive and hollow.

'I'm going into the garden. Unless there's anything else you'd like to say to me.' He's playing the end of a Noël Coward scene. 'I so enjoy these Sunday morning conversations.'

Fuck Noël Coward.

'I think we should see a marriage counsellor,' I blurt out.

He looks me up and down. 'Feel free.'

'But we need to go together.'

'Louise, you are the one with the problem. My marriage is fine.'

Once again, I find I'm alone in the barren wasteland of the living room. The torn paper is the only evidence of life.

The words, 'If you are wise, then you will allow it to pass unnoticed' swim around and around in my brain. I'm not wise. But I don't know why.

I go into the bedroom and look out of the window; he's pulling weeds in the back garden. How can he do that? How can he carry on with basic domestic tasks when everything between us is deteriorating? But he does.

I watch him rearranging the garbage bins at the back of the building in order of size and fullness. He does it carefully, earnestly. He needs to. He needs to believe it matters. That he's protecting us from all sorts of chaos – the chaos of dusty surfaces, the violence of unevenly stacked books, the irreparable damage of a fruit bowl found to contain an onion next to an apple. He's an errant knight, on a quest to save a lady who doesn't want to be saved. Who doesn't even want to be a lady and who'd rather sleep with the dragon than sleep with him.

And that's when it hits me. I go back to the moment when he comments on my weight loss. I freeze-frame it in my mind's eye. And there, there it is, clear as day. The truth is I don't want him to notice me, to cuddle me, or touch me, or say how pretty I am. I just want him to leave me alone.

After all that, I don't want to fuck him either.

We have both been blind.

I'm sitting on the edge of the biggest bed you can buy in the United Kingdom.

The zip has come undone, the beds are drifting and soon the walls of the bedroom will not be able to contain the sleeping figures that are floating apart.

In the weeks that follow, I become obsessed by Oliver Wendt, otherwise known as The Man Who Can See Me.

I spend inordinate amounts of time wandering around the theatre on the off chance that I'll encounter him and then running away when I do. I find myself lurking, like a stalker, outside his favourite pub, standing across the street in the darkness, glued to the spot by desperate, confused lust. The weird thing is (and I don't really get this at the time), is that the lust I feel is for myself – the self I see in his eyes. I don't really want to talk to him, or know him; I just want to be seen by him.

'Do those reports need to go downstairs? I'll take them.'

'But, Louise, you've only just come back from there. We can take them down later.'

'Oh, it's no trouble. No trouble at all.'

And I'm off, roaming around the building like a creature from a fairy tale, doomed by some evil curse to wander the earth forever in search of her own reflection.

This continues for a while, we see each other, we stare at each other and I run away. And then one day, when I absolutely can't stand it any more, I invite myself out for a drink with him.

He's smoking in the foyer. It's the opening night of a new play and the revolve on the stage isn't working properly. He's got all the techies putting in overtime while he works his way through a pack of Marlboro Lights.

I'm meant to be gone, or rather, I'm not even meant to be in today, but that's how it is for me during this time. I find myself 'popping into work' for no reason, hanging about in the foyer, walking around the halls, possessed and saucer-eyed, one millimetre away from hysteria at all times.

I spot him and then race immediately to the Upper Circle Ladies and check my make-up. Then I check it again.

I take deep breaths, pray and then saunter over to my Nemesis.

'Hey, how are you?'

What this costs me, you'll never know. My voice is about three octaves higher than normal and my hands are shaking. This doesn't prevent me, however, from imagining that I'm the sexiest, most alluring creature on the planet and that I'm in fact, part of a living movie, complete with thrilling sound-track, mood lighting, and a cracking script.

He eyes me in that way smokers do when they exhale,

not quite winking, not quite frowning, just avoiding the stinging smoke of their own fags. 'Great, Louise. What about you?'

Ah! He speaks! My heart convulses, palpitates, chokes on secondary smoke.

'I'm, well . . . I'm thirsty,' I rejoin, tossing my hair back. 'That's how I am.'

He stares at me like I'm demented. 'Thirsty?'

I smile. How different it is when he looks at me like I'm demented than when my husband does!

'Yes,' I persist. 'Ever so thirsty. One might even say parched.'

And then the penny drops, almost audibly. He laughs and swings the door open. We walk out in the cool evening air and cross the road to his favourite pub. He buys me a drink and we sit on dangerously high barstools, attempting to make conversation.

Alas, every relationship has its Waterloo. Conversation proved to be ours.

It's difficult to have a conversation if your basic premise is not to reveal anything about yourself. He asks me a question, for example: where do I come from or what am I doing in London, and I try, in the most charming and amusing way possible, not to tell him point blank that I'm married. I twist my hand around like a claw on the bar, trying to hide my wedding band. I don't know why I don't take it off. I guess I can't. It's as simple as that. So I sit there, with my hand in a casual fist, giggling maniacally and volleying each question with another one.

'So, how long have you been in London?'

'I don't know – ages. What's your favourite colour?'

'My favourite colour?'

(It's charming to be infantile . . . isn't it?)

He lights another cigarette. 'Ah . . . well, that'll be green, I guess. What about you?'

'Hot pink and the colour of gold sequins.'

'That'll be gold, won't it?'

'Well, not really. Not flat gold. I only like sequined gold.' Oh God, I'm trying *way* too hard. I shove the claw that passes for my hand into my hair and examine the bottles behind the bar like an alcoholic out of change. Please, please don't let there be a moment of silence! What can we talk about, what can we . . . 'What about your father?'

He raises an eyebrow and gives me what I take to be the Look of Total Riveted Fascination. 'What was he like?'

'Old. What about yours?'

That was quick.

'Honest,' I say, forlornly, caught off guard. 'My father's a very honest man.'

And because I've said something true, he looks at me with real interest.

'That's a good quality.'

'Yes . . . I suppose it is.' And I stare at my drink like it's a crystal ball, going to tell me my future.

We last about twenty minutes before Oliver excuses himself on the grounds that the opening night won't occur if he doesn't sort a few things out. Like the set.

We walk back as slowly as possible without actually stopping in the middle of the road.

'So, when can I buy you a real drink?' he ventures, squinting sideways at me through a stream of smoke.

'I'm . . . I'm not sure . . .' I stammer.

Strange as it seems, I'm caught off guard. It's one thing for me to fantasize and project like a mad woman; it's quite another for the object of my delusions to respond. And besides, what am I doing? I can't make a date, I'm married! But there's another voice in my head, a soft, compelling voice whispering, 'Hey! What's the problem? Chill out. It's not like you're sleeping with him . . . you're . . . you're just . . . having a drink, that's all. Right?'

And then I'm back in the movie again, trying my best to play the femme fatale.

'I think I'd like to go somewhere I've never been,' I parry, smouldering at him from behind a sheaf of Veronica Lake hair.

The 'Are you demented?' look is back.

'Well,' he sounds irritated, 'how am I meant to know where you've been?'

Good point.

I shrug my shoulders nonchalantly and walk straight into a restaurant hoarding.

'Oh, Jesus! I'm so sorry! Fuck! What am I doing? I'm apologizing to a wooden sign!' He watches as I struggle to detach myself from the specials of the day. Once free, he takes my arm with the kind of solicitous authority usually reserved for the elderly and steers me back safely to the theatre entrance.

'About that drink . . .' He waits, but I can't think. It has to be somewhere perfect, somewhere private, somewhere away from restaurant hoardings and people who know me . . .

He's starting to get restless.

'Why don't I give it some thought?' I suggest.

'Please do.'

He smiles and, with that, disappears into the rapidly filling foyer. I stand transfixed on the front steps, my heart pounding, palms sweating. The crowd engulfs me, swirling around me like fast moving water around a stone in a brook.

I've done it. I've taken hold of my life and, for better or worse, nothing will ever be the same again.

A week later, I drop a small note into Oliver Wendt's mailbox. In the bottom right hand corner of an emerald green card I've written,

I've never been to the Ritz

The days pass and I hear nothing.

Nothing at all.

I

Ideal Wardrobe

For an Elegant Woman:

9 am. *Tweed skirts in the brown autumn shades and harmonizing sweaters, worn under a fur coat of one of the casual varieties. Brown shoes with medium heels and a capacious brown alligator bag. (A really elegant woman never wears black in the morning.)*

1 pm. *A fur-trimmed suit in a plain colour (neither brown nor black) and a matching fur hat. Underneath the jacket, a harmonizing sweater, jersey blouse, or sleeveless dress.*

3 pm. *A wool dress in a becoming shade that matches or contrasts with: A pretty town coat in a vivid colour.*

6 pm. *A black wool dress, not very décolleté. It will take you everywhere, from the bistro to the theatre, stopping en route for all the informal dinner parties on your social calendar.*

7 pm. *A black crêpe dress, this one quite décolleté, for more formal dinners and more elegant restaurants. A white mink hat.*

8 pm. *A matching coat and dress that is called a 'cocktail ensemble' in Paris, but in reality is often far too dressy for the occasion, although perfect for theatre first nights and elegant black-tie dinner parties.*

10 pm. *A long formal evening dress that can be worn all the year round (which means you should avoid velvet and prints).*

9 am and I'm at the top of Whitehall, wearing a navy gabardine suit, with a brown V-necked knitted top from Kookai and a pair of black T-bar shoes. The Kookai top is beautifully form fitting but has a tendency to unravel under the arms. Must remember to keep my jacket on. Am popping into Sushi Express for my breakfast – a fruit smoothie and an order of green tea to take away. Part of my new regime. I will not eat sugar today. I will not. I buy an extra banana, just in case. The sun is blinding as I race across the street to catch the light. I'm good at running in high-heeled shoes now – I have to be. I've been promoted to manager in the box office and spend all day running up and down the stairs between the window in the lobby and the office upstairs. A bit of a wild-card candidate for the job, no one was more surprised than I was when I got it. It's been a huge boost to my self-confidence. And the constant activity is a godsend. My husband and I have, as far as I can tell, stopped talking. The new job makes it easier for us to pretend that we are too busy or just too tired to communicate. Neither of us is ready to hear what the other has to say.

1 pm and I'm in the changing room of the gym, along with about thirty other women, all of whom have only an hour to squeeze themselves into their lycra ensembles, work themselves up into a sweat, shower, dry their hair and tear back to the office. Since I renewed my membership several months ago, I've managed, miraculously, to show up four times a week. Not since my dancing days have I pursued any form of fitness with this much success. And it's starting to show.

The gym locker room is also where you learn about the reality of other women's bodies and wardrobes. We all spend as much time surreptitiously examining one another as we do on the treadmill. Everyone freezes simultaneously as the tall, tanned blonde emerges from the shower. We pretend to be adjusting our hair but really . . . yes! She does have cellulite!

Life is full of surprises. Who would've guessed that the newsreader with the Armani suit and the mobile phone attached to her ear ('I'm at the gym! T-H-E G-Y-M!'), would wear dingy white M&S knickers with a black see-through bra? But the surprise transformation of the week goes to the mousy-haired, be-fringed girl in the 1984 Laura Ashley floral ensemble who undresses to reveal a bright pink silk bra and knicker set with matching garter belt, stockings and a pair of legs that would make Ute Lemper weep. Even the tall blonde stands agape in the centre of the shower room. I pull on a bright blue crop top, a matching pair of stretch trousers and some hideously expensive Nike trainers. I'm sure I burn more calories just trying to squeeze myself into this outfit than the whole workout put together.

3 pm and I'm back in the office, showered, hair not quite dry (competition for the three blow-dryers is fierce) and back in my navy suit. The only difference is, I've given up on my black T-bar shoes. There's only so long a woman can be expected to bounce around on the balls of her feet before someone has to die. The temperature has shot up and my jacket is hanging over the back of my chair, leaving the unravelling Kookai top in full view. I will repair it. I will. Tomorrow. In the meantime, I'll just get rid of this stray thread that's hanging down . . . I watch with a strange sense of detachment as half the remaining sleeve comes undone in my hand.

I'm meant to be completing a weekly sales report but have hit my mid-afternoon slump. This is a biological glitch that renders me incredibly depressed between the hours of three and four o'clock each afternoon without fail. My theory is that I'm genetically programmed to have a nap at this time but unfortunately don't live in a climate that favours siestas. The consequences are dramatic. The will to live seeps away and, instead of focusing on figures and performance breakdowns, I'm visualizing various methods of suicide. Dangling from a rope, passed out on a bed, floating in a stream. Or a drastic haircut.

The phone rings on the desk opposite, and as I scramble to get it, my foot catches on an invisible snag in the grey carpet tiles. My stocking runs and I still manage to miss the call. Luckily, Colin puts the kettle on (he's intuitive in this area) and magicks up a box of Jammie Dodgers. ('Two for the price of one, darling. Only *slightly* crushed.') I desperately grapple for my spare emergency banana and find it at the bottom of my handbag, beaten into a kind of brown pulp. Fuck it. Spirits rise with the sugar intake and Colin assures me that Sinéad O'Connor was a fluke; that most women would be unable to successfully carry off a shaved head with any real sense of style. Unless they had ambitions of a professional wrestling career.

6 pm never fails to bring with it an inevitable second wind. The malaise that immersed the office at 4:45 – that hopeless hour when going home seems like a cruel, unsubstantiated rumour – evaporates and at 5:55 is replaced by a carnival atmosphere. There's dancing, singing, the telling of jokes. Colleagues pat each other on the back and hold the door open for one another as they run, laughing and singing, out of the office. The night shift takes over, looking like they've just been sentenced to life imprisonment. I've got just over an hour to go home and get changed before I'm due at the theatre for the opening night of my husband's new play. He's having dinner after the show with his agent and the director and they expect me to be there, proud and supportive in my role as 'the wife'. I feel a headache coming on just thinking about it. I decide to take off my stockings, as the run is just too bad for public display, and force my swollen feet back inside the T-bar shoes. On goes the jacket and I'm tearing out the door, flapping my way down Whitehall towards home.

7 pm and I've had a quick shower and am reapplying my make-up. In an effort to look striking and sophisticated (I was reading *Vogue* on the loo), I've pencilled in my brows with kohl pencil and now look like I have Down's syndrome. I try to compensate for my uni-brow by applying a thick coat of red lipstick and before I know it, am a dead ringer for Bette Davis in *Whatever Happened to Baby Jane?*. As I'm frantically wiping it all off with wads of toilet roll, it occurs to me that ten minutes before you're due somewhere is obviously a bad time to experiment with your look. I manage to tone my make-up down to a Joan Crawford level and am searching through my underwear drawer for a pair of matching hold ups. Will I ever get out of the habit of saving runned tights, 'Just in case'? Finally locate matching pair and step into my new Little Black Dress, a strappy, short Karen Millen design in thick, black stretch satin, which was the very first purchase I made after my promotion. I'm Audrey in this dress and love it more than anything in the world. However, do NOT feel the same way about black T-bar shoes, as I slip them back on my aching feet. Grabbing a little black satin evening bag I found in the sales, I try unsuccessfully to cram the entire contents of my purse inside and then relent, telling myself that it's OK, I probably won't need my address book, a needle and thread, and seven tampons for a single evening out. (My period isn't due for a week.) Force myself to make do with a lipstick, a compact and my change purse, but not before doing a brief visualization exercise I learnt from reading *Feel the Fear but Do It Anyway*. I'm only fifteen minutes late as I hail a cab to the theatre.

8 pm. I'm standing alone, like a total lemon at the theatre bar, when I magically spot two old friends, Stephan and Carlos. Stephan's a set designer and Carlos works in the wig department of the RSC. They're buying and suddenly things start to look up. After all, I'm going to need a few drinks to make it through the entire evening as half of the happiest, non-speaking couple on earth. The bell goes. Go on then, just one more.

God, that bartender is cute.

10 pm. Supper with husband's agent and the director at The Ivy. A little bit tipsy. My husband is still not talking to me (this is Advanced Silence) but did rescue me from drowning in the tub. Don't normally bathe this much but seems I kept missing my mouth at dinner.

May go back to acting. Flirted all night with the director, who couldn't keep his eyes off me. Think I made quite an impression.

3 am. Wonder what Oliver Wendt is doing and who with.

J

Jewellery

The contents of a woman's jewellery box are a chronicle of her past; more telling than her underwear drawer, bathroom cabinet or even the contents of her handbag. The story the jewellery box tells is a romance and hopefully for you, it is a grand and passionate one.

Jewellery is the only element of an ensemble whose sole purpose is elegance, and elegance in jewellery is a highly individual matter. It is therefore impossible to say that only a particular kind of jewellery should be worn. One thing however is certain: an elegant woman, even if she adores jewellery as much as I do, should never indulge her fancy to the point of resembling a Christmas tree dripping with ornaments.

Finally, a word to would-be husbands: an engagement ring is often the only genuine jewel a woman owns, so please, invest in one of a respectable size. The shock of paying for a good quality ring will *evaporate the instant you see your thrilled fiancée proudly displaying it to all of her friends and relations. And secondly, do not underestimate the advantages of buying only from the very best. A ring box from Cartier, Asprey, or Tiffany's will be prized almost as much as the ring itself. And this is one occasion where you do not want to be accused of economizing!*

I close the book and lean it softly against my chest. Imagine receiving a box from Cartier or Asprey! As for Tiffany's, I've never been in — not even to browse. I wonder what it looks like inside. Or what it's like to walk in on the arm of a man who loves you, knowing that when you come out, you'll be wearing a diamond ring or maybe a sapphire surrounded by brilliants. I gaze at my hand resting on the duvet and try to envisage a sparkling, bright diamond solitaire on my fourth finger. Closing one eye, I concentrate as hard as I can but still, all I see is the pink, slightly wrinkly flesh where my finger and knuckle meet.

I look over at my husband, who's reading in bed next to me, and watch as he furiously gnaws away at a non-existent hangnail on his thumb. He's reading the evening paper as if it's written in code, scowling as he diligently scours its pages for clues.

He never gave me an engagement ring.

It slipped his mind.

He had planned to ask me to marry him, but evidently in much the same way that you plan to keep a dental appointment. Later, he claimed not to know that when you propose, it's customary to present the woman with a ring.

I told myself at the time that we were beyond romantic gestures; unorthodox; unique. And we congratulated ourselves for not indulging in any of the common, more banal expressions of love. I even looked up the word romance in the dictionary once, obsessed with justifying its absence from our relationship.

'A picturesque falsehood,' I read out, closing the book triumphantly. 'See, it's not real. Romance is a lie.'

And he nodded sagely. How reassuring, to know the emptiness surrounding us is real.

But, as I sit here, pretending I can see a diamond on my bare finger, it occurs to me that intellect can be a terrible, deceptive thing.

I remember the day he asked me to marry him. We were in Paris in the middle of a heatwave. He'd just finished the run of a play where he was a dog, scrabbling around on all fours, and had badly hurt his knee. He was limping around with a stick and I had a cold. The French love suppositories. All the cold medicines seemed to involve inserting something into your bottom, so I preferred to sniffle and sneeze as we stumbled around the great city, determined to absorb its beauty.

The relationship had come to a standstill several months ago. I knew he was going to propose because there was nowhere else for it to go and I was deeply irritated that he hadn't asked me yet. I was tired and ill and wanted to go back to the room, take off my dress and lie down. But I knew he was measuring each place we went as a potential setting for the proposal. So I stumbled on, pretending to find everything charming, lest my bad attitude spoil the moment and delay it further.

And I wore a dress because that's what you wore when someone proposed to you.

We drifted through the landscape of Paris, hoping to find on a bench or in a narrow alleyway the reason for our continued association. Eventually we came to sit under the shade of some trees in the Jardins du Luxembourg.

'You're not happy,' he said at last.

'I'm afraid,' I conceded.

He waited patiently in the stifling heat.

'Remember when we first met,' I began, feeling a wave of nausea building, 'and you had a . . . a friendship . . .'

He pressed his eyes closed against the burning sun. 'That's over,' he said. 'You know that's over.'

'Yes, but it's what's behind it that scares me.'

He kept them closed. 'There's nothing behind it, Louise. We've been all through this.'

But it wouldn't go away; it was like a third person on the bench between us.

'I'm only saying, I mean, as a reflection of your true self . . .' I persisted.

He opened his eyes. 'There is no "true self". I am who I make myself to be. It was a normal friendship.'

'But you had to break up with him. When we met, you broke up with him. Friends are pleased when you meet someone. They stick around, get to know them. You don't meet them in the park one wet Wednesday afternoon and quietly inform them that "things have changed". They don't disappear – not when they've been calling you every day for years . . .'

He grabbed my wrist. 'What do you want from me? What is it that you actually want? Do you want me to pretend it never happened? Is that it?'

'No, but don't you understand? How do I know it won't happen again?' I tried to pull away, but he held on tightly.

'Because I won't let it. I just won't let it.' His voice was defiant but his eyes looked exhausted, lost. 'I promise you, Louise, I promise I won't let you down.'

He let go and my arm dropped limply by my side. I stared at the sandy walkway. Everything inside me was telling me to leave, to walk away.

We're in Paris. It's romantic. A French family walks by, complete with small children and grandparents, as if they'd been cued in by an unseen director.

I say it quietly, but I say it. 'What if that's your true

nature. You cannot, no matter how hard you try, deny your true nature.'

He rises slowly and holds out his hand. 'I'm not going to have this conversation again. Either you accept me the way I am or not. It's up to you.'

I get up. I tell myself I'm crazy, stupid. He loves me, doesn't he? He says the words, doesn't he? I have a cold; I'm being dramatic.

And I don't want to be alone.

We walk. We stumble on, into the heat. It never becomes more comfortable.

The next night he proposes to me in the middle of Le Pont Des Arts and I accept.

I close the book and look again at my husband. He's completing the crossword, methodically crossing out each clue as he goes, writing the answers in pen.

He has kept his promise; he has not let me down.

1. We've always lived comfortably, in the best neigh-bourhoods, often within walking distance of the West End.
2. He has never been rude to me in public or, to the best of my knowledge, unfaithful.
3. He has looked after me, managing the household finances, taking care of me when I've been ill, and constantly seeking to improve our home.
4. He does the laundry. I regularly come home to find

my clothes neatly folded and stacked on the bed.

5. When he's working in the West End, he picks up the Sunday papers outside Charing Cross on his way home on Saturday night so that we can stay up late and read them together.

6. We often go for long walks together late at night, all over London, when the city is transformed by stillness.

7. He is a good companion.

8. And he has brought me the perfect cup of tea every morning in bed for the past five years.

Who am I to say this isn't love?

The first time I saw him, it was at the opening night party of *The Fourth of July*. It was my first big professional role and I was ecstatic with the feeling that I'd made it; I'd arrived. The audience had given us a standing ovation and everyone was certain the play would transfer into the West End. I was wearing my favourite red dress, a long swirling concoction of silk crêpe that flowed and clung to the body. The lilting, pulsating rhythms of Latin music filled the house in Ladbroke Grove where we were celebrating and some of the guys were mixing pitchers of margaritas in the kitchen. The rest of us were dancing on the patio, swaying and turning with our arms outstretched, laughing too loudly in the cool, early autumn air.

When he appeared, a gatecrasher from another theatre, tall and slender, with light hair and pale blue eyes, I barely noticed him. He wasn't my type. He was in a new play at the Albery and doing well for himself. But I had other plans. My live-in boyfriend had cheated on me a few months earlier. I ignored it at the time, but tonight, wearing my red dress and drinking too many margaritas, I was determined to pull.

I don't know how or why I came to be kissing him. But the next morning, nursing a violent hangover and lying very, very still on the cold, flat futon in the bed-sitting studio I shared with my cheating boyfriend, I realized I'd made a mistake.

I called to let him know I'd fucked up, that it was just something stupid and to laugh it off but instead he must've heard the confusion and fear in my voice. 'Let's meet for a coffee,' he said. 'Tell me what's really bothering you. Maybe I can help.'

And so we met in a little Polish tearoom off the Finchley Road, where they served lemon tea in glasses and the air was thick with the fug of goulash soup. It rained and we sat at a tiny corner table and he listened while I told him the whole, sordid tale of my unfaithful boyfriend. I apologized for 'behaving badly' and he nodded his head and said it was all understandable under the circumstances. And then we walked, very slowly and for a long time through the quiet streets of West Hampstead. He told me he'd ring me again, to see how I was doing.

The next day we met in the outdoor café in Regent's Park. It was too cold to sit outside, but we did anyway. Moving indoors required more commitment than we were prepared to make, so we perched gingerly on the edge of the wooden benches, shivering. And again, I told him things I hadn't intended telling anyone and he listened. All the feelings that had been bottled up for the past six months came crashing forward and I didn't think I'd be able to bear it.

The day after that we met on the other side of Regent's Park and walked until we came to a street in Fitzrovia. He stopped and said, 'This is where my flat is.' I followed him up the winding stairs and we sat on a sofa in the front room. It was a tiny flat but everything was immaculate, spotless. It was so different from the bed-sitting room I shared with my boyfriend, crammed full of books, papers and clothes. There was space to breathe here; everything was visible. We talked and I cried and told him I didn't know what to do. He held me, and I stayed curled up in his arms for a very long time.

Then we went into his bedroom.

The bed was made so tightly, so perfectly, that there were no creases anywhere. The books on the shelf were in alphabetical order. Everything was white – the bedclothes, the carpet, the bookshelf, the desk. He took out a volume of poems. We sat on the bed and he read to me 'The Love Song of J. Alfred Prufrock'. And when he finished, there were tears on his cheeks.

And there, in the clean, white, untouched room, we tore at each other's clothes, grabbing and pulling, twisting the perfect sheets, shattering the silence.

When it was over, we dressed again, quickly, without looking at one another, and walked back into the safe neutrality of the park.

And, there, under the sheltering boughs of a chestnut tree, an hour after we made love, he told me that he had been thinking . . . that when he had broken up with his previous girlfriend, it was because he suspected . . . that he was afraid he might be . . . well, that there might be something wrong with him.

We didn't speak for weeks after that. The play transferred into the West End. I left my boyfriend and slept on the sofa in a girlfriend's flat. But every day I thought of him, of how he'd listened to me and held me and how peaceful and serene the cool white world was where he lived.

And then he rang.

We met in the same outdoor café, only this time we moved inside where it was warm. After an embarrassed silence, I started to say, fumbling for words, how I thought we could probably still be friends, when he reached across the table and took hold of my hands.

His eyes were feverish and the words came spilling out on top of one another, in a disjointed torrent I struggled to keep up with. Never before had he been so animated, so passionate, or alive. He had just been afraid, he said, he could see that now. For so long – too long – he'd been on his own in the apartment; day after day, just waiting for something to happen, for some sign. He'd been over-whelmed by depression, suicidal even and hadn't known what to do. Which way to go. The men ... he'd tried, but it had repulsed him. He'd been disgusted. Ashamed. But it had all been just a red herring, nothing more than a phantom. The truth, the real truth, was that he had just been afraid to love anyone.

But that was over.

Now he loved me.

He held my hands tighter. He'd tried to forget me, but he couldn't. I haunted him, whispered to him, thoughts of me swam around in his head day and night.

He pulled me closer and looked into my eyes. I'd never know how desperate, how lonely, how hopeless it had all been. Or how I'd changed him. Changed him to the very core.

Laughing, suddenly euphoric, he showered my face with kisses and told me how he knew, as soon as he saw me in my bright red dress, that I was the one for him. And how all he wanted to do was to help me, take care of me, look after me.

'Please, Louise! Rumple the bed sheets! Pile the sink high with dirty dishes! Hang your red dress from the centre of the ceiling in my cold, empty bedroom! But most of all stay.'

I smiled, leant forward and kissed him.

He seemed the kindest, most gentle person I had ever known.

'You look tired,' Mrs P says, breaking the silence between us.

I stare up at the ceiling. 'I'm not sleeping very well,' I say at last.

She expects me to go on but I don't. I'm too tired to talk, too tired to do anything but curl up on the dreaded daybed and fall asleep. There's a tiny spider attempting to scale the elaborate moulding in the corner; I watch as it slips back over the same few inches, again and again.

'Why do you think you're sleeping so badly?' Her voice is frustrated, tense. I feel for her, having to play such an active role in our session. She must've imagined herself as a kind of female Freud, curing patients of deep-seated traumas and neuroses. But instead she gets to watch me take a nap.

'My husband . . . we're . . .' I yawn and force my eyes to stay open. 'We're falling apart. The whole thing is falling apart. And I can't sleep any more when he's there.'

'What does that mean? "Falling apart?"'

I shift onto my side and pull my knees up towards my chest. I can't get comfortable. 'It means the glue that used to stick us together isn't there any more.'

'And what glue is that?'

The answer flashes in my brain almost instantly, but I think a moment longer because it's not the one I'm expecting.

'Fear,' I say.

'Fear of what?'

The spider tires again. And fails.

'Fear of being alone.'

She crosses her legs. 'And what's wrong with being alone?'

The spider has given up. I watch as it descends slowly from the ceiling on an invisible silk thread.

'I don't know. I used to think everything was wrong with being alone. That I would die, kind of literally implode with loneliness. But lately, lately I'm not so sure.'

'Louise, do you love your husband?' Her voice is challenging, hard.

I'm quiet for a long time. A gust of wind blows through the open window and the spider wavers, dangling precariously. It couldn't be more fragile.

'Love isn't the point. As a matter of fact, it only makes it more confusing. It's not a matter of loving or not loving. I've changed. And it isn't enough just to be safe any more.'

'And is that what you were before? Safe?'

'That's what I thought. But now I see that I was afraid.' I close my eyes again; I'm getting a headache. 'It's like that thing, that thing that when you know something, you can't ever go back and pretend you don't know it. You can never go back to the way you were before.'

'But you can move forward,' she reminds me.

Yes, I think. But at what cost?

*　　*　　*

Weeks later, I come home from work to find my husband sitting, still in his overcoat, on the living room sofa. He looks dreadful, as he has done for weeks. By some strange, sick law of nature, as I become more attractive, he declines. It's as if only one of us is allowed to be appealing at a time. His eyes are ringed with dark circles, his hair wild and unkempt and he seems to have forgotten that razors exist. He should be gone, at the theatre getting ready to go on, but he's not. He's here instead.

'Oh!' I say when I see him sitting there, staring into the middle distance. 'You'd better go, hadn't you?'

But he just looks at me, like some feral animal that's been trapped in the house by accident.

I should feel concern, or worry, but the truth is I'm more irritated than anything else. We have an unspoken agreement, an arrangement that each of us has been honouring for months now: I go to work in the day and he's gone in the evening when I get home. He's now on my time and I don't want him here.

But I sit down anyway, in the green chair, and wait.

'We need to talk,' he says at last.

Here it is; the conversation we've been avoiding for months. I feel sick and yet strangely exhilarated, calm even. 'Fine,' I agree. 'You start.'

He stares at me for another long moment and when he speaks, his voice is accusatory. 'You're different. You've changed. And I feel like I've done something wrong but I don't know what it is. What have I done wrong, Louise? What is it that I've done?'

I take a deep breath. 'You're right; I have changed but it's all been good. Surely you can see that?'

'All I see is that you're more concerned with the way you look.'

'But that's good. I look better than ever before – you should be proud of me.'

'I liked you better before. You were easier to be around.'

'You mean less demanding.'

'I mean less vain,' he contradicts. 'Less self-obsessed.'

It's starting to get ugly. I can feel myself baulking at every word he speaks. It's hard to believe that this is the same man that only six months ago, I would've given my right arm to please.

'You know what, people are supposed to change,' I remind him. 'It's a good thing. You're just used to me not giving a shit what I look like. The truth is, you like me better when I'm depressed. Well, I don't want to be depressed any more. I don't want to spend my whole life hiding and feeling ashamed and apologizing for myself. I have a right to look good and to be happy. And I have a right to change!' I'm shaking, my whole body quivering with the force of my declaration. 'Anyway, the problem isn't about me changing. I think the real problem is that we don't really want the same things any more.'

'Like what?' He sounds crushed.

'Like . . . I don't know . . . everything. I mean, we're not going to have children, right? So what are we going to do? Just sit around in this flat of ours, hunting for the perfect lampshade and growing old?'

'Is that really so bad?'

He just doesn't get it. 'Yes! Yes, it is that bad! Can't you see that it's bad for us to be sitting around here like two pensioners with no surprises, no passion, no hope, just waiting to die? I mean, doesn't that strike you as bad?'

For a moment it looks as if he's going to cry, and when he speaks, his voice is hoarse. 'Is that really the way you see our life together? Is that really what you think? That we're like two old pensioners?'

I know I'm hurting him. But if we don't speak honestly now, we never will. 'Yes, that's exactly what I think.'

He sits, motionless, cradling his head in his hands. Silence stretches out before us, vast and insurmountable. Then suddenly, quite suddenly, he pulls himself onto his feet and I watch in horror as he crosses the floor and kneels in front of me.

'I should have done this earlier, Louise. I'm so sorry, I've been very selfish.' He's looking up at me, his eyes two enormous pools. I feel sick.

He reaches in his pocket and pulls out a tiny, clear plastic bag.

'Perhaps we haven't been very passionate . . . I'm not very good at showing you how important you are to me.

I'm sorry. I'd like to make it up to you.' And he puts the little plastic bag into my lap.

There, floating amidst the emptiness, are three tiny coloured stones. It's a surreal moment; I can't quite figure out how we went from discussing our life together to this bizarre, make-shift proposal.

'I got them from Hatton Garden. We can have them made into a ring.'

I should say something – act surprised or pleased, but instead I just stare at the packet, unable to form any cohesive thought other than shock and dismay.

'Louise, I'm here . . . on my knees before you. I know we've been having difficulties. And . . .' I have the uneasy feeling he's rehearsed this; he's looking down now, taking a pregnant pause. 'And I want you to have this, to know that I love you, that I'm sorry.'

He looks up at me again.

It's my cue. My head is pounding; say something nice, something conciliatory, it screams at me. But when I speak, my voice is cold and flat.

'Exactly *what* do you want me to have? Some coloured stones in a bag?'

He blinks at me.

'This isn't a ring, is it?'

'Yes, but . . . but it could be.'

'But it isn't. What kind of stones are these?'

He shakes his head. 'I don't know the names.'

And then I find myself doing something very unexpected; I hand the bag back to him. 'Why don't you get up,' I say.

He stares at me in amazement. 'Louise, please!'

'Please what?' I'm suddenly overwhelmingly angry. I want him off the floor. I don't want to be a part of this charade anymore. It's offensive. All of it; the stones, the speech. 'Why are you doing this?' I demand. 'Why are you doing this now, after all this time?'

'I . . . I'm doing it because I don't want you to leave.'

'Why?' I persist. 'What difference does it make whether I stay or go?'

He just kneels there, staring at me.

'Be honest, you don't really want me, do you? I mean, it's not like you want to *touch* me, do you?'

'I do want to touch you,' he says, his eyes not meeting mine.

'Then why don't you?'

But he just shakes his head, over and over.

And I snap.

'Why are you doing this?' I shout, my voice so loud and shrill it doesn't even sound like it's coming from me. 'Just tell me! Say it! Why?'

'Because,' he whispers, his hands trembling as they cover his face, 'I cannot trust myself when you're gone.'

My husband and I are having a 'trial separation'.

Colin is looking for someone to rent his spare room. I tell him that person is me and he blinks in surprise and asks, wide-eyed, if there's anything he can do. No, I say, there's nothing to be done. And of that, I'm sure.

It's been months now – months of conversations, arguments, silences, tears. We have 'given it one more week' again and again and again. It's like trying to amputate a limb with a spoon.

We make it to the end of the month, to the end of another excruciating month, and then I move out.

It's a Tuesday. My husband offers to help me pack my bags.

'I'm not going on holiday,' I tell him, repulsed and amazed that he can imagine us standing side by side, taking things off hangers and folding them into piles. He stares at me, numbly.

'I'm leaving you,' I explain, saying the words slowly and

loudly, the way you speak to a deaf person. 'This is me packing my bags and leaving you.' But he just blinks.

'I'll pay for the cab,' he says. He reaches for his wallet and examines the notes. I watch as he calculates in his head how much he can spare. He puts back the twenty for later. And I want to hit him, to cry, to tear through the fabric of our life together like it's a badly painted backdrop and get to the point at last. He fumbles. Pulls out a tenner. And we've been here before; we've been right here, in this same, exact spot for a very long time.

I let him put the money on the table. I turn and walk into the bedroom and take down my suitcase, the one I brought to England when I thought I was going to be a famous actress, and start filling it with clothes.

My husband goes out for a walk and when he comes back I'm gone.

Colin lives with his flatmate Ria, a glassblower and gallery manager, in South London, beyond the urban chic of Brixton. Gone are the exclusive cafés and lunchtime concerts of Westminster, replaced by the gaudy splendour of the Streatham Mega Bowl and the late night Mecca Bingo parlour.

The cab driver helps me to unload my bags and haul them up the front steps. I ring the bell and the door opens to reveal Colin in his bathrobe, hair wet from the shower and Madonna blaring in the background.

I stare at the misshapen collection of bags, suddenly too overwhelming and unwieldy to move. 'I'm sorry, Col. What am I doing? What have I done?'

He wraps an arm gently around my shoulders. 'Come inside. Sit down. And I'll make us a nice, hot cup of tea.'

K

Knitwear

Few women can resist the temptation of a soft new pullover in a luscious shade, and how right they are! If you feel the cold, as I do, then it is really the only garment that will keep you comfortable and content from morning till night, in all kinds of seasons, in both the country and in town. The sweater is the grand-mère of the fashion world: warm, loving, and totally forgiving. (Unless, of course, you are afflicted with a very large bust. Then it is in your interest to stick to less clinging fabrics.)

Made from silk for the warmer days and of cashmere when it becomes bitter, a good sweater has no rival. And with a little care and attention, it will last years and years without the slightest sign of age. In these whirlwind times of changing fashions, it is reassuring to know that a camel or navy twin set will continue to be elegant for seasons to come. It is a perfect example of the modern trend towards ease and comfort.

During the first days at Colin's, I fall into a kind of stupor, going to work in a daze and returning to spend the evening rolled into a little ball on my bed, crying and staring at the ceiling. The garment of choice during this bleak period is, morbidly enough, a worn navy cashmere jumper of my husband's. For years I've had a clandestine relationship with this jumper, curling into its warm, forgiving softness like a child clings to a favourite blanket. I used to sneak it from his cupboard when he was out at the theatre; racing to return it when I heard his key turn in the lock.

I hadn't intended to steal it and I'm not even sure why I did. It was draped over a chair in the corner of the bedroom and I just slipped it into my case along with the rest of my clothes. It's his favourite; it will be missed. And maybe that has something to do with it. Perhaps I'm waiting to see which one of us he wants back first.

Then the blue envelopes started to come, letters from my husband.

I'm sorry . . . I've failed you . . . so sorry.

They go on and on, saturated with regret and remorse, but not one of them asking me to come home.

I had expected something more. A grand gesture: he'd appear in a cab in the middle of the night and insist upon taking me home. Or he might ambush me as I left the theatre, his arms filled with roses. Part of me dreads the idea of spotting him, thin and haggard, smoking on a street corner, waiting for me. But I dread even more the empty corners that appear, with haunting regularity, as the days go by, and the consciousness of the resigned ease with which he's let me go. The letters are not declarations of love or pleas for resolution or even promises for the future but persistent, miserable apologies to which there is really no reply. He's letting me know, in his own quiet way, that all the street corners will be empty from now on.

I sit in my room crying, choking and spluttering, rocking back and forth, blowing my nose on roll after roll of toilet tissue. I cannot go back but I cannot bear to be where I am. Colin tries to coax me out with various culinary delights; nearly new bourbon biscuits, slightly crushed chocolate éclairs, and chicken korma made fresh from a jar (special offer, two for the price of one). But I've lost my appetite. Instead, I stagger down to the Indian shop on the corner to buy single cans of spaghetti, eating them, more often than not, straight from the tin.

Even Ria, who's never met me before and who has more than enough reason to be wary of the obscene lack of mental health in her new flatmate, makes a few tentative overtures. She offers to help me unpack my bags and make my bed up with some pretty linen and even lends me a delicate, 1930s lamp from her collection of prized objects. But it's no use. I don't want to unpack my bags. My bed is far too small to bother with pretty sheets and as for decorating the room, who cares. It's over. I'm finished. Over the years I've transformed from a budding, young actress into a bitter, disillusioned box office manager, selling tickets to plays I could have been in. I'm thirty-two years old, living in a broom cupboard with a theatre queen and a spinster.

I take a few days off of work. And then a few more. When I do show up, eyes red and swollen from crying, I have the concentration of a three-year-old. The same things must be repeated three and four times before I can take them on board. I make mistakes. My colleagues cover for me, finally delegating simple, manual tasks for me to blunder instead. All decisions seem completely overwhelming, even simple ones, like what kind of sandwich to have for lunch. I side step this quandary by not eating at all. My weight plummets and I can't find the energy to wash my hair or organize clean shirts. I wear the same dress day after day, like a uniform. But I don't care. All I want to do is go home, close my bedroom door, and fall asleep in the jumper that still smells of him, feels like him, reminds me of him.

And then, well into my third week of unbridled wretchedness, the jumper goes missing.

One morning it's where I left it in a loving, crumpled heap on the corner of my bed and by that afternoon, it's gone. I search frantically throughout the whole of my tiny room, flinging the contents out of my half unpacked bags and tearing the sheets off my bed. Then I expand my hunt to the living room and its environs, overturning sofa cushions and rifling through the laundry basket. It isn't until I've exhausted every possibility and am bordering on hysteria that it occurs to me; I'm not dealing with a simple case of a misplaced jumper, I'm dealing with a kidnapping.

Suspiciously, both of my new flatmates have retired early for the night. I knock on Colin's door first.

'It wasn't me!' he shouts over his new Robbie Williams CD.

'But you know about it, you traitor!' I rage, stamping down the hall to pound on Ria's door.

'Ria, I believe you have something that belongs to me and I want it back!'

A tiny, sullen voice answers firmly. 'No.'

I'm flabbergasted. 'What do you mean "No"! That's *my* jumper! You have to return it!'

'No. It's bad for house morale.'

Now I'm stunned. 'You cheeky, little fart! How can it be bad for house morale? It's got nothing to do with house morale!' I rattle the doorknob threateningly.

She opens the door a crack. Five feet tall in her stockinged feet, Ria peers at me like a mischievous elf. 'It has everything to do with house morale when one person has completely given up even trying to pull themselves together.'

Colin's head pops out from behind his door too. 'She has a point, Ouise.'

It's more than I can bear. My eyes sting and my throat's

so tight, I can hardly breathe. 'I don't want to discuss it. Just give it back to me. I'm not in the mood for jokes.'

Ria takes my hand. 'But, darling, believe me, this . . . this . . . over-indulgence is not the way to mend a broken heart. You're doing yourself more harm than good.'

I pull my hand away. 'What does it matter what I do, as long as I'm quiet and pay my rent? What difference could it possibly make to you! Why should you care, anyway?'

'Louise . . .' She's taken aback but I can't help myself.

'Don't! Don't even pretend you care about what happens to me! Do you realize . . . have you even *noticed* that my own husband hasn't rung once since I arrived? Do you know what that means? Do you have any *idea?*'

'Honey, I'm sorry . . .'

'He doesn't want me back!' I point out to her, tears rolling down my face. 'He doesn't even want the fucking jumper back!'

I run into my room and slam the door. I'm acting like a child, throwing a temper tantrum. Shocked as I am at the violence of my reaction, any shred of self control has disappeared. I curl up on the bed, sobbing pathetically into my pillow, beating my fists into the mattress. I'm as power-less and impotent as a child.

Suddenly, I'm seized by an overwhelming sense of *déjà vu*. And memory from long ago.

This isn't the first time I've stolen a jumper.

The first one was my father's; an ancient moss green pullover of his which hung in the laundry room by the garage. He wore it to do chores in but in its heyday, it had been to countless fraternity parties and dates during his college years. It was his constant companion during the long nights of studying for law school and the more it deteriorated, the more he loved it. When my mother finally exiled it from his daily wardrobe, it lingered on, waiting patiently for him, like a once fine show dog grown old in all its shabby, soft splendour.

The most enduring image I have of my father, is of distraction. His mind was always elsewhere. A whirlwind of activity, he could lose weight just getting dressed in the morning. 'I have a list of things to do today,' was his constant refrain. 'A list of things to do.' And he'd be off. He'd set himself heroic, impossible tasks to accomplish. 'I'll rewire the house by dinner time.' (My father was not an electrician.) Or 'I'm sure there's a way of building an indoor pool by yourself.' And then he'd disappear. There was always one more job that had to be done, some final thing that needed urgent attention, one more essential bit of home improvement that absolutely must be completed by dusk. With only his faithful green jumper to keep him warm, he'd vanish into the sunset, never to be seen again, lost in a blur of perpetual motion.

It wasn't easy to get my father's attention, but you could steal his jumper if you were desperate.

Trouble is, we were all desperate and the competition for that jumper was fierce.

Traditionally, my mother had first dibs. But she had other, more effective ammunition in her armoury. She had perfected a fail-proof technique to grab my father's attention that the rest of us could only marvel at. Since my father loved to fix things, she'd deduced that the best way to secure his attention was to be broken. Accordingly, she suffered from strange, debilitating headaches that could strike without a moment's warning and last anywhere from twenty minutes to two weeks, as required. It was genius. If he was going to be distracted, he could be distracted with her. As a consequence, she pretty much had a copyright on any form of illness in our family. Occasionally my brother or sister would do a weak imitation, a kind of tribute to the master, but it's hard to compete with someone who isn't afraid to pass out.

Effective as it was, it had its downside. By the year I turned seventeen, my mother had got fed up with the invalid routine. It must have dawned on her that she was worth more and that made her angry. So angry that she stopped talking to my father altogether. It was known as the Year of Silence.

It was a dismal time aggravated by their refusal to admit it was happening.

'Mom, why are you and Dad not talking?'

'We are talking. We just don't have anything to say.'

His voice was on a frequency she no longer registered. Anger hung over the household like a thunderstorm that refused to break, the pressure building day by day. My father still fixed things, probably even more so now that he didn't have all the diversions of conversation, but my mother greeted each accomplishment with Sphinx-like indifference. We were all horrified to see how easy it was to vanish from her affections. The invisible man had finally disappeared altogether.

During this time, my dad and I became friends. We drove into school together in the mornings and there, in the sanctuary of the car, he listened to my endless Bowie compilation tapes and quizzed me about my studies. When I read Dickens, he bought a volume and read it too. And that's when I started to wear the moss green jumper by the door.

One day I came home from school with it on and my mother saw me.

'Don't wear that again,' she warned. She had a way of saying things.

I tossed my hair out of my heavily lined eyes. 'Why not?' I challenged.

My mother said nothing. Her silence could spill out in all directions.

'What difference does it make to you, Mom,' I persisted. 'It's not like you wear it any more.'

She gave me a look. 'Just don't.'

The next day I wore it again.

This went on for some weeks. My mother warned me. I ignored her. My father was nowhere to be seen.

And then, on my seventeenth birthday, I came home from school with my father and my best friend. My mother was standing in the kitchen with a birthday cake she'd picked up on her way home from work and as I walked in, her face fell. There I was holding my father's hand, laughing, and wearing the jumper. She brushed past my father, grabbed my arm, her fingernails digging into my flesh, and dragged me into the hall.

'That doesn't belong to you!' she hissed, barely able to control the venom in her voice. 'Do you understand me? *That doesn't belong to you!*' She stared at me, a strange, fierce stare. At last she let go of my arm.

I didn't wear the jumper after that. It went back on its hook in the laundry room and hung there uneventfully for several months.

Then one spring afternoon, I noticed my mother wearing it while she and my dad washed the car. My father was Hoovering the interior, all his attention on the task in hand, and my mother was emptying out a pail of dirty, black water. To anyone else they looked like a normal couple engaging in a traditional Sunday afternoon chore. But I saw a different picture.

My mother had given up. The Year of Silence had failed. My father probably didn't even notice she'd nicked the jumper, he was so intent on completing his list of things to do. But she was back to stealing what she could from him; moments of companionship and the intimacy of the jumper.

She was right; it didn't belong to me. Things you have to steal never do.

Now the sun is setting outside. I sit up on my bed and blow my nose. When I open my bedroom door there, neatly folded on the floor, is the navy blue jumper.

Stepping over it, I walk into the living room where Colin and Ria are watching a late night chat show about royal impersonators. Colin mutes the sound and they both look up at me.

'I'm sorry,' I begin. 'You were right about the . . . the jumper thing . . . it isn't helping.' I'm staring at my shoes. I've never had to apologize as an adult for having a temper tantrum before. It's much harder and more humbling than I thought. 'The truth is, I'm not very good at being on my own . . .' Even as I say it, this seems like the understatement of the year. 'I don't really know how to . . . you know, do it.'

For a moment, I think they're going to laugh. And then Colin reaches out and takes my hand.

'None of us do. But you're not alone, Ouise. We're here and we've been where you are now. Two years ago when Alan left me, all I wanted to do was open a vein.'

'And believe it or not, I was actually engaged at one time,' Ria adds quietly.

I look at her in surprise. Tiny, capable, emotionally concise, Ria seems above the messy realm of failed relationships. 'And what did you do when it was over?' I ask. It's almost impossible to imagine her wading through the same histrionic wreckage I'm having such difficulty navigating.

She smiles at Col. 'I cried, like you. And then I came here, like you. I knew Colin through a friend of a friend and when Alan left, he needed a housemate. The rest is history.'

Colin gives my hand a little squeeze. 'Welcome to Mother Riley's Home for Wayward Women. It gets better, kid. Believe me. The trick is to stay in the game long enough to be around when the good stuff starts happening again. You'll see. Suit up and show up. Even if you feel like the whole world can see that you're made of little pieces, badly glued together.'

Ria nods. 'And, when in doubt, bathe.'

And so, in the absence of any direction of my own, I take their advice.

Ria runs me a tub with lavender oil in it while Colin grills us up some sausages and mashes potatoes. He and Ria argue over which CD to listen to (the Goldberg Variations vs. Massive Club Hits Volume 2) and the Bach wins, but only on account of me being suicidal. Colin sets the table with the mismatched silverware and china his favourite grandmother left him when she died. And while I bathe, Ria makes my bed with the pretty linen sheets she offered earlier and even begins to hang up some of my clothes. When I emerge, freshly scrubbed in my bathrobe, they both applaud.

That night the bed seems softer and more comfortable than before, the street outside more tranquil. Moonlight shines through the narrow slats of the Venetian blind, forming little rectangles of pale light on the carpet, and the gentle rustling of the wind through the leaves is the only sound to be heard. I fall into a heavy sleep, no doubt induced by the potent combination of a hot bath and sausages, and when I wake up, I feel oddly refreshed, despite the constant, aching heaviness in my heart. After ironing a shirt, I put on a clean trouser suit and catch the bus into work with Colin on time. I may still feel like a hollow shell but at least I don't look like one.

A week later, I post the jumper back to my husband with a brief note.

I took this by mistake. Sorry for the inconvenience.

As comforting as it's been, I don't want it any more.

After all, it never really belonged to me.

I sit, very deliberately, on the edge of the daybed in my therapist's office. She's upped my sessions since I left my husband and the last few times I've simply refused to engage in the conversation about lying down. I've decided there's nothing wrong with wanting to sit up and am tired of wasting sessions talking about it. I find my decision liberating but there are consequences, ripples in the dynamic of the relationship that all have to do with status.

Mrs P closes the door and sits down. She waits for me to lie down and I don't. I smile at her but she doesn't smile back. Instead, she looks at my shoes.

'Those shoes are very high,' she says. I'm wearing the pair of black suede T-bar shoes from Bertie. They are high, but also very sexy.

'Yes, that's true.'

She can't take her eyes off these shoes. I cross my legs and one foot dangles elegantly, making my ankle seem fragile and tiny. I love it, but Mrs P seems disturbed.

'They must be very hard to walk in,' she adds.

'They're fine once you get used to them, not nearly as treacherous as they seem. But no, they're not really walking shoes,' I laugh. Her smile is tense. Why are we talking about shoes?

Of course, I can't help but look at her shoes now. They're from Marks and Spencer's, the kind you try on while you're nipping in to buy pre-shelled peas. They're flat and beige with a crêpe sole. She catches my eye and shifts her legs defensively.

'Your fashion sense has changed dramatically,' she concludes.

'I think that's a good thing.'

She peers at me over her glasses.

'I'm dressing more like a confident woman,' I explain.

'And how does a confident woman dress?' Her voice is challenging.

'Like she knows she's a woman and she likes it. Like she expects people to notice her.' I smooth a crease out of my suit skirt. 'Also, I have a more demanding job now,' I remind her, 'and I'm required to look a bit more professional.'

'Yes.' She nods her head, but gives the impression of being somehow unconvinced. What am I trying to convince her of?

'So why didn't you dress "like a confident woman" before?'

'Because I wasn't confident, I suppose. And there was

no one there to notice anyway.' We've been down this road before and I don't like it. Automatically my eyes scan around for the tissues. There they are on the faux mahogany coffee table; all I need to do is reach across. How handy. Do they teach that at psychiatry school – where to place the tissues? If they're too close, is that considered enabling?

'What about your husband?' She's staring at me but I can't decipher the look. It's neither kind nor indifferent. I feel a mass of pressure building in my chest, tearing at my throat. I swallow, breathe, and then I say it, out loud to another person for the first time.

'My husband is gay.'

It comes out sounding like a very mundane fact, like I've said 'I'll have some chips.' This strikes me as odd and I find myself flashing her this funny, little smile, a kind of awkward half smirk. I know it's inappropriate, but knowing that only seems to fuel it. I try to will the corner of my mouth down with some success but it pops up again, this time accompanied by a little fart of a laugh. My hand shoots up instantly to cover my mouth but it's too late. The smirk explodes into a fit of giggles, hysterical and oddly hyena-like.

Mrs P stares at me impassively. She reminds me of every nun who ever taught me at school. 'Louise,' her voice is stone cold sober, 'why are you laughing?'

I'm six again, in church.

'I'm not,' I say, stupidly, pressing my hand into my mouth.

'Yes, you are.'

'No, not any more.' I straighten up. Think sad thoughts, car crashes, dead parents. Dead parents, dead parents, dead parents.

'Louise . . .'

Oh fuck! My face explodes again and I throw myself into a ball on the daybed. 'Excuse me,' I stammer.

'Louise . . .'

I'm making noises I've never even heard before.

'Louise!'

'Yes?'

'Why are you laughing?'

I manage to lift my head up. 'Wouldn't you?' I whisper hoarsely.

'Wouldn't I what, Louise?'

The temperature seems to have plummeted ten degrees in the last second. I feel small and cold; my voice sounds like a child's. 'Laugh if you married a gay man.'

The silence that follows is crushing; it's the silence of my childhood, my mother's silence, which isn't silence at all, but the howling vacuum of the absence of response.

She's looking at me again with that look I can't quite get and then she says, 'No. I don't think I would.'

The light has drained from the sky. My face is wet and my eyes stinging. 'Try it,' I mumble, dabbing my eyes with one of the recycled tissues. 'It's hysterical.'

'What makes you think your husband is gay?' she asks.

I'm tired. I want to go home.

'He told me. He said he thought he was gay, or at best bisexual when we met.'

I'm leaving here and going straight to the off-licence.

'But that does not mean he's gay.'

I've got mascara in my eyes and it's burning. Am I deaf?

'Pardon?'

'I said,' she repeats, 'that it doesn't mean he's gay.'

Oh.

'What does it mean then?'

'Well.' She's the one crossing her legs now. 'It means that he's questioning his sexuality, what it means to be a man. It does not mean he's gay.'

Wait a minute.

'I'm just telling you what he told me. Don't you think he knows if he's gay or not? Also, we didn't fuck. Don't you think that's significant?'

'There are many reasons why sexual relations cease in married couples.' She adjusts her glasses and cocks her head to one side. 'Why do you think they stopped?'

'Well.' I cock my head too. 'I think they stopped because my husband is gay and because he's not interested. Let's face it, if you want to do something, you usually find a way of doing it. We didn't fuck because we didn't want to; it's as simple as that.'

She arches an eyebrow. 'So you didn't want to fuck either.'

'Being rejected twenty-four hours a day is not an aphro-disiac. It's humiliating.' And then I add, somewhat defen-sively, 'There's nothing wrong with me.'

She cocks her head the other way, like a parrot. 'And yet you claim to have married a gay man.'

'Yeah, well, apart from that.' What is it with her? This isn't at all what I expected. I feel like I've fallen into an episode of *Perry Mason*. 'And I'm not *claiming*, I'm telling you what I know to be true.'

She's looking at me over her glasses again.

'Look,' I continue, 'he doesn't want to be gay, it's damned inconvenient for him – he's a very conservative guy, from a very conservative family. And I come along and we fuck and he tells me this thing and I'm so crazy with fear of being alone and I say, "No, you're not. Look, I've fixed you." And he loves that because that's his problem solved and we get married and someone's got to be crazy because you can't marry a straight woman to a gay man without someone going mad, so it gets to be me. Get it?'

She says nothing.

I hate her.

'Well, I do. And that's something.'

'You seem angry,' she observes.

I'm clutching handfuls of chenille throw in both fists. 'Angry? Yeah, just slightly. Just slightly pissed off.'

She removes a piece of lint from her skirt. 'And why do you think that is?'

I can't believe her. I want to throw things, to rip those lousy pictures off the wall and smash them into her face. 'Why? Haven't you heard a thing I've said? *I'm married to a gay man!*'

She considers this. 'That's your perception of the situation.'

I can't stand it. 'What does that mean, "my perception"? You know what, it's a lot more than my perception, it's my *experience* – my hard-earned experience of the situation, whether you believe it or not. *I'm not crazy!* My experiences are real. I don't need you or anyone else to verify them for me. If ever I was crazy, it was when I believed that someone like you, with your . . . your incredible mediocrity, could help me!'

I'm on my feet.

'Anger can be very healthy,' she says.

'Fuck you,' I say, putting on my coat.

Her kids' university fees are walking out the door. She stands too. 'I think we're making real progress, Louise. But you may be feeling a little unsupported at the moment and we should think about increasing your sessions.'

I turn and take her hand in mine. We've never touched before; I feel her recoil but don't care. 'Thank you for all your help. Extra sessions won't be necessary. You've taught me that my biggest mistake is giving my power away to people who haven't got a fucking clue.'

I let go of her hand and it drops limply by her side.

She's speechless. Only she manages to talk anyway. 'Louise, what are you doing? You can't finish your therapy just like that! We should discuss this over a series of sessions . . . we need to resolve the relationship.'

I feel sorry for her; she's pathetic.

'No, no we don't. We don't need to talk, we don't need to discuss, or resolve. Send me a bill. Buy yourself a decent pair of shoes. Do something for a change. Talk is cheap.'

I open the door.

And walk through it.

Why is it easier to walk away in high heels?

L

Lingerie

The number of articles worn by a fashionable woman has considerably diminished since the beginning of the century. However, even though a woman's lingerie may be reduced to two pieces, they should at least be matching. It is the height of negligence to wear a white brassiere with a black girdle, or the reverse. Bright-coloured undergarments are charming, but of course can only be worn under dresses which are opaque or dark. In the summer, it is preferable to stick to white. If you are extremely refined and rich, your underclothes might match the colour of your outer ensemble.

Women are making a mistake in neglecting this potential added attraction to their charms. In short: when you dress, think always that later on you will be undressing and in front of whom. After all, nothing betrays a woman more than her lingerie; it is infinitely more revealing than a thousand hours spent on a psychiatrist's couch.

One final word: this is not an area in which you
throw discretion to the wind. Do not confuse beauti-
ful lingerie, the kind that supports well and remains
fresh, with the cheap, vulgar stuff of men's magazines.
Fascinating? I'm certain. But elegant it is NOT.
A man likes to think that his wife is attractive and
discerning even when he is not looking, and surely,
that is the image you want him to have at all times
and the one that will excite his deepest admiration.

One day, after I'd hung out my washing on the kitchen
drying rack, Ria takes me aside.

'Louise, what are these?' She points to a pair of ancient
Sloggi briefs that are clinging in grey, exhausted resignation
to the line. (No matter how many I toss out, The Curse
of The Dingy Knicker haunts me, mysteriously refilling my
drawers with shabby pants.)

Not since my early childhood, when I was young enough
to wet my pants, has anyone called such dramatic attention
to my knickers. I look them over closely.

'Knickers?' I offer, hesitantly. (Even I have to question
their identity.)

'No,' she says firmly, taking me by the hand. 'Those
are not knickers. Come with me, I want to show you
something.'

And she leads me into her room; a sanctuary not to be

violated for anything less than fire, burglary or extreme acts of God. Within its walls she's created the most wonderful of girly havens. Her bed is antique mahogany, covered in a collection of tapestry cushions and swathes of fabric she's gleaned from markets all over London. The walls are covered with photographs, and original paintings, and everywhere there are objects chosen to entice and delight: milky bone china cups, slender hand-blown champagne flutes, printed silk scarves, satin Emma Hope slippers, piles of multi-coloured hat boxes and stacks of art books upon which she's placed scented candles and fresh flowers. The window box is planted with a vast collection of herbs and flowers that perfume the air through the enormous sash window. And, although it's a small room, Ria has managed by a thousand clever touches to pay tribute to each of the senses which have been deprived during the other ten hours of the day.

I watch as she kneels by the bed and pulls out a flat pink box tied with a black silk ribbon from Agent Provocateur.

'These,' she says, opening the box carefully, 'are knickers.'

And there, wrapped in gauzy tissue paper, lie a black lace bra and panty set, hand embroidered throughout with the tiniest, most delicate scarlet poppies. The poppies, flowers of intoxication, of vibrant sensuality, are so minuscule, so exquisitely, mind-achingly small, that they're nothing but a whispered *double entendre*, a knowing little wink of a sexual joke. They glow in luminous silk thread against the inky, flat blackness of the hand-finished lace, weaving their way sinuously around the curve of each breast and fanning outward, almost sprouting from the crotch of the panties. Here is lingerie which is cunningly, knowingly erotic, with or without the company of a man.

We worship in silence for a moment.

'Do you actually *wear* those?' I whisper. (I don't know why I'm whispering; maybe because I've never had another woman show me her underwear before.)

'No.' She places the lid back on the box and carefully re-ties the ribbon. 'I mean, I hope to some day.'

I'm fascinated. 'Did you buy them for yourself?'

She blushes. 'No, someone bought them for me.' She says it with such finality, that I know it's pointless to ask who. 'But in a way,' she continues quickly, 'that's not the point. Of course, not every pair of knickers is going to be gorgeous – you wouldn't even want that. But . . .' and here she looks me sternly in the eye, 'everything you own should do its job with some semblance of grace and dignity. Underwear isn't just underwear, Louise; it's the true garment of your secret sexual self. And nasty knickers completely sabotage your sexual self esteem.'

I nod solemnly and try to figure out why my mother didn't initiate me into these feminine mysteries years ago. Then I recall the state of her underwear drawer.

'You have seen greatness,' Ria smiles. 'Now please, go and buy some proper pants.'

We walk back into the kitchen to make dinner and I watch in wonder as she unpacks her groceries: tuna steaks she'd selected from the fishmonger, new potatoes authentically covered in black Jersey dirt, fresh mint, fragrant and soft, and perfect raspberries for the dressing on her salad. Ria never does bulk shops; she only buys food on the day, depending on her mood. Preparing each course languidly, in a kind of meditative state, she arranges her plate with careful aesthetic consideration.

Everything is specific and sacred in Ria's world. That's the mark of a true artist.

The most remarkable thing is she's only cooking for herself. I can imagine going to such trouble for a dinner party or a special occasion, but just for me . . . ?

I reach for another tin of Safeway's own brand ravioli and look up at the drying rack on the ceiling and the worn collection of undergarments that normally fill my lingerie drawer. I can only describe them as 'Catholic knickers', that is, garments specially designed to repel the lustful advances of the opposite sex. Ria's right: I can't possibly continue to wear them.

I think of Madame Dariaux and her enigmatic advice fills my mind, 'When you dress, think always that later on you will be undressing and in front of whom.'

Undressing. With my husband, that always meant changing into my nightgown in the bathroom and scuttling to bed with the lights out. I close my eyes for a moment and try to imagine slowly undressing in front of Oliver Wendt, his dark eyes watching me steadily through a cloud of silver smoke. But before I know it, the fantasy short-circuits and I'm back in the bathroom again in my Snoopy nightshirt.

Right. Actions speak louder than words. I reel the drying rack down from the ceiling, pull the offending articles off the line, and stuff them into the waste bin. There's no way I'm undressing in front of Oliver Wendt in a pair of grey Sloggi pants.

The next day, I head off for Agent Provocateur, in search of a new, improved sexual identity and a decent bra. It proves much more difficult than I imagined.

The shop is all hot pink and black lace – a tongue-in-cheek version of a naughty lingerie store. The girls behind the counter are voluptuous, sexy and indifferent, their blouses unbuttoned to expose the curves of their ample bosoms, and the gasping vocals of 'Je t'aime' play in the background. Gingerly, I sift through scraps of sheer lace and satin floating on pink silk hangers; tiny slips in pastel candy colours with white marabou trim and matching g-strings, saucy lace bras and suspender belts, boned bustiers that finish just below the breasts, French knickers and sheer peek-a-boo bras. Under the pink glow of the lights, everything has a slightly sinister, Barbiesque feel to it. I don't know when Ria received the embroidered set she showed me, but they're gone now. I contemplate a fairly conservative silk camisole and knicker set but cannot bring myself to try them on. The truth is, just looking at it makes me feel shy and awkward, let alone wearing it. After half an hour of loitering about like a dirty old man in a video shop, I leave with nothing.

Walking across Soho, I try to recall the last time I had sex and draw a blank. Standing stock still in the centre of Soho Square, I really, *really* concentrate and still nothing. If this isn't bad enough, I expand the field to include 'even with myself' and my memory remains a flat, empty screen. Apart from my childish fantasies about Oliver Wendt, which always end in a kind of slow fade, Vaseline kiss, I'm nothing more than a kind of second-hand virgin. A prude. Frigid.

Depressing as this is (and it is deeply depressing), I'm faced with an even more pressing problem: I've chucked away all my knickers.

There's nothing for it. Having failed to identify my sexual self at Agent Provocateur, I have no alternative. Let's face it, when your secret sexual self resides at Marks and Spencer's, things are looking pretty grim.

I'm dragging myself across town to Marks when the sky begins to darken ominously. I quicken my pace. When the raindrops harden into a torrent of hailstones, I dodge into a doorway for cover. After standing there for several minutes, wincing and pressing myself against the window for protection, I notice that the shop is none other than La Perla.

Despite being convinced that my destiny now lies firmly within the walls of a convent, I go in.

Now this is lingerie of a completely different class. There's nothing seedy or vulgar here. The shop itself has the bright, golden sheen of a very expensive pearl, with creamy white walls and pale marble floors. La Perla carries no peek-a-boo bras or crotchless panties and not a hint of black lace or marabou in sight. This is the genuine article. Luxurious lingerie that's attractive and comfortable enough to wear everyday – if only you could afford it.

A man and a woman are shopping together. They're a handsome couple, youngish and probably Italian, both beautifully dressed in the kind of flawless, casual tailoring the Italians excel at. He's selecting various panties for her to try on: silk g-strings, hipsters, and the tiniest of thongs, while she's tossing her long, dark hair and looking rather bored, as if they do this every day and she'd much rather be at home, watching TV. I feel slightly voyeuristic watching them shop but still make a mental note of each item he selects. Is this what men like?

But you can't expect to walk into a shop like La Perla and just browse. Moments after I step across the threshold, a saleswoman descends upon me. Disturbingly, she's the very image of Madame Dariaux on the back of my book, with the same aristocratic nose, imperious gaze, and sculptural Margaret Thatcher hairstyle. She clears her throat and looks down at me while I stand, gaping up at her.

'You look as though you may need some help.' She speaks slowly and carefully, as if she's weighing even these simple words.

I cannot get over the resemblance. 'I . . . yes . . . I need some new knickers, ah, I mean lingerie,' I stumble, 'and I can't decide which ones . . .'

Before I know it, she's got her arms around my chest and is measuring me.

'You are a 32 B and,' she looks me up and down, 'I'd say a size 10 should be adequate below. What would you like them for? Are they to go with a specific outfit? A strapless dress, perhaps?'

'No, no, just for real life.'

'Well then, white is best, I think.' And she points me away from the exotic silks the Italians are admiring and in the direction of a distinctly modest range.

I'm back where I started, but at five times the price. I follow her anyway and she hands me a white bra and a pair of briefs. 'Would you like to try them on?' she asks.

Oh, hell, why not? 'Yes. Fine.'

She shows me into a changing cubicle the size of my bedroom, complete with a little white velvet settee and soft, amber lighting.

'See how you get on,' she says, closing the curtain brusquely.

Just being in the changing room is soothing and relaxing. I sit down on the settee and peel off my coat, shaking the rain from my hair. Then I slip off my shoes and begin to undress. The La Perla pieces fit well, smooth and seamless, and have an attractive clean shape, with tasteful lace detailing. They're sleek and figure enhancing. But are they sexy?

I turn and look at the back view. No problems there. I do a little twirl. Very nice really. I shorten one of the bra straps. Stroking the smooth silk of the cups, I adjust my breasts so that they sit a little bit higher and smile approvingly at my reflection. And that's when I notice that the curtain hasn't quite closed and the handsome Italian is watching me, quite unashamedly, while he waits for his wife to emerge.

I see him and he sees me. However he doesn't move or look away. Instead, he smiles very slowly and gives me the slightest nod. His wife is calling him and he answers, quite calmly, without averting his gaze.

My heart is pounding, I feel flushed and at the same time unusually languid. My conscious mind protests, 'How dare he!' but there's another, much more mischievous side that's secretly excited and thrilled. There's a rattle of the curtain and the sales woman clears her throat outside. 'What do you think?'

'Fine,' I say, my voice much softer and deeper than normal. She pokes her head round the corner.

'Um,' she nods approvingly. 'Perfect. How many would you like?'

'Well . . .' I look back in the mirror.

The Italian has gone.

I buy three sets in white, two in nude, and two in black. I'm overdrawn for a month but it's worth it.

I have, at long last, found my secret sexual self and she's a little naughtier and a great deal more expensive than I anticipated.

Now when I'm dressing, I'm only too happy to think that later on, I'll be undressing. The only question that remains is, in front of whom?

ℳ

Make-up

Ah! Wouldn't it be marvellous if none of us needed it? But, alas, while some beauties are born, most of us are made. Make-up is a kind of clothing for the face, and in the city a woman would no more think of showing herself without make-up than she would care to walk down the street completely undressed. Nothing is more effective for brightening a woman's visage and putting that final bit of polish to her look than a dash of lipstick, a sweep of black mascara or a rosy hint of rouge.

However, while fashions in make-up may come and go, there are some things that remain forever déclassé. To be perfectly frank, too much is always too much. It is worth noting that people are meant to be complimenting you on the beauty of your eyes, not your eye make-up. And if you find you cannot embrace a man without leaving a trail of powder on his suit lapel (an event too hideous for words!), then it's time to recon-

sider your motives, as well as your methods. Make-up is capable of many ingenious enhancements but it will not make you impervious to age or disappointment or a thousand other insecurities that plague the female mind. By all means, be quick to make the most of what make-up can, reasonably, do for your appearance but also be clever enough to know when to stop.

Suddenly I wake up one morning to discover, that in addition to dealing with a failed marriage, a new job, a, shall we say, challenging financial independence, and the certainty that I will end up alone for the rest of my life, I now, just as a *pièce de résistance*, have the skin of an adolescent girl – pink, oily, and erupting in spots.

Not only is my life veering dangerously out of control but now my face is as well. A girl can happily avoid any connection with reality as long as she looks OK. But when that fails, drastic action must be taken.

And that means make-up. Lots of it.

Rising at daybreak on my day off, I catch a bus into town and arrive at Selfridges's cosmetic emporium just as the store opens. Hidden behind sunglasses, head bowed, I weave through the maze of displays and bored perfume promotions girls until I arrive at the only cosmetic solution I know for Problem Skin.

There's the same clinical, freshness about the display, the

same assistants dressed in white lab coats, the same pale green and frosted glass bottles. After so many years and half way around the world, I'm back where I started.

My mother, also a traumatized survivor of teenage acne, first steered me towards an identical counter when I was twelve. She was not about to let me suffer the way she had all those years ago, in the age before oil-free make-up formulations and mildly medicated soap bars. Her hand firmly gripping my shoulder, she guided me through the make-up department of Horne's Department Store until we arrived in front of the same glowing white stand. 'Pardon me, my daughter has acne,' she announced, to my intense mortification. 'And we'd like to know what you can do about it.'

Of course the worst thing you can do is march up to a sales counter and announce that you need help.

The first hour we were there, the make-up assistant, who was at least forty-five and appeared to be wearing all the products in the range at once, insisted on diagnosing my skin type using the then high-tech Skin Analysis Station, which was on a separate little island in the centre of the cosmetics room. It consisted of two high white stools and a plastic, illuminated box with some sliding panels on it, under the headings of Oily, Combination and Dry skin. We sat on the stools and she put on a white lab coat and took out a pad and pen and began asking me a series of very serious questions like, 'Is your skin dry and flaky?' To which my mother persisted with the refrain, 'She's oily! Oily! She's got really oily skin!'

The assistant nodded knowingly and slid the panel in the illuminated box over to the pale green, astringent-coloured section marked, 'Oily'. Then she moved on to the next question. 'Would you say your pores are small, normal, or large?'

'Well, just have a look.' My mother gave my head a push and the next thing I knew, the assistant and I were staring at each other's pores.

'Yes, large,' she confirmed, just as I was thinking hers were the size of a house. And again she pushed the panel over to the oily section.

By now a small crowd was gathering, so novel was the sight of the Skin Analysis Station in action, especially for one so young and so in need of emergency attention. The assistant, deftly playing to the crowd, raised her voice, shouting the next question across the entire ground floor. 'So, how many times a day do you need to moisturize?'

'Moisturize?' My mother shouted right back. 'You don't understand; she's oily! OILY! The last thing she needs is moisture!' And the women in the crowd, indeed, even a few of the men in the gentleman's shoe department across the aisle, shook their heads in sympathy.

When every panel had finally, scientifically revealed that, yes, I did indeed have oily skin, the assistant tore the sheet off her pad, removed her lab coat, and led us back in a cloud of perfume to the purchase counter. 'Fortunately, we have a number of extremely effective products to combat the oily skin condition,' she began. The next forty-five minutes are a blur.

And that's how I came to look like a twelve-year-old version of Joan Collins.

Now, hovering just beyond the jurisdiction of the white lab coated assistants, I'm on the verge of doing it again. I remove my glasses and take a deep breath. Desperate times require desperate measures.

An hour later, I'm armed with a new collection of lotions, astringents, smudge-proof foundations, cover-up sticks, oil-removing blotting pads, blushers, a quad of eye shadows (three of which I don't like) and a free lipstick in a shade I'll never use. From now on, the words 'fresh faced' are just a distant memory. So is the balance in my bank book.

However, there are some things that even one's best Joan Collins impersonation can't remedy.

The next day at work I check my mailbox and discover nothing. Yet again. No note or sign from Oliver Wendt, who I haven't seen in weeks. What have I done wrong? Upstairs at my desk, I stare blankly at my e-mail screen, replaying the whole sequence of events in my head. Over and over.

It's been ages since I left the note, the note I now seriously regret. I feel like a complete twat. Worse, I still think of him all the time, still wander the halls of the theatre hoping to see him, still fail to find any other man attractive, still cling to this old obsession.

If Oliver Wendt can see me, I must exist. This is the philosophical premise upon which I've built my new life. And now that I exist, I'm allowed to participate in the whole dynamic of living without apology – to take up space and time, to want things, to reach, to try, to fail. However, it seems impossible to me that I should come this far, make so many changes, and yet miss out on possessing Oliver himself. He's the prize, the reward I get for so much effort, the reason that I've gone to all this trouble.

I must love him. I think about him all the time.

Or am I really thinking of him thinking of me? Is Oliver merely a reflective surface in which I've caught sight of my own image for the first time?

Suddenly, my phone rings. Could this be it, at long last? I take a deep breath, my heart pounding as I reach for the receiver.

'Phoenix Theatre box office,' I purr, in the smoothest, calmest tones I can manage. 'How can I help?'

There's a pause.

'It's me,' my husband says. 'We need to talk.'

I meet him for lunch at the Spaghetti House restaurant next to the theatre. We're both unable to conceal our shock at seeing each other. He looks drained, thin and exhausted, and I resemble a pantomime dame. We stand together by the doorway, awkward, uncertain of how to greet each other and afraid to look each other in the eye.

Now we're seated in a corner booth. The food we order arrives and sits there, untouched. After what seems like hours of painful chit-chat and loaded silences, he finally asks, 'So, what are we going to do?'

This isn't a subject I'm ready to discuss, although I suspect we both know the answer. I toy with my cutlery, trying to balance my knife on its flat edge. 'I'm not sure,' I stall. 'What would you like to do?' The knife falls and I catch sight of my reflection in the blade. The distorted face of a fun house mirror stares back at me.

'I take it you're not coming back.' He's trying to force my hand. It's all too abrupt, too sudden, and too real.

The waiter brings us our coffee. I wrap my hands around the warm china cup for comfort.

'Nothing's changed,' I say at last. I sound vague even to myself.

He sighs in frustration. An awkward silence ensues.

I pick up my teaspoon and am about to stir in some milk when, again, my image, pale and warped, is reflected back to me in the curved bowl of the spoon. I bury it immediately in the sugar bowl.

'I've been to see a lawyer.' He's undeterred by my eva-siveness. 'Just as a precautionary measure.'

I open my mouth to say something. Nothing comes out.

'Tell me honestly, have you met someone else?'

I look up, startled. And there, in the darkened glass behind him, I see myself again, my face red and flushed, almost unrecognizable behind the mask of make-up.

'You're blushing.'

'No! No, I'm just shocked that, that you would even think such a thing!' I fumble, certain he can read my guilty thoughts.

'Well, then maybe we can repair the damage, don't you think?' He reaches across the table and touches my hand.

'I'm sorry.' I struggle to push my chair away from the table. 'I really . . . really can't do this right now.' My head pounds and my hands shake as I reach for my bag.

'Louise, we need to talk about this!'

'Yes, yes, I know.' I stand up. 'But please, not now!' The words trail over my shoulder as I head for the door.

I run all the way back to the theatre and into the safety of the Upper Circle Ladies. Splashing my face with water, I fill the palm of my hand with cheap, pink hand soap, and scrub my face clean. My make-up dissolves, mascara running and lipstick smearing to form grotesque shapes. And suddenly I'm sobbing into the warm water.

It's all gone wrong. And all the make-up in the world can't hide it.

That night at home, I lock the door and sit, with my pen and Post-its, making notes of Madame Dariaux's words of wisdom. If I just concentrate, if I can just get it right, everything will become clear. And I'll know what to do.

The next day at work, I get a call from the foyer to say there's someone waiting to see me. 'Is it a man?' I ask cautiously.

'Nope.' The security guard suppresses a burp. 'It's some old tart.'

Mona stands imperiously in the centre of the lobby, smoking a cigarette and peering disdainfully at the poster for the season of new lesbian writing we're hosting next month. She has a grey fox-trimmed cashmere wrap thrown around her shoulders and a tiny green Harrods bag dangling from her wrist.

Every inch of me wants to turn and run back up the stairs before she can see me.

No such luck.

She turns, looks up, and her face expands into a slow, Cheshire cat grin.

'Louise!' she cries, as if we're not so much mother and daughter-in-law as two long lost lovers, and a moment later, I'm enveloped into a full Mona embrace, a kind of suffocation by cashmere and Fracas.

When I disengage myself, she holds me at arm's length and gestures dramatically. 'But, darling, you're not well, are you? All this nonsense is clearly making you ill. Look! You're nothing but skin and bone! Doesn't that Calvin you're staying with have any food?'

'It's good to see you, Mona,' I lie. 'And it's Colin; my flatmate's name is Colin.'

'Well, that's settled! I'm definitely taking you out to lunch! We'll go anywhere you like – The Ivy, Le Caprice . . . you name it and we'll go get some *proper* food into you!'

She pulls me across the foyer but I manage to twist free. 'I'm sorry, Mona, but I can't. I just got on duty and I don't have another break for ages.'

'Well then, a coffee. Just for five minutes.' Her hand is on the small of my back, pushing me firmly towards the door. I feel like a leaf, small, brown and weightless, being forced downstream in the direction of some treacherous waterfall. In the five years that I've known Mona, I've never managed to defy her and it doesn't look as if I'll be able to start now.

We sit in Café Nero across the street from the theatre. Mona orders a double espresso and I drink still water, turning the glass bottle around and around, peeling the label off in long strips while she talks.

'Louise . . .' she begins, and I know, just from the tone of her voice, that this is not a conversation I'm going to enjoy. Sensing this, she stops and starts again. 'First of all, this is for you!' She places the Harrods bag grandly on the table between us and my whole insides collapse with mortification.

'Really, you shouldn't have.' My voice is as flat as a pancake.

The last thing I want to do is have to go through the whole dumb show of pleasure and gratitude in front of Mona. Not today. Not ever.

'Well, it's not actually *from* Harrods . . . I got it in a little shop in Hampstead but I had the bag at home and I thought it might be *fun*.'

I'm not sure why it's fun to make something look like it comes from a different, more expensive store but it does somehow make the whole charade easier to bear; the knowledge that the gift is not, in fact, an extravagant gesture, but only a trinket parading as such. Inside the bag there's a tiny tissue paper parcel. I unwrap it to discover a silver brooch in the shape of a fish.

'Oh. How thoughtful. Really, really lovely.'

'I thought you might like it, you being a Pisces and all. I don't know if you believe in that sort of thing but . . . it's *fun*.'

Everything's fun today. We're having a wonderful time.

'How lovely,' I say again, re-wrapping the fish and putting it back in the Harrods bag. I haven't got the energy to tell her my birthday's in June.

I peel another bit of the label and watch as she takes a small, enamel vial from her purse and carefully shakes two tiny saccharin tablets into her coffee. Her spoon clips the edge of the cup with a brisk, clicking sound.

'Well, I won't ask how you are, Louise; this whole thing has clearly affected you very badly. And of course, I'm here to offer you my help and guidance. There comes a time in every woman's life when she needs the advice and assistance of, shall we say, a more *experienced* confidante.'

I continue peeling.

She clears her throat. 'Let me be frank with you. All marriages go through bad patches – that's just part of the deal, isn't it? For better or for worse. Am I right?'

She pauses but without effect.

'Louise, I know my son can be difficult. He's sensitive, an artist. His father, God rest his soul, was the same way. But you and I are women, we're the adults here. Am I right? Certainly, we'd all like life to be about romance and flowers and all the rest of it but sometimes it just isn't that way. There's a lot more to making a relationship work than just sex!' She laughs awkwardly. 'Sometimes marriage is more about kindness, shared interests; a kind of sympathy for one another . . .'

It's not working. She stares into the small, black darkness of her coffee for a moment and when she speaks again, her voice is tired and drained.

'I know my son. I know he's . . . difficult. But he does love you, Louise. In his way.'

I stare at the table.

She sighs heavily and looks me in the eye. Her voice turns bitter. 'You're not making this very easy are you?'

'It isn't easy,' I say.

She smiles, lips stretched across teeth. 'No, no of course

not. But have you thought about where you're going to go? What you're going to do? This situation may not be ideal, but after all, you're old enough to realize that there's more than one kind of love in the world. You're going to have to learn to take the rough with the smooth.'

I push the chair away from the table and stand up. 'I'm sorry, Mona, I really have to go. Thank you very much for the pin.'

She doesn't move. 'You're very welcome, Louise. It's a pleasure.' Then she reaches out and grabs my hand. 'Just think about what I said. Sometimes the best thing to do, the *smartest* thing, is to just kiss and make up.'

She lets go and I turn and walk out of the coffee shop.

That night, Colin and I are riding home on the bus, when he looks at me and says, 'Stay still, there's something on your cheek.' And he reaches out a finger and begins brushing away at something.

I recoil violently. 'Don't touch it!' I snap. 'Just leave it alone.'

But he won't. 'No, Ouise, there's just this little dark mark,' and he licks his finger, the way your mother used to do when you were a kid, and begins to rub even harder. 'Hold still, I've almost got it.'

But I know what he's after and it isn't a mark, it's a suppurating boil that's taken a good ten minutes and two different products to hide and now he's only making it worse.

I push him off. 'Just leave it I said! Can't you understand English? Get off me!'

The bus lurches up to our stop and I race down the aisle ahead of him, while he struggles, laden with shopping, behind me. 'What's got into you, anyway?' he says, as we clamber off. 'Why are you so touchy?'

'I'm not touchy. I just don't want to be touched,' I retort, walking, or rather running as quickly as I can down the street away from him.

'Fine! If you want to walk around with a big, black mark on your face, then great. I was only trying to help. God, Louise, you are really getting to be hard work, do you know that?'

'Who cares,' I hiss, suddenly irritable beyond all reason. I turn the key in the front door and stomp upstairs.

He catches the door as it swings closed with his foot. 'I care!' But by then I'm in the flat and halfway to my room. I make it just as he reaches the landing, and slam the door behind me. But he follows me, bursting in with all his shopping before I can stop him. 'I care!' he shouts again.

And then stops.

And looks around.

Everywhere, on the mirror, on the wall, are little yellow Post-its.

Reminding me of what is elegant.

And what is not.

'Jesus, Louise, what's all this about?'

'Nothing,' I say, suddenly quiet. 'It has to do with a book I'm reading.'

'What book?' He puts his shopping down. 'Honey, this ain't normal.'

'Yeah, well, I'm not normal, not normal at all. There's something wrong with me.' I lift up my hair and show him my cheek. 'See that? That isn't a mark, it's a spot. Loads of them. If Oliver Wendt should see me like this . . .'

'Oliver Wendt? What's he got to do with anything?'

'Nothing.'

I've gone too far.

Oh, fuck it.

'Only I met him for a drink and he said he'd take me out, so I left him this note, and I haven't heard anything. Nothing. He's obviously avoiding me. He probably saw me and thought, "What am I doing with this loser?"'

Colin sits carefully on the edge of the bed. 'He's in Australia, Ouise. He was sent to direct *Gale Force* in Australia.'

'Oh,' I say, stupidly. It never occurred to me that he might be away.

'What's all this?' He gestures to the yellow Post-its. And before I can stop him, he reaches out and plucks one off the wall. ' "Beauty is no guarantee of happiness," ' he reads aloud, ' "strive instead for elegance, style, and grace." What is that supposed to mean? Louise?'

He's talking to me but his voice seems far away. I've been here, exactly here, before.

'Ouise?'

But the only thing I can say is, 'It isn't working. No matter what I do, it isn't working. I'll never be elegant. Never get it right. It's all gone terribly, terribly wrong.'

'Honey, sit down.' Colin yanks my hand and my knees bend forward, landing me abruptly on the bed. 'Tell me, what's this all about?'

I hand him the book, my bible, from where I keep it, in pride of place, on my bedside table. And then, almost immediately, I regret it.

'*Elegance*,' he reads out loud, flicking the pages open. 'What is this? Some sort of ancient self-help book?' He riffles through it, as if it were nothing more than an amusing oddity.

'Never mind.' I try to take the book back but he holds it aloft, just beyond my reach.

'Not so fast! Are you honestly telling me you think this woman, this, what's her knickers, Madame Dariaux, knows what it means to be elegant? That she's got something you lack? By the way, she has Margaret Thatcher hair.'

'Does not!' I punch his shoulder, a little harder than I'd intended.

He swats me back. 'Does too! Listen, Ouise, that book is just one woman's opinion. And by the looks of it, one woman's opinion from a completely different age! What does she know anyway? Has she ever had to go through what you're going through? Has she ever left her husband and had to build her life from scratch? Why are you torturing yourself? Because that's what all this is; torture. Don't you have any confidence to trust your own instincts? So what if you make mistakes or have a few spots! Jesus, if I'd just left my husband I'd have a whole lot more than just a few spots!'

'You don't understand! None of you! It isn't about a few spots! Or about taking the rough with the smooth! Or any of that crap! Now give it back to me!' Again, I grab for the book and again, he holds it just out of my reach.

'No. First tell me, why is being elegant so important anyway?'

'Because . . . because . . .' My mind goes blank, folding in on itself, collapsing with frustration. 'Jesus! Why don't you just fuck off, Colin!' I explode. 'Stop being so fucking self-righteous and leave me alone!'

He stares at me a moment. Then he thrusts the book back at me and stands up, gathering his shopping together. 'Fine.' His voice is cold. 'Have it your way.'

He strides out of the room and the door slams behind him. And I'm alone, with my book, my Post-its, my spots and my faux Harrods fish pin.

I've never been so rude to anyone in my life. Clutching the book, my hands shaking, I try to grasp what just happened. Why am I overreacting this way? Why can't I answer his question like a reasonable person? And, why, after all that, is it so important to me to be elegant?

And then it comes, emerging slowly out of the darkness of my mind. Perhaps if only I'd been more of a woman, maybe he would've been more of a man.

When I finally dare to step out of my room, I find Colin making a shepherd's pie and listening to the football on the radio in the kitchen. I stand in the doorway a while, watching him mash potatoes and he ignores me. So I move into the centre of the kitchen, where I become a real obstacle and refuse to budge.

'Forgive me. I was wrong. And rude. And a bitch.'

He stops what he's doing for a moment, and stares at the floor.

'I was wrong and rude and a bitch,' I repeat.

He looks up. 'It's not just that. I'm worried about you. You're acting crazy.'

'I know. I *am* crazy. Please, Col. Don't hate me. I'll get rid of the Post-its, put the book away. Only, please, forgive me! Say we're still friends.'

'Come here.' He steps forward and wraps his arms around me. 'Listen, Ouise, no matter what happens between you and me, no matter what we say or do, there's one thing I can promise you. We will *always* make up.'

He held me for a very long time.

A week later, my husband and I decide to file for divorce.

And shortly afterwards, my face begins to clear.

N

Négligées

One of the most baffling points of inconsistency in many otherwise elegant women is the way they completely neglect their appearance during the hours of intimacy in their own homes – which is the very time and place where they ought to be at their most attractive.

For every woman who, at the end of the day, removes her make-up and replaces it with a lighter one, ties a ribbon in her well-brushed hair and slips into a pretty, long dressing-gown or housecoat with matching slippers, how many dress for an evening at home in a shabby dressing-gown, their heads bristling with curlers, cream spread over their faces (when it isn't a green or black masque), and with huge shapeless mules on their feet? It makes you wonder whom the result of all this beauty care is meant to impress – undoubtedly the trades-people they will see when doing their shopping the next morning. In the mean-

time, the poor husband learns to avoid looking at his scarecrow-wife and fixes his gaze instead on the sports page of the newspaper or in contemplation of the television screen.

After all, isn't this really what beauty parlours were created for – so your poor, dear husband might be spared the horror of having to see everything?

I'm thirty-two and for the first time in my adult life I'm living with people I'm not sleeping with, commonly referred to as flatmates. We share the kitchen, bathroom and living room.

Communal living doesn't come easily for me. At first I make a few *faux pas*. I don't understand how to shop for myself, or how to sit in the living room with the others and watch TV. I am, however, very good at doing the washing up and taking out the garbage. Every day is a learning experience. I learn from Colin how to organize three people's shopping in a single fridge, ('Stack from large to small, sweetie. Think upwards, upwards!') And Ria teaches me how to take a bath, with candles, special soap, bath salts, and loofa scrubs. 'You're communing with yourself,' she instructs. 'The water is your emotional life. If you're in and out, your relationships will never succeed.'

Oh. OK.

The one thing they both do is chip in and buy me a new

robe, under the guise of an extremely belated Christmas gift.

'We have something for you,' Colin says one evening, when we're all making dinner together. And he presents me with a bulky, wrapped package. Ria's smiling and looking at her shoes.

'Oh, my God! Guys! You shouldn't have!' I'm thrilled to bits, giggling and tearing the paper like a kid. When I open it up, it appears to be a giant towel.

'Wow,' I say, wondering why they've bought me a towel. 'This is great. You shouldn't have.'

'I'm glad you like it,' Colin says, looking at Ria, who's trying so hard not to laugh, she has to turn away. 'By the way, Louise, it's a robe.'

'Ahh! Yeah, I can see that now! It's great,' I say, noticing how enormous it seems. And blue. And shapeless. 'Yeah, fantastic but, you guys, I already have a robe. My little white one. You've seen it, haven't you?' I look at both of them, but they're not looking at me. All of a sudden the floor is deeply intriguing.

This is weird.

'You have seen my robe, Col? Haven't you?'

Colin clears his throat. 'Yes, darling, we've all seen it. As a matter of fact, when Mick was over the other night and you were coming out of the bathroom, he saw it too. And he's straight. The thing about that robe, is that it's fine if you're trying to seduce someone . . .'

'But,' Ria finishes his sentence, 'not really appropriate for communal living.'

I can feel my face burning, my hands tingling. 'What are you saying? What's wrong with it? Is it see-through? What?'

'What we're saying,' continues Ria, 'and maybe we're not you doing it terribly tactfully is . . .'

'We can see your tits,' Colin concludes.

'Absolutely,' Ria says.

'Oh my God!' I curl up into a little ball of shame on the floor, clutching the enormous, thick, terry cloth robe. 'Oh God! I'm so sorry! How . . . how embarrassing!'

'Calm down, sweetie.' Colin strokes my hair and laughs. 'They're lovely, really. Just a bit distracting when you're having your tea in the morning.'

I look up sheepishly. 'I'm so sorry, really, I had no idea. All these years I've been wearing it, no one's said anything . . . nothing's ever . . . I mean . . .' I drift off, not sure how to continue.

Apparently, I'd been strolling around in a see-through garment for months, but like a modern-day, sexual version of the Emperor's New Clothes, I'd been oblivious to my nakedness. After years of living with a man who's completely immune to me physically, I've apparently concluded that everyone is. In the absence of any response, I've pretended to be clothed, but in fact, I've been just begging for some kind of reaction.

And here it is.

Thing is, it isn't the first time. When I go out dancing with Colin and his friends, he shimmies around me, pulling up the straps on my Morgan halter neck. And Ria has met me by the door a few times, brandishing a cardigan and refusing to let me leave until I cover up. Until now, I've managed to ignore these unrelated incidents, but suddenly the focus has been pulled in, sharply, and I can see clearly. It's like my radar's broken. After so many years of hiding, the pendulum's swung completely the other way and I'm an overnight exhibitionist, shouting, 'Look at me! Notice me! I'm alive! Here are my tits to prove it!' How pathetic and degrading. And yet I've done it again and again.

And now I'm the subject of some bizarre flatmate intervention.

I bury my head underneath the mountain of terry cloth Colin's calling a robe. I want to hide here forever – to pass out from embarrassment and never come to.

There's just one thing I want to know before I do. 'Are they really lovely?'

'I'm sorry?' Colin asks.

I clear my throat. I shouldn't need to know this, but I do. 'I said, are they really lovely?'

'Are what?' Ria and Col look at each other, confused.

I'm staring intently at the blue swirl that separates the red rectangle on the Oriental rug. The pattern repeats itself again and again, all along the edge of the design.

'My breasts.' My voice is suddenly choked, just barely above a whisper. 'You said . . . you said they were lovely.'

There's a long, astonished silence. And I find that I'm crying – the blue swirl is melting into the red rectangle. I blink and they separate again.

It's Ria who says, 'They are lovely and you're lovely. Lovely enough to put your clothes back on, Louise.'

O

Occasions

There are numerous occasions in life when even the most unassuming, least clothes-conscious woman realizes that it can be of real importance socially for her to be well dressed. Suddenly seized with panic at the idea that she will be the centre of attention, she wonders in anguish, 'Whatever shall I wear?' and rushes out to buy any kind of new dress she can find.

Whatever the ceremony at which you or your husband may be required to play a leading role – such as godparent at a christening, committee member of a charity ball, or merely as a guest at the Christmas office party – you should always adopt simplicity as the best policy and not try to radically transform your appearance for this special event. It would only astonish everyone, and on this particular occasion you do not want to cause a sensation, but simply to present a pleasing and attractive appearance.

One Saturday morning, I awake to the sound of muffled voices. Shuffling into the hallway, wearing my new, guaranteed opaque robe, I pause to listen by the living-room door.

'And you think they're getting a divorce?' This is a woman's voice, but one I don't know.

'Yes,' Colin says, 'it's pretty much certain now.'

The woman sighs. 'Sex or money, darling. Mark my words. It always comes down to sex or money.'

I knock gently. 'Hello? Sorry to disturb you.'

Colin rises and the woman, slim and tiny with flaming red hair, smiles at me. She's wearing a tweed skirt with an emerald green twin set and she sits with her ankles crossed, her feet arched delicately.

'Morning, Ouise! Did we wake you? I don't believe you've met; this is my mother.'

I grin apologetically, aware of how bedraggled I look and badly in need of coffee. 'It's a pleasure to meet you, Mrs Riley.' I cross and shake her tiny hand.

'Please, call me Ada.' Her voice, smooth and cultured, betrays just the slightest hint of an Irish accent.

'I'm about to make some coffee, can I get you some?' I offer.

'No.' She rises. 'I really should be getting on before your father misses me. It was lovely to meet you, Louise.'

Colin holds her coat out and she steps into it. 'I'll see you out, Mum.' And I hear them whispering as they make their way down the steps.

When Colin returns, he joins me in the kitchen.

'Your mum's an early riser. What was all that about?' I ask, pouring a bowl of cereal.

He leans his head on the door frame and closes his eyes. 'It's my father,' he sighs. 'He's playing up again.'

Colin's father, Patrick Riley, was once a famous Irish tenor and his mother Ada, a dancer in the Royal Ballet. They met at Covent Garden in the fifties and were married shortly afterwards. Very quickly, five children followed, of which Colin is the youngest. However, Patrick's career came to a sudden and tragic halt when he lost his voice during a performance of *Cavalleria Rusticana* in the late sixties. Unable to conceive of a career in anything but music, he struggled to support his family as a voice coach and music teacher, but never fully recovered from the loss of prestige from his Covent Garden days. Always highly sensitive, he began to succumb to dark periods of depression and lock himself away in his study for days on end. As he grew older and his children left the family home, his mood swings became increasingly violent; sudden, uncontrollable outbursts were followed by tears and pathetic promises that he would 'pull himself together'. But he was unable to effect any real or lasting changes on his own. The family rarely spoke of 'Da's condition', but lately things had been worse and Ada was beside herself. And he was always particularly bad around the anniversary of his final, devastating performance, which was in a month's time.

'Mum thinks that maybe we should organize some kind of tribute to him. You know, gather all his friends and family and have a party to celebrate his career, but I don't know. It could go either way; either he could really enjoy it or it might just send him into another bad bout of morbid reflection – though, chances are, he's going to no matter what we do.' He shook his head. 'I just don't know, Ouise. I really don't know what to do.'

'It's a tough one.' I poured him out a cup of coffee. 'I wish I could help.'

'Well, there is one thing . . .' he hesitated.

'Just name it.'

'If she does decide to go ahead with this whole thing, will you come with me?'

'Sure, Col. No problem. Although she might just want family only, don't you think?'

He studied the kitchen floor a moment. 'And their partners,' he added quietly.

'Partners?'

He looked up. 'You see, I've never really told them I'm gay.'

For a moment I thought I would laugh. 'And you don't think they know?'

He sighed heavily. 'It isn't a matter of them knowing, Louise. But they're not of a generation that find it necessary to discuss these things. Do you understand? What they know or don't know is not really my concern. My *telling* them doesn't help. We all get along better when it just isn't an issue.'

'And how do you accomplish that?'

'I just don't put it in their faces and they don't ask.'

'That's fine now, while you're single, but what about when you have a boyfriend?'

'Louise,' he seemed tired and irritable. 'Trust me on this one. They don't want to know. They want me to be happy but they don't want to know. Some things are just better left unsaid.'

Three days later, Colin confirmed that his mother had decided to go ahead with her plan; the party was to be held in their large family home and would be a surprise. And in the weeks that followed, Colin spent every spare moment coordinating arrangements between his mother and fellow siblings. They planned a buffet supper, a jazz trio for dancing, and Ada had arranged for some of Patrick's star pupils to sing. Family and friends were scheduled to arrive from as far away as Dublin, and Colin's brother Ewan had managed to find some old film footage of his father singing in *La Bohème*, which he'd had restored, to be screened at the end of the evening. The phone rang constantly and there was a buzz of real excitement in the air. The energy and enthusiasm with which the Riley clan launched themselves into Patrick's party was unparalleled.

A week before the big night, Colin cornered me as I

was doing the washing up. 'I think we ought to talk about what we're going to wear.'

I handed him a tea towel. 'Good plan. Let's start with you.'

'Well,' he polished off a few glasses, stacking them on the kitchen shelf. 'I'm thinking maybe my navy pinstripe, a pale blue shirt, and a red tie. You know, something very conservative, formal but not too formal . . . what do you think?'

I looked at him in surprise. 'You own a navy pinstripe suit? I can't imagine you wearing anything so sombre!'

He smiled. 'Well, I'll have to have it cleaned, but yes, it does exist. Alan bought it for me when he was trying to persuade me to go into banking. I tried to convince Mum to make it a black tie evening – everyone looks better in black tie – but she says that not everyone will have a tux and I'm sure she has a point.'

'*Banking!* I can't imagine you trying to control anyone's spending, Col!'

He laughed. 'Now it's your turn. What did you have in mind?'

'Well,' I hesitated, 'I'm not really sure. I've got my little black Karen Millen dress.'

'Hummm.' I could tell by the way he was concentrating on the drying that it wasn't quite what he had in mind.

'But then again, it may be a little . . . how do you say it?'

'Tight?' he volunteered.

I turned to face him. 'Tight?!'

'Well, then, form fitting. A little close, shall we say.'

I glared at him. 'Colin, there's absolutely nothing wrong with that dress. Or the way it fits me!'

'Yes, yes, yes, yes! Of course! I love it, Ouise! Really, I do. But I'm thinking something a little more subdued, a little more restrained . . . what's the word I'm looking for? A little more Catholic.'

'Like what? A habit?'

He sighed and put the tea towel down. 'You have to understand, Louise, this is my family we're talking about. When it comes right down to it, they're a little old fashioned. Traditional even. Despite the showbiz roots. You and I are going as kind of a team, right? I'm wearing the blue pinstripe and you can wear something that goes with that look . . . don't you think?'

I frowned at him. This was not the Colin I knew. Suddenly it was as if he'd been abducted and replaced by an evil twin – one that wanted us to perform some sort of bizarre charade for his parents.

And then it hit me.

'Colin, did you by any chance tell them that I was your girlfriend?'

He picked up the tea towel again and started drying as if his life depended on it. 'No! No, of course not!'

'Really? 'Cause you're acting really weird.'

He avoided my gaze and began stacking plates together. 'Absolutely not, Louise! Really!'

'But you didn't *not* tell them I was your girlfriend either. That's it, isn't it? You were going to just say nothing and let them draw their own conclusions.'

He put the plates down. 'Is that really so bad?'

I shook my head. 'Why are you doing this, Col? You do know, don't you, that you have nothing to be ashamed of?'

He closed his eyes and passed a hand wearily over them. 'This is not the occasion, Louise, when I come out to my family. Can you understand that? This party, this night, is not about me. All I'm asking is that we blend in, that we remain anonymous. Just for this one night. Look, I'm not going to try to pass you off as my girlfriend, OK? As far as anyone's concerned you're my friend and my flatmate, all right? But all I want is for this one night to go smoothly. Can you understand that?'

I can.

I wrap my arms around him. 'Listen, I'll wear anything you like, OK? And we'll have a good time and the whole evening will be a terrific success. Just wait and see.'

He gives me a squeeze. 'I did take the liberty of borrowing something from the wardrobe department.' He dives into the living room and comes back clutching a shopping bag. He hands it to me. 'Go on, see if you like it.'

I reach in and pull out an original Diane Von Furstenberg wrap-around dress in a bold crimson print. 'Wow,' I say, holding it up against me. 'It's kind of incredible.'

He beams at me. '*Now* you look like a banker's wife!'

However, Colin and I never get to wear our carefully chosen outfits.

Two days before the party, while Colin is delivering spare plates and cutlery to his mother, they hear a strange noise from Patrick's study. They discover him, slumped in a heap on the carpet, having swallowed a fatal dose of tranquillizers. There is no note.

Colin spends a week at his mother's, helping with arrangements, and then, after the funeral, Ada departs for Ireland, to stay with family.

The day Colin comes back to the flat, Ria and I both take the day off. He comes in and goes straight to bed for four hours, while Ria and I busy ourselves baking scones. (She bakes. I watch.) When he finally wakes up, eyes swollen and red, we make a fresh pot of tea and try our best to force feed him the scones, and when that doesn't work, we just sit there, in the living room, watching the sun melt behind the London skyline and listening to an old recording of Patrick singing famous Italian arias. The record ends and we sit in silence in the dark. And then Ria turns a light on and goes into the kitchen to make us all cheese on toast. Colin lies down and rests his head in my lap.

'He was so much trouble,' he says at last. 'So unpredict-able to be around. And yet I don't know what we'll do without him.'

I gently stroke his hair.

I want to tell him I understand, but I don't. I'm one of the lucky ones.

When I was thirteen, I came home from school one day to find my mother sitting in one of the living-room chairs in her nightgown. She should've been dressed. And at work. But she wasn't. She was here instead — pale, drawn, her eyes glassy and swollen. The nightgown she was wearing was faded and damp. It clung to her thin frame and there was some sort of stain on the front. My mother was never home when I got back from school.

I asked her if she was all right and she ignored me, staring straight ahead, her head wobbling on her neck as if it might fall off at any moment. I stood directly in front of her and asked again, but she looked at me as if she didn't recognize me and blinked slowly. Far too slowly. Then her mouth just fell open and, in a single, horrible instant, I realized she was dying. The world seemed to move in slow motion; I felt my back pack slide off my arms and onto the floor and although I was running, my feet were made of lead. I pulled at the phone on the wall and dialled a number. A voice came on the line and I could hear myself screaming our address, telling them to hurry, and as I turned, I saw her slump forward, head on chest, a thin, strand of drool sliding its way slowly down her chin. I let go of the phone and it crashed against the wall, as she crumpled to a heap on the floor.

Minutes later, the ambulance team arrived. I was rocking her back and forth in my arms, trying to get her to wake up. They pulled her away from me, strapped her onto a stretcher, and put an oxygen mask over her mouth. Then they searched the bathroom until they found some bottles. In a matter of minutes, they were gone. A neighbour came over, Mrs Klavinski, and rang my father. She was Polish, and although she was just trying to be helpful, her English wasn't very good. When my sister and brother came home, she greeted them with the news that my mother had a 'sickness of the head and was taking to hospital'.

It was months before she came home.

And when she did, she was different. Better.

And as I held Col, I thought of all the secret preparations that had been made over the past month and of how he and his mother found Patrick too late. And I thought again, for the thousand millionth time, of what would've happened if I'd been late home from school that day – if I'd loitered by the bus stop, staring at the boys from St Andrew's or landed myself in detention.

Later that night, I rang home. Sitting in the darkness by the window, I listened to the phone ring, thousands of miles away. Then I heard a click and my mother's voice came on the line.

'Hello?'

'Hello, Mom.'

'Louise! What's the time? It's kinda late there, isn't it?'

'A little.'

'Are you all right?'

'Yeah, Mom, I'm fine. I just called to see how you are.'

'Great, Kiddo. Couldn't be better. Your father's a bit of a pain *dans le derrière* but I'm being very firm with him, so we'll soon have that under control. It's all about this new shed he wants to build in the back yard. Did you know your sister's trying for another baby? No luck yet, but I'll keep you posted. How's the job? I spent the whole day planting bulbs, which I have a feeling the deer are just going to eat again. But I try every year, so I can't start giving up now, can I?'

'Absolutely not.'

'So, Kiddo.' I hear her lighting a cigarette. 'What's the occasion?'

I look out the window. The world outside is still and black.

'No occasion, Mom. I just called to hear your voice.'

P

Pounds

Every springtime the fashion magazines and women's pages invent new diets which, if they are followed to the letter, guarantee a slender figure and, consequently, elegance. Although it isn't necessarily indispensable to be as skinny as a mannequin in order to be elegant, it is probably true that the list of the Ten Best Dressed Women is also a list of the Ten Hungriest Women.

Slimming is practically a new religion. It used to be practised very discreetly, almost clandestinely, and the early followers contented themselves with a moderate slenderness which still allowed for a few soft curves. But the sect has gained new converts every day until it now confidently decrees that salvation is impossible for the few remaining infidels who do not believe in the string bean silhouette and the skinny look.

Should you or should you not convert to this new

*religion? Perhaps, but at what cost? Dieters can
become drearily obsessive about their new found
vocation. I recommend that you weigh not just yourself but your priorities as well. After all, God made
you the way you are and there is no point fighting
nature to the extent that you alienate all your friends
and family with endless rules and regulations concerning what you can and cannot eat.*

*Being slender is undoubtedly elegant but neurotic
self-obsession is NOT.*

I'm standing in the queue at Starbucks, trying to figure out
the fat grams, calorie content, and carbohydrate index of a
fat-reduced blueberry muffin. All I really want, though, is
a slice of double fudge chocolate cake. I'm irritable and
confused, looking at the cake like a hypnotized lemming.
Ria's asking me what I want so that we can order and the
queue behind me's getting restless and the girl behind the
counter is rolling her eyes. What I want to do is to punch
through the glass case and grab the whole cake and run
howling into the street with it like a creature from a Ham-
mer Horror film.

But I don't.

No, I do the right thing. Because the world is divided
into right and wrong, good and bad, fat and thin. So I order
a double espresso instead with no sugar.

And when Ria asks, 'Are you sure?' because she saw me eyeing the cake, I snap at her, 'Yes, yes that's it!' like I hate her, because I do. I hate her and anyone else who can order anything they want without going through a thousand mental gymnastics – who can walk up to the spotty Spanish girl behind the counter and say, 'I'll have an iced latte and a slice of double fudge chocolate cake', without taking a rollercoaster ride to hell and back from waves of guilt and panic.

So. I order the double espresso instead, get completely psychotic on caffeine, and walk around in a sweaty, twitching cloud of resentment all day long because yet again, I've denied myself. And there are three meals in a day, a day's twenty-four hours long and they follow each other, day after day after day, until you die. And that's an awfully long time not to have what you want.

I went on my first diet when I was nine. Being a dancer, we were encouraged to starve ourselves. I remember our teacher sitting us down, talking to us about how it was time to start watching our weight. She taught us how to carry little jars of honey and teaspoons in our ballet bags so that when we'd been dancing all day with nothing to eat and felt like fainting, we could pop a teaspoon of honey into our mouths to keep us going. So we all carried leaky little jars of honey that came undone and coated our leotards in thick, sugary goo.

We used to sit in the changing room, listening avidly to

the diet tips of the older girls. You must eat only low fat yoghurt, Diet Coke, coffee, and baked potatoes with nothing on them. Or only protein and vegetables, as much as you want but less is better. However, all too often we ended up eating hamburgers at McDonald's after class, and if you were going to have a hamburger, you might as well have fries and a shake. But that was OK, because we'd all learnt from Melissa Formby the wonderful invention of throwing up everything after you ate. She'd only just discovered this magical solution herself and was now giving master classes on how to best achieve the results you wanted with the least amount of effort.

'Always drink a glass of water very quickly beforehand,' she instructed us. 'And then use your longest finger. A little nail doesn't hurt. And think of something gross. If you can think of something *really* gross, then you don't have to waste too much time and that keeps your mother from getting suspicious.'

We nodded. How wise she was.

'Oh, and use a private toilet. Especially until you learn how to do it quietly.'

Good one. We were, after all, as dancers always learning how to do things quietly – how to jump across a room and land without a sound, how to bourrée on bloody point shoes without so much as a whisper, how to stretch your leg up around your ear without screaming. Piece of cake.

By the time I was thirteen, I'd developed my own little

variation on this theme. I'd have one meal a day, usually something completely disgusting and devoid of any nutritional value, like chocolate cake, covered in M&M's, with ice-cream and chocolate sauce for breakfast, and I'd take speed, coffee, and Diet Coke the rest of the day. If I had any food after my one meal, I'd chuck it up in the guest room toilet.

This went on for quite a while, until one night, high on speed and having just watched a particularly depressing Bergman film about necrophilia, I scoffed down a whole box of nasty, white sugar biscuits and then threw them up again. I sat, shaking on the bathroom floor, certain that I didn't want to live any more. Or, at least, that I didn't want to live like this. I could no longer bear the twenty-four hour obsession about what I was going to eat, when I was going to eat it, and worst of all, what I wasn't allowed to eat. (I'd already tried laxatives, with disastrous results.) So, I resolved that whatever I ate would stay down, for better or worse. And a new chapter in my dieting history began.

When I got married, I kept my eating habits a secret. But with my husband away every evening on stage, it was easy to get into a routine of bingeing in his absence.

We're in Stratford; he's with the RSC. We have a new place to live, he has a new job, and I'm on a new diet. It's like the Hay Diet, only it's with organic food. Every day I eat about twenty-six pounds of grimy, misshapen, hairy fruits and vegetables. I have wind constantly and smell like a cabbage.

The rules are easy. (Diets have rules, like games. There's no difference really, this one's Twister with food.) You can have carbohydrates with vegetables and dairy but not with protein. And you can have protein only with vegetables. And fruit, well, fruit's so dangerous that you can only have it on its own, several hours before or after eating anything. So, that's steak and salad, chicken and salad, fish and salad. But not cheese. Cheese is evil. The devil's work. I'm allowed some strange form of organic goat's cheese curd but there's only one shop in Notting Hill that sells it and it tastes like glue. And for lunch, salad. Salad with rice, salad with nuts, salad with bread. When I say bread, what I really mean is a gluten-free yeast-free loaf of millet and linseed. It looks like a brick but if you toast it, it's really quite crunchy. (In the absence of any taste, texture will have to do.) And no sugar of any kind, no caffeine, and no fat.

The book makes it seem quite simple. Actually, more than just simple; like you'd be an idiot to eat any other way. There's a couple in their seventies laughing hysterically on the front cover and running a marathon. Completely caffeine free. I feel inadequate just looking at it. There's a strong emphasis on beans. Bean and cabbage soup, flavoured with garlic. They could've warned me that I was going to explode. I have to lock myself in my room with the window open. My husband sleeps on the couch.

You're meant to eat as many things raw as you can. I'm munching on a fortune's worth of crudities all day long and all I manage is to feel bloated and hungry at the same time. I'm dreaming of hamburgers, chips, shepherd's pie. I wake up gnawing at my pillow. Watching other people eat becomes an erotic experience for me. Staring in the window of McDonald's like a Peeping Tom, I'm glued to the spot, ready to kill for a Happy Meal.

It's meant to get better. I'm meant to be full of life and energy. My skin's meant to glow. But all that happens is I get a vicious case of irritable bowel syndrome. I'm doubled over with pain and my husband takes me to the doctor.

'What are you eating?' the doctor asks after he's examined me.

'Well, today I had gluten-free muesli and rice milk, broccoli and chicken stir fry with ginger, some raw carrots, a little rye toast with soya spread and sugarless raspberry jam . . .'

He raises a hand to stop me; he's already late for his golf.

'Good God!' He looks at me in disgust. 'Eat a potato, woman! Have a sausage roll! No wonder you can't stand up straight.'

'But . . . but . . .' I can't believe it. Doesn't he want to be running a marathon when he's seventy?

Apparently not.

By the time I came to live with Colin and Ria, I was so confused from a lifetime of dieting that I felt beyond repair or redemption. The only difference was that now there was no place to hide it. We shared a kitchen, often ate together, and while Colin was happy to tease me about my strange meals and occasionally force-feed me chicken curry and steamed jam pudding, Ria observed my eating habits in silence, quietly noting all the things I would rather she'd forgotten.

Then one night, she finds me in the kitchen.

It's half past two and I'm sitting in my pyjamas, stuffing cookies into my mouth. They're her cookies; she'd been given them at Christmas, several months ago, and, not having much of a sweet tooth, she'd let them sit there, going stale on a shelf above the sink. Normally I wouldn't touch her food without asking her, but I'd woken up, suddenly scared and starving and didn't have any of my own food left. I was afraid to buy it in case I ended up eating it all in one go. I hate myself for stealing stale biscuits. They're the kind I normally would've gone out of my way to avoid. But here I am, crouched in the dark, cramming them into my mouth when she comes in and turns on the light.

I blink stupidly, like a wild animal caught stealing from a garbage pail. I can't bear to be seen eating, even at the best of times, but it's absolutely essential that these midnight raids remain secret.

'What are you doing?'

I scramble up from the floor and try to smile. 'I'm sorry. Really.'

'But what are you doing?' she asks. Again.

I want to die, to disappear, to be sucked away into the ether. I'm still holding the bag, so I put it on the counter, my hand moving in slow motion, as if not holding it will make it all go away.

'Those are old,' she says. 'Why are you eating them? And why are you eating them in the dark?'

'I was hungry. I'm sorry. I'll replace them. Buy some more.'

'Louise, I don't like those biscuits; that's why I never ate them. The biscuits don't matter. But what you're doing is strange.'

'I know. I'm sorry. I won't do it again.'

She looks at me carefully. 'Yes. Yes you will.'

It's half past two and there's nothing, no noise of passing traffic, no distant drilling to whisk the words away. They hang there, solid between us, and for some reason I can't explain, I don't lie or wheedle, laugh or protest.

'You're right,' I hear myself say.

How odd that you're saying that, I think in my head. No one's meant to know and now here you are, saying it out loud. But it doesn't stop there.

'I can't eat,' the voice goes on, speaking through me, like a ventriloquist's dummy. 'I don't, don't really know how.'

We stand there. A breeze blows in through the open kitchen window, out of the solid blackness that presses against the house. Cold and fluid, like mercury, it races between us, running its fingers through Ria's hair and making it dance around her face. Her white cotton nightgown billows up around her like a sail and for a moment she isn't earthbound at all but weightless and floating, like an apparition pasted against the poorly fitted kitchen cabinets. Then it darts away, brushing past us impatiently on its way to more exotic locations and we're alone again. Ria's nightgown drifts silently back around her ankles and her hair lands gently in place on her head.

'Are you still hungry?' she asks.

'No.'

'Well, why don't we go to bed then.' She holds out her hand and I take it. 'You think too much, Louise. You're not really meant to think so much.' And she leads me back through the darkness to my room.

The world is full of advice about how to eat, but here's a novel idea.

Have three normal meals a day. Eat what you really want. Stop when you're full.

I'll admit, sometimes that's easy and sometimes it's very, very hard.

But, in Madame Dariaux's immortal words, 'God made you the way you are.'

And in Ria's, 'Get over it.'

Q

Quality/Quantity

One of the most striking differences between a well-dressed Englishwoman and a well-dressed Parisian is in the size of their respective wardrobes. The Englishwoman would probably be astonished by the very limited number of garments hanging in the Frenchwoman's wardrobe, but she would also be bound to observe that each one is of excellent quality, expensive perhaps by British standards, and perfectly adapted to the life a Frenchwoman leads. She wears them over and over again, discarding them only when they are worn or outmoded, and she considers it a compliment (as it is meant to be) when her best friend says, 'I'm so glad you decided to wear your red dress – I've always loved it!'

Foreign visitors are often shocked by the high prices in the Paris shops, and they wonder how a young career girl, for example, who earns no more than her British counterpart, can afford to carry an

alligator handbag and to wear a suit from the Bal-
main boutique. The answer is that she buys very few
garments: her goal is to possess a single perfect ensem-
ble for each of the different occasions in her life,
rather than a wide choice of clothes to suit every
passing mood.

I wonder if the Englishwoman wouldn't profit by
replacing once in a while her penchant for quantity
with a quest for quality. She might find that not only
is her elegance increased, but also the enjoyment and
even the confidence that she gets from her clothes.

Colin and I have adopted a new catch phrase and a new
philosophy, which is essentially this: life's too short. Not
staggeringly original, but nevertheless, it fits the bill.

I'm not sure quite when we reached this conclusion, but
the pivotal moment might well have taken place on the
top deck of the number 159 bus. We were riding into work
together one rainy morning, jammed in with all the other
rush hour commuters. Everything was wet; the windows
were fogged up, the seats soaking, sopping umbrellas littered
the aisles. Colin was squashed into the seat next to me. On
his lap he balanced a large plastic bag filled with Patrick's
old suits to drop off at a charity shop, while simultaneously
trying to keep his backpack and umbrella from rolling into
the aisle with each jolt of the bus. I was sitting next to him,

my feet damp and freezing inside a pair of newly ruined suede loafers.

I opened my post to discover yet another batch of divorce papers as the bus lurched forward and then screeched to a sudden halt, pitching me into the back of a well dressed black man in the seat in front. 'So sorry!' I apologized, gingerly retrieving my letters from where they had landed on the floor.

'That's quite all right,' he smiled amiably. 'Not your fault.'

I smiled back.

'If I may disturb you just a moment longer,' he continued. 'I'd like to tell you about the joy of living in the light of the salvation of Christ.'

And that is the exact moment I think it happened. I looked at Col and he looked at me.

'Life's too short,' he said, perhaps the first full sentence he'd uttered that day, and I was inclined to agree.

'What are we doing anyway?' he continued, suddenly unstoppable in his indignation. 'What are we waiting for? I'm tired of death. I'm tired of taking the bus into work. I'm tired of sitting at home in the evening, waiting for the right guy to come up and knock at my door.'

'I'm tired of divorce!' I chipped in. 'And I'm tired of wet shoes!'

'To hell with wet shoes!' He stood up and pushed the bell. 'I'm tired of playing it safe! Goddamit, Ouise, we're young, we're sexy, we're talented! You know what, life's just too fucking short and I think it's about high time we had some fun!'

'OK.'

We got off the bus and caught a cab instead.

And that's how it began. Suddenly being a grown up was just too difficult, so we gave up. At the same time, I decided to give the sane, sober, fashion advice of Madame Dariaux a break as well. The thought of saving all of one's pennies for the perfect cashmere cardigan seemed too old, too responsible, and to take far, far too long. I wanted to be one of the girls with as many outfits as she had men for a change – gay, dazzling, voracious, and in the thick of life. Like Colin, I was tired of waiting for time to heal my heart and make me feel normal. And, like Col, I was ready for drastic action.

That's when I decided that trying to be elegant wasn't working any more. I wanted to be fashionable instead.

It's a Thursday night and Col and I are out with twenty of our new best friends at a bar called Cube. Cube is just like Mink Bikini, only Mink Bikini was hot last month and Cube is hot now. The place is packed, heaving with spiky-haired media types dressed in grey, unisex clothing; sulking, lanky would-be models in torn Chloe style tee-shirts and spike heels, and ad men in black Armani suits with bold, neon ties – all shouting, jostling, spilling drinks on one another and tripping over the Swedish style lime green ottomans that constitute the lounge area.

The soundtrack is surreal, spacey French re-mixes of KC and the Sunshine Band, dubbed over by Vanessa Paradis. And there are loads of saucy little features to keep the customers amused, including a discreetly hidden video camera tucked away in the men's toilet and a not so discreetly displayed video screen transmitting all the evidence in the ladies (forewarned is forearmed). There's also a large electronic billboard above the entrance that projects different messages every time someone walks in the door. 'Jesus loves you but he won't leave his wife,' it bleeps, like an automated fortune cookie. 'Is it love or is it lust?' it bleeps again, as a young woman ducks in out of the black rain, shaking her hair and pulling down her micro-mini. Someone calls out 'Lust!' across the room and we all laugh while she stands, frozen like a rabbit caught in headlights, unaware of the cartoon captions lurking just above her head.

There's a definite buzz. We've all made it. We survived the doorman and the two Gucci clad female bouncers, who stand poised, dripping with boredom and fatigue, ready to reject anyone too ugly, too fat, too old, or too 'yesterday' (retro looks not withstanding). We celebrate this fact by waving twenty pound notes furiously at the blue-haired, tattooed barmen, giggling at the drunken media men peeing (unbeknownst to them) on video and flirting with the obnoxious ad men, who in turn, flirt with the sulking models, who in turn flirt with no one.

I'm wearing a black pencil skirt from Kookai that's

almost exactly like this season's Prada, a tiny, sheer layered vest top like the one they're showing at Versace (only mine's from a stall in Brixton Market), and a pair of painfully high single strap hot pink mules from Office, which are the spitting image of the Manolo's Kate's wearing in this month's *Vogue*. My hair's blown dry into a single sheet of heavy, blond straightness, with a 'natural' looking centre parting that took me only fifty minutes and three different hair products to achieve. My lipstick is Mac, my toenail polish Chanel and I smell like a mixture of wild figs and French wisteria, which is meant to be both sexy and unisex at the same time. I've come a long, long way from the navy pinafore dress. And I'm as hot as they come.

Unfortunately, not everyone I invite is. A few of my friends almost don't make it past the doormen. They simply just don't understand that you need to look the part.

Darren's a music student; he's carrying an old smelly black gym bag and wearing a yellow Rupert Bear scarf. If this weren't bad enough, he's got on a bright red Gap puffa jacket that's easily ten years old and is holding his travel card like it's a Press Pass at a catwalk show.

The Gucci brigade salivate as he ambles unsuspectingly up to the door. I lurch into action, descending upon him like a tornado, whisking off his jacket and scarf, quickly tucking his bus pass into his breast pocket (he whimpers when I suggest we put it in his bag), and smoothing down his white boy afro rather unsuccessfully with the palm of my hand. Then I hand the whole bundle, bag and all, to the repulsed Norwegian coat check boy, who touches the Rupert Bear scarf as if it were medical waste and insists on giving us a separate ticket for each item, as if to punish us both for Darren's appalling lack of taste as well as his complete inability to travel light. The Gucci Girls narrow their eyes and one is about to speak, but she relents, waving us on and pursing her lips in a terse little smile as if to say, 'You owe me one'.

I'm left with Darren, bemused and bewildered, and not a little overwhelmed, who turns to me, clutching his bouquet of coat check tags and says, 'I didn't know, Louie . . . you know, that it was *that* kind of place.'

I laugh like Cruella De Vil and shove him towards the bar. 'Don't be silly, darling!' I scream above the lethargic intoning of Ms Paradis. 'Let's get you a drink and look! You can watch people come in and laugh at the things above their heads!'

'Really?' He looks up at the billboard with all the *savoir faire* of a special needs child. 'Soooo cool! Louie, walk in so I can see what it says!'

'No, Darren,' I say firmly, pushing him harder in the direction of the bar and away from the Gucci danger zone. 'You only walk in once. You have to wait for someone new to come in. Those are the rules.'

'Wow,' he says, reverently. 'We're in a place with *rules*.'

Fashion is all about rules, as are fashionable places. We

didn't want to have drinks at the local pub across the street from work. We wanted it to be different. Rules make it different – give us something to do, something to focus on instead of one another. And it's a success. Everyone's thrilled to be here, shouting to one another at point blank range, spending too much money on expensive rounds of drinks, trying to dance between the tables and falling into strangers' laps. We get drunker and drunker, run out of cash and the credit cards come out. I'm flitting between groups of people, having half conversations – catching a verb here, an adjective there and throwing out my fair share in return.

'Fantastic!' I shout, blowing air kisses across the room to a man I saw peeing on video.

'Absolutely *screaming* at each other!' I interject, stealing the punch line from Colin's story, along with a sip of his Martini.

'Really, *really* repulsive!' I stage whisper behind my hand to a girlfriend as we watch one of the models ooze her way across the room to the Ladies.

Everything I utter comes with an exclamation point attached to it. I talk to no one for very long but we hug each other a lot and say things like, 'We really must get together sometime!' And later on in the evening, when standing upright is becoming a bit of a challenge, we grab each other, bury our faces in each other's necks and sob, 'I love you! I really, really do!' And then attempt to look each other meaningfully in the eye, which isn't easy when you're seeing double.

The next morning I'm trying to recover from my hangover, drinking coffee and munching on piles of toast with Ria. She couldn't make it last night. I went round to the gallery where she works to meet her, but she cried off at the last minute; said she wasn't in the mood for all those people, all that noise.

'You're never going to meet anyone if all you do is hang around the house,' I lecture, waggling a finger at her across the kitchen.

She turns another page of the magazine she's reading. 'And who did you meet?'

I have a hazy recollection of a loud agent pulling at my arm, a married photographer who wanted to do some 'art shots' of me and another girl, a bisexual ex-army man . . .

'That's not the point,' I snap, finding it difficult to butter my toast without shaking too much. 'I'm out there; I'm in the game. You've gotta be in the game, Ria. Take it from me, I know.'

'Aha,' she murmurs, turning another page and smiling like the Mona Lisa.

She's looking at *Vogue* and as I sit down, I note, with considerable irritation, that they've dumped the whole seventies retro look and are now pushing a bouffant debutante meets punk rock chick story that renders all my carefully researched knock offs completely useless. The models are photographed skulking around in £700 Pucci shifts with torn fishnets and fat, absolutely enormous hair. It's not just a new look but a whole new ethos. I feel unnerved. How can they do this? I've only just learnt how to blow-dry my hair flat.

'I don't know why anyone would even bother to spend that much money on designer pieces!' I fume, wondering if I still have any fishnets lurking in my lingerie drawer. 'In another few months, that look will be dead anyway. What's the point of spending seven hundred quid on something you can get from Top Shop for £35 in two weeks' time? Pass the sugar, please.'

Ria pushes it across the table without looking up.

'I'm serious. What's the point?' I continue, furiously filling my coffee with spoonfuls of sugar. 'Who would bother to spend that sort of money just to stay in fashion?'

'Well,' she says quietly, sipping her tea, 'first off, fashion is not the same as style. Secondly, a person might easily spend £700 on something that was the real thing.'

The real thing? Is she being condescending?

'And what exactly is the real thing?' I ask. I can feel myself just picking a fight; someone has to pay for all the time I've wasted in Miss Selfridge.

'The real thing is what remains when fashion is gone,' she continues, pouring herself a second cup of tea. 'It has staying power, character. It's a pair of well tailored trousers, a perfectly fitted suit, a black cashmere polo neck . . .'

'Oh, right! You mean *boring* clothes!' I correct her, frustrated beyond belief that my new red snakeskin ankle boots are already passé and she's talking to me about black polo necks as if they were the Zen of fashion.

'Classics,' she parries.

I glare at her. Has she been reading my book? Either that or she's actually channelling for Madame Dariaux. 'Classics are for when you've given up,' I point out. 'Given up going out, given up dancing, given up being fashionable. If you want to be sexy and young, you have to be fashionable.'

'Or perhaps,' she says, eyeing me slyly, 'they're the kinds of things that appeal to you only when you've grown up.'

A weighty silence descends between us. I hate her. And I despise black polo neck jumpers.

'So, how was it last night?' she asks, quickly changing the subject.

I let her score her point; after all, I reason, she's obviously one of those people who's already given up and it would be rude to continue.

'It was great last night. Really, really good. Everyone was there – Colin, Sanam, Nelson, Darren.' I have a flash of inspiration. 'You should come next time. I think you and Darren would really get along.'

She wrinkles her nose at me. 'We'll see.'

I shrug my shoulders. 'Sure. Maybe next time.'

And I think about how staid she is with her home-cooked dinners and her piles of art catalogues, bless her. Doesn't she know the clock is ticking? I pat her affectionately on the head before I disappear down to Brixton Market in search of something vaguely Pucci that I can wear next Friday night.

Then, one Sunday, I find myself alone in the house with Ria. I'm suffering from a particularly irritating and persistent cold and have reluctantly cancelled all my weekend plans in favour of sleeping, face down on top of my duvet all afternoon. I linger in a coma-like state most of the day until the afternoon wanes and the sun sets. When I finally pad into the kitchen to make some dinner, I run into Ria, who's emerging for the same purpose after an afternoon of reading. We move effortlessly around the narrow galley together, ducking out of each other's way, sharing utensils, talking when we want to and comfortable in our silence when we don't. I'm struck by the easy calmness that I'm enjoying in her company.

We turn the television on and, as luck would have it, a huge costume drama is airing its first episode that night. We nestle into the enormous, sagging sofa together and settle down to an evening of heaving bosoms and bursting bustiers.

A heated debate ensues over whether or not the oppressed virgin should really have a fringe or not and we disagree violently about the sexiness of the leading man. (Is it possible to love a man whose hair is bigger than yours?

I think not but Ria believes it's all a matter of proportion.) And we agree unequivocally that there are, in fact, only three extras in the whole series that the production team just dress in different clothes and force into the back of each shot.

When the evening's over, I discover, much to my surprise, that I feel better and more refreshed than I have in a long time and yet we've done nothing, gone nowhere, said very little. I find myself eagerly looking forward to next Sunday and then the Sunday after that.

And very quickly Sundays become the most cherished day of the week.

Fast forward to a year later.

It's Ria's birthday. Colin and his new boyfriend, Andy, and I are taking her out to dinner. I'm wearing my red silk Joseph dress, and a matching cashmere cardigan. I've worn it a thousand times already this summer; it's my 'summer outfit'. But it's so perfect, so beautifully cut, that I don't mind if everyone's seen it before.

Ria's already waiting outside our favourite restaurant, Villandry, when I arrive. She, Andy and Colin are sipping champagne and chatting in the warm glow of the late afternoon sun. She's holding a bouquet of flowers they gave her at work and she looks crisp and fresh in her white linen shirt and trousers. It's not a big party, just the four of us, but her face is beaming as I get out of the cab and she's so excited that when we sit down, she can hardly eat. I've asked them to make a cake for her, which they bring out with coffee. It's a solid, almost impenetrable block of pure chocolate with 'Happy Birthday Ria' written on it in pink icing and a single, slender candle. When we sing 'Happy Birthday', she turns bright red and starts to cry.

I've seen Ria a thousand times since I first met her. We know each other so well now that we can finish each other's sentences. I hand her my gift. It's a book about Barbara Hepworth that she's been wanting for a long, long time.

And I know this. I know that she's wanted this book. I know that she'll order fish to start with and fish for her main course. I know she'll only have one glass of champagne because she doesn't really drink and that she's been lusting after that crisp, white linen blouse she's wearing for ages. I know what shoe size she wears, why she doesn't like the Underground, and how anything, beautifully done, can make her cry.

She's the real thing. A classic. A real black cashmere polo neck of a friend.

And after all, life's too short for anything else.

R

Restaurants

The question, 'Where are we going tonight?' is never an idle one. It provides valuable information that will allow you to tailor your appearance to best suit the surroundings in which you find yourself over the course of the evening, and it is just as unthinkable for an elegant woman to arrive at a restaurant for dinner in the wrong attire as it would be for her to turn up an hour late.

For example: if you are being treated to a glamorous evening in a fashionable bistro, prepare yourself for food that is really quite average but clientele that are sure to be wearing the very latest styles. You will feel most comfortable if you follow suit and choose something along the lines of a chic, little black dress, augmented with very fashionable, up-to-date accessories. If, however, your escort has selected a celebrated, well-established venue, then I would suggest you dress in whatever you own that's conservative, luxurious, and perhaps even a little banal. By all means, fling a mink stole over your shoulders and deck yourself in diamonds – this is exactly what he would expect. And besides, your more avant-garde, stylish ensemble will most likely be wasted on the older, affluent clientele, who are really only there to eat.

Never forget that when you are dressing for dinner, you are dressing not just for yourself, but also for the pleasure and comfort of the gentleman taking you. And when a man is spending a small fortune on an evening, he usually likes to be surrounded by lavish décor, delectable cuisine, and a companion who looks as if she blends in perfectly with both.

And then it happens. Long after I'd left the fateful note, Oliver Wendt makes a rare and brief appearance in the lobby. I'm on my hands and knees counting programmes in one of the storage cupboards when I suddenly become aware of the smell of cigarette smoke behind me. I turn to find him staring down at me, lounging against the door frame and blowing a trail of hazy smoke rings into the dusty sunlight that filters in from the stained-glass window above the main door. He looks tanned and relaxed in his pale blue shirt and jeans.

'I guess you'd have to wear a tie at the Ritz,' he ponders,

gazing reflectively at the slowly dissolving rings and flicking his ash into one of the battered brass urns with a practised flick of the wrist.

I swallow hard. Easy does it, girl. Cool and aloof. Cool and aloof.

'I suppose so,' I answer, arching an eyebrow. 'That is, of course, if a person were actually going to the Ritz.'

I smile coyly.

He smiles coyly.

And then suddenly my hands begin to shake. I turn bright red and try to mask it by gripping the stack of programmes as tightly as possible. But somehow it only makes it worse. I'm possessed; my hands have a life all their own and I can only grin stupidly as the pile suddenly erupts and shoots across the foyer as if under some supernatural attack.

'Shit!' I say, as coolly and aloofly as possible, scrambling to pick them up. Oliver grins, places his cigarette carefully in the corner of his mouth, and stoops down to help me.

'You really have a knack with inanimate objects,' he observes.

'I'm not normally this bad,' I defend myself, furiously piling the programmes together. I wish I were dead. 'There are times, believe it or not, when I'm downright graceful.'

'Let's hope Friday is one of those times,' he replies, piling the programmes swiftly into a spare box.

I freeze.

'Friday?' I try to sound casual and nonplussed. Unfortunately, my voice takes on a strange vibrato and it comes out more like Edith Evans delivering the famous handbag line in *The Importance of Being Earnest*. He appears not to notice.

After we finish stacking the programmes, he lifts up the box. 'Where would you like them?' he asks, ignoring my question.

'Ahh . . .' I'm having difficulty concentrating. 'Ahh . . . here. Just here is fine.'

He looks at me. 'Here,' he repeats.

'Yes, please, that would be great,' I smile.

'But you just took them from here.'

'Oh! OK . . . Well, what about there then.' I point wildly to a spot across the foyer. 'Let's take them over there!'

He hauls them over to the designated spot and puts them down.

'Thank you so much! That's terrific!' I gush. I'll have to wait until he leaves before I can move them back again.

'You're welcome.' He draws hard on his cigarette.

We contemplate the box in silence for a moment.

'So, Friday,' he begins; now it's his voice that sounds oddly Edith Evans. He shifts from one foot to the other. 'I mean, that is, unless you have other plans.'

'No.' I stand numbly, trying my best not to throw up or fall down or destroy anything. 'No.' I pretend to be going over my social diary in my head. 'I guess I could do Friday.'

'Right then. Shall I collect you?' He makes it sound like a parcel.

'No, no!' I'm horrified at the thought of him seeing my home, especially my broom cupboard bedroom and Colin's dubious collection of *objets d'art*. 'Why don't I meet you there.'

'Seven o'clock?'

My mouth is dry. 'Seven is fine,' I croak.

'Then I'll see you there,' he says, heading into the auditorium.

Suddenly I feel like the victim of a hit and run. 'Yes, but where?' I call after him.

He turns and grins. 'Somewhere I've never been before, Louise. The Ritz.'

And then it's all over. He's gone. And there's only an impossibly tidy box of programmes and a bit of fag ash left to confirm that he's been there at all.

'I guess you have to wear something pretty swell when you go to the Ritz,' I chirrup to Colin when I arrive home that evening, eyes sparkling.

He's dusting the flat, and in particular, his prized collection of china figurines. There they all are, carefully lined up on the dining table; the naughty shepherd and shepherdess, the leaping tiger, the emaciated Don Quixote tilting at a windmill. He looks up.

'The Ritz! Well, I suppose, darling. Boys like me don't get much past Walthamstow KFC on a good night out. And who,' he adds, grinning slyly, 'would be taking my little Americano to the Ritz?'

I skip gleefully into my room. 'Oh no one. Only his name starts with an *O* and ends in *liver Wendt*!'

'My lord, he *is* straight! Hallelujah! Oh Ouise! My own little Ouise!' He clutches the dust rag he's holding dramatically to his chest. 'My little girl's all growed up! Next thing I know you'll be leaving me!'

'Col, stop rehearsing for *Coronation Street* and come help me.'

'I don't know why I should,' he sulks. 'You never let me finish a scene.'

A moment later he pokes his head round the door to find me tossing everything I own out of my wardrobe onto the bed.

'So, what are you going to wear?' I can feel him examining my room. The Post-its are gone now, but that's not the only thing troubling him. 'Lord, don't you *ever* dust?' he despairs, his eye falling on my overcrowded bedside table. Shaking his head, he perches on the edge of the bed and starts wiping my perfume bottles with an air of quiet resignation. It's Colin's curse that he's unable to pass by any surface without inspecting it for dust.

'I just don't know,' I fret. 'I have nothing . . . absolutely nothing!' I chuck another pile onto the bed.

'I have an idea. When you're done throwing everything, we can put it all back arranged in colour-coded sections. Look,' he smiles, holding his handiwork up to the light. 'Now, just look at that and tell me it doesn't look better! You can even read the name on it now, *Amarige*.'

'Colin! You're not paying attention to a word I'm saying! I don't have a thing to wear!'

'Don't be such a silly moo, of course you do!' He flicks his cloth over the lampshade in a single, absent minded gesture. 'But I can tell right now we're going to need a cup of good strong tea before we can make any real progress. Oh Ouise!' He shakes his head in disbelief as I throw another blouse onto the bed. 'I don't know how a girl like you can still be using wire hangers! One would think you were raised by a pack of gypsies.' And with that, he disappears into the kitchen to put the kettle on.

A few minutes later he's back with two 'doubles', as he calls them, which are like espressos, only with tea; a speciality of his achieved by cramming a whole handful of PG Tips into a very small tea pot and allowing it to brew until the colour of tar. He claims it's how the British won the war, which brings troops of twitching, sweaty caffeine junkies to mind.

'Now,' he settles onto the only available corner of the bed left. 'Let's proceed logically. Option number one, please.'

'Well, there's this.' I hold up a tweed suit. 'With this

little top,' I add, pointing to a black lace button down shirt.

'Hummmmmm.' He purses his lips and taps them with his forefinger. 'Very mixed messages. Very "I'm a prude, oops! No I'm not," if you get my drift. Kinda "Do I, don't I". A little bit, "Why, Miss Jones, you're beautiful!" And just a touch "Ooooooh, matron!" Which, personally, I like. Only thing is, they don't seem to match.'

'All right. What about this one?' I hold up a black evening dress.

'Louise, it's got a bow on it. How can a woman in her thirties own anything with a bow on it?'

'I thought it made me look young,' I protest weakly.

'Young is one thing; infantile is another.' He waves it away.

'OK, fine. There's always my Pucci look skirt and halter neck.' I hold them up. He dismisses them as well.

'Ouise, that look is soooooo dead.'

'What can I do?' I sink into a dejected mass on the floor.

'Whatever happened to that little black dress of yours? You know the one.'

I shake my head. 'The Karen Millen. I ripped a seam dancing at Mink Bikini and never had it repaired.'

'Well, what would Madame What's Her Knickers say in a case like this?'

I look at him. 'Col! You're the last person I would expect to send me back to Madame Dariaux!'

'Well, angel, you don't *have* to be completely psychotic

about it – you could just read it and take the advice with a pinch of salt like a normal person.'

I stick my tongue out at him. 'I don't think so.'

He shrugs his shoulders. 'Then there's really nothing for it. You're going to have to borrow something from Ria.'

'Ria! You must be joking!' I try to laugh, but a hollow choking sound comes out instead. Colin blinks at me unmoved.

'Face facts, Ouise. It's a class joint and you, I'm sorry to say, ain't got no class clothes. No offence, sweetie, you're cute and sexy, but when we're talking about a £200 evening, we need Audrey Hepburn not Barbara Windsor. And,' he goes on, raising a hand to silence me, 'no matter what you think of our tiny dictator, you must admit, she's always beautifully dressed.'

'She wears *old people clothes*!' I shout, trying very hard to resist the urge to pitch my tea at his head.

'Ahhaa! But that's just where you're wrong, my little bargain basement friend! Ria wears classics and the Ritz is a classic kind of place. Your aim is to blend into your surroundings, angel. Blend and become, blend and become . . . repeat after me. Ouise,' his look is stern, 'trust me on this. I'm an old queen, I know what I'm talking about.'

'You're thirty-five, Colin.'

'Yes, but in gay boy years that's sixty-five and shopping with a trolley.'

'You're missing the point entirely! I don't want to blend

in; I want to stand out! I've been waiting months for him to ask me out. I want him to notice me!'

'No.' He shakes his head and waggles a finger at me as if I were an erring dog. 'Not at the Ritz. Believe me, darling, you really *do* want to blend in, you just don't know it. And he has noticed you or else you wouldn't be going there in the first place.'

'But if he saw how sexy I was . . .' I begin. But Colin continues to shake his head 'no'.

'I'll think about it,' I sulk.

'Do. Now,' he stands up eagerly. 'Shall we colour code these clothes?'

'No, not now. I want to be alone.' I push him towards the door.

'Now, Ouise, you're not angry are you? Babe?'

I shove him out and slam the door shut.

'Ouise?' He presses his eye to the keyhole but I put my hand over it. 'Don't be mad, it's for your own good. Even Audrey was nothing until she met Givenchy.'

'With all due respect,' I respond haughtily, 'I am thirty-two years old, Colin, and I think I can dress myself. Now, if you don't mind, I'd like a little privacy.'

Ask Ria for clothes! Honestly!

As I pick up my faux Pucci mini and rummage around for my sheer layered vest top, my eye falls on the copy of *Elegance* where it sits on top of a stack of books balanced against the windowsill. Perhaps Colin's right. Maybe it wouldn't do any harm to consult the oracle one more time.

I pick it up and hold it a moment, staring at the well-worn grey cover and feeling the familiar weight of it in my hands. I think of all the hours I've pored over its pages, searching for answers and advice. I was desperate then. But I'm not desperate now. After all, he's asked me out, hasn't he? I must be doing something right.

Still, I hesitate. Flipping the book open, I riffle through until I come to 'R'.

'Dress in whatever you own that's conservative, luxurious and perhaps even a little banal.'

I look again at the tweed suit on my bed. OK. Why not give it a try? Moments later, I'm examining my reflection in the wardrobe mirror. Adorned top to bottom in brown tweed, I look not just conservative but positively *embalmed*. Attack of the Sexless Librarian. I take off the suit and throw it back on my bed in frustration. There's nothing for it; rummaging around in the back of my wardrobe, I locate the damaged Karen Millen dress. I'm just going to have to repair it myself. And while I'm here, I toss my copy of *Elegance* behind a stack of old tee-shirts and close the door.

I've waited far too long to let this opportunity go to waste.

And I don't need help from anyone.

*　*　*

It's Friday night. I emerge from Green Park tube station waxed, shaved, depilated, exfoliated, refined, defined, moisturized, and volumized. I am, in supermarket terms, washed and ready to eat.

Getting dressed was nothing short of a nightmare. I figured I had one shot at this and one shot only; therefore, I'd better not leave anything to chance. If I was going to successfully seduce Oliver Wendt, I'd better bring out the big guns. So, I've highlighted a few of my assets.

Although I'm not the world's greatest seamstress (or even in the top five thousand), I have managed to stitch together the torn seam of the black Karen Millen dress. Exhilarated after completing my task with such a relative amount of ease, I then decide to go that one step further. After all, if the dress looks sexy just above the knee, imagine how much more effective it will be if I take it up a few more inches. So much more Versace. And tonight I'm determined to give even Liz Hurley a run for her money in the glamour stakes. To finish the look off, I've got on strappy high heels to make me look taller, fishnets to make my legs look thinner, and a new, inflatable push-up bra aptly named, 'Vavoom'. Then I backcombed my hair to make it look fuller, sprinkled my eyes with gold glitter dust to bring out their colour, and dusted my cleavage with a little blush. I'm not dressed so much as armed. He cannot fail to appreciate my natural charms.

However, impressive though I am in an MTV kind of

way, I'm attracting a little more attention than I'd like travelling on the tube from Brixton. I'm practically chased down the platform by a Rasta who wants to sell me his travel card, calling out after me, 'Oooo, I think you look *fancy*, girl!' This isn't quite the reaction I'm after.

I stand outside Green Park tube station with my black overcoat buttoned to the chin feeling more than a little peculiar. Compared with the hysteria of blow drying, plucking, ironing, etc., showing up seems something of an anticlimax.

It's seven o'clock. I turn and make my way towards the Ritz.

I walk in from the cold, damp, darkness of the park, past an army of uniformed doormen in coats ornamented with gleaming brass buttons and stiff epaulettes, bellhops in pillbox hats, and foyer attendants in morning suits.

The first thing I notice is how golden everything is. The light is, in fact, blinding, bedazzling. It sparkles across mirrors, bounces off crystal chandeliers, glitters over gilt surfaces. I stop for a moment, clinging to a corner of the front desk like a drunk while I catch my breath and allow my eyes to gradually adjust.

The second thing I take in is the sheer grandiosity of the place – the bold, unassailable authority of so many rococo flourishes gathered unblushingly into a single location. Pudgy, rosy-cheeked cherubs romp across pale blue skies on cream-coloured clouds not unlike junior members of the

Conservative party set loose at a party conference. Chandeliers blaze above velvet-covered Louis Quatorze furniture. The atmosphere vibrates with self-assurance. There's the sound of a piano playing unobtrusively in the next room. 'Isn't It Romantic?' it enquires softly. And it is.

And then I become aware of something else; it's as if gravity pulls harder at the Ritz. Everyone seems to be moving just a little bit slower than normal people do. I notice a blond woman sitting at a small table in the corner. She's dressed in an off the shoulder black cocktail dress, ornamented by a single strand of pearls. She could be twenty-five, thirty-five, an immaculate forty. She's engaged in conversation with an elegant man in his fifties, who could equally be her father, her husband or her lover. He's handing her a small turquoise Tiffany bag which seems to float between his hand and hers. She smiles. He smiles. She opens the box and laughs a little before closing it again, and they exchange a knowing look. There is nothing hurried or impulsive about the transaction – they move in a kind of emotional slow motion, brought about by a drug more potent than Prozac or Valium. It's affluence itself that evens out their lives into a single, pale sheet of fine water-marked paper.

Gradually I become aware that all around me life defining moments are being played out against the plush emerald velvet seats: proposals, anniversaries, infidelities. It's no wonder that everyone is moving so slowly.

And here I am, about to join this exclusive club and engage in a life defining moment of my own.

I see him before he sees me. He's sitting, forlornly, at one of the small round tables in the lounge, drinking beer from a glass and pulling awkwardly at his tie. It's an old school tie – I can tell by the bizarre combination of colours. And at that moment I realize, with a dreadful, sinking feeling in the pit of my stomach, that I've made a terrible mistake.

S

Sex

Unconsciously or not, men and women indulge in all sorts of artifices in order to attract each other, and the sad truth is that women almost always employ far less discretion than men. In fact, it is often in attempting to exploit their natural advantages that they destroy all hopes of elegance. So called 'sexy' styles are never truly elegant, but only suitable for the vamps of gangster films or comic strips.

A kind of mythology seems to have been built up concerning men's preferences in fashion, with the result that many a young woman who deliberately dresses to attract masculine admiration often inspires only astonishment. To separate once and for all the fact from the fiction, this is:

What Is Really Attractive To Men:
  – full skirts, tiny waists, and a long-legged look
  – clothes that are in fashion, but not avant-garde;

men follow the fashion trends more than you may realize
— furs, and a general air of luxury
— almost any shade of blue; white; very pale and very dark grey; certain men hate to see their wives in black; others adore it
— perfume — but modern men appreciate lighter perfumes than their fathers did, subtle sophisticated blends rather than simpler scents

What Men Think They Like:
(but only in the cinema)
— revealingly tight skirts and aggressively pointed bosoms
— false eyelashes
— 'femme fatale' lingerie
— musky, oriental scents
— spike heels
— yards of black fringe and miles of red chiffon flounces

In short, men enjoy being envied, but they hate feeling conspicuous. And they particularly dislike vulgarity in the woman they love.

I ring Ria from the telephone in the Ladies loo.

'Louise? What is it? Where are you?'

'Ria, Ria, I've made a mistake, a terrible mistake!' I'm choked with tears.

'Calm down, baby. Where are you?'

'I'm at the Ritz.'

'The bastard hasn't stood you up, has he?'

'No, no, he's here but . . .' I can almost taste the shame, 'it's me. I . . . I'm *all wrong!*'

'Wrong? What do you mean?'

'I look like something out of Studio 54! I'm wearing my black Karen Millen dress.'

'Yes? What's wrong with that?'

'I've . . . I've shortened it, Ria'

'By how much? An inch? Two inches?'

'Try five,' I whisper.

There's a long silence.

'Oh Louise!' I can actually hear her shaking her head.

'Ria, you've got to help me!' I plead. 'He's my destiny. I know it. But I can't go to dinner at the Ritz like this!'

She sighs. 'All right,' she says at last. 'Stay where you are. I mean, no, go out, speak to him; it's rude to keep him waiting. But whatever you do, don't take your coat off! I'm on my way.' And then she hangs up.

When I walk back to the lounge, he's still there. He stands up to greet me, holding his tie to his chest as if he fears it might fall off into the cocktail peanuts. I smile a frozen head of death smile, pull my coat more tightly around me, and laugh like a hyena on helium.

'I'm so sorry I'm late . . . I just had to . . . to . . .'

'Quite right,' he smiles, pulling out a green velvet chair for me. 'Please.' He motions to the chair again and then moves behind me. 'Shall I take your coat?'

I recoil as from a hot flame. 'No! No!' I hiss, coming over all Glenn Close. Then, seeing the look of shock on his face, force my mouth back into the death grin and say with as much softness as I can muster, 'It's just that I'm so awfully cold.' I thud into the chair like a sack of potatoes.

He motions to the waiter. Act like a normal person, act like a normal person, I berate myself in my head. Pull yourself together.

Right, I think. I'll fake it. He doesn't know what I'm wearing underneath this coat – I could be draped in Dior and dripping in diamonds. From this moment on, I am the blond woman with the Tiffany's box.

'And what would Mademoiselle like?' purrs the waiter.

I straighten my shoulders, sit up, and cross my legs. 'I'd very much like a glass of Chablis please.'

Oliver smiles. 'A glass of Chablis for the lady and another Heineken for me,' he orders.

'Very good, sir.' He dissolves into the golden ether.

Oliver looks at me admiringly and straightens the top of his tie. 'I think we're going to have a good time tonight. I mean, I had my doubts about coming to a place like this.

I'm not really a suit and tie kinda guy. To be honest with you, I like the atmosphere, the way people look. I guess I'm really a secret snob,' he laughs.

I laugh gaily, fighting the desperate desire to sob outright. 'Who isn't?' I parry lightly. I am the Tiffany woman, I am the Tiffany woman. 'I love the Ritz. It's so quiet and discreet.'

He looks at me carefully. 'I thought you'd never been here before.'

I am still the Tiffany woman, still the Tiffany woman. 'Ah, yes, well now that I'm here, I find I love it. And it is discreet,' I flounder. 'Discretion is so undervalued, don't you think?' I sound like the straight man in an Oscar Wilde play.

'True enough.' He passes me the peanuts.

I decline with a gentle wave of the hand. Women with Tiffany boxes do not require peanuts; they've undoubtedly had smoked salmon sandwiches at lunch.

The threat of a silence stretches out in front of us. When in doubt, ask a question. 'Tell me about your day,' I invite him, eager to abandon any more metaphysical discussion of the merits of discretion.

'Well,' he begins, 'everyone at work teased me today because I was wearing a suit.' He smiles. 'They wanted to know who I was trying to seduce.'

My heart skips a beat. 'And what did you tell them?'

'I told them I was meeting someone at the Ritz and that

since they couldn't understand the concept of a suit and tie, they'd better just leave it. Of course, it didn't keep them from following me around all day trying to prise your name out of me.'

Sudden panic. 'And did you tell them?' I try to sound light and easy.

He sips his Heineken. 'Well, I don't know about you, but I think discretion is so undervalued nowadays. Besides which, I decided that a girl with such refined tastes wasn't to be revealed lightly.'

I want to say, 'Not all my tastes are refined,' but I sip my Chablis instead. And then I spot Ria's diminutive figure scurrying past us, glaring at me significantly. The Cavalry has arrived!

I jump up. 'Will you excuse me a moment?'

'Ah, sure . . . are you all right?'

'Oh, yes! Absolutely! It is a little warm in here after all. So I will check my coat.' I smile and speed off to the Ladies where Ria's leaning against the sink, trying to catch her breath.

'Sorry, I ran all the way from the gallery,' she gasps, fanning her face with her hand. 'He's a bit of all right, isn't he? How's it going?'

'Uh, OK. Fine. I think. Truth is, I don't know.'

'Hum, maybe you just need to relax. OK, let's see the damage,' she sighs.

I open my coat, feeling very much like a flasher on a

Sunday afternoon jaunt. She shudders and seems to deflate inwardly for a second, then rallies and looks me sternly in the eye. 'I just want you to know I have never done this before and I will never, I repeat, *never* do this again. Right,' she continues grimly, 'there's only one thing for it; we'll have to swap. Get your kit off.'

And she begins to undress. The ancient cloakroom attendant is completely unfazed by this bizarre transaction. Ria's come straight from work. My heart sinks at the austerity of the black Sonia Nuttal skirt and fitted gabardine top she's wearing. But then again, she's none too thrilled by the home-made micro mini I hand her and flatly refuses to wear it under any circumstances. 'If I die in a car accident, I'd rather people found me wearing nothing but my underwear,' she says, slipping it into her handbag.

Three minutes later, I'm magically transformed from Sweet Charity into a real life Tiffany woman. The skirt, which seemed so stark in its simplicity, drapes across the moving figure with stunning fluidity. And the fitted top's bateau neckline frames my creamy pale shoulders in a subtly sexy way.

Ria regards me uncertainly. 'Here.' She hands me a tissue. 'Rub off your lipstick. Hurry!' Then she carefully removes the gold, glitter eye shadow from my lids.

'My face looks chalky and washed out,' I protest.

'Hush!' She pulls out a soft crimson lipstick and paints on a sweet red mouth. To my surprise, I actually look younger. Then she wets her hands and begins to smooth down my hair. I watch in horror as she undoes in thirty seconds what's taken forty-five minutes of blow drying to achieve. But as she flattens my hair into a sleek little bob, it occurs to me I look more confident without my rigidly coiffed mane.

'Now, what else?' She eyes me carefully. 'This has to go.' And she strips me of my sparkling necklace and earrings, slipping her own Georg Jensen silver cuff on my wrist instead.

'There!' Standing back to admire her handiwork, she pulls her overcoat around her. 'You're a woman. Not a Barbie doll. Let that be a lesson to you. Now get out there or he'll think you're a drug addict.'

I hug her and force a twenty into her hand for the cab ride home. 'Ria, I can't thank you enough, you're so kind, so amazing. You've worked miracles!'

She pushes me towards the door. 'No one else but you, Louise. And remember, we must never, *ever* speak of this again.'

At last, almost an hour after I arrived, I'm finally able to check my coat. As the decaying attendant hands me the tag, she leans forward and whispers, 'Now that's a real friend.'

I sashay forth in my chic reincarnation and sit down once again next to the would-be man of my dreams. Only, something strange happens, something unexpected. Clothes make the woman and Ria's clothes certainly transformed me. I feel more vulnerable. More exposed. No big hairdo, no sexual trimmings, no cartoon make-up mask to hide behind.

Oliver seems different too. He's ordered another Heineken in my absence and he's smoking a cigarette, playing with his lighter.

'You look stunning. I'm glad you decided to take off your coat.' He smiles and it occurs to me that he's proud to be seen with me. However, his next question catches me off guard. 'May I ask you something?'

'Of course.'

'Are you married?'

There you have it; proof that gravity does pull harder at the Ritz.

'Yes.' I feel awkward and detached – like the gig is up; I've been found out posing as a young, single woman. 'We're getting a divorce. Right now we're separated.'

He looks at me intently. 'What happened?'

'Nothing happened.' I don't really want to go down this avenue. 'We didn't get on.'

Any hope of sexual frisson drifts away. An uncomfortable cloud of seriousness descends. 'And what do you want from me?' he demands.

And to this day, I will always shudder when I think of my response.

I look at him, sitting in the Ritz, sucking on a cigarette,

and I think of all the times I've wandered around the empty theatre, hoping I'd run into him, imagining he felt the same way.

'To play,' I say. It sounds plaintive, so I smile and try to make it seem cute, sexy and enticing. 'You know, like when you were a kid – just to play, have fun.'

He's looking at me very seriously, not at all like a kid having fun.

'I see,' he says at last and leans back in his chair again.

I'm an actress. I've auditioned for the role of mistress but the director remains unconvinced.

'I was with someone for seven years,' he begins.

I feel as if I'm falling, very quickly, from a great height. This is not the conversation I imagined during all those months of obsession. Apparently we're not about to embark on a romantic, sparkling, magical evening. We're going to talk about the exes instead.

'We almost got married.' He taps a packet of Marlboro Reds against the table. 'Mind if I smoke?'

I shake my head 'no'. After all, he's already started.

'She was pregnant. And lost the baby.' He motions to the waiter. 'Want another drink?'

I stare at my untouched glass of Chablis. 'No. Thank you.'

'Another Heineken,' he orders. 'And a whisky chaser.' The waiter nods and vanishes once more.

'Her name was Angela. She was amazing.'

And suddenly it's all over.

Before it's even begun.

He smokes and drinks and tells me about how accomplished Angela was, of her courage and poise. He shows me the lighter she bought him one year for Christmas and makes me feel how heavy it is to hold. He talks about how difficult it is to pay two mortgages – she still lives in the house they once shared, while he moved out to a tiny studio flat not far away. And how she criticized his drinking; told him he was an alcoholic but he's sure it's just a phase.

I smile and nod my head and play with the Georg Jensen cuff on my wrist. And in the golden light of the music-filled lobby in the world's greatest hotel, impeccably dressed, beautifully coiffed, and ten pounds lighter than I've ever been, I finally realize I'm not going to get what I want. I'm not going to be saved by a thrilling, all consuming relationship with Oliver Wendt. And even looking like the Tiffany woman can't protect me from all the gross realities that loom before me. I've left my husband and it's too late to scuttle back. I'll go home tonight and wake up tomorrow and there will be nothing there to distract me.

I'm alone. I've lived in absolute terror of just this moment and here it is – as cool and detached as a note scribbled in an appointment diary.

Friday, March 18th, 8:21 pm – you discover you are alone.
Really.

Thing is, what happens at 8:22?

And for the first time, perhaps, since I've laid eyes on him, I have a real look at Oliver Wendt. He has a paunch. There are heavy, dark circles under his eyes. He's chain smoking and ordering another drink. But most of all, he's sitting with a beautiful woman, talking about someone who left him four years ago.

I have to smile.

Friday, March 18th, 8:22 pm – you discover you're better off. Really.

I think this is what's known as a moment of clarity. My grandmother used to comfort my widowed aunt by saying, 'Better to go alone than to be badly accompanied.' That always used to frighten me. But tonight, it starts to make perfect sense.

After a while I stand up, put my hand out and thank Oliver for agreeing so kindly to meet me.

'But I thought . . .' he stammers, rising, 'I thought that we might actually have dinner together – get to know one another.'

'You're still in love with Angela,' I remind him.

He seems genuinely shocked to hear it. 'No, I'm not! I'm sure I'm not. I mean, I'll always love her, of course . . .'

'Besides which,' I interrupt him, 'I think that on this occasion, I'd rather dine alone.'

264

And as he stands, swaying slightly in front of me, I realize he's drunk.

'I made a mistake,' he says, blinking. 'I . . . I've fucked up, haven't I?'

I don't know what to do or say. He seems pathetic, baffled and out of his depth.

'Would you like a cab?' I ask him quietly.

'Yes, yes, I guess that's the thing to do,' he mumbles, searching in vain for a coat he didn't bring, unable to look me in the eye.

We walk outside into the bracing cold and the doorman waves down a black cab and opens the door for him. He stands in front of me for a moment, wavering, and then suddenly demands hoarsely, 'Kiss me.'

There they are, the words I'd dreamt of. I feel myself go numb inside. And automatically, without thinking, I tilt my cheek towards him. He blinks, obviously shocked by my reading of this request, but he kisses it anyway, brushing his dry lips against my skin. Then he falls into the cab and the doorman slams the door shut. I watch as it lurches away into the darkness.

I walk slowly back inside. This isn't at all what I'd planned. What do I do now? I stand alone in the centre of the lobby. Should I just get my coat and leave?

What would a woman of substance do in a case like this?

The *maitre d'* smiles as I approach. 'Good evening, Madam.'

'Good evening.'

'Table for one?' he asks, as if it were the most natural thing in the world.

'Yes, please,' I say. 'Table for one.'

T

Tan

Although I sincerely hope that I don't need to warn you about the dangers of over sunning yourself and ruining your complexion, I hardly imagine my own advice will dissuade you, especially if you are intent upon spending your summer holidays looking like a burnt piece of toast. There used to be a time when a deep tan was absolutely essential upon returning from holiday to excite the envy of all of one's poor friends who were condemned to spend their summer months in the city. But modern travel means that nowadays everyone has access to sunny climes and a tanned complexion is in no way unique or exclusive. So really, what is the point?

While a lightly sun-tanned complexion creates an agreeable impression of health, an overcooked epidermis is very ageing and even inelegant upon one's return to the city at the end of the summer. In order to be attractive, a deep tan requires the open air, very décolleté necklines, and bright, clear colours (particularly blue, yellow, and white). The rather neutral shades of town apparel often make a sun-tanned bathing beauty look more like an anaemic African and there's nothing even remotely elegant about that!

There comes a time in every woman's life when she's finally ready to move on.

The débâcle with Oliver Wendt helped. But now, two weeks later, my Decree Nisi has arrived in the post, as stark and impersonal as a gas bill. The message is more than clear. I'm single – not just waiting for someone to return my phone call – but completely unattached to anyone in any way, either by old, lingering ties or by any shred of hope for the future. And, now that the focus is firmly on me and my life, it's become clear that my time at the Phoenix Theatre Company is drawing to a close too.

Once this job was a haven. I started out as an usher, working weekends for extra pocket money when I first got married. Now I was one of two rotating box office managers (or rather, Deputy Head of Sales, as they liked to call it). I can't deny that if things had worked out a little differently with Mr Wendt, I might still be happily compiling sales reports with a ridiculous grin on my face, but now that the thought of bumping into him in the hallway fails to fill me with delight, I'm forced to concentrate on the job in hand. And the job in hand is dull.

'I'm thinking of making a career move,' I say to Colin one lunchtime.

'Oh?' He picks at his lunch. 'Fireman or policeman?'

'Well, there's a position going in the development department of the Royal Opera House.' I hesitate. 'Actually, I applied for it a while ago. And I've got an interview next week.'

I wait anxiously for his response; after all, we've been working together for years. But he just sighs wearily. 'Sounds perfect, Ouise. Let me know how you get on.'

He pushes the same forkful of leftover fish pie from one side of his plate to another. Something is definitely wrong. I expected him to be disappointed or excited but nothing prepared me for his complete and utter disinterest. 'Col, I can't help noticing that you seem a bit distracted today. Are you all right?' I ask.

He shakes his head sadly. 'Nothing for it, I'm afraid.'

'Nothing for what?' I persist.

He looks up at me with the most wayward, hopeless expression I've ever seen. 'Oldest story in the book, Ouise. I'm in love.'

I laugh with relief. 'But that's wonderful! You should be over the moon! Right?'

He pushes his plate away and looks more despondent

than ever. 'Yeah, right. Thing is, he doesn't even know I exist. To him, I'm just some filthy old queen.'

I have visions of a seventeen-year-old still shambling about in his school uniform. 'How old is he?'

'Twenty-three,' he confirms, with all the enthusiasm of a prisoner repeating his sentence.

'But that's fine, darling. What's wrong with that? You frightened me. I thought for a moment you'd been loitering by the school gates.'

He shakes his head again. 'You don't understand, Louise. This boy's an Adonis; an absolute god. The only way a boy like that's ever going to look at me twice is if I'm a rich sugar daddy. And let's face it, three Armani tee-shirts, a flat in Streatham and a monthly bus pass do not a sugar daddy make.'

I can't believe what I'm hearing. 'Shame on you, Col! How dare you speak like that! Not only are you demeaning yourself, but you're also being incredibly harsh on him. Do you really think so little of both of you? If that's the way you honestly think he is, I wonder that you're bothering to pursue him at all!'

'I'm not pursuing; I'm pining,' he corrects me. 'Which is exactly why I'm allowed to form bitter and twisted judgments about the object of my desire. Besides, I don't expect you to understand,' he adds grandly. 'I'm suffering from a condition that you can only guess at, Louise – a love that dare not speak its name.'

I ignore this last bit of drama. 'And where did you meet this Adonis?' I imagine some gyrating figure at Heaven or one of the pulsating pelvises from GAY.

But Colin blushes and begins fumbling with the strap on his backpack like a fourteen year old. 'He's . . . I met him the day you sent me over to Copy Cat with the autumn season proofs.'

'The printer man?' I can't believe it. 'Col, are you in love with Andy the printer man?'

He looks at me in surprise. 'You know his name?'

'Of course! He's a total sweetie! He looks after our account; I've known him for ages.'

'Andy.' He repeats his name softly, as if invoking some magical being.

'Col, this isn't a love that dare not speak its name; it's Andy the printer man! He's a darling. Just ask him out!'

We're back to more fourteen-year-old mumbling. 'Well, I'll . . . I'll certainly think about it . . .'

'Don't think, act!' I urge him.

He mumbles a bit more and the words 'but', 'can't' and 'Adonis' are tossed around a few more times.

'Anyway, what's all this about an interview?' he says suddenly, obviously desperate to change the subject.

'I'm sorry I didn't tell you earlier, but I thought there'd be no point in mentioning it if I didn't get one.'

'And in the development department.' He's really listening now. 'Very posh!'

I smile and he reaches out and takes my hand.

'So you're leaving us, are you?'

I nod. 'Time to move on, darling. Time to move on.'

In the days that follow, I proceed to do what I always do when big changes are afoot: I panic. I panic about my background, my age, my lack of experience, my qualifications, my hair, my outfit for the interview, what will happen if I do get the job, what will happen if I don't, what they might ask me, and, most of all, how I'll respond to all these fictional questions. I sit alone at a table in the staff canteen, answering them at some length, until one of my colleagues confesses I'm starting to frighten them and asks me to stop.

Colin, in the meantime, seems to have taken on a new lease of life. Not only has his depression lifted, but he positively glows with renewed health and vigour. When at last I lift my head long enough from my own obsessions to notice, I'm amazed to find him a man transformed.

'You seem well.' I eye him as he bounces from his desk to the stationery cupboard in a single bound.

He just smiles at me.

'Have you lost weight?' There's something about him I can't quite place; a subtle difference I can't put my finger on. It's infuriating. I'm actually starting to feel jealous of him. And in my already heightened state, it's more than I can bear.

'C'mon,' I snap. 'What is it? What have you done?'

'Jesus, Ouise! Take a chill pill, why don't you!' he giggles, and then, seeing the look of psychopathic dementia cross my face, adds gently. 'I was going to tell you about it anyway. It's a new self-tanning solution and it's amazing; makes you look ten years younger and ten pounds lighter overnight! I'll tell you, darling, it's just the boost you and the rest of rain-soaked London needs.' He leans forward. 'I'm even going to stop by the print shop on my way home and see if I can't lure Andy out for a drink! Really, you ought to try it. It's done wonders for my self-esteem.'

I look at him sceptically. 'You can't be talking about that orange stuff in a bottle?'

He taps the side of his nose. 'When I get home tonight, IF I get home tonight, I'll show you everything. I promise.' And he skips away from me before I can respond.

That night, sitting alone on the bus home, I wonder if, on the eve of my interview, I might not avail myself of a little bottled self-esteem too. Having rehearsed every conceivable outcome and scenario I can think of, including those involving fire, acts of terrorism, and the sudden, debilitating loss of feeling in one's limbs, I'm still no closer to feeling comfortable or confident about my big day. Besides, it's transformed Colin so completely and subtly, that what could be the harm? I decide to take him up on his offer.

By 12:30 that night, Colin still hasn't come home. If ever I needed proof that the self-tan works, this is it. However, having waited patiently for him for three and a half hours, I'm now reaching a fever pitch of anxiety about sleep deprivation and the importance of getting an early night. So, in a fit of hysteria and more determined than ever to appear for my interview as a sun-kissed goddess, I decide to raid Colin's bathroom shelf myself. After all, I hardly need an instruction manual and personal assistant to help me slap on a little fake tan.

Colin's shelf in the bathroom is stacked with more beauty products than Ria's and mine combined. It's not easy being a gay man. In the cut-throat world of Soho bars and one-night stands, only the youngest and fittest survive. There are toners, moisturizers, blemish sticks, foundation, cover-up crayons, and pot after pot of anti-ageing creams, along with all the normal male grooming products of shaving creams, deodorants, and a stunning, completely comprehensive range of after shaves and colognes that he arranges in alpha-betical order, from Armani to YSL along the bathroom window ledge. It takes me a while to find what I'm looking for but eventually I discover the magical bottle of self-tanning lotion, tucked away behind an extra-large bottle of Regain shampoo.

I sit down on the side of the tub to read the instructions.

'*First prepare skin with exfoliating scrub and moisture-surge skin balm.*'

I search again through Colin's massive collection of lotions and potions; they're nowhere to be found. Typical. You buy one product and they always make it sound as if you need to buy ten more. Well, if Colin has achieved such stunning results without them, so can I. I move on to the next section.

'Then apply tanning lotion in smooth, even strokes, one limb at a time to prevent streaking. The use of plastic gloves is highly recommended.'

Plastic gloves? I look around the bathroom. Apart from a pair of old yellow Marigolds crumpled in a heap by the bathroom cleanser, there are no other gloves to be seen. It's probably not that big a deal. They're most likely just being overly cautious in case someone suffers from some strange allergy. Besides, I can always wash it off.

'Avoid contact with all fabrics and surfaces until completely dry. Formulation should be completely dry within ten minutes.'

Sounds easy enough. Let's get cracking!

I strip off my clothes and begin slathering the stuff on. It looks a lot darker than I anticipated, as a matter of fact, it's like covering myself in oily mud. I consult the bottle again.

'Colour will appear initially darker but will rinse off in the morning to reveal silky, smooth skin and a golden, natural looking tan.'

Great. Right on target. I smooth some onto my face and neck and then stand, naked, in the middle of the bathroom waiting for it to dry. A half an hour later, it's still tacky to the touch but after 45 minutes I decide that the definition of 'dry' can probably be stretched to include 'not absolutely sopping wet'. Finally, somewhere around 1:30 or two in the morning, I fall into bed and drift into a deep, exhausted sleep.

The next morning, I stumble into the kitchen for a cup of coffee and am greeted by a horrified scream. 'My God, Louise! What have you done to yourself?'

I'd almost forgotten. 'Don't panic, Ria,' I reassure her, 'it's this fantastic new tanning lotion. As soon as I have a shower, you'll see. It washes off and all I'm left with is a glorious, golden glow.'

'You look like an extra from *Quest for Fire*.' She shakes her head sceptically. 'And your hands, Louise, they're orange!'

I look down; my palms are at least two shades deeper orange than the rest of my hands, obviously from slathering the lotion on without the recommended plastic gloves. The effect is disturbingly simian. My confidence is starting to wane. I put my coffee down and jam them into my pockets. 'I'm telling you, Ria, it all washes off! Look, I'll prove it to you.' And I stride into the bathroom and turn on the shower.

Ten minutes later, I emerge, wet and triumphant. 'See,' I gloat, 'what did I tell you? Do I look ten pounds lighter and ten years younger or what?'

She continues to stare at me in horror. 'You're orange,' she says at last. 'A kind of *stripy* orange.'

She's starting to really annoy me. 'Ha ha ha. Very funny, Ria.'

But she just shakes her head. 'No, Louise. Not ha ha ha at all.'

I run into my room and stare at myself in the mirror. She's right. My body's covered in bizarre orange tidemarks that don't make me look either ten pounds lighter or younger but definitely do give the impression I might easily glow in the dark. 'Shit! What am I going to do?' I panic. 'Ria, what can I possibly do?'

An evil little smile creeps across her face. 'Apply for a job in Willy Wonka's Chocolate Factory?'

I glare at her and then, much to my shame, start to cry. 'I have an interview at eleven o'clock!' I wail, two huge tears rolling down my cheeks. 'At the Royal Opera House and they probably don't hire orange people!'

'OK, OK, calm down. No more jokes, I promise. Come on.' She takes my hand and leads me back into the bathroom. After ferreting around in a wicker basket for a few minutes, she comes up clutching a giant loofa. 'Get back in the tub,' she orders. 'If we're lucky, we might be able to scrub it off.'

I've never been treated for radiation contamination, but I imagine that standing, naked and shivering in a tub while somebody you never, *ever* intended to have see you naked scrapes off the top three layers of your skin with a dry, rough object is all just part of the fun. Memorable as this attempt is in the humiliation stakes, it hardly puts a dent in the ginger tinge that's masquerading as my 'natural-looking golden tan'.

Finally we both give up. 'Look, Louise, much as I've enjoyed this rare chance to indulge in some serious female bonding, I've got to go to work and you've got an interview. Face it: you're just going to have to tough it out.'

I wrap my raw limbs carefully in a bath towel. 'I could always reschedule. Say I got food poisoning or something.'

She shrugs her shoulders. 'It's up to you. Though, if they're interviewing today, they might easily find someone before they meet you. And it always looks a bit dodgy when someone can't turn up for an interview.'

She's right. I have to go.

To minimize the damage I wear a navy trouser suit, hiding my monkey hands in the deep pockets. The pretty red dress I'd had dry cleaned and the new pair of Kurt Geiger shoes I'd splashed out on beckon but involve far too much skin exposure. Besides, as Ria points out, red and orange don't really mix. After buttoning my blouse right up under my chin, I'm left with only my curiously carroty face to deal with. Foundation only makes it look chalky, but luckily a thin dusting of translucent powder does wonders to tone down the neon quality of the tidemarks.

By ten to ten, I'm out of the door, heading for the bus stop, just praying I won't be interviewed in a room with fluorescent lighting.

An hour later, I've been installed on a bench outside one of the private bars, waiting to be called in. Eventually a woman in her mid-forties emerges, shaking the hand of another candidate.

'Lovely to meet you, Portia,' she smiles. 'We'll be in touch. And please, do send my love to your father!'

The girl, at least ten years younger than me and sporting a perfectly normal skin shade, lopes off down the corridor, her long blond hair swinging behind her. My heart sinks. I wish I'd called in sick with food poisoning after all.

Then the woman turns to me. 'Louise Cassova?'

'Canova,' I correct her, standing and holding out my hand. 'It's Italian.'

'How lovely.' She eyes my monkey paw warily and I jam it back in my pocket. 'Would you like to come through?' I follow her into the empty bar. She gestures to a table and chairs by the window. 'Please have a seat. My name is Charlotte Thorne, the Head of Human Resources. The Head of Development, Robert Brooks, will be joining us in a moment but I thought I might ask you a few questions myself.'

I nod eagerly and feel my face stretching into a petrified grin of sheer terror.

She sits down and opens the file of résumés in front of her. 'I see you were one of the lucky ones who got away over the Easter break.' She makes small talk while she rummages through her pile of papers. 'Where did you go?'

'I'm sorry?'

'I couldn't help noticing your tan. Did you go some-where nice?' She's located what she was looking for and now gives me her full attention, folding her hands neatly in front of her on the table.

I freeze. Where do people who went away over Easter go? The Cayman Islands? Skiing? She sits there blinking at me. I can practically hear time slipping away while I stare blankly at her. 'Well, no. No, I didn't get away this time . . . it's just . . . just . . . well, you know how we Italians are! A few sunny days and we're as brown as can be!'

I laugh inanely and she smiles, launching swiftly into her standard line of attack. 'Lucky you. So tell me, Louise, what makes you think you'd like to be part of our team here at the Royal?'

Fortunately, this *is* one of the questions I've prepared for. I take a deep breath. 'Well, Charlotte, I guess the bottom line is, I'm just so passionate about the arts . . .' and I go on to bludgeon her with my enthusiasm until Mr Brooks appears.

All in all, it goes better than I could've imagined, though, after Ms Thorne introduces me as 'multi-cultural', there are a few sticky moments when he insists on speaking to me in Italian (of which I'm entirely ignorant) and regales me with stories of his student adventures in Florence (where I've never been). But somehow my total ignorance escapes him; he's on a mission. And, despite the fact that I giggle nervously each time he addresses me, he seems to have taken a shine to me.

'Although we're a great British institution, we're also one of the world's leading international houses, Ms Canova.' (He rolls my surname out with such zealous attention to what he imagines is the authentic pronunciation that I barely recognize it.) 'And I feel that it's about time we reflected that in our personnel.' He pumps my hand vigorously. 'I'm certain we'll be seeing you again.'

I exit the building as quickly as I can, before he has time to recall another secluded art collection or remote café in Florence I really must be familiar with.

Having made my escape, I stand panting with relief on the front steps, when a handsome young man stops me.

'Excuse me, do you have a light?'

I'm so shell shocked that I just stare at him. 'A light?' I repeat, as if he's speaking in code.

'Yes, you know, for a cigarette?' he prompts.

'Oh!' My mind kicks into gear. 'Yes, of course! Let me have a look.' And I rummage around in the bottom of my bag until I find a battered box of matches, bizarrely enough, some I'd pinched from the Ritz. I fumble to strike one and notice, to my embarrassment, that my hands are shaking violently.

I strike one and my hand wobbles dangerously towards his face. 'Pardon me,' he intervenes, gently steadying my wrist before leaning in. 'I hope you don't mind.'

'No, no. I'm sorry. I've just come out of an interview and I'm still a little shaky,' I confess.

He smiles. 'Please, allow me to return the favour.' He offers me one of his cigarettes. 'You look like maybe you could use one.'

I hesitate. 'I'm not really a smoker.'

'Quite right,' he nods. 'Filthy habit. Absolutely disgusting.'

I watch as he takes a long, luxurious drag.

'Well, maybe just one wouldn't hurt.'

He lights it for me and we stand a moment, smoking. It's only 12:30, but it's already been quite a long day.

'So, how'd it go?' he asks, leaning casually against a poster for *Swan Lake*. And suddenly, as he smiles in the warm sunlight, it strikes me that he's easily the most beautiful man I've ever seen. Slim and not terribly tall, he's graced with a mass of wild, dark hair and even darker, enormous black eyes. When he smiles, his full lips relax into a sanguine grin that's both mischievous and completely benign.

I realize I've been staring at him. 'I'm sorry,' I apologize, coming to. 'You were asking?'

'The job . . . do you think you got it?'

I shake my head. 'I have no idea. Impossible to say. Do you work here?'

'Only for the summer. I'm a classical pianist. My sister works here and she managed to wangle me a job playing for the Royal Ballet rehearsals. I'm studying in Paris this autumn and the money's really quite good.'

'Gosh, the Royal Ballet, Paris. You must be wonderful!'

He grins, suddenly shy. 'I'm lucky,' he confesses. 'Have you been to Paris?' He quickly changes the subject. 'It's my favourite city in the world! You haven't lived unless you've idled away an entire afternoon sipping champagne and smoking cigarettes in a café on the Boulevard St Germain!'

I laugh. 'I've been to Paris but somehow I never got around to that.'

'Then you must go again,' he says softly.

I look up and catch his eye. He smiles again and I feel myself blushing.

'Do you like the ballet?' he asks.

'I love it. Or at least, I used to love it, many years ago. I haven't been in a very long time.'

'Here.' He reaches into his back pocket and pulls out a ticket. 'I don't know what you're doing for the rest of the afternoon, but there's a dress rehearsal for *Swan Lake* going on at the moment. They give me these tickets and I always forget about them until it's too late. Speaking of which,' he checks his watch, 'I was due in rehearsal five minutes ago.'

'That's so kind of you . . .' I falter, caught off guard by his generosity.

He stubs his cigarette out under his heel and turns to go. 'Enjoy! And you never know, maybe you will get the job and I'll get to see more of you!'

A moment later, he's gone.

I take another drag. This is certainly turning out to be an unusual day, especially for one that had started off so disastrously.

I had planned to go straight home and hide for the rest of the afternoon. I look again at the ticket in my hand.

It's been a long time since I've been to the ballet. Eighteen years, in fact. That was the summer I stopped dancing. The same summer my mother tried to commit suicide.

I'd been asked to audition for the local ballet company that year. But when the day came, I never showed up. I blamed my mother; told myself I had too much to think about, that I needed to look after her.

Perhaps I couldn't bear to try and fail. Or perhaps I just wanted to be a normal teenager for once, without the pressure of establishing a whole career before the age of sixteen. It was her dream that I become a dancer. But after that summer, there seemed no point.

I'd failed.

Taking a deep breath, I exhale slowly and close my eyes. Long rows of girls stretch their legs in impossible positions on the barre. Rosin crunches beneath my feet. The air is thick with sweat and concentration. And there's music. Always music.

I flick my eyes open again.

Eighteen years is a long time to feel like a failure.

I take one last drag on my cigarette before throwing it away. Then I turn and walk inside.

'I'm afraid you're too late to take your seat,' the young girl ushering informs me. 'However you are allowed to stand at the back of the dress circle until the end of the first act.'

As I follow her up the grand central staircase, I notice how her jacket is just that bit too big, the way mine was when I used to usher at the Phoenix.

'Are you a student?' I ask, as we reach the top.

She nods. 'A singer at the Royal Academy. Only one year left.'

I think about all the plays I've watched, standing at the back of the stalls in my ill-fitting jacket.

'Good luck!' I whisper as she opens the door and I slip inside.

And there, tucked into the warm, black curve of the circle, surrounded by the overwhelming music of Tchaikovsky, another, equally unexpected thing happens.

As I stand there in the darkness, watching some of the finest dancers in the world, it gradually occurs to me that it's OK that I'm not one of them.

I could never have changed my mother anyway. No matter how hard I danced.

Darcy Bussell leaps across the stage, defying gravity – defying all the laws of nature – and a soaring, light-headed joy overwhelms me.

I haven't failed anyone. Least of all myself.

*　　*　　*

Two days later, I'm called in for a second interview. And that afternoon, I become the first orange person to be hired by the Royal Opera House.

U

Uniformity

Thanks to the high standard of living in the Occident and the perfection of mass-produced Western fashions, an untrained observer must have the impression that every woman is dressed exactly alike. I do not know the origin of this modern form of modesty, which has swept through the feminine population from San Francisco to Paris, and which seems to cause all women to want to resemble each other — even though at the same time they are spending more and more on clothes, cosmetics, and hair dressers! But if you really enjoy being dressed exactly like everybody else, then your future is rosy. Uniformity is the natural by-product of an automized society, and — who knows? — perhaps one day individuality will be considered a crime. In the meantime, you can always join the Army.

We don't dress for who we are, so much as who we would like to be.

In London, different streets and different parts of town have different uniforms. Soho has a dress code just as much as the City or the Kings Road. And then there are places where these worlds collide. The theatre is one of them.

A really hot production will have an audience as mixed as they come – conservative business men, ageing Sloane rangers, hippie chic students, Notting Hill bohos, Prada and Armani-clad minimalists, gay, straight, young, old, all mashed in together and yet as clearly defined as if they're wearing big-labelled tee-shirts.

It's a Friday night in early June. I'm sipping lukewarm white wine, being jostled to and fro in the bar of the Royal Court in residence at the Ambassadors Theatre and chatting to my friend Sandy, who, in a Cassandra-like fit of foresight, managed to book these tickets ages ago. It's a full house and the bar is heaving when the bells start to go and Sandy decides, the way certain women must, that two minutes before curtain up is the ideal time for a trip to the loo. The throng oozes its way slowly towards the auditorium and suddenly I catch a glimpse of a profile that seems familiar. It belongs to a smartly dressed man. He's leaning forward, listening with great intensity to what another, younger man is saying to him.

My mind is strangely blank. Yes, I *do* know him but from *where*?

And then that thing happens that sometimes occurs in great and dreadful moments where everything falls away – the crowd, the noise, the bells, and there is only the horrific, curious detail of the moment.

I do know that man.

It's my ex-husband.

I stare, mesmerized, as he turns around and laughs, slapping his friend on the shoulder.

I wouldn't have recognized him.

Couldn't have recognized him.

Everything about him is utterly, completely different. His hair is cropped short. Not cut, mind you, as in, I popped down to the barber's but *cropped*, as in I just nipped into Nicky Clarke's. And dyed; pale, honey-coloured highlights. He's wearing a pair of fitted dark brown velvet jeans and a Hugo Boss pale blue roll-neck jumper with the neck worn slouchy and high, as if he's just this moment pulled it on over his head. Slung casually over his arm is a softly tailored black leather jacket and his feet are adorned with a pair of Camper bowling shoes.

He isn't just dressed; he's groomed, styled.

Here is the man whose wardrobe consisted of shirts his mother had bought him from Marks and Spencer for Christmas, worn without being pressed, cuffs frayed and tattered until they literally fell off his body. Who found it physically painful to buy a new pair of shoes. And now he's transformed, floating butterfly-like over to the crowded bar to leave his glass, and wearing this season's hot item – the bowling shoes – without so much as a glimmer of discomfort or a trace of irony.

He's a changed man but one I recognize.

It's the uniform. I know it. I've seen it before.

My head is a vacuum, imploding. If I don't move, he won't see me. So I freeze, standing so rigidly that even the tables and chairs look animated in my presence. And I watch, holding my breath, as they press their way into the auditorium, chatting easily, completely unaware of my existence. He moves with unexpected fluidity, almost gliding up the stairs. I'm sick and fascinated at the same time.

Suddenly Sandy is by my side again, searching for the tickets in her wallet, panicking that she doesn't have change for the programme seller, wondering out loud if she should fold her coat and put it under her seat or if she should pop it into the coat check. And before I know it, we're sitting, crammed next to a couple of German tourists clutching their knapsacks on their knees. The lights are dimming when I realize I'm still holding my glass of warm wine.

I can't remember anything about the first act. Intent on locating the silhouette of my ex-husband's head, I spend the whole of it looking through the audience, trying to discern his distinctive new haircut from the haircuts around him. I think I see him and then I don't. And I want to see him. To stare at him. I cannot – or rather won't – believe my eyes. So I stare into the blackness of the auditorium rather than at the brightly-lit stage. The audience leans forward in fascination, laughs in all the right places, gasps during the climax, but still I can't find him.

Finally the first act ends and the lights come up.

'That was amazing!' Sandy gushes, completely enthralled. 'Don't you think that was absolutely amazing?'

I spot them. There they are, walking up the centre aisle. Laughing.

'Incredible,' I murmer.

Sandy's standing up, brushing off her skirt. 'Shall we?'

It's his friend I'm looking at now; same cropped haircut, same Camper bowling shoes, but young, younger than I'd realized. His face has that hyper neatness. Does he pluck his eyebrows? And he's wearing a pair of Diesel jeans and a tight black tee-shirt. They're walking past now. I hold my breath. Sandy's pushing me towards the end of our row and we slot in behind them. The cologne the young one's wearing wafts around me, clean and light, and then I watch as he reaches up and places his hand briefly against the back of my ex-husband's neck.

It's a small gesture: quick, casual. But it stops me dead in my tracks. A kind of slow motion close-up shot of the thing I never wanted to see. I'm staring, not at the hand, but at my ex-husband's reaction.

There is none. It's apparently normal for him to be touched this way.

I cannot make my feet move forward any more. The crowd is clogging up on the steps behind me.

'Are you all right?' Sandy asks, giving me a gentle shove. But I'm glued to the spot.

'I forgot my programme,' I croak, turning back against the tide, away from the bar. 'I just want to grab my programme.'

And I stumble down the steps, past my row, to the front of the stage, where I lean, heart pounding, against the front of the orchestra pit.

I know. I know now.

I always knew, but now I really know.

You can't tell a book by its cover, but you can learn a lot about a person from their shoes.

V

Veils

Somewhat out of fashion at the moment (and I cannot imagine why), veils are one of the most flattering feminine adornments. If you wish to appear at once seductive, mysterious, and incredibly sophisticated, a veil will serve your purposes admirably. The unique charm of this accessory is that it allows even the most plain, uninspiring creature to look as if she's Anna Karenina, or at the very least, Garbo. And the very fact that part of the face is hidden from view creates a certain frisson that is both exciting and intriguing. Whether you choose a large, coarse veil, or a fine, delicate wisp of tulle, makes no difference. Women who wear veils are creatures with a past, a secret. And what could be more elegant than that?

'But I don't wear hats,' I protest. 'No one wears hats any more!'

'They do at Ascot,' Colin says firmly. 'You won't even get in unless you have a hat on your head, so you might as well get over it. Now, be a darling and pass me that piece of sandpaper, will you?'

I bend down and riffle through the collection of tools, dirty rags, and toxic potions Colin's using to strip the paint off the living-room door. I come across something rough and brown and hand it to him. 'This is such a total bore!' I sulk. 'I don't even know why I have to go to this stupid event anyway. Corporate entertaining is turning out to be incredibly dull!'

'Well,' Colin douses a toothbrush in turpentine and works it vigorously into the moulding, 'you didn't need to take the job at the Royal, did you? You could've always turned down the chance to make more money, work in a thrilling environment in one of the leading artistic institutions in the country and own even more fantastic pairs of shoes. No one's twisting your arm. Utter mediocrity and a return to a life of ass-aching boredom is only a short phone call away.'

'Fine, I get your point.' I flounce into an armchair.

Colin looks up at me sternly. 'Don't you flounce at me, Missy. What's got into you anyway? You should be pleased, excited! Most girls would be thrilled to be going to Ascot and getting paid for it!'

'Most English girls,' I correct him bitterly.

He frowns. 'What has that got to do with anything?'

'Everything! Oh God, you just don't understand, do you!' I bury my face in my hands dramatically.

Colin puts down the toothbrush and eyes me warily. 'Ouise, is someone maybe just the tiniest bit pre-menstrual?'

'No!' I snap. 'And don't be so condescending!'

'I think I'm doing pretty well,' he counters. 'Especially considering that I'm rooming with Dr Jekyll and Mrs Hyde. One minute you're thrilled to bits to get the job of your dreams and the next you're spitting flames because someone's taking you to one of the most sought after social events of the year and all you have to do is shove a hat on your head! Quite frankly, you've been in a foul mood all week and if your period isn't coming, you'd better have a pretty damned good excuse.'

We sit in silence, glowering at one another.

'I'm sorry,' I say. Finally. 'It's just much . . . much harder than I thought.' How can I explain it to him? 'The trouble is, Col, I'm not English.'

'I've got news for you, Louise. You never were.'

'Ha ha. No, I'm serious. These girls, they're like, how can I put it? Professionally English. Like the whole point of them is how English they are. For starters, they've all got names like Flora, Poppy, Hyacinth and Ginista. It's like working in a herbaceous border. And this is just something they do to pass the time before they marry their city boyfriends. A job they got through Daddy, who either knows the artistic director or *is* the artistic director.'

'Meeeeeeoooooooooooow, Ouise! Put the claws away!'

'It's not that they're not nice,' I acquiesce, trying to control myself (and not succeeding). 'They're fine in a sort of inbred, mutant kind of way. It's just that all we seem to do is entertain the fathers and mothers of their old school chums. For example: the head of Investment Banking at Goldman Sachs is Flora's best friend's Dad. They spend all evening talking about his son at Eton and her brother at Harrow. The next day he books a season box and donates a cheque that's so large they're obliged to engrave his name all over the building – I'm talking on *every* conceivable surface!'

'And what, exactly, has this got to do with you?'

'I can't compete, Col! I just can't compete! Plus,' I add bitterly, 'they've all got legs *and* tits, which is just too, too unfair!'

He smiles at me. 'You're jealous.'

'Of course I'm jealous!' I rage. 'But I'm also out of my depth! I can't do all this public school stuff. I've never been shooting, or to the races, or to Annabel's or Tramps or had my picture in *Harpers & Queen*. No one's ever invited me to their place in the country and I wouldn't know what to do once I got there! I'm from Pittsburgh, for Christ's sake! And now we're going to Ascot to entertain clients from BP and Reuters I just know it's going to be like a kind of living hell, with hats and rules and strange insider knowledge I know absolutely nothing about.'

He squeezes my knee. 'Louise, that's why these girls are so useful in that profession; their upbringing and education guarantees that they have a certain number of connections. But they hired you for a reason. I suggest that you keep your eyes on your own paper. You're too old for this kind of bullshit. Plus, my dear, I hate to be the one to tell you, but it's really rather unattractive.' He looks at me significantly. 'Now, why don't you do me a favour and clean up that awful mess you made in the kitchen. Andy's coming round later and I don't want him thinking I live in a tip.'

And with that, he goes back to his toothbrush and turpentine.

Two days later, I'm languishing at my desk, picking soggy tomatoes out of my calorie controlled BLT sandwich and attempting half-heartedly to jazz up my standard corporate begging letter without sounding too pathetic, when Poppy lurches over, all five foot ten inches of her, and invites me to join her for a session of hat shopping. A tangled assortment of arms and legs, she resembles an embarrassed giraffe as she tosses her long fringe out of her eyes and smiles at me shyly.

'I have absolutely *nothing* I can wear!' She slouches against my desk, pulling at the cuffs of her blouse in a vain attempt to make them cover her wrists. 'I mean I have this really poxy hat from my sister's wedding last year but she insisted it had to be lilac.'

Suddenly there's a shriek from behind the felt partition that separates the desks. '*Nooooooo!*' Flora's neat little blond bobbed head appears. 'You *so* didn't tell me that Lavender was married!'

'Tell you!' Poppy rolls her eyes. 'Flora, you were *there*!'

'Oh!' She's shocked to hear it. 'Did I give them silver place-card holders in the shape of pigs?'

'Pineapples,' Poppy corrects her.

'I gave them pineapples? That's not like me.' She frowns, chewing vigorously on the end of her pen. 'Who did I go with?'

'Flora! You are such a cadet! Went to boarding school at, like, three,' she whispers to me behind her hand. 'You gave them silver *pineapple* place-card holders from Smythson's and you went with Jeremy Bourne-Houthwaite. Remember, you were practically engaged to him once.'

The light goes on in Flora's pale blue eyes. 'Oh! Lippy Houthwaite! Of course!' And they both start giggling uncontrollably.

'Lippy Houthwaite?' I'm not certain I really want to know.

'I'm telling you, Louise, he had the most *enormous* lips,' Flora explains. 'I mean, kissing him was like being attacked by a Labrador. I've never been so damp in all my life!'

And they giggle even harder until Poppy begins to choke. I pat her on the back.

'So, if you gals are going shopping, I *soooo* need to come with you,' Flora pleads.

'Fine, where shall we go?' I ask.

'Locks,' they chirp in unison and then shout 'Snap!' at each other, falling into hysterics again and pounding their feet into the floor.

Any minute now, I think, I'm definitely going to have an out of body experience.

'Lock's in St James's Street,' Poppy explains. 'It's *the* place to go for a good, proper hat.' She eyes me sternly, which, I must say, is odd coming from Poppy; she and any form of gravitas are not natural partners. 'You don't want a *fancy* hat, do you?' (She says 'fancy' the way that football thugs say the word 'poof'.)

'Well, no . . .' I hesitate, secretly thinking that a fancy hat is exactly what I want; the fanciest, most stunning hat money can buy.

'No, you want a *proper* hat!' Flora nods her pale head with surprising vigour. 'A proper English hat!' she adds significantly, like a Mason dropping a code word into casual conversation. There it is – the E word. I give way immediately.

'Oh yes! Absolutely!' I agree, overwhelmed by the strange feeling that any moment they might launch into an impromptu version of 'Rule Britannia' and I don't know the words. I smile and they smile back at me. (This is my latest defence mechanism for dealing with anything that goes completely over my head. It also means I spend most of my day grinning like an idiot.)

I'm not quite sure what they mean by 'proper' or 'English', but it's clearly the opposite of 'fancy', which, for reasons I'm too foreign to understand, is definitely beyond the pale. If I can just survive this latest shopping excursion, I'm bound to be initiated into some of the most elusive elements of the English upper class social code.

'No fancy hats for me!' I cry gaily. And perhaps just a little prematurely.

It's not until later on that afternoon, when I come face to face with Flora and Poppy's idea of a proper English hat, that I begin to regret my earlier enthusiasm. They're all the size of small planets.

'Here, try this one,' Flora says, jamming a colossal pink candy floss confection on my head. It slides down below my eyebrows and when it comes to a stop, the enormous brim sags listlessly over my shoulders.

They stand back in admiration.

'That is stunning!' Poppy gasps. 'Simply stunning!'

I try to position myself in front of the mirror so that I can see the whole thing but only manage to knock over a pile of foldable Panamas some two feet away with my incredible brim.

'It seems a little large,' I point out.

'Large!' Flora frowns. 'But that's the whole point!'

'A big brim makes your hips look smaller,' Poppy

explains. '*And,*' she whispers conspiratorially, 'you don't have to fix your hair.'

'And if it's mammoth,' Flora adds brightly, 'you don't even need make-up!'

'I see.' Hat as one stop dressing.

And then they try on a couple of equally daunting head meringues and I notice that, even when we're standing brim to brim, there's a good three feet between our bodies. Then I get it. Like hedgerows and newspapers on the tube, these hats are primarily there to protect one's privacy – just another manifestation of that impenetrable English reserve.

I'm far more attracted to a small collection in the corner: trim, chic little creations to be worn at a jaunty angle by a confident woman. Brilliant jewel colours: emerald green, sapphire blue, ruby red, are decorated with feathers, curling in bold shapes around the head.

'What about these?' I venture.

Poppy wrinkles her nose at me. 'A bit fancy, don't you think?'

Flora reaches over and picks one up. 'That's going to do absolutely nothing for your hips.'

'I like them.' (What is it with English women and their hips?) In a fit of defiance, I try one on.

To be honest, it looks a bit silly. Even I can see that. The emerald feather that had seemed so striking on the white, hairless mannequin sprouts like some bizarre growth from the back of my head. It dangles eerily over one eye with a razor sharp point that threatens to stab anyone who comes too close. No matter where I put it, it retains the same sculptural rigidity, making me look more like an amateur performance artist than a sophisticated *femme fatale*.

Poppy curls her lip. Flora narrows her eyes.

'Quite frankly, it just tries too hard,' Poppy says.

'She's right,' Flora agrees.

And then she delivers the *coup de grâce*. 'It looks a bit *common*.'

There can be no insult more scathing than the accusation of being common. Even I, puppy dog exile from the home of the free, land of the brave, shudder inwardly at the finality of this sentence. And of course there are few things considered more common among the English upper classes than something that tries too hard. After all, effort itself is working class. Shamefaced, I whisk the hat off and the subject's dropped.

Poppy and Flora make their selections in a matter of minutes, deciding only between huge hats and obscenely huge hats, while I linger listlessly.

'Coming back to the office?' Poppy asks, while Flora flags down a cab. (They're unable to walk and carry their hatboxes at the same time.)

'I, ah . . . I think I'll just have a peek at Fortnum's,' I stall. As I watch them lumber merrily into their cab and head towards Piccadilly, I'm more disappointed than ever.

I wander up to Fortnum's. On the first floor they have

a hat department rather like the one at Lock's, and once again, I try to make a selection from one of the wide-brimmed varieties. I'm peering sheepishly out from underneath a particularly vile pastel creation when I hear a voice behind me exclaim, 'My dear, with all due respect, that really isn't you.'

I turn around to face a very elegantly dressed, diminutive older woman. She has on a cream cashmere coat, draped over a classic, ivory Chanel suit and is carrying an alligator Kelly bag. She smiles at me and her remarkable blue eyes sparkle mischievously.

'It is none of my business, of course,' she says, in a very refined Austrian accent. 'However, I hate to see such folly in one so young. I must say,' she continues, 'it is rare to see someone of your age even looking at hats. I was of the impression that they were considered *très passé*.'

'I'm going to Ascot,' I explain, removing the offensive article from my head. 'I need a hat and the girls I'm going with are all wearing these. I'm not quite sure of what's expected, of what's . . . best.'

'I see,' she nods. 'You are American?'

'Yes, that's right,' I confess, as if it were my guilty secret.

She pulls herself up to her full height (which puts her at about five foot). 'Those sorts of hats are good on English women; they are tall and don't like to attend to their hair properly. I would suggest that you wear something a little chicer, smaller. Something perhaps with a veil.' She turns and hands me a small navy cloche with a dramatic loosely woven veil attached to the brim. 'Something like this.'

I put it on. Instantly, I'm perfectly aloof. The veil intervenes between myself and the outside world, creating a superior modesty that is at once seductive and impenetrable. And incredibly chic.

She smiles triumphantly. 'Now, you see! That's much better.'

I can't take my eyes off myself, I look so film star-ish. But still I hesitate. 'It's just, well, the other girls won't be wearing this sort of thing,' I falter. 'It might be a little out of place, a little too . . .'

She raises her hand to stop me. 'As I said, it is none of my business. But in my experience, it is best not to try too hard to be like the English. Being English is, after all, a club not even the English can get into. And they will not respect you for it'.

And with that she turns and disappears among the women's lingerie, vanishing completely somewhere between the cashmere bathrobes and the Egyptian cotton nightdresses.

Suddenly, I panic – the only voice of sanity I've encountered all day is disappearing. 'Wait!' I call out and run after her.

Almost instantly I find myself face to face with what appears to be a transvestite member of the senior sales staff. (I say transvestite because she's built like a linebacker for the New Zealand All Blacks squeezed into an outsized polyester suit.)

Folding her enormous hands across her chest, she glares at me. 'And would Madame like to *buy* the hat?' she demands significantly, raising a single, omnipotent hairy eyebrow.

I reach for my head and as my hand lands on the navy cloche, my heart sinks.

'Oh! I'm sorry! I didn't realize . . .' I stammer, feeling my face flush. I smile in what I imagine must be a winning fashion. 'I was just . . . just looking for someone and I forgot I had this on my head and . . . and I . . .'

It isn't working. She's looking at me like I'm a criminal. I'm beginning to feel like a criminal.

I giggle stupidly. 'Oh, really! You can't honestly imagine that I meant to . . .' (How can I put this?) 'to . . . *abduct* the hat!'

She stares at me unblinkingly and exhales in a kind of snorting fashion reminiscent of a bull just before it charges.

I try a different tack.

I whip the hat off of my head and thrust it at her defiantly. (When in doubt, act like a spoilt child.) 'Here!' I roll my eyes and do my best to seem indignant and superior. 'Here is your hat! Now, I am sorry but I really must go!'

And just as I'm about to flounce past her and hurl myself headlong down the steps in a frantic, suicidal bid for freedom, my little Austrian friend re-emerges.

'So. Are you taking it?' she asks, oblivious to the embarrassment of my current situation. 'It is really quite the best one.'

I'm about to respond, when I notice that something is happening to the sales woman. She blushes and flounders. 'Lady Castle!' Her monstrous eyebrow shoots up to her hairline. 'I do apologize . . . a simple misunderstanding, I'm sure . . . I mean . . . what a pleasure it is to see you!'

Lady Castle nods in her direction, otherwise ignoring her. 'It is the best one, don't you agree?'

'Oh, yes . . .' She's desperate to appear accommodating. 'It's undeniably a very sophisticated . . . a very . . . uh, unique design . . .' I watch as my former foe melts to a jelly on the floor.

'Lady Castle, I want to thank you so much for helping me to make a selection.' I pluck the hat back triumphantly. 'Your advice has been invaluable.'

'It is no trouble at all,' she assures me. 'I have a great deal of experience in these things. I have found a hat with a veil very useful in the past. It's flattering and a little mysterious. That sets one apart.'

'Well, that's just it,' I confide. 'I already feel set apart – a little too set apart in fact. What I was trying to do was to fit in.'

She shakes her head vigorously. 'Fitting in is for schoolgirls. Being different is not a crime, my dear, but an asset.'

I shrug my shoulders and smile wryly. 'I'm not so sure.'

Lady Castle looks appalled. 'But of course it is! You are an individual! A woman with a past, a history. No one can take that away from you!'

I'm intrigued. She speaks so passionately, with such assurance that, once again, I'm flooded with the feeling that I don't want to let her go.

'Would you allow me to buy you a cup of tea?' I offer, sounding, even to myself, like an archaic figure from a P.G. Wodehouse novel.

She accepts my invitation without a moment's hesitation, as if it's only natural that she should be invited to tea by a total stranger that she's just met in the hat department of one of the better department stores. This remarkable self-assurance is exactly the quality I feel I lack. And, so, after I've bought my hat we go downstairs to the splendour of Fortnum's tea room, where Lady Castle promptly and unapologetically orders a full afternoon tea, complete with toasted tea cakes and scones.

I watch and listen in complete fascination as she recounts her history in England, while effortlessly negotiating the business of serving tea with all the ease of one for whom it is a daily habit.

'The English are wonderful people. I adore them,' she says, adding a slice of lemon to her tea. 'If it weren't for the English, I wouldn't be alive. It's as simple as that. During the War, I was sent from Austria when I was just a child. My mother put me on a train and I left. The only one to

307

make it out alive. The only one,' she repeats softly. 'I do not know why I should be so lucky, only that I am. The English are my family now.' She carefully presses the lemon against the side of her china cup with her teaspoon. 'But like most families, it is not always easy.'

'But you are a Lady now,' I point out emphatically. 'Surely that makes all the difference.'

Again she looks surprised. 'But, my dear, I always *was* a lady! Even when I was a scrawny, immigrant child who couldn't speak a word of English! I did not need to wait for a Lord to ask me to marry him before I became a Lady!'

'But what I mean,' I struggle to put it into words, 'what I mean is, now that you are a Lady, you're one of them . . . you're not an outsider any more.'

'Outside, inside . . . you make too much of this thing.' She takes a sip of Darjeeling, her sharp eyes never leaving my face. 'What people respond to, what is such a mistake, is not that you are different, but that you are *ashamed* that you are different.'

She smiles and pops another fruit tart on her plate. 'These pastries! Really, they are too good! I shall have to fast this evening to make up for it. Do things with style, Louise. Your own style. And believe me, no one will care where you come from.'

Back at the office, the hat is more of a miss than a hit with the girls.

'It's ever so serious.' Flora turns it over in her hands like it's a bomb.

'Yes, it's certainly very adult,' Poppy agrees. 'You're a braver man than I,' she adds, handing it back to me quickly.

I put it back into its box, undaunted.

'Cup of tea, anyone?' I offer.

'Oh yes please!' they chorus, ecstatic in the way only the English can be about tea.

That night, as I manoeuvre the hat box in place on top of my wardrobe, I'm struck by the persistent feeling that I've met Lady Castle somewhere before. I sit down on the edge of my bed and concentrate. Who does she remind me of?

Then suddenly, it comes to me. I open my wardrobe and unearth my volume of *Elegance*. Flicking it open, I browse through the gems of timeless advice. Lady Castle reminds me of Madame Dariaux and I realize with a twinge how much I've been missing her. She'd become real to me and even when I resented the unfailing accuracy of her wisdom, she never let me down. I've been foolish to exile her and now carefully dust the book down and return it to its place of pride on my bedside table.

When the big day arrives, I discover that Lady Castle is right. I pair the hat with a very simply cut navy raw silk dress and matching jacket; the hat is, of course, the star of the show. Sure enough, amidst a sea of three-foot brims,

I'm distinguished and aloof. And I have the additional bonus of being able to slip easily through the crowd, which is undoubtedly more elegant. The veil itself has the most surprising effect. It bestows upon me an instant status that's beyond anything I could have predicted. Men are incredibly solicitous, fascinated by it, and women intrigued. And as I walk towards Flora and Poppy across the Royal Enclosure, I see Flora's jaw drop, even from beneath the formidable brim of her candy-floss creation.

'Oh Louise!' she cries, clutching at my arm forlornly. 'You look exactly the way I would've liked to if only I could!'

And for the first time, I see them in a completely different light. They seem strangely vulnerable amidst the daunting crush of morning suits and designer dresses; small and young with only their huge hats to protect them. And I think of Lady Castle's words: inside, outside, it makes no difference.

It's a long, thrilling, and exhausting day. The weather, so often grey and dismal in early June, turns out to be stunning and the clients genuinely appear to be having a good time. It's almost four o'clock before I can slip away for a few moments' peace on my own. I'm strolling slowly through the crowd, wondering if I dare to place a bet, when I catch sight of a familiar face.

'Hello!' I say. It's the young man who'd given me the ticket on the opera house steps, only this time he's dressed in full morning suit.

'Hello!' he beams back. 'What happened, did you get the job?'

'Yes, yes I did, and I just wanted to thank you so much for giving me that ticket. I can't tell you how amazing it was!' The crowd presses around us, pulling us in opposite directions as the bells sound.

'Look, I've got to quickly place this bet for my grand-father before the next race,' he shouts over the noise of the throng. 'Fancy a drink?'

'I can't,' I shout back, just as the bells sound again. 'I've got to get back in a minute. Run or you'll miss your chance!'

He pulls away, fighting his way to the shortest queue, but before I lose sight of him completely he turns and yells across the betting hall, 'By the way, you look absolutely incredible!' Which results in a flurry of good natured 'Hear, hears' from some of the gentlemen around him.

He stands grinning at me and a moment later, melts into the crowd.

My whole body's tingling, and as I make my way back to the Royal Enclosure, there's a definite spring in my step.

Ascot is a feast of fashion statements, some disastrous, others delightful. However, despite the vast variety, I'm surprised to see very few women wearing hats with veils. As a matter of fact, Lady Castle is wearing the only other one I spot all day. It's a small silver-grey pillbox with a stunning swathe of black net falling across the face. Just below, her perfectly drawn matte red lips smile playfully and she gives me the slightest hint of a wink.

'I am really quite impressed!' She takes my arm as I approach. '*You* look like a lady – these others may *be* ladies but you look like one. A real Wallis Simpson! Horrible woman, of course, but so beautifully dressed, you cannot imagine! Now,' she steers me towards her box, 'you must allow me to introduce you to some people. I have a feeling you might find them interesting.' She swings me around to face a small, squat, red-faced man who's holding his glass of champagne as if it's a beer mug. 'This is Fredrick Von Hassel, Louise. Mr Von Hassel has a passion for early music.'

He thrusts a swollen pink paw at me, which I shake.

'Fredrick collects Caravaggio's,' Lady Castle continues. 'I understand that the Royal Opera is mounting a new production of *Orfeo*. Is that correct?'

Before I have a chance to speak, Mr Von Hassel is away.

'Nobody stages Monteverdi correctly!' he barks. 'They are always trying to make "a statement". To update the story. It is a great tale of love and death!' he shouts, his face growing redder by the second. 'I cannot stand to see these productions! I object to them! I really object!'

Here is a moment when a veil really comes in handy. I blink. I smile. I take the liberty of brushing some of Mr Von Hassel's spittle off my lapel and then quietly say, 'That's such a shame. Especially as Caravaggio is the inspiration behind the design of our new production and I would love to have your opinion of it.'

I think it's the exaggerated glamour of the veil that gives me the courage to turn away. Bold gestures as well as lingering silences come more easily behind a wall of mesh.

He's by my side in an instant.

'Caravaggio?' he stammers. 'Please, I am most eager to hear more!'

The Von Hassel productions of early music are really one of the highlights of the winter season each year. They're thoughtful, intimate, and beautifully produced. More often than not, they're completely sold out months in advance. So book early.

And you might want to ask for seats in the Castle box.

W

Weekends

After five days of gradual asphyxiation in town, an ever increasing number of city dwellers escape to the country for the weekend to fill their lungs with forty-eight hours' worth of fresh air. As a result, an entire industry has been built around this desire for pastoral leisure, and never before have so many sports clothes been sold.

However it's important to note that forty-eight hours in a country house require almost the same number of clothes as a holiday abroad and, if one is to be a pleasant and social guest, not one of the items in your overnight case will be optional.

These will include an attractive suit of the sporty variety, either of tweed or linen in the summer for travelling down, sensible, flat-heeled shoes, a sturdy pair of boots for walking, a pretty silk dressing-gown – never sheer or revealing in any way for breakfast, a pair of trousers with a matching fitted shirt, a warm sweater or cardigan, a long evening dress for formal suppers or a shorter, more casual one for evenings en famille, a lightweight cotton dress and matching sandals for exploring the countryside, a pair of mannish silk pyjamas, and above all, a hot-water bottle in a soft cover, some of your favourite soap and a secret supply of biscuits. (It is impossible to know when and if you will ever be fed!)

This list will be longer and more complicated if your hostess expects you to engage in any kind of sport. Naturally riding will require that you come prepared with riding boots and jodhpurs, tennis means you should be dressed in a clean, white skirt, shirt, and shoes, and, whatever you do, don't forget to bring along your racquet, golf clubs, or any other equipment that's necessary for a good game. You will not endear yourself to anyone if you're forced to borrow bits and pieces of the appropriate attire from either the hostess or other house guests.

So be warned and be prepared. Weekends away are the Waterloo of many a friendship. And you may ask yourself if it's worth all the trouble. I'm not an outdoor woman myself but I'm always incredibly refreshed and pleased after a weekend away, if only because I realize how wonderful and easy living in town really is!

After Ascot, I acquire a reputation in the office as a sophisti-cate. I nickname Flora and Poppy the Flower People, and they in turn call me Shanghai Lil in honour of my veiled success.

'It took more than one man to change my name to Shanghai Lil', Poppy intones at me every morning as I stroll in, clutching my double café latte. I wink at her, force my voice down two octaves and sing the opening lines of 'Fall-ing in Love Again' until it becomes too murderously low for me to continue. And bit by bit, we grow accustomed to each other, then to appreciate one another, and, finally to be friends. Despite our different backgrounds, I soon discover that my little Flower People have just as many secret vices as I do: Poppy's sole ambition in life is to meet a man she can wear high heels next to, hopefully while seducing him at her weekly salsa class, while Flora harbours a dangerous obsession with old re-runs of *Dallas*. When we get bored (which is often), she regales us with stunning impersonations of Sue Ellen emerging from blackout, which Poppy claims are just a bit too realistic for comfort.

So it's not a complete surprise when, one steaming Thursday afternoon in August, Poppy casually asks if I'd like to spend the weekend with her and Flora at her family's country home in Berkshire.

'Nothing fancy,' she says. 'But it will give us a chance to get some fresh air and it's very relaxed down there. We can just laze about . . .'

The thought of escaping from London into the cool, green oasis of the English countryside is too intoxicating for words. I have visions of tea tables set up under a leafy canopy of chestnut trees, of hammocks swinging gently in the breeze, of dinner al fresco under the stars, accompanied only by a chorus of crickets, of girls in white dresses with blue satin sashes . . . essentially, I lose the plot.

'That sounds amazing!' I sigh.

'Great!' Poppy says. 'We'll go tomorrow night after work. Flora's driving, so I'd suggest no solid food until we arrive . . . *if* we arrive! Really, Louise,' she beams, 'I'm so pleased you're coming! It's only a small house party.'

'House party?' I come to with a jolt. A weekend away is one thing; a house party is another animal altogether.

She sees the terror on my face. 'But only small, teensy even,' she assures me quickly. 'Just my brother and his wife, Mum and Dad, my sister Lavender and her husband, who's a terrible bore and a bit of a letch, so stay clear, my other brother Tarquin, who's just been expelled from Eton so you're not to mention anything to do with school, school friends, academic hopes for the future, gap years, books, uniforms, Prince William, rugby, or alcohol in front of my parents. As a matter of fact, best to shun him altogether. It's what we'll all be doing. It's easier that way. Then there's you, me, and Flora, Flora's brother Eddie, who plays the piano, my grandparents, my mother's sister Hazel, my cousin Daisy, her friend Sacha, and possibly the Drews, who are friends of my aunt's and are thinking about getting a divorce.' She smiles brightly. 'So no one, really. It will be *so* cool!'

'Cool,' I echo. 'Really, really cool.' But my heart sags like an empty, old Wellington boot.

I've never been good at staying at other people's houses. Even when I was a kid, I was terrible at sleepovers. And what is a house party if not one great big adult sleepover? I panic if I can't eat what I want, when I want, and I'm extremely bad-tempered about sharing bathroom facilities. Creeping around corridors in the middle of the night, listening at bathroom doors for any sign of life, trying to pee as quietly as you can in case the walls are paper thin, all send shivers down my spine. In addition, I'm terrified that I'll be expected to participate in one of those country sports that requires years of training. And special clothes. Like riding, shooting, or golf. I can see everyone else in impeccable hunt gear flying over fences while I plod along on an aging mule half a mile behind them.

'It will be brilliant,' Poppy enthuses. '*And* we can play charades!'

Life can be so cruel.

'What can I do?' I duck down behind the felt partition and whisper into the phone to Colin. 'I already said yes!'

'Sweetie, you go, of course. Honestly, don't be so silly. The whole trick of it is just to be prepared.'

'Col, you don't understand!' I hiss. 'I'm not good at communal living. It took me months just to get used to you and Ria!'

He sighs. 'Fine. Tonight when you get home, we'll go over it all and I'll help you pack, all right? But no backing out! Truth is, with Ria at her sister's this weekend, Andy and I can finally have the house to ourselves – he's already gone to Marks and Spencer's and I get to choose which videos we're watching.'

'OK, OK. It's a deal,' I agree. Nice to know that at least one of us has a love life.

When I arrive home that night, Colin greets me at the door with an ice-cold glass of Chablis.

'Oh, you angel!' I collapse gratefully onto the couch. 'How did you know?'

'I always know,' he grins, settling down next to me. 'Now look, I hope you don't mind but I borrowed your fashion book, Madame Thingy, just to have a look through. And I've come up with a few ideas. Here's what I think you're going to need, as a kind of bare minimum.' And he hands me several pages of A4 paper.

I look at him. 'You've got to be kidding.'

He smiles. 'Have another sip and try to keep an open mind, will you?'

The list is thoughtfully divided into 'style sections':

For travelling down:

1 pair jeans – not too tatty

1 simple cashmere pullover

1 plain white tee-shirt (+ 2 spare)

1 pair loafer-style driving shoes

'I won't actually be driving, Col.'

'It's just a suggestion. Want some crisps?'

'Yes, please.'

He disappears into the kitchen.

For Country Walks:

1 pair Wellington boots

1 Barbour or Barbour style coat

Previous jeans, new tee, cashmere jumper

'This is impossible! I don't have a pair of Wellingtons, let alone a cashmere jumper. And Barbour jackets stink to high heaven!'

'When in Rome, Ouise. Plain or cheese and onion?'

'Cheese and onion, please.' I return to the list, which I'm beginning to hate.

For Town and Evening:

1 casual linen dress (for going into town)

1 simple jersey evening sheath for formal meals

'A simple jersey evening sheath? Have you ever *seen* a simple jersey evening sheath? I haven't.' This is getting grim. 'Col, you don't actually think they're going to dress for dinner . . . do you?'

He emerges with a bowl of crisps and hands them to me. 'Well, you never know.'

For Bed:
1 pair mid-weight pyjamas and matching robe
Slippers
Clean and matching bra and knickers – just in case someone walks in on you by accident

'Col!'

'It could happen to anyone, Louise.' He stretches out his long legs and pops a crisp in his mouth.

Sport:
Tennis whites, tennis shoes and racquet
Riding boots (can borrow)
Bathing suit

I put the list down, my head reeling.

'This is just too much! I can't just go out and buy a tennis outfit or riding boots or even Wellingtons. I mean, surely they'll let me off the hook if I don't have all this gear . . .'

He stares at me. An unyielding silence settles between us.

I try a different tack. 'There must be other people in the party who aren't going riding, or shooting, or whatever they do in the country. A special outfit to walk in? I just don't get that. I mean, not everyone's robe is going to match their pyjamas, not everyone is going to spend tonight bleaching their knickers just in case the lock on the bathroom door doesn't work. I can't be the only one!'

He shrugs his shoulders. 'Look, you asked for my help. Here it is. I can't help it if that's what people wear in the country, can I? You're welcome to go down there with nothing but a fresh pair of knickers but what if they do dress for dinner, huh? What are you going to do then?'

I'm just about to tell him when Ria lets herself in the front door.

'What's all this about?' She throws herself down on the sofa next to me and helps herself to some crisps.

I sigh heavily. 'I've been invited by Poppy for a weekend at her country house and it turns out it's a whole house party full of strangers and I'm not sure what to take or what I need and Colin's trying to help me . . .'

She takes a sip of my wine. 'Well, I just hope you've got a pair of Wellingtons.'

Shit.

Later that evening, I unearth my sky-blue nylon overnight bag and plop it on the bed. I bought it in LA airport some time in the eighties when I'd stocked up on too many plastic flip-flops to fit into my suitcase. It sags open in all its garish glory, like a soiled, battered mouth, covered in airline stickers and boarding tags. I strip off the excess tags but it still looks cheap and ridiculously bright. I'm distinctly uninspired.

Next I open my wardrobe and consider what I own that might actually be suitable. A pair of flared Diesel jeans, a cropped Morgan cardigan, a leather shift dress that makes more noise when I move than a military demonstration in Red Square.

Then I remember that Colin had consulted my old friend, Madame Dariaux when making his list. Sitting on the bed, I open to 'W' and read her advice.

'*Be warned and be prepared.*'

My heart sinks. Colin is right after all.

And as I sit there, holding my book, I begin to wonder if I will ever graduate from Madame Dariaux's tutelage. Just when I think I've got it sussed, some new, unexpected dilemma comes careering along. Part of me longs to chuck a few pairs of clean pants into my blue nylon bag and be done with it. And yet I can't. I've come too far. If I've learnt one thing, it's that being elegant is just a matter of being willing to make an extra effort and enter into the spirit of things – of life – with enthusiasm and grace. And after all, if this is how people dress for a weekend away, then it's not going to kill me to give it a try.

I knock on Ria's door.

'Yep?'

I poke my head round the corner. 'Do you know anyone who has a pair of Wellingtons I could borrow?'

She smiles. 'I think my sister has a pair. I'll see what I can do.'

Come Friday afternoon, after a day of frantic bargaining and begging, I've finally managed to pack a reasonable sized bag (that's using the word reasonable liberally). I'm pretty well prepared for just about every occasion, except for tennis, which I've resolved to solve by posing as a fascinated bystander. Although I'll never be accused of demonstrating the height of casual country chic, I can console myself that at least my pyjama tops match my pyjama bottoms, and I've managed to pack a dress that shouldn't crease too badly and both an outdoor and an indoor pair of shoes. As a matter of fact, I'm inwardly congratulating myself on how well I've done, taking everything in my stride, when Flora pulls up outside the office in her aging sunshine yellow Beetle convertible and toots the horn.

'She's here!' Poppy's whole face shines with joy as she leans out of the office window and waves. And then I suddenly remember the one thing I've forgotten.

'Shit! Shit, shit, shit! I can't believe it!'

'What is it?' Poppy says, rushing to turn off her computer and set the answering machine.

'Listen, I've forgotten to get a gift for your mum and dad.' I grab my wallet from my massive cherry-red straw handbag and race towards the door. 'Be an angel and pop my bag in the boot for me. I won't be a minute, I swear! Tell Flora to wait!' And I run down the steps towards the staff exit.

One of the brilliant things about working at the Royal Opera House is that you're right in the centre of Covent Garden. It takes me just fifteen minutes to pop into Penhaligon's, buy a gift-wrapped box set of scented candles and tear back to the car where Flora and Poppy are waiting.

'Ready?' Flora's revving her engine and slipping on her pink plastic shades.

'Ready!' I shout, throwing myself into the back seat.

The car lurches forward, barely missing a *Big Issue* seller and we're off, speeding out of London, racing towards a greener, pleasanter land in the dappled light of the warm evening sun.

Somewhere between Oxford and Reading we turn off the main road and fall, like Alice in Wonderland, into the surreal, impenetrable rabbit warren of secondary roads that weave across the countryside, hugging the hedgerows as they twist from one bizarrely named enclave to another. Three Mile Cross, Rotherfield Peppard, Nettlebed, Russell's Water, Gallowstree Common – the names are not so much destinations as roads not taken in a mystical, magical journey worthy of J.R.R.Tolkien or C.S. Lewis. We pass Tutts

Clump, narrowly escape Rotten Row and are headed towards a fate known as Sheffield's Bottom when Flora takes a sharp right. We skid off the road and onto a paved driveway that extends for a quarter of a mile through parkland bordered on either side by an avenue of ancient chestnut trees. As we near the house, the parkland gives way to a rolling green carpet of immaculately manicured lawn and there, sprawled before us is Poppy's family home – a huge Queen Anne house of red brick and leaded glass windows, complete with two narrow turrets and a set of snarling gargoyles poised above the solid oak door.

I'm not certain if it's the unbelievable size of the place or Flora's driving, but suddenly I'm finding it very difficult to catch my breath.

'We're here!' Poppy jumps out of the front seat with surprising agility for a girl of her size.

'My God, Poppy!' I gasp. 'You live here?'

'It *is* nice,' she concedes. 'But it's full of damp and costs a fortune to heat . . . not a patch on my little cubbyhole in Notting Hill.'

She pushes the car seat forward and I try to step out. However, my knees are shaking so much that I collapse onto the drive instead.

'Upsy-daisy!' Flora picks me up off the gravel, completely unfazed (people evidently always fall out the cars she drives). 'Deep breaths, Louise; it will pass. Isn't this air terrific?'

And the next thing I know, I'm surrounded by dogs. Not just two or three but easily twelve of various breeds and sizes, jumping, barking, licking and sniffing in that over-intimate way you dearly wish they wouldn't and all smelling quite distinctly, quite strongly of dog. In the midst of this canine cloud, a woman with absolutely no sign of ever owning a chin emerges, towering above even Poppy in a pair of old Wellingtons and brandishing a pair of lethal looking secateurs.

'Down!' she booms, in a voice that could rule an empire (or destroy one). 'Down boys! Jasper, No! NO! Just push him off,' she instructs me. 'He hasn't been done yet and he's a *terrible* nuisance.'

'Mummy!' Poppy leans forward across the sea of waggling tails in an attempt to kiss her mother on the cheek. However, this noble effort is thwarted not just by the dogs but by Mrs Simpson-Stock herself, who performs a swift side step, thus neatly avoiding any form of physical intimacy. The move throws Poppy off balance and she lands heavily on her mother's shoulder.

'Honestly, Poppy!' she snorts, pushing her away. 'Still as clumsy as ever!'

'Yes, Mummy,' Poppy giggles. 'You know me!'

'Hello, Flora.' Mummy's hand shoots forward as if it were spring-loaded. She shakes Flora's hand so violently that her blond bob bounces up and down and her sunglasses fly off her head, lost in a sea of dog. Next she turns her fearsome hospitality to me. 'And you must be The American!' she bellows, giving me the same brain-addling handshake.

'Louise, Mummy. Her name's Louise,' Poppy corrects her.

'Yes, well, Louise, welcome to Lower Slaughter. Just make yourself at home. We have only a few rules here. First off, supper is 7:30 for 8 pm. Sharp. And secondly, no feeding the dogs! They're fat enough, aren't you, boys, aren't you, my lovely little babies! Yessssssss! And thirdly, no strangers in the gun room. If someone's going to get their head blown off, I'd prefer it was a member of my own family. Understood?'

'Absolutely,' I joke. 'We have similar rules about guns in my family too.'

She stares at me stonily.

No one makes a sound. Even the dogs sense I've made a *faux pas* and freeze mid-wag. Somewhere in the distance a peacock cries eerily. Wind whistles through the chestnut trees. Time, who waits for no man, is apparently quite accustomed to standing still for Mrs Simpson-Stock.

'Yes. Well. Be that as it may,' she says finally, and the film starts rolling again. 'Poppy will show you to your rooms. I expect that you will actually *sleep* in yours this time, Flora,' she adds, raising an eyebrow significantly, to which Flora responds by turning several shades of crimson and giggling nervously.

In a desperate bid to repair the damage I've already done,

I thrust the Penhaligon's gift box towards her. 'These are for you,' I smile, the very essence of obsequiousness. 'Just a little something to say thank you.'

'Very much obliged,' she replies brusquely, taking the box and tucking it neatly under her arm without so much as a glance. 'Bound to be scented candles or soap. All anyone ever brings me is scented candles and soap. I'm certain I'm the cleanest, freshest smelling woman in Christendom. But you're very kind. A well brought up young woman. Don't expect such civilized manners from an American. Now, I must finish pruning these rose bushes before supper. Remember, 8 pm sharp! And Poppy, for Christ's sake! Don't slouch! Come on, boys!'

And she tramps off, engulfed in the cloud of dogs.

We stand in silence a moment, more shell shocked than anything until Poppy heaves a long sigh. 'Isn't she a darling? I think she adores you already.'

'Bit of a favourite,' Flora confirms. 'It was two years before she even spoke to me.'

Poppy unhands the bags from the boot. She slams it shut and gathers her things. 'Shall we go in and I'll show you around?'

I stare at the pile of luggage. Something's missing. 'Where's my case?'

She and Flora look at each other.

'What case?' Flora says.

The whole bottom of my stomach falls away. 'The blue

nylon case I brought to the office. The one I asked you to put in the boot for me.'

There's that damned peacock again.

Poppy opens her mouth, then shuts it again. She looks confused. 'But when you said put your bag in, I thought you meant that,' she explains, pointing to the cherry red straw bag. 'I thought that was your weekend bag.'

My throat is dry. '*That* is my handbag,' I croak.

Silence.

'It *is* an awfully big handbag.' Flora's trying to be helpful. She's not.

'Oops!' Poppy laughs awkwardly, slapping me on the back a little too roughly. 'Never mind! You can borrow some clothes from Flora and me. I'm sure we'll find you something!'

I'm drifting into a coma of despair. All my easy adaptability instantly vanishes.

'Come on, Louise! Don't look so glum!' Flora says. 'It's not the end of the world! I'm sure I've got a pair of knickers you can borrow and those trousers you're wearing –' she eyes my 'not too tatty' jeans – 'well, I'm sure they're just fine . . . dinner isn't, well, *too* formal and as long as you don't go riding in them . . .' Her voice tails off as she begins to comprehend the reality of spending a whole weekend at Lower Slaughter with nothing but a pair of jeans and a cardigan.

We stand in silence for a moment, staring at the blank space on the driveway where my bag should be.

'I *am* sorry,' Poppy apologizes softly, putting her arm around my shoulders and easing me gently towards the front door. 'We'll sort something out, I promise.'

But, well meaning as they are, all I can think of is how they're at least six inches taller than I am. How will I ever manage without my borrowed Wellingtons and my carefully folded crease-proof dress?

Poppy shows me to a room on the east side of the house that's decorated in pre-war Liberty prints and has the kind of sloping ceiling and uneven floorboards that conspire to attack even the most docile visitor. The bed groans in protest when I sit on it.

'There's a lav just down the hall and Flora and I are right next to you.' Her voice is gentle and kind, as if trying to console an elderly relative. 'Why don't you have a rest and I'll knock on your door when it's time for dinner?'

'Wonderful!' I force a smile. 'I'll just have a lie down.'

They leave and I sink onto the bed. A gentle breeze wafts in through the open window and suddenly I deflate like a balloon, utterly worn out. Much to my shame, stinging tears well up in my eyes. The tears of a disappointed eight-year-old who wants to go home. Resistance is useless. I curl up into a little ball and surrender. All my expectations of another dazzling Ascot-type triumph dissolve. For all my fastidious planning, I couldn't have reckoned on this. I'm going to end up being uncomfortable and badly dressed all weekend, shambling about like a homeless person in the same outfit for three days. I punch the pillow in frustration and a blizzard of feathers spurts out, covering the duvet and part of the floor.

That's all I need. Sobbing bitterly now, I crouch down and try in vain to gather up the dusty feathers whirling around me.

So here I am, scrambling around on my hands and knees, drowning in a sea of self-pity and non-waterproof mascara, when slowly I become aware of the sound of piano music drifting in through the open window. It begins softly, delicately, building in a series of intricate themes. Slowly it gathers strength and force, finally exploding in a pile of octaves, furiously stacked one upon another, and then subsiding, softening, melting, and beginning the cycle all over again.

I kneel on the floor, transfixed. Perhaps it's a recording or maybe someone's listening to the radio. But after a while the piece ends and then a particularly tricky bit is repeated; it's played over and over until the pianist gains confidence and clarity. And I realize with a shock that the music is live.

I stop crying. Or rather, I simply forget to continue. Getting up from the floor, I push the bedroom door open and creep downstairs, following the music like a hypnotized child trailing after the Pied Piper, moving as quietly as possible so as not to break the spell.

Most of the guests are out on the lawn, playing croquet

or collapsed into loungers. The house itself is abandoned. A warm zephyr blows in through the open windows, gathering and releasing the sheer curtains with silent, invisible hands, almost in time with the music.

At the bottom of the stairs, I turn a corner and follow the corridor along until I come to a long narrow room, bordered on one side by a wall of windows and on the other by floor-to-ceiling bookshelves. At the far end of the room, there's an elegant early-twentieth-century Steinway grand piano. And there, unmistakable, even with his back towards me, sits the young man from the opera house steps.

Playing with a kind of tremendous fury, oblivious to everything around him, his long fingers glide over the keyboard with unbelievable speed; one moment attacking, the next caressing in a dazzling display of technical and interpretative brilliance. The total assurance of his playing is nothing less than heroic. Nothing is measured or hesitant. Even the softer passages display a level of involvement and commitment uncommon in everyday life. I hover a moment in the doorway. Nothing, not even an act of God, is likely to distract him, so I steal in.

And as I stand, listening in the corner, a remarkable transformation takes place. My shoulders release and sink forward. The tight thread knotted in my head begins to unravel. And gradually I'm aware of the even, steady sound of my own breathing. The last rays of the shocking pink sunset glow over the lawn, outlining his shoulders and highlighting his dark hair. They radiate around his fine features like a halo of golden light; too beautiful to be real.

Only he is real.

And then, incredibly, even the all-pervading smell of dog vanishes and is replaced instead by the delicate perfume of the late summer roses that wind around the open glass doors.

I don't know how long I've been there, maybe a few minutes, maybe half an hour, but after a while he stops playing and turns around.

'Oh, hello,' he smiles. 'Fancy seeing you here! Have you been there long?'

'Yes, well, no . . .' I hesitate, 'not long enough. That is, you play so beautifully.'

'Thank you.' He tilts his head shyly. 'Fourth Ballade. Chopin. My favourite. Or, actually no,' he corrects himself, apparently unable to let such a shocking inaccuracy slide. 'Beethoven's my real favourite, and then Chopin, Brahms, and you can't beat Rachmaninoff. Do you like him?' He plays a few bars of Rachmaninoff's Third Piano Concerto. 'Isn't that amazing? And this bit . . .' He launches into another passage. 'This is the absolute best bit of all!' he shouts above the crashing chords. 'You've gotta love it!'

'Yes, it's amazing,' I agree, laughing. His eagerness and delight is infectious.

'See and wait! Wait! Listen to these octaves!' He pounds away, fingers flying. 'I saw someone break a finger once playing those – isn't that incredible! Ruined his whole career.' And he smiles again as if it were the most wonderful news in the world. 'Do you know any Prokofiev?'

'Only *Romeo and Juliet* and *The Love for Three Oranges*,' I admit.

'I love *Romeo and Juliet!*' For a moment I think he's going to explode with excitement. 'Mercutio's death scene – so tragic!' Again, he begins to play, filling the room with the dramatic, halting, march that characterizes the end of Act Two, replacing a whole orchestra with an intricate transcription for single piano.

Curling up in a nearby armchair, I make myself comfortable and bask in the light of his enthusiasm and astonishing talent.

I can't recall the last time I saw someone enjoying something so much, so openly. Perhaps it's my age or just the people I hang out with, but almost everyone I know seems to be an aspiring cynic. We stand at the edges of our experiences, smoking cigarettes and trying to convince each other that we've seen this, done that and it isn't so hot anyway. It's considered un-cool to be passionate, if not downright gauche. And on the occasions when one of us does become excited, it's under duress, both embarrassing and brief. It's considered unrealistic; a kind of madness that descends and has to be apologized for the next day. 'Real life' is, after all, a serious and rather dull business. And the more serious and dull, the more 'real' it is.

I don't know how we all collectively came to the conclusion that this is the way adults behave but, as I watch him play, I feel an aching in my chest: an intense longing to let go of my eternal pessimism and trade it instead for the easy joy before me. The rapture I hear right now.

He finishes Mercutio's death scene and is launching into the flowing, ominous passages of the balcony scene when I hear someone crossing the wooden floor.

'There you are!' I look up to find Flora standing over me, wearing a floral dress. 'I've been looking for you everywhere. It's almost time for supper.' She offers me a hand, pulling me out of the armchair with a good, solid all girls hockey team yank. 'I see you've met my brother Eddie. Eddie!' she shouts. 'Eddie shut up, for Christ sake!' He stops playing and swivels round indignantly.

'Oh, it's only you, Old Bag,' he says, giving her a wink.

'Nice to see you to, Waste of Space,' she counters, grinning. 'I hope he hasn't been boring you senseless. He can pound that piano until you just want to bludgeon him to death, can't you?'

He nods happily.

She looks at me and frowns. 'Geez, Louise, what's happened to you? You look an absolute fright! You're covered in feathers and there's mascara all down your face! What've you been doing to her, you brute!' She turns to Eddie, hands on hips.

'Nothing, I swear!' he protests. 'It's the music! My music

has been known to bring tears to the eyes of many a lovely lady! And to cause the occasional moult,' he adds.

I'd completely forgotten about the exploding pillow tantrum. I catch sight of myself in one of the huge gilt mirrors hanging between the pairs of French doors. I look like I've been tarred and feathered by a group of minimalists. 'Shit!'

'Well put!' Eddie laughs.

I'm blushing.

'Well, there's only a few minutes before supper,' Flora says, glancing at her watch. 'So I'd clean up if I were you. I put a spare skirt on your bed.'

'Thanks,' I murmur, racing towards the door. I can't get out of there fast enough.

My mind is reeling as I bound up the stairs. Eddie, the man from the opera house steps, is Flora's brother! And he's here! Why does this have to be the weekend I have no decent clothes?

I dive into the bathroom, splash my face with water, rinse away the trails of mascara and pull the feathers out of my hair. Three minutes to eight. Shit, shit, shit! I tear off my jeans, pull on the skirt Flora left for me and look in the mirror. Barefaced, without a hint of make-up, and dressed in a tee-shirt, elasticized floral skirt and loafers, I look like an escapee from a special needs home. I sob in despair. One more minute to go. Damn it! I pull the tee-shirt out to cover the ruched waistband, grab the red lipstick out of my handbag and paint on a lovely red clown mouth, which I dab down desperately with a tissue. The grandfather clock in the front hallway chimes ominously. Eight o'clock. Fuck! I grab my cardigan, throw it around my shoulders and tear out of my bedroom.

I skid down the main staircase, coming to a halt at the bottom, unsure of which way to go. There's laughter somewhere to my left. As I speed down the hallway, the noise becomes louder and louder. The doorway to an open lounge is only ten feet away. The clock is just striking eight. I might just make it! Rounding the doorway, I prepare to smile winningly at the assembled guests when suddenly I'm hit by a wall of jumping dogs. Before I know it, I'm down on the Aubusson, covered in canines.

'No running in the house!' Mrs Simpson-Stock roars. 'How many times do I have to say it! Down, boys, down! Heel! Sit! STOP! Here,' she offers me a hand and pulls me up. 'You're late. Everyone, this is Poppy's friend, Eleanor.'

'Louise, Mummy.'

'Yes, well, whatever. She's American,' she concludes by way of explanation and they all nod their heads knowingly.

Poppy comes to my rescue. 'Why don't I get you a Pimms and introduce you to everyone later?' she suggests, taking me under her arm and guiding me to the drinks table.

'Thank you, that would be lovely,' I rasp, shamefaced. As we cross the room in total silence, I scan its borders as discreetly as I can for any sign of Eddie. Is it possible that I've escaped humiliating myself in front of him for a second time? My heart lifts at the thought. I search the room once more just to be sure. He's definitely missing. I'm so relieved, I even manage a smile when Poppy hands me a glass filled to the brim with fruit salad and cucumber floating in a sugary amber liquid.

'Cheers everyone!' she toasts, raising her glass.

'Cheers!' they shout back, manoeuvring their faces so that they're able to drink the liquid without disturbing the complicated mass of foliage. It's like taking a sip out of a vase full of flowers. With my track record, I decide it's best for everyone if I give it a miss.

I stand there holding my glass, trying to blend in with the other guests when a youngish man with very blond hair and no discernible eyelashes swaggers over. He has on a purple and white pinstriped shirt and a pair of canary yellow corduroy trousers that, like the sun, can't be looked at directly without severe damage to the eyes.

'Yah hello. My name's Piers, Lavender's better half,' he introduces himself, gesturing to a drained, angry looking young woman in the corner, who's clutching her drink so violently, she might easily shatter the glass. 'So,' he smirks at me. 'You're American. Tell us why your presidents are all such dumb pricks?' He tries punctuating this sparkling opening gambit by taking a swift swig of his drink, but miscalculates and lands a bit of cucumber in his eye instead.

I hesitate. 'Well, politics isn't really an interest of mine . . .'

'Well, what I want to know . . .' he continues, undeterred, 'is how they can be allowed to continue in office when it's clear that they're all total liars? I mean they're all a walking mass of contradictions . . .'

'I really don't follow the Presidential follies,' I interrupt, wishing he wouldn't stand so close. 'It's not a topic upon which I have an opinion.'

'Well, regardless of that,' he waggles a thick, pink finger in my face, 'the thing that gets me, is how the most powerful man in the world, I mean, we're talking about a man who's got more nuclear capability, right? than all the other world powers combined, can be allowed to say whatever he wants, even lie directly to the Supreme Court of America, on, like, national television! It's like everything in America is one great big bloody Oprah Winfrey Show! And that's another thing I hate!' he rants, his voice filling the room. 'This whole country is getting to be just like America! We've completely lost our national identity. We're just like some faded, secondhand rip off of Your Country!' He points at me accusingly. 'Like we're just some unofficial, bastard fifty-third state! I mean, how do you explain that?' He turns to the rest of the room for affirmation. 'Special relationship with Britain! "Special relationship" my arse! As far as I can see, the whole "special relationship" is built around us doing what you tell us to do! And what's more . . .'

'Oh, shut up, Piers!' Lavender hisses across the room. 'You're boring the poor girl senseless. And everyone else.'

He rolls his eyes. 'No, I'm not, darling. Elsie and I are having a very nice, very civil conversation about her president. And, for your information, politics is not boring, yah? It's just boring for you because you have a brain the size of a pea and don't understand, like, long words all strung together in a row.'

For a moment I thought Lavender was going to chuck her glass at his head. 'Piers! How can you be so rude!' she screams. 'If you ask me, the President of the United States isn't the only one who's a prick!'

'Language, Lavender!' Mrs Simpson-Stock glares at her. 'A lady never swears!'

'But Mummy!'

'*Never*!' her mother growls and Lavender sits down abruptly, like one of her mother's dogs.

A mortified silence ensues. The rest of the guests, too daunted to speak, sit holding their drinks like third-class trophies, staring with pretend fascination as the dogs savage what appears to be a small woodland animal in the centre of the floor. Piers pokes his tongue out at Lavender. She responds by sticking two fingers up at him when her mother isn't looking.

Mrs Simpson-Stock twists her wristwatch around, frowning at it intensely, the way people do when they haven't got their glasses. 'Flora, honestly! Where is that brother of yours? We can't sit around here all day making polite conversation!'

'Certainly not,' Flora giggles nervously and Mrs Simpson-Stock shoots her a look Medusa would be proud of.

'I'll go get him!' I offer, desperate to get away from Piers' searing political insights. 'I think he might be in the piano room.'

'Yes, well, whatever.' She waves me on. 'But no running in the halls! Understood?'

I nod obediently, hand my glass to Poppy and make my escape.

I wander through the long corridors until I reach the music room, only this time it's empty. I walk out of the French doors onto the lawn and there, sleeping in a lounger, is Eddie.

He's the only person I've ever seen who sleeps with a smile on his face.

His eyes flick open and he smiles even wider. 'I'm late, aren't I?'

I nod. Even this piece of information seems to please him enormously. He stretches his arms out languorously above his head. 'Shall I kidnap you? We can escape down to the local pub instead and finally have our drink. I'll even buy you a packet of crisps,' he offers.

I'm sorely tempted. 'I don't dare. I'm already in trouble. I've been caught running in the house.'

'No!!!' he gasps in mock horror. 'Not actually *in* the house! Were you pulled over?'

'Worse. The dogs got me.'

He winces violently. 'Oooo! *Nasty!* Smelly little vermin.'

'Too right,' I confirm. 'They just went for me.'

He leans in and lowers his voice. 'Rumour has it that she gets a new one every time *He* has an affair. They're really just walking, wagging, weeing versions of her own pent up fury and betrayal.'

'Noooooooooooo waaaaayyy! I didn't even know there was a *He!*'

'Only a rumour, mind you.' He taps the side of his nose.

'About the dogs, you mean?'

'No, about the husband,' he winks. 'See! See what a fount of knowledge I am! How dashing and debonair! And full of malicious gossip! How can you turn me down? How can you miss this enchanting opportunity to be alone with me over a Scotch egg and a game of darts?'

'But I'm dressed like a 'tard.' I point out, completely baffled and thrilled by his persistence. 'And besides, I . . . I just can't . . . they're all waiting in there with glasses of . . . I don't know . . . fruit salad and sugar water. We can't just *leave*.' I sound pathetic even to me.

He surveys me sadly. 'Now, is this the spirit that won the West? Walked on the moon? Bombed the shit out of Vietnam?'

'No,' I admit.

343

'I didn't think so,' he comments gravely. 'What *is* the world coming to! Come on,' he sighs. 'Well, then. Here's to the Voice of Reason. If only she'd mind her own bloody business!' He stands up and offers me his arm with exaggerated formality. 'Shall we?'

I take it and we walk back, through the empty hallways to the lounge. Just before we enter, he gives my hand a little squeeze. 'Just between you and me,' he whispers, 'I think we missed a wonderful chance to really fuck these people off.'

'Just between you and me,' I whisper back, 'I think you're absolutely right.'

And with that we sweep into the lounge and on to one of the most painful meals of my life.

It's not just that there's more cutlery surrounding my plate than I know what to do with, or that the 'Summer Gazpacho' soup turns out to be cold tinned Campbell's cream of tomato with additional chunks of raw onion, or even that a cloud of floating dog hair descends upon every course. No, the most painful aspect is the halting, stilted attempts at conversation, made more tortuous by the rigid social observance of turning first to your right and then to your left to ply your neighbours with half-hearted queries about summer holiday plans and observations on the state of the weather.

The dining room, which possesses all the dark grandeur of an Italian morgue, is surprisingly cold, despite the time of year. I perch, shivering, next to Poppy's deaf grandfather on one side and an increasingly drunk Lavender on the other.

In a show of resolute social decorum, she swings round to face me. 'Going on holiday?' she snaps, her gaze glued to the white wine bottle as it makes its way around the table. (Despite the number of guests, only two bottles of wine appear, one red, one white, and the mounting tension as they're passed from hand to hand is almost unbearable.)

'I don't think so. What about you?'

'Never go anywhere,' she spits bitterly. 'Piers thinks we ought to save money. He's under the impression that we're going to have children, although I can't imagine how.'

Not really sure what to say, I watch as her hands clutch and un-clutch the linen napkin in her lap.

'At least the weather's been nice,' I hear myself bleat.

'Fucking fantastic.' She grasps the bottle eagerly with both hands when it finally arrives, draining the remains into her glass. 'Thank God!' she gasps, her whole body collapsing in relief.

The Summer Gazpacho is followed by a fish course that looks like a medical sample on a Petri dish. Minuscule shreds of smoked salmon are dotted on piles of shredded iceberg lettuce, then completely overwhelmed by generous dollops of mayonnaise and chopped gherkin. In the corner of each plate is a little triangle of dried brown bread with curly corners where the crusts have been cut off. After that, shavings of lamb are accompanied by tinned peas and roasted potatoes, which manage the culinary distinction of being both simultaneously burnt and undercooked. We're rationed to three per plate; they stand, sentinel-like around the grey, cooling slivers of meat. There's an even more violent scramble for the gravy than the wine, with the result that half the table have plates swimming in the stuff while the rest of us are left to negotiate the horror unaided. We poke, push and pull at the lamb until it snaps into rubbery little parcels, that can be chewed for fifteen minutes or more without dissolving.

Poppy's grandfather turns to me and smiles. 'Going on holiday this year?' he shouts.

Having survived a stint at a local community theatre, where the over-sixties used to yell at the actors if they couldn't hear, I fancy myself as a bit of an old hand when it comes to dealing with the hard of hearing. I smile. 'No!' I bellow back. 'I'm not going this year!'

He recoils and straightens his tie defensively. 'You don't have to shout!' he booms. 'I'm not deaf, you know!'

The whole dining room freezes, focusing its collective horror upon me.

'Oh! I'm so sorry!' I flounder. 'I didn't mean to offend you . . .'

'What?' He fiddles with his hearing aid. 'Stop mumbling, girl! Filthy American accent! You people always slur your words! What is it Churchill said, "A people divided by a common language!" Ha, ha, ha! Too right!'

Suddenly a green grape bounces off his head.

'Hey!' he dithers indignantly.

I look in the direction of the grape's flight path, at Eddie, who's staring at his plate and pushing his peas around with incredible intensity. He doesn't dare glance up at me, but looks as though any minute his face might explode.

'What's going on here?' Poppy's grandfather demands. 'Is that a grape? Why don't I have a bloody grape! I fought in the war! I *deserve* to have a grape! Who's hoarding the grapes!'

'Father,' Mrs Simpson-Stock rolls her eyes heavenward, 'no one's hoarding the grapes. They're in the centre of the table. Centre of the table!' she shouts automatically. 'And don't scream, you're upsetting the dogs.'

'Bugger the dogs!' He lurches forward and appropriates a bunch, clutching them protectively to his chest. 'Next bastard to chuck a grape is going to get more than he bargained for!' he threatens, eyeing the assembled party suspiciously. 'Never saw a grape during the war. Or even a tomato. Here.' He passes me half a handful. 'If it weren't for your scruffy doughboys, none of us would even be here, let alone eating grapes!'

'Thank you.' I've obviously risen in his estimation, though why remains a mystery. Perhaps the 'special relationship' between Britain and America only really flourishes under attack.

Pudding is a large, gooey sherry trifle, followed by thimbleful of lukewarm Nescafé. At 9:47, we're finally released. Mrs Simpson-Stock rises and sweeps back into the lounge, escorted by her furry entourage. The rest of us bolt after her, leaving only her father behind, popping grapes into his mouth, savouring the possession rather more than the flavour.

Once in the hallway, Poppy turns to me. 'Fancy a fag on the terrace?' she whispers. Flora opens her cardigan and flashes a hip flask she's tucked into the waistband of her skirt.

'C'mon!' she giggles and the three of us bypass the rest of the party, slipping out into the moonlight.

'Head for the oak!' Poppy hisses and we kick off our shoes and run across the cool, damp lawn to the enormous, ancient oak in the centre. Under its canopy of branches, we throw ourselves down, panting and laughing.

'God! What I wouldn't give for a packet of Smarties!' Flora sighs, passing the flask.

'Ahhh! Or a giant box of Cadbury's chocolate biscuits!' Poppy says.

'So' I laugh, 'I'm not the only one who's starving!'

'As a matter of fact,' Poppy says, 'that's one of the main reasons we come down here. When I've put on a few pounds, I just head home for the weekend. Cheaper than a spa and much, much more effective.'

'Actually, Pops, your mother's true calling may be saving

chronic overeaters,' says Flora. 'A few family dinners at Lower Slaughter and you'll never look at food the same way again. And she could put the dogs on patrol at night to keep clients from escaping to the nearest all night mini mart.'

'There's an all night mini mart?' I say, sitting up.

'Miles away,' they chorus.

'Oh.' I collapse once more. 'Poor Poppy! Please don't tell me you were actually raised on this food!'

Poppy takes a long swig and passes the flask. 'What can I say? I was the only kid at boarding school who thought that school dinners were heaven. I used to weep with joy over boiled cabbage, stringy beef and semolina pudding. Never wanted to go home for the holidays.'

We lean back and gaze up at the stars through the branches of the oak, leaves fluttering in a soft, cool breeze. A chorus of crickets sings gently. And all is quiet except for the sound of our grumbling stomachs.

The next morning, I awake to the thunderous chords of Beethoven's *Hammerklavier*. Eddie's obviously an early riser. However it goes rapidly downhill from there. I do my pre-coffee stagger into the bathroom, only to discover that there's no hot water. Evidently, Mrs Simpson-Stock is a passionate morning person. She rises at dawn, refreshes herself with a quick splash, and can't understand why anyone would require more, taking an unnaturally hostile view of people whose morning routines include such extravagances

as hot baths and showers. Like many British raised during
or just after the war, she regards a bath as the ultimate
luxury and hot water as downright frivolous. If you really
want to inflame her, all you need to do is mention the
disturbing trend amongst the young to wash their hair every
day and she's catapulted into a hysteria second only to her
feelings on animal quarantine laws and the decline of the
Women's Institute.

So I crouched naked in the tub, shivering as I sprayed
myself with icy water from the hand-held shower attach-
ment. It's one way to wake up fast.

I prefer coffee.

Now dressed in the jeans and tee-shirt, I make my way
downstairs in search of food. If there's one meal the English
excel at, it's breakfast. I'm dreaming of silver urns filled
with steaming piles of scrambled eggs, sizzling sausages,
bacon, grilled tomatoes, creamy mushrooms and piles of
warm toast. The dining room, however, is completely
empty. Not a sausage in sight. I wander tentatively into the
kitchen, where I find an enormous woman wading through
piles of washing up.

'Hello?' I venture. Where did all these plates come from?

'Hello, to you.' She doesn't bother to turn around.

'Ah, so, what do people do around here for breakfast?'
I wonder aloud.

'They turn up on time,' she says brusquely. 'Need to be
down here by eight am at the latest.'

'Oh.' I spot the remains of crispy bacon and fluffy eggs being scraped into the bin.

'There's cereal on the table and some milk in the fridge,' she dismisses me.

And that is that.

I eat and make my way into the music room.

'Hey!' I shout to Eddie, who's pounding away.

'Morning!' he shouts back, not slowing his pace.

'Where is everyone?' I yell.

'Out killing things! Louise! Just listen! This theme is the best!'

'Killing things?' I echo.

'It's what they do in the country to have fun,' he beams. 'You know, chase 'em, shoot 'em, fish 'em, trap 'em . . . otherwise known as the joys of country life.' He pauses a moment, seeing I'm at a bit of a loss. 'Not everyone's out butchering the wildlife. I think Flora and Poppy are sunning themselves in the garden. At least, that's what they're calling it. More likely they've passed out trying to recover from a couple of very mysterious hangovers.'

'I'd better join them, if only to offer them my sympathy.' I don't want to disturb him further. 'Thanks, Eddie.'

'Or,' he stops and looks up at me, 'we could always take a walk.'

'Are you sure?' Do I sound too delighted?

'Absolutely,' he says. 'There's only so much of me that Beethoven can take in a day and I think he's had it up to here.'

'Then I'd love to,' I agree, 'only, I'm warning you, I'm not much of an outdoors person.'

'You'll be fine,' he assures me. 'Only, I don't suppose you have a pair of Wellingtons, do you? It's just you never know what you're going to walk into out there.'

'Well, no.' I think of the pair I'd borrowed, comfortably installed in my office, next to my dinner dress, fresh tee-shirts and clean knickers.

'What a relief!' he grins. 'There's a certain type of girl who owns her own Wellingtons and I'm glad you're not it!'

'And what type of girl is that?'

'The same type of girl who always has a clean hankie, the right bus fare, and matching socks. A girl who owns her own Wellingtons is afraid of looking ridiculous, afraid of getting mud on her feet and that's a terrible thing.'

'But you said we needed them!'

'Absolutely – it's perfectly foul out there, Louise!' He stands at the French doors, hand shading his eyes: a dauntless explorer looking towards the woodland beyond the lawn. 'But just because we need them, doesn't mean we *want* them. We shall use them under protest, under duress, and with the complete understanding that we welcome mud, wouldn't be caught dead using a clean hankie when we have a perfectly good shirtsleeve, and would catch a cab over the bus every time. In short, with our integrity intact.'

'Our integrity?'

'Yup, our integrity demands that we have boots but recoils at them being ours.' He's leading me down a corridor I haven't seen before.

'That's a bit tenuous,' I trip along, laughing beside him. 'Amusing, but you're not making sense.'

'There you go again! Sense, sense, sense! What is this obsession with sense! Nothing of great beauty in this world makes sense! Now, "Let us go then, you and I,"'

He quotes Eliot and I join in '". . . when the evening is spread out against the sky like a patient etherised upon a table."'

We arrive at the boot room. It's a kind of giant closet filled from top to bottom with mouldy pairs of mismatched Wellingtons in all conceivable colours and sizes. Along the walls, wooden pegs hold row after row of waxed Barbour coats; my eyes water from the stench of the waxed coating.

'My God, Eddie! How can people wear those things!' I gasp, pinching my nose. 'I can't even get anywhere near them!'

'Why, the Barbour waxed jacket is the very emblem of English country life!' he proclaims, as he chucks various rejects across the room. 'They repel not only water, but also any form of human contact. Perfect!'

We find one black and one green welly for him and two left footed red wellies for me. It's not easy to walk with two left feet; there's a distinct tendency to move in a circle.

Only by turning my right foot outward, at a 90-degree angle do I manage to make any progress at all.

I start to sulk.

'*Courage, mon amour!*' he cries. 'Remember our integrity!'

'I've got two left feet,' I remind him. 'You haven't got two left feet!'

He gives me one of his fetching, quirky looks. (Already I'm building a file of his expressions to go over when I'm not with him.) '"You grow old, you grow old, you shall wear the bottoms of your trousers rolled."'

I stick my tongue out at him.

We tramp (or rather he tramps, I limp) across the lawn until we come to a grassy lane leading to the riverbank.

'Smell that air!' Eddie sighs.

Someone has been riding that morning and the air smells of horse manure.

'Look at that view!' he cries.

We stop for a moment, look up, and then continue to shuffle along.

'Feel the sun on your face!' he beams exuberantly.

We both turn our faces upwards and walk straight into a cloud of midges. We dodge the manure. We duck the midges. We run off the trail to avoid the midges but the horses have been there too. Both midges and manure are remarkably adhesive.

Piers, Lavender's self-proclaimed better half, is fishing by the river's edge. Somehow he's managed to bag the only matching pair of Wellingtons, has exchanged his brilliant canary yellow corduroys for moleskin trousers and is even sporting a tweed fishing cap. It's all very Constable-ish. He clearly shops at a store with a 'What to Wear in the Country' section. He waves a be-Barboured arm, signalling for us to be quiet. This is what it's all about: a man, a stream, a smelly coat. A moment of almost overwhelming pastoral beauty. Moments later, he reels in a fish and begins clubbing it to death with a small leather bat he keeps in his pocket.

I had no idea that fish screamed but they do.

'Well, that was lovely. Just lovely,' Eddie says. 'Shall we go back?'

'Yes, why don't we,' I agree.

Fifteen minutes of rural bliss is enough for anyone.

Back at the house we peel off our boots and flop down on the grass. Lunch seems miles away. On the lawn, a heated game of croquet is going on between Mrs Simpson-Stock, her father and Lavender. The game is considerably hampered by the participation of the dogs chasing after each ball and who the elderly man regards as a free target, whacking his mallet around indiscriminately and with some effect. They in turn feel free to savage his leg. Under the old oak, the dozing figures of Poppy and Flora are pretty much where I left them the night before.

'Now what should we do?' I ask, pulling lazily at a blade of grass.

'Let's take a nap,' he suggests.

And that's what we do. He takes off his jumper, bunches it up in a ball and slips it under our heads. Side by side, our eyes closed, we bask in the warm heat of the sun. After a while, I'm aware of the sound of Eddie gently snoring next to me. And it's a wonderful sound; a soft, whistly little sigh of a snore. I open one eye to see if he's still smiling, and he is.

I smile too and close my eyes again.

How strange! I think, just as I'm dozing off. Why is it that I can sleep next to Eddie and yet I needed a bed the size of a football pitch to sleep with my husband? And as I snuggle closer to him, he turns and throws an arm over me. It must be the country air, I conclude, dreamily. It obviously has an intoxicating effect.

And that's how I learnt that the great secret of surviving a country weekend isn't the right clothes or the right equipment or even an enormous secret stash of food. It does, however, have everything to do with the company you keep.

The next evening, Poppy, Flora and I drive back to London. Sitting in the back seat, I stare out of the window at the patches of green countryside as they flash by. I feel strangely melancholic and agitated. I should be overjoyed to be returning to civilization but I'm not.

'So.' Flora looks at me significantly in the rear-view mirror. 'You and Eddie were thick as thieves. You really like him, don't you?'

'*No way!*' Poppy laughs. 'Oh, he's a cute kid but too young for you! I mean, he's twenty-four and still doesn't have a proper job! All he cares about is his music. You can't be serious, Louise!'

'I know that. She's just teasing me, Poppy.' I'm longing to change the subject. 'Hey, why don't we turn on the radio?'

'Sure.' Flora fiddles with the dial. I catch her eye in the mirror and she smiles.

No, I can't be serious, I think, as we beetle down the motorway. Everything Poppy says is absolutely true.

So why do I feel so miserable?

Two days later, I arrive at work to find three white roses on my desk along with a note from Eddie.

'*You still owe me a drink,*' it says.

A moment later, my phone rings. It's him.

'Hello, Louise?' There's the sound of crowds, train announcements. 'Can you hear me?'

'Yes, yes where are you?'

'I'm at Waterloo. I'm about to catch the train to Paris in a few minutes. Did you get my flowers?'

'Yes, they're gorgeous! I didn't know that you were leaving today . . . Eddie . . . can you hear me?' The line fades, his voice crackling inaudibly. 'Eddie?'

'I was saying, I wanted to buy you more, a whole desk full of roses! Next time, Louise! When I get back we'll . . .' and the line goes dead.

I put the roses in a glass on my desk. When they start to wilt, I dry them upside down. And when the petals fall, I collect them and keep them in an envelope.

A month goes by.

I throw the envelope away.

After all, I can't be serious.

X

Xmas

Christmas is a very special occasion. If there's one time during the year when you ought to feel good, affectionate, kind-hearted, thoughtful, and generous, it is certainly at Christmas.

It is only natural to harmonize your physical appearance with these beautiful moral qualities and this for the average woman means a new dress, a lovely hairdo, and perhaps a beauty treatment. According to the type of Christmas party you may be invited to attend, the ideal costume is a long or short evening dress, and, without going so far as trying to out-sparkle the Christmas tree, it is perfectly appropriate for you to make a special effort to create a splendid appearance.

The point to remember is that this is a very special evening, and it merits the honour of a special manner of dress.

'Are you sure you're going to be all right on your own?' Col is standing by the front door with his suitcase in one hand and his coat in the other.

'I'll be fine,' I say. 'It's only for a couple of days.'

'But it's Christmas. It isn't just a couple of normal days. It's a couple of Christmas days!' he frets.

'I'll be all right,' I assure him.

A car horn sounds outside and Ria emerges from her bedroom, dragging a bulging overnight case and two large shopping bags full of carefully wrapped presents.

'The cab's here, Col, we've got to go! Are you sure you're going to be all right, Louise? It's not too late to come to Dorset with me – my family would love to have you. Honestly, the more the merrier.' Ria hates travelling and has accelerated into a total panic. I watch as she buttons her coat up wrong, puts her hat on backwards, and drops her gloves. 'My keys! I can't find my keys! Damn it, Col! The meter's running! We'll miss the train and I'll be locked out of the house when I get home!'

'Have you checked your pockets?'

'Oh. Yes. Here they are. Now, the meter's running. Col!'

'Darling, it's a minicab. It hasn't got a meter.' He gives me a hug. 'Goodbye, honey, take care. Don't forget to put the alarm on and call if you get lonely. The numbers are by the phone. I still feel dreadful about leaving you but I'd better get this one to the train station before she explodes with anxiety.'

I kiss Ria on the forehead and turn her hat the right way round. 'Travel well, sweetheart, and Merry Christmas.'

'I'm going to call you!' she shouts as she hauls her luggage and shopping bags down the steps. 'I'm going to check in with you every hour on the hour to make sure you don't do anything silly!'

I watch as they pile into the cab. They wave. I wave. Even the cab driver waves. And a moment later, they pull away into the dull mist of the freezing morning air and are gone. I close the door and collapse against it. Alone at last!

Moments like these are so rare when you have flatmates. And, much as you love them, there's still nothing like the wonderful, luxurious sense of freedom that descends when you're by yourself. I walk into the living room, switch on the Christmas tree lights and pour myself another cup of tea. Then I snuggle down on the sofa and contemplate my liberty.

It's December 23, 8:32 am. Very cold, but dry. Both Colin and Ria have now officially gone home for the holidays – Colin to meet Andy's parents for the first time in their home in High Wycombe and Ria to her parents' cottage in Dorset. Being recently divorced and virtually penniless, a trip to the States during peak rate time is off the cards for me. But no worries. This is my first Christmas alone and I feel oddly excited. I sip my tea and allow myself to become mesmerized by the lights on the tree. I could do anything, absolutely anything. I can listen to my own music, watch what I want to on TV, leave the washing up stewing in the sink for days. I have all the time in the world.

Three hours later I'm in the office.

'What are you doing here?' Flora demands. 'You're the lucky one, remember? The one who gets to have Christmas off.' She's making paper chains out of old programmes and has glue in her hair.

'Oh nothing,' I lie. I don't want to tell her I have nothing to do and so end up hanging out at work on my day off. 'I was just passing and I thought I'd pop in and check my e-mail. Need a hand?' I can't remember the last time I made a paper chain. As a matter of fact, I don't think I've ever made a paper chain, but she looks like she's having fun and it's surprising how quickly the anticipated joys of leaving your washing up in the sink can pall.

'Sure.' She passes me a pile of strips and some glue. 'Wow. If I were you, I wouldn't be anywhere near this place. I'd be out doing my Christmas shopping. I haven't done any and I don't know when I'm going to find the time. I've promised to take my mother, my sister, and her two little girls to see the *Nutcracker* tonight, I've got a charity ball to go to tomorrow night . . . I might as well shoot myself!'

'But instead you're making paper chains.'

She looks at me. 'Louise, I take my job very seriously. God forbid I should be skiving when I have an obligation to maintain office morale and to spread goodwill via the ancient art of paper chain making. Or paper chain *fashioning*, as we skilled artisans like to call it. Do you realize how many holiday suicide attempts could be avoided by the simple addition of a paper chain to the depressed person's surroundings? At least five, I should think. Which is why I'm hanging them up around here.'

'So, that's you, me, Poppy and what, two moody bystanders?'

'Face it, no one ever visits our department. We'd have to lure a couple of depressives up here.'

'Or we could invite Crispin and Terrance from Finance.'

We paste in silence for a moment.

'A charity ball, eh? Sounds very grand!'

She shifts uncomfortably. 'Well, not really a ball . . . more like an *event*.'

'Could you be more cryptic? My Pritt Stick's dead.'

She hands me hers. 'The use of the Pritt Stick marks the pro from the amateur every time.'

'OK, you can stop doing that now.'

'Just one more joke.'

'No.'

'I *sooooo* don't want to go,' she moans. 'I've been bullied into the whole thing by Poppy, who started on about the rampant commercialism of Christmas last February until I couldn't stand it any more and has been practically forcing me, by the sheer multitude of her arguments, to take rash and drastic action!'

'Calm down, girl!'

'You don't understand! She sang "Do They Know It's Christmas?" to me until I snapped! She used to hobble around the office pretending to be Tiny Tim and pasted Post-its to my lunch box saying things like, "Feed me!" and "Don't worry . . . I'll survive . . . somehow!"'

'Flora, you're hyperventilating! What has she made you do?'

'I said I'd go with her to feed the homeless.' She hangs her head in shame.

'But that's admirable,' I assure her.

'It would be, except I'd give my right arm not to go. I am evil! I am!' Her lower lip trembles and she covers her face with her hands.

I eye her suspiciously. 'Have you been watching re-runs of Dallas again?'

She peers at me between two of her fingers. 'Maybe just a little bit.'

'Anyway, it will be fun if the two of you go,' I point out, trying to paste a paper strip around my wrist as a makeshift bracelet.

'Ahh! But that's the problem! Poppy's had to go home now for the funeral.'

The paper strip snaps off my wrist and flies across the room. 'Funeral? My God, what happened?'

'One of her mother's dogs died at the weekend. Poppy says natural causes but her mother's convinced it was murder. You remember Albert, the terrier with the overbite and the bladder infection? Evidently the old man's been having a go at him lately because he used to pee in his slippers.' She sighs. 'But that's all over now.'

I stare at her. 'They're having a funeral for the dog?'

She nods. 'Open casket. I was going to send a wreath, if you want to go halves.'

The English and their dogs share a bond that foreigners like myself can only marvel at. I decide to stick to more familiar ground.

'So you have to go on your own to feed the homeless.' I try to draw her back to the subject.

She glances at me sideways. 'That is, unless you don't have anything better to do?'

'You are evil.' I chuck a paperclip at her head.

'Come on, Louise! It will be fun, I promise! And it's only around the corner in the basement of St Martin-in-the-Fields. We'd be the early shift, from eight 'til ten and then you'd have the whole rest of the evening to yourself . . . pleeeeeeeease!'

I think about the washing up in the sink at home. What else have I got to do?

'Sure.'

She squeals with delight and throws her arms around me. 'You're a perfect angel! Which reminds me, every year the volunteers have a costume competition. It has to be seasonal but I thought we could go as angels. The card shop across the road is selling little silver plastic angel wings you slip over your shoulders with matching tiaras and I've got some old white nightgowns we can throw over our jeans.'

'Perfect. Why don't you go and buy some wings. And while you're at it, make a dent in that Christmas shopping of yours. I'll hold the fort till you get back.' I wave my Pritt Stick as if it were a magic wand. 'Now go and be free!'

There's nothing like a little charity to make a girl feel warm and fuzzy all over.

We meet the next evening at the opera house and change into our makeshift angel outfits in the loo, slipping the faded flannel nighties over our jeans and donning our plastic tiaras and wings. The mood's festive as we make our way down Long Acre towards Trafalgar Square. It's raining rather than snowing and sharing an umbrella, we shuffle in time with our arms wrapped around each other's waists. We arrive in the basement of the church to find it buzzing with activity. Elves are dishing out turkey dinners, reindeer pass out bowls of soup, partridges with or without pear trees are busy slicing up thick helpings of Christmas pudding. We're quickly assigned to coffee and tea duty by the Ghost of Christmas Present, a man named Reg in an impressive crimson velvet robe and ginger beard.

For the next two hours we don't stop. We make countless pots of tea and coffee, refill cups, sing Christmas carols, and wash stacks of dishes. We help unload the seemingly endless supply of provisions that flood in from local businesses: deliveries of sandwiches, fresh fruit and veg, whole turkeys, clothing, blankets, tinned goods, cigarettes and shoes. Stacking them up in tall piles, they're quickly removed and reorganized by a whole other army of volunteers before being distributed, sometimes to kitchens in less central parts of London where they're more desperately needed. People wander in off the street, curious about all the activity and end up staying to help: groups of students, tourists, and those who aren't homeless but somehow displaced. The way I feel. And for a couple of hours we're part of something.

I'm aware of a feeling of incredible abundance – not just of supplies, but of energy, joy, and hope. As I rush to fill cup after cup, smiling and laughing with people I don't even normally make eye contact with in the street, I realize I'm happy. This is the very stuff of happiness and yet it's always eluded me in the past.

Suddenly, amidst a sea of unshaven faces, a familiar smile appears.

'So, you think you can just sleep with me and then bugger off without a trace!' Eddie grins. 'Cup of tea, please while you're at it. Chop, chop! My audience is waiting!'

He's wearing a tea towel on his head and has a large faded blue travel rug wrapped around his body.

'Eddie!' I'm conscious of the eyes upon me, especially one giggling old grandpa in the corner, who's been trying unsuccessfully to seduce me all night. 'Firstly, what are you doing here? I thought you were in Paris. And secondly, what are you wearing?'

'We're wearing costumes, right? Well, I'm the Baby Jesus and these are my swaddling clothes.'

'You've got a tea towel on your head. Wait a minute, that's our tea towel! Eddie, you've nicked our tea towel!'

He pulls himself upright. 'Someone of my class doesn't nick a tea towel, he embezzles it. But you're in luck. I'm willing to rent it out to you for a small fee. Though you may have to part with your halo.'

I blush. 'How long have you been back? And will that be one or two sugars?' I ask, chucking a couple of cubes at him.

'NO FOOD FIGHTS!' Reg booms across the hall.

Eddie leans across the counter and looks round furtively. 'Look, I'm a Baby Jesus, you're obviously an angel, what you say we go lie down in a manger?'

'He he he!' the old grandpa giggles.

'My thoughts exactly,' Eddie grins.

I look into his enormous, smiling black eyes. 'Eddie!' I'm at a complete loss for words.

'Yes, my angel?' he whispers softly.

'Hey! I thought you were here to play the piano!' Reg shouts.

'As I said, my audience awaits me!' He steps aside to let the queue flow again and disappears into the crowd.

Flora leans over. 'I probably shouldn't tell you this, but he was completely uninterested in volunteering tonight until he heard that you were coming along. I think he really likes you, Louise. You have been warned!'

I'm blushing again. 'But Flora, when did he get back? And what could he possibly want with an old fart like me?'

'He got back yesterday, with what looks like four months of dirty laundry, and I don't even want to *think* about what he wants to do with you!'

My heart's racing. 'But I'm *nine years* older than he is!'

'He likes older women, Louise.'

'Gee, thanks.' I've never had the dubious pleasure of thinking of myself as an older woman before. I'm not sure I like it.

'Well,' she says, mopping up a warm puddle of spilt tea, 'if you don't like him, fair enough. But honestly, I haven't seen him this excited since Lara.'

'Lara?' An unexpected wave of jealousy overtakes me. 'Who's Lara?'

She smiles slyly. 'Just some cello player who broke his heart last spring.'

'Oh,' I imagine a beautiful, talented, Jacqueline du Pré lookalike.

'Bit of cow, if you ask me.' She squeezes her rag out into the sink.

I look across the room. Eddie's pulling a chair up to an old upright piano in the corner. Then the sound of ragtime jazz fills the hall, as infectious and buoyant as Eddie himself.

When the ten o'clock shift arrives, Reg holds up a hand to silence the room. 'Hey! Quiet, everyone! Thank you! It's around this time that we take a minute and vote on the best costume!'

There's a generous cheer.

'Now everyone line up and when I put my hand over your head, we'll let the audience decide!'

The volunteers form a misshapen, unruly line and Reg works his way down. Eddie plays snatches of appropriate carols for each contestant and when Reg gets to Flora and me, he plays 'There Must Be an Angel' by the Eurythmics.

In the end it's Reg himself who wins; with his flowing red velvet robe and booming laugh he's the perfect Ghost of Christmas Present. But we give him a good run for his money.

'Well, I guess that's it,' Flora sighs, as we emerge from the basement of St Martin's. 'We're officially good people now.'

'What do you say I buy you two lovely ladies a drink?' Eddie wraps an arm around each of our necks.

'Like this?' I say. 'It may be Christmas Eve but not even an angel is going to get served looking like this!'

'But you forget, I *am* the Baby Jesus. I have connections! Taxi!' He hails a cab. 'To the Ritz, my good man!'

'No, Eddie! We can't! Not the Ritz!' I protest. 'Not like *this*!'

Flora giggles. 'Chill out, Louise. It'll be fun!'

'No, no. Not for me. I think I'll just bug out and go home. To tell the truth, I'm pretty tired.'

'I'll take off my swaddling clothes if you come.' Eddie pulls me towards the open cab door. 'As a matter of fact, I'll take off all my clothes if you come!'

Suddenly I'm nervous, out of my depth. What does this handsome, talented, young man want with me anyway? Why is he so keen? I have the sudden compulsion to run away and escape before I can destroy whatever mistaken, wonderful delusions he still harbours about my character.

'Look! There's a night bus! If I run I might catch it! Good night and Merry Christmas!' I give them each a swift peck on the cheek and begin running across Trafalgar Square, my plastic wings flapping in the wind.

'Wait a minute!' Eddie runs after me, which isn't easy wrapped in a large woolly blanket. He catches my hand. 'I'm having a get-together next weekend on my boat. Will you come?'

'Your *boat*?' I don't know what to say.

The bus lumbers forward, groaning under the weight of a particularly festive top deck.

He holds my hand tighter. 'Please come, Louise, and don't run off now; we can drive you home if you like.'

My stomach contracts with fear. I like him. I like him more than I should. That's the trouble.

The bus grinds to a halt and starts to fill up. 'No, please

don't worry . . . it's just here!' I look into his eyes. 'Happy Christmas, Eddie, you make a wonderful Baby Jesus . . . you make a wonderful . . . anything!'

'Does that mean you'll come?' he persists.

The conductor rings the bell and the bus heaves away from the kerb. I pull my hand out of his and race to jump aboard. 'I'll see . . . I'll speak to Flora and let you know! Happy Christmas!' I shout.

And as the bus lurches forward down Whitehall, I turn back to see him standing forlornly in the middle of Trafalgar Square, the tea towel still on his head.

I stumble up to the top deck and find a seat next to a man wearing a red paper Christmas cracker hat, who's passed out and drooling with his head against the window. I yank the halo off my head and wriggle out of the wings. Everyone's yelling, laughing, shouting into their mobiles.

We trundle past Big Ben, the Houses of Parliament, and then the street where I lived for so many years with my ex-husband. I wonder what he's doing and if the place still looks the same. Shall I get off at the next stop and see? What would he do now if I were to show up on his doorstep dressed in an old nightgown? Would he even recognize me? Or would I be as indistinguishable to him as he had been to me that night in the theatre?

The next stop comes and goes. But I don't get off. Not even for a look. The bus crosses the bridge into Lambeth and the moment is gone.

When I get home, I run a bath and put on a CD of Ria's, Chopin ballades that remind me of Eddie. I heat some soup on the stove and sit at the table, dipping water biscuits into my cream of tomato and staring at the lights on the Christmas tree.

It's a silent night.

And I think about how I'd come all this way to be sitting here, eating soup alone on Christmas Eve and how I didn't even want to get off the bus and about the people at St Martin's and I wonder what Reg does when he isn't being the Ghost of Christmas Present and if I'd recognize him if I passed him on the street and about Flora and Eddie and if they went to the Ritz and were they there right now and then I think about Oliver Wendt and how certain I'd been that he was the man for me and about the way he looked in the back of the cab when it drove away and about my job and how frightened I'd been and how wrong I was about everyone and then about Colin and Ria, at home, celebrating Christmas with their families and about our funny little home here in London.

And an unexpected wave of happiness washes over me.

It's been worth it.

It's all been worth it. To be sitting right here, right now. Alone.

And that night, I slept in heavenly peace.

Υ

Yachting

The only thing that should float in the wind on board a yacht are the ship's colours. A dress or skirt that does the same would be quite out of place. Consequently, a simple, even slightly masculine style of clothing is most advisable. Adventures on the high seas only happen rarely in one's life, so seize the opportunity. Be quick to discard your evening gowns and high-heeled shoes but keep your sense of humour and enter into the spirit of things by remaining, above all, a good crew member and a good sport.

Now is your chance to show everyone that you are not afraid to be seen without make-up, that you never leave a trail of disorder in your wake, that you have a wonderfully even disposition, and that your elegance is based on utter simplicity. If this is the case (and if you are not prone to seasickness and know how to swim), you will surely have the most wonderful time of your life.

The next week, when I come into work, there's a card waiting for me on my desk.

YOU ARE CORDIALLY INVITED TO EDWARD JAMES' BOAT CHRISTENING PARTY

2PM THIS SATURDAY AT THE CHELSEA PIER

R.S.V.P. 07771283112

Flora and Poppy giggle as I prop it up against the front of my computer.

'Are you guys going to this shindig?' I ask.

'We weren't invited,' Poppy says. And they giggle again.

That night when I come home, I ring Ria, who's still in Dorset.

'What should I do?'

'What do you want to do?'

'I don't know. It's just . . . he's so young. My God! *Twenty-four!* What's he doing asking me out anyway?'

'Do you really think that's any of your business? After all, he's an adult. You've got to trust that he knows his own mind. And why do you think age matters that much anyway? Look at Colin and Andy.'

I think a moment. 'I guess I always imagined the man should be older . . . older and preferably not quite so attrac-tive. If I'm honest, I want to be the young attractive one, the one in control. I mean, what future could it possibly have and why would I even bother to get involved now if I knew there couldn't be any future? Ria, when he's thirty-four, I'm going to be *forty-three*! He'll be young and lithe and I'll be fumbling about for my HRT!'

'Slow down, cowboy. You keep repeating all these numbers like they mean something. Let's start at the beginning. Do you like him?'

I smile; I can't even think about Eddie without smiling. 'Oh, he's brilliant! Really bright, *so* talented and the best thing about him is his incredible enthusiasm! Everything with him is an adventure. And the way he plays the piano, Ria – you'd love him!'

I hear her laughing on the other end of the line. 'Listen to yourself, Louise! Why don't you just focus on that for the time being and go along and see what happens?'

I hang up, still agitated, and decide to get a second opinion. Col is lying on the couch, flipping through a body building magazine called *Pump*. (At least, I hope it's a body building magazine.) I fling myself into an armchair.

'Col, what would you do if you were me?'

'Fuck him, of course. He sounds gorgeous!'

'Col! No, really! What would you do?'

He looks at me in all seriousness. 'Fuck him. Why do you think I'm joking?'

God, gay men. Or rather, men. Period.

'But what if I get involved and then he dumps me for a younger woman?'

He raises an eyebrow. 'And . . . ?'

'Damn it, Col! I'd be *devastated*!'

'But that's not a reason to duck out of life, sweetie. So, you'd be hurt. Big deal. That's the chance we all take. What's the point in being alive at all if you're so afraid of pain that you can't appreciate the rare gems when they do come along?' He closes the magazine for a moment. 'We all want to protect ourselves but the bottom line is: we can't. It's as simple as that. You can either enjoy this wonderful, exciting young man for who and what he is or you can hide away, waiting for some dull, average, shmuck to emerge that will make you feel safe.' He starts to laugh. 'Remember Oliver Wendt?'

'You are so cruel! And there's nothing wrong with wanting to feel safe . . . is there?'

'My darling, there's *nothing* safe about love!'

'Well, I don't know about love.' I blush. 'It's a bit early for that.'

He smiles. 'Yes, well, whatever. Take it from me, Ouise, if you don't take a chance, you'll regret it for the rest of your life.'

I spend the rest of the week in a daze, staring at the invitation, wondering how I should respond.

A boat christening party. I don't like boats. And I've always dreaded the sea. I hate the thought of being stranded with nothing but water around me and losing sight of the shore.

377

Besides, what does a girl wear on a boat in the dead of winter?

'It'll be cold,' Ria warns. 'I'd go for something warm, like a big fisherman's type jumper and a navy peacoat.'

'This is not a look I'm loving,' I grimace. 'You'll be telling me I need a skipper's hat any minute now.'

'Well, no . . . but a cute little woolly hat and maybe a thick pair of wool trousers wouldn't go amiss.'

'How am I supposed to seduce anyone looking like an extra from *Peter Grimes*?'

She shrugs her shoulders. 'Out on the water, it's going to be freezing. I'd forego trying to seduce anyone and settle for being a good sport.'

Being a good sport. There's that phrase again, first from Madame Dariaux and now from Ria. It echoes round my head. A good sport knows their place, accepts things at face value, loses gracefully, keeps trying, doesn't sulk or take their toys and run home. A good sport is not the same as a winner.

Do I have the courage to be a good sport in love? Or is it best just not to play at all?

On Thursday, I finally ring the number on the card.

'Hello, Eddie?'

'Hello, Louise.'

'It's Louise.'

'I know,' he says.

'I just thought I'd ring to say I'd very much like to come

to your party.' My hands are shaking. Does my voice sound all right?

'Brilliant!' I can hear the smile on his face. 'Oh, you've made my day! Do you want me to pick you up or anything?'

'Oh no!' Keep cool, I tell myself. 'You're the host, after all, and there'll be masses to do. I'll meet you on the pier like everyone else. But how will I know which boat is yours?'

'Oh, you'll know,' he laughs. 'It's not terribly big, it's red and it's called the *Hammerklavier*.'

I hang up. Red's an awfully strange colour for a yacht.

It's Saturday; I'm bundled into a pair of black trousers and a thick cream jumper I borrowed from Colin. Incredibly chunky but also extremely warm. My hair's tied back into a long pony tail; make-up's minimal, in case the wind makes my eyes water. Hardly my idea of a woman embarking on a first date. I look completely nondescript and anonymous. I panic and am about to exit in a pair of black, kitten heel ankle boots when Ria stops me at the door.

'You can't wear heels on the deck of a boat,' she explains. 'They'll ruin it.'

She sends me back to my room like an errant child. I emerge in a pair of old trainers, put on my woolly cap and coat, and she sends me off again looking more like the Michelin Man than a chic guest at a yacht party.

It's a stunning clear day, bright with a high wind. I stop

by Woolworth's and buy a copy of *Titanic* and then pick up a bottle of vintage champagne. At ten past two, I'm wandering around Chelsea Pier searching for a red yacht, hoping I'm not going to be the oldest person there.

I am.

I find the *Hammerklavier* wedged neatly between two gigantic sun cruisers and probably wouldn't have noticed it at all if the sound of piano music hadn't caught my attention first. I look down and there it is, all fifty feet of its slender deck, decorated with Christmas lights and tiny British flags: Eddie's canal boat. There doesn't seem to be a lot of activity; I check my watch again. Maybe I'm early. There aren't any doorbells on canal boats, or at least none that I can see, so I call out and after shouting his name at the top of my lungs for several minutes, the piano playing stops and Eddie surfaces on deck. He's wearing a beautifully tailored navy suit and brilliant pink silk tie.

'You came! You look absolutely stunning!' he says.

All I can do is laugh. 'I know for a fact that I don't. I don't know how, but I seem to have misunderstood your invitation. As you can see, I'm dressed for a voyage out on the high seas!'

'Would that please you?' He reaches out his hand.

'I'm not certain, really. I'm a little afraid of the water. And I'm sorry I'm here so early. Maybe I can help you set up for the other guests.'

'Ah, well. Yes.' He smiles and looks away. 'That's a bit of a point. But why don't you step inside out of the cold.' I take his hand, climbing down into the warm hull of the boat.

Inside it's exactly like a narrow little house. There's a galley kitchen which leads into a bright, surprisingly generous living room and a door beyond which (I assume) goes through to a bedroom at the front. The living room is charming. Its walls are lined with books and stacks upon stacks of sheet music. Against one wall there's an upright piano, piled with even more music. The floors are layered with worn Oriental carpets. More of his vast collection of CDs are stacked against the windowsill, massed on top of books, heaped in piles on every conceivable surface. The only clear area to be found in the whole room is a small, round mahogany table. There, elegantly arranged, is a luncheon set for two.

'Oh!' I stare at the table in surprise. 'Is that for me? For us, I mean.'

He smiles shyly. 'If you'll stay.'

I can't quite get my head around what's happening. 'So, no one else is coming to your party?'

'No, Louise. Just you. I hope you don't mind.'

'I see.' I sit down on the arm of the sofa. 'Just me.'

He nods.

I don't want to say it, but I feel I have to. I look down at my hands, at the space where my wedding band used to be. 'Eddie, you do know how old I am, don't you? I'm thirty-three. That's nine years older than you are.'

'Isn't that brilliant?' He smiles.

'But that's not all; I'm divorced. I haven't dated in years. I'm . . . I'm from Pittsburgh! I'm sorry if I in any way misled you into thinking that I was younger or . . . I don't know . . . different from how I am. You're an amazing person and I admire you so, so much.'

He stops me there. 'Are you breaking up with me? We haven't even gone out yet.'

In the pit of my stomach a hollow, hopeless loneliness begins to grow, a pounding, dull familiar feeling.

'No, I didn't mean to sound so arrogant. It's just that . . . I'm a little confused as to why you would even want to do a thing like this. I mean, I don't know who or what you think I am but I'm not . . . I'm . . .' My voice starts to falter. 'It's just . . . I'm . . . potato.'

He blinks at me. 'I'm sorry; did you just say you were a potato?'

I nod. I cannot do this; suddenly I'm back in the Twentieth Century Galleries, a bloated, sexless woman in her early thirties, dressed in a shapeless grey dress, staring longingly at a black and white world of unimaginable beauty and glamour. Eddie is more beautiful, more talented, more elegant than all the famous faces combined.

My throat is tight and my eyes stinging, suddenly welling up with tears. 'Potato, Eddie, potato!'

There are no elegant potatoes.

'Take it easy, Louise.' He moves closer. 'What does that mean . . . what's potato?'

I stand up, desperate to leave. 'Potato means I can't do this. Potato means . . . I have to get out of here, that I'm sorry . . . I've got to go . . .'

He wraps his arms around me. 'Is this a Pittsburgh thing? Come on, take it easy. There, there,' he whispers.

He smells of flowers and warmth, just like he did the day we napped in each other's arms, and everything inside me melts with an overwhelming longing to lose myself, to fall deeper and deeper into his embrace.

But it's too much.

You're being foolish, the voice in my head says over and over. This is wrong. And suddenly I'm drowning, from the inside out. I've lost sight of the shore and there's nothing but water on every side. I panic and push him away.

'I'm sorry, Eddie, really I am.' I bolt past him and clamber back to the safety of dry land.

He doesn't follow me.

And it isn't until I'm sitting in the back of the cab, crying, that I realize I'm still holding the video and the champagne.

Colin and Ria are out when I get home. But a package has arrived for me from the States and is sitting on the dining room table.

It's a belated Christmas present from my mother. Neatly wrapped in gold paper and tied with a white silk bow. She's slipped a little card under the ribbon:

> Hey Kiddo,
> Found this in the loft the other day and thought of you.
> Do you remember?
> You always did have a style all your own!
> You have a lot of courage, Louise. I've always been proud of that.
> Don't give up now. The best is yet to come.
> Love you. XXX Mom

I unwrap it.

And there, carefully preserved in layers of translucent tissue paper, is the cream-coloured marabou jacket she bought me when I was twelve.

Z

Zips

Zips are the beginning and the end. Every evening begins with a wife pleading for her husband to zip her up, which he does in a frustrated hurry. However, if she is lucky and smart, that same evening will end with him impatient to unzip her again!

'Eddie! Hello! Eddie!'

It's dark now and the wind is up, forming the water into choppy black waves that slap against the side of the boat. A light is on inside but there's no music playing. Perhaps he's gone out, maybe even with someone else, and I'm too late.

'Eddie, are you in there? *Eddie!*'

But there's no reply. It occurs to me that he might even be in there, able to hear me, but just not willing to speak to me. Ever again.

I've ruined it.

There's nothing left for me to do. I turn and make my way back along the pier, head bent against the tremendous wind, struggling to press forward against the invisible hands that force me back. Everywhere moorings are straining, lamps and tackle swinging to and fro as if at any moment they might be whipped away into the night.

A great gust buffets me. Losing my footing, I lurch forward, stumble in the darkness, and fall. I land, abruptly, as if the ground's shot up and hit me in the face. I scrape my hands as I throw them out to brace myself and my bag explodes as it hits the earth, its contents rolling out in all directions.

Damn! I curse myself for changing my shoes, groping my way like a blind man for the missing spare change, lipstick and keys. Stupid of me to come back in the first place. What kind of idiot runs away from her date and then re-emerges several hours later and expects him to be at home, waiting for her? My hair comes undone, dancing around my head, making it almost impossible to see. Gathering what I can find into my bag, I struggle to my feet and am brushing myself off when a man in a hooded coat walks towards me through the gale.

'Are you all right? Have you got everything?' he calls.

I know this voice. We're standing face to face. 'No, no I'm not all right,' I say. 'Not at all.'

He looks down at his shoes. The wind whips around us like a thousand voices, filling the air with whispers.

'In fact, I've been extremely stupid and made a terrible mistake,' I continue.

For a long moment, he says nothing.

At last he looks up. His face is sad. 'I can't be anything other than what I am, Louise. If this is going to be a problem for you, there's nothing I can do. It's up to you. I can't do or say anything that will make you feel safe.'

'Oh, Eddie! But I don't want to feel safe any more! I was wrong! Really, badly wrong!'

I reach out and bury my face into his chest, wrapping my arms around him and holding him tight. 'Please forgive me. Even if you don't want to go out with me any more . . . even if you just want to be friends. I'd rather know you and have you be part of my life on any terms than none at all.'

It seems I'm standing there for ages, holding him, before he wraps his arms around me too. We stand there, clinging to each other in the dark.

And then he picks me up and carries me home.

'There's to be no more mention of potatoes ever again in our relationship.' He kisses my shoulder, pulling me closer.

'No, never.' I nuzzle my face into his chest.

'What does it mean, anyway?'

'Nothing. It's a code word. A get-out clause. It means it's time to leave.' I kiss the back of his hand and his delicate, clever fingers one by one.

He withdraws them and leans back against the head-board, looking at me intently. 'Parsnip,' he whispers, softly. 'Parsnip, Louise Canova.'

I laugh. 'And what does that mean?'

'Stay.' He kisses me softly on the lips. 'Stay.'

Six months later, I'm unpacking my books, slipping them in beside all Eddie's CDs, when I happen upon an old friend of mine: a slim, grey volume entitled, *Elegance*.

I sit down on the edge of the sofa and open it. The spine is worn, the cover frayed at the edges. The book collapses open to one of the early pages, which, perhaps fittingly enough, is headed:

Age

> There is a saying in France, 'Elegance is the privilege of age' — and, thank heaven, it is perfectly true. Between childhood, youth, maturity, and old age, there are no particular birthdays on which a woman automatically graduates from one to another. And she generally retains her youth to the same degree that she retains the same interests as young people.

One should, of course, defend oneself vigorously against the attacks of extra pounds, wrinkles, and double chins, but it is a battle that should be undertaken philosophically, for even the most skilful plastic surgery cannot recapture our youth. It is far better to settle down without vain regrets to a life filled with the rewards of past efforts and the joys that we at last have the means to give to others, instead of sulking like little girls when we are far too old to cast ourselves in such a childish role.

Elegance can be acquired only at the price of numerous errors that are best remembered with good humour. And in the end, it is in the moments when we forget ourselves entirely that we are at our most beautiful.

I close the book.

Here's the perfect home for it, between a biography of Glenn Gould and a copy of the Forty-eight Bach Preludes and Fugues.

I like to think that Madame Dariaux would approve.